Praise for the novels of Erin McCarthy

HARD AND FAST

"Sizzling hot, jam packed with snappy dialogue, emotional intensity, and racing fun."
—*New York Times* bestselling author Carly Phillips

"*Hard and Fast* was an absolute winner . . . a contemporary erotic romance with a perfect balance between the erotic and the romance. A definite must read for lovers of sports themed romance, smart heroines, and delicious heroes with a taste for the naughty."
—*Romance Novel TV*

"McCarthy has done it again! This follow-up to *Flat-Out Sexy* is a thrill ride that's unexpectedly funny, sentimental, and thoroughly entertaining. It's full of real women and sexy men, and these authentic characters, their unexpected love, and a few twists will make you a stock-car racing fan."
—*Romantic Times*

"Erin McCarthy writes stories guaranteed to draw you in."
—*The Long and the Short of It*

FLAT-OUT SEXY

"A steamy romance . . . Fast paced and red hot."
—*Publishers Weekly*

"This is one smart, sassy, steamy, and flat-out sexy read. McCarthy will have you giggling on page one, fanning yourself by page twenty-five, and rooting for the hero and heroine the whole way through. Buckle your seat belt and hold on—this is a fast and fun ride."
—*Romantic Times*

"A fast-paced read . . . The action starts on page one and doesn't stop until the last page. Erin McCa‍‍‍‍‍‍‍‍‍‍‍‍‍‍‍‍‍‍‍‍‍ sexy read. The love scene ‍‍‍‍‍‍‍‍‍‍‍ memorable. Pour yourself ‍‍‍‍‍‍‍‍‍‍‍‍‍‍‍‍
Today

"An engaging, often humorous contemporary romance."
—*Midwest Book Review*

"A treat. The characters were totally believable, and since it's Erin McCarthy, you know it's sexy! No one writes this type of story better than Ms. McCarthy. As usual, this author delivers."
—*Fresh Fiction*

HEIRESS FOR HIRE

"If you are looking to read a romance that will leave you all warm inside, then *Heiress for Hire* is a must-read."   —*Romance Junkies*

"Two enjoyable, empathetic people . . . make this romance shine."
—*Booklist*

"Amusing paranormal contemporary romance."
—*The Best Reviews*

"One of McCarthy's best books to date . . . Characters you will care about, a story that will make you laugh and cry, and a book you won't soon forget."   —*The Romance Reader* (5 hearts)

"An alluring tale."   —*A Romance Review* (5 roses)

"The perfect blend of sentiment and silly, heat and heart . . . Priceless!"   —*Romantic Times* (Top Pick, 4½ stars)

"An enjoyable story about finding love in unexpected places, don't miss *Heiress for Hire*."   —*Romance Reviews Today*

A DATE WITH THE OTHER SIDE

"Do yourself a favor and make a date with the other side."
—*New York Times* bestselling author Rachel Gibson

"One of the romance-writing industry's brightest stars . . . Ms. McCarthy spins a fascinating tale that deftly blends a paranormal story with a blistering romance . . . Funny, charming, and very entertaining, *A Date With the Other Side* is sure to leave you with a pleased smile on your face."   —*Romance Reviews Today*

"If you're looking for a steamy read that will keep you laughing while you turn the pages as quickly as you can, *A Date With the Other Side* is for you. Very highly recommended!"

—*Romance Junkies*

"Fans will appreciate this otherworldly romance and want a sequel." —*Midwest Book Review*

"Just the right amount of humor interspersed with romance."

—*Love Romances & More*

"Ghostly matchmakers add a fun flair to this warmhearted and delightful tale . . . An amusing and sexy charmer sure to bring a smile to your face." —*Romantic Times*

"Offers readers quite a few chuckles, some face-fanning moments, and one heck of a love story. Surprises await those who expect a 'sophisticated city boy meets country girl' romance. Ms. McCarthy delivers much more." —*A Romance Review*

"Fascinating." —*Huntress Book Reviews*

Praise for the other novels of Erin McCarthy

"Will have your toes curling and your pulse racing."

—*Arabella*

"The sparks fly." —*Publishers Weekly*

"Erin McCarthy writes this story with emotion and spirit, as well as humor." —*Fallen Angel Reviews*

"Both naughty and nice . . . Sure to charm readers." —*Booklist*

Titles by Erin McCarthy

A DATE WITH THE OTHER SIDE
HEIRESS FOR HIRE
FLAT-OUT SEXY
HARD AND FAST

The Vegas Vampires Series

HIGH STAKES
BIT THE JACKPOT
BLED DRY
SUCKER BET

The Deadly Sins Series

MY IMMORTAL
FALLEN
THE TAKING

Anthologies

THE NAKED TRUTH
(with Donna Kauffman, Beverly Brandt, and Alesia Holliday)

AN ENCHANTED SEASON
(with Maggie Shayne, Nalini Singh, and Jean Johnson)

THE POWER OF LOVE
(with Lori Foster, Toni Blake, Dianne Castell, Karen Kelley,
Rosemary Laurey, Janice Maynard, LuAnn McLane, Lucy Monroe,
Patricia Sargeant, Kay Stockham, and J. C. Wilder)

FIRST BLOOD
(with Susan Sizemore, Chris Marie Green, and Meljean Brook)

THE TAKING

ERIN McCARTHY

BERKLEY SENSATION, NEW YORK

THE BERKLEY PUBLISHING GROUP
Published by the Penguin Group
Penguin Group (USA) Inc.
375 Hudson Street, New York, New York 10014, USA

Penguin Group (Canada), 90 Eglinton Avenue East, Suite 700, Toronto, Ontario M4P 2Y3, Canada
(a division of Pearson Penguin Canada Inc.)
Penguin Books Ltd., 80 Strand, London WC2R 0RL, England
Penguin Group Ireland, 25 St. Stephen's Green, Dublin 2, Ireland (a division of Penguin Books Ltd.)
Penguin Group (Australia), 250 Camberwell Road, Camberwell, Victoria 3124, Australia
(a division of Pearson Australia Group Pty. Ltd.)
Penguin Books India Pvt. Ltd., 11 Community Centre, Panchsheel Park, New Delhi—110 017, India
Penguin Group (NZ), 67 Apollo Drive, Rosedale, North Shore 0632, New Zealand
(a division of Pearson New Zealand Ltd.)
Penguin Books (South Africa) (Pty.) Ltd., 24 Sturdee Avenue, Rosebank, Johannesburg 2196,
South Africa

Penguin Books Ltd., Registered Offices: 80 Strand, London WC2R 0RL, England

This is a work of fiction. Names, characters, places, and incidents either are the product of the author's imagination or are used fictitiously, and any resemblance to actual persons, living or dead, business establishments, events, or locales is entirely coincidental. The publisher does not have any control over and does not assume any responsibility for author or third-party websites or their content.

THE TAKING

A Berkley Sensation Book / published by arrangement with the author

PRINTING HISTORY
Berkley Sensation mass-market edition / January 2010

Copyright © 2010 by Erin McCarthy.
Excerpt from *Hot Finish* by Erin McCarthy copyright © by Erin McCarthy.
Cover art by John Blumen.
Cover design by Rita Frangie.
Interior text design by Laura K. Corless.

All rights reserved.
No part of this book may be reproduced, scanned, or distributed in any printed or electronic form without permission. Please do not participate in or encourage piracy of copyrighted materials in violation of the author's rights. Purchase only authorized editions.
For information, address: The Berkley Publishing Group,
a division of Penguin Group (USA) Inc.,
375 Hudson Street, New York, New York 10014.

ISBN: 978-0-425-23021-3

BERKLEY® SENSATION
Berkley Sensation Books are published by The Berkley Publishing Group,
a division of Penguin Group (USA) Inc.,
375 Hudson Street, New York, New York 10014.
BERKLEY® SENSATION and the "B" design are trademarks of Penguin Group (USA) Inc.

PRINTED IN THE UNITED STATES OF AMERICA

10 9 8 7 6 5 4 3 2 1

If you purchased this book without a cover, you should be aware that this book is stolen property. It was reported as "unsold and destroyed" to the publisher, and neither the author nor the publisher has received any payment for this "stripped book."

For Heather Graham,
a wonderful friend and mentor,
who loves New Orleans as much,
if not more, than I do

ACKNOWLEDGMENTS

To Kathy Love, Jamie Denton, and Christy Carlson, a huge thank you for helping me with the plot of this book and for all the words of encouragement (I need those frequently!).

To Chris Nelson, the best concierge in the French Quarter, who inspired the character of Chris Davidson. Thanks for keeping me from falling off the balcony and for all the late night chats!

To Jen Dengler, thanks for years of friendship and for letting me borrow your name. Just for the record, you're much more fun than the Jen written in this book.

Prologue

❧

NEW ORLEANS, 1878

The latest yellow fever epidemic held the city in its iron grip for nine days and nights, the bodies piling up like corded wood in the cemeteries, in the hospitals, and in the streets themselves, as ordinary business and cheerful living bowed in deference to death. With nary a streak of sun in the sky, the shrouded city was quiet save for the constant clatter of carriages carrying corpses and the roar of cannons in the square to clear the putrid air. The tally of dead rose daily—dozens each hour—and the endless opening of doors to bring out a parade of victims to the carts and wheelbarrows waiting on the streets contributed to the weary denizens of despair, darkness, and numb drudgery.

No stores, businesses, or banks were open, as those who could had fled to the country, and all conveyances were pressed into service as hearses, while the cloud of the smoke from burning bodies created a stinging mist that lingered for days. The

agony of melancholy and the silence of profound
grief crept into every corner, every house, as the
disease swept mercilessly from block to block,
taking the young, the old, the rich, and the poor
with equal enthusiasm—the sick, the dying, and the
dead all intermingling.

I performed innumerable last rites from morning
to night each endless day as the plague raged on,
both on those I knew and victims I had never before
laid eyes on. Children I had only recently baptized,
adults seeking absolution for their final sins on
earth, those with no one to grieve them, and whole
families who left this earth together—all received
my prayer.

Specific tales of tragedy abound everywhere,
such as the unfortunate end of the wealthy and
proud Comeaux family who had dominated
Louisiana business and politics for decades.
Seven members of the Comeaux family sat down
to dine, hearty and hale and confident in their
place of power in our city, on the second day of the
infestation, and twenty-four hours later all save
one were dead. Camille, the Comeaux's youngest
and unmarried daughter, was left at the tender
age of twenty void of her entire family. One can
only ask what such a loss would do to the state of
one's mind and heart, and how many survivors
came to the same sad conclusion as she did in the
epidemic's aftermath.

—From the diary of Father John Henri, Catholic priest

Camille Comeaux lit the candles on either side of the
French doors to the gallery, igniting taper after taper and
watching with pleasure as the flames cast dancing shad-

ows on the wall behind, framing the doors with a moving, undulating arch of darkness.

"Don't light too many," Felix said from behind her, his hands coming to rest on her shoulders. "You'll risk a fire."

Enjoying the press of his strong fingers on her bare shoulders, Camille lit another candle and still one more, pleased with the effect, excited by the danger. If the draperies caught on fire, it would only be fitting. Conjuring the dead deserved drama.

"I want to be sure it works," she told him. She wanted that more than anything.

She knew that Felix didn't understand her drive, her need, but then she knew he was using her, the same as she was using him. He wanted her wealth, and perhaps her body, while she wanted—needed—his power. His magic.

"It will work," he said, leaning around her and snuffing the last two candles she had lit, squeezing the flames between the tips of his thumb and forefinger. "I don't perform any ritual that isn't successful."

It was easy to believe such confidence, and Camille studied his profile, pleased with her choice of voodoo practitioner. Daring, bold, and successful, Felix was also singularly beautiful, with the thick dark hair and rich skin tone that revealed the African heritage of his mother's family, along with the narrow, aquiline nose of his French father.

At some point soon he would take her virginity along with the vast amounts of her money he had already acquired, she knew that. Perhaps even tonight. Regardless of when it happened, it was inevitable, given the course she had set them upon, and she could not regret it. The future had been altered irrevocably when her entire family had perished in the fever four months earlier, and every day, every decision, had led her here to this moment.

This was the night she would call forth her mother and father and sisters from the grave.

Felix stared at her, and she stared back, a smile playing about her lips. There was a question in his brilliant blue eyes, a doubt that she could see the ritual through to the end, and it made her laugh out loud. She had no doubts, none whatsoever, and she would do whatever was necessary to speak to her family, to express her love, her loneliness, her grief and desperation.

"Are you sure?"

"Yes." Perhaps he thought she was mad. Perhaps she was. Certainly twelve months earlier she would never have imagined that she would be standing in her parents' bedroom *en chemise* with a man such as Felix, the expensive chest of drawers from France converted to an altar for his implements to aid in the ritual. A year ago, Camille had been a pleasant, content young woman of wealthy means, her days busy with embroidery, playing her instrument, receiving callers with her mother, and doing acts of charity in the hospitals of less salubrious neighborhoods.

But she was no longer that girl. She was a woman now, a manic angry woman with no one to love her, and no one to live for. Camille grabbed the open wine bottle off the altar and drank straight from it, the sweetness sliding down her throat. "I am absolutely certain."

Felix didn't hesitate. He closed the distance between them and kissed her, a hot skillful taking of her mouth that had Camille's head spinning and her body igniting as the candles had. He gripped the back of her head, his tongue tasting and teasing, his thumbs brushing over the front of her chemise, finding her nipples and stroking them.

Camille was always surprised at how good it felt when Felix touched her, how wonderfully free and alive it made her feel. She ran her fingers over his bare chest, excited by the hard muscles, by the power his body contained. Whether it was the wine, or the excitement, or the sexual desire stirring to life, she didn't know and didn't care, but she could see through half-closed eyes that the room was in motion, the shadows pressing in and back out again, the furniture crisp and sharp, the candles appearing pliant and alive.

Everything was dark and warm, the yellow glow of the tapers plunging the altar into light, yet leaving the corners of the room black and secretive. Felix slid his tongue across her bottom lip and she shivered, her body aching deep inside, between her thighs. He stepped away and turned his back to her, leaving her breathing hard and reaching up into her hair to pull the pins away, to let the blonde tresses tumble over her shoulders. Her bare feet dug into the rug and she licked her moist lips, the heat from the sultry September night, from the candles, from her own pleasure and excitement, creating a deep flush on her face along with a dewy sheen between her breasts.

When Felix turned around to face her again, he had a snake in his hand, its long brown body wriggling in an attempt to escape, but its captor brandished it high in the air, chanting lowly. Camille hadn't known about the snake, had never guessed one of the baskets was holding a living reptile, and she gasped. Not from fear, but from excitement. This was right. This was magic.

Felix's hand moved the snake so skillfully that it looked as if it were dancing, its body moving to a rhythm its master created, a decadent, primitive form of expression. A glance down the length of Felix's hard chest and past his trousers showed that his bare foot tapped out a beat, and with his free hand he pulled a stick from his pocket and hit the chest of drawers, the sharp rap of the rhythm loud in the closed room. The hand tapped out time, the snake did his dance, Felix's foot went up and down, but the rest of him held still, a hard, lean body of control.

"Dance for me, Camille," Felix commanded, his eyes trained upward.

She did, first swaying softly, hands in her loose hair, then closing her eyes and letting her body feel the rhythm.

It started in her feet and worked its way up to her hips, her shoulders, until she was careening to the staccato beat, feeling it from inside her, springing to life, wanting out, needing air to fan the flames.

"You have the power," he told her. "The magic comes from you. Reach for it."

It did. She could feel it, boiling up in her body, and she would have it. Camille opened her eyes as she moved, dancing in a pounding circle, her arms reaching up and out, sweat trickling down her back, and she loosened her chemise in a sharp tug at the ribbons, wanting the air, wanting the brush against her bare skin, wanting Felix to see her, wanting to connect with her very essence, the heart of who she was.

Felix brought the snake to her, and where she would normally have recoiled, Camille didn't flinch or retreat, but danced for Felix while the reptile twisted and turned in front of her. They moved together, and she tore at her chemise with trembling, excited hands until she was completely naked, writhing like the snake, her fingers in her hair.

"You *are* ready," Felix said.

She was. She was ready for whatever this night would bring.

Chapter One

Regan Henry wanted to leave her husband tonight. She wanted to leave him so desperately that the mere sight of him mingling across the room at his law firm's Christmas party made her palms twitch, her heart race, and a cold trail of sweat trickle down between her breasts.

Get out.

That's all she could think, and it took everything in her to not turn around and run from the room.

He wasn't a bad guy. Some would call him the perfect man, the perfect husband. Attractive, successful, charming.

But perfection demanded perfection, and Regan was exhausted from the effort of trying to live up to that expectation.

When she realized he was making his way to her, a smile on his face as he adjusted his tie, she took a gulp from her glass of wine to fortify herself.

"You could try to smile," he said, his own smile still in place, the words light and teasing. To anyone around them, it would seem as if he were trying to cheer her up, include her, but Regan heard the censure behind it.

"I have a bit of a headache," she said, which was the truth. Her temples were throbbing, and a dull pain jabbed above and below her eyes. The room was cold, and she was wearing a sleeveless black cocktail dress. Between the chill and her own stress, every muscle in her body was tense.

"Do you think maybe you should lay off the wine then?" He reached out and took her glass. "That's your third."

She wasn't sure if it was or not, but she felt compelled to argue. "It's only my second."

He gave a laugh, which to Regan's practiced ear held no true amusement. "It's okay. I'm not criticizing. I knew you were a lush when I met you."

His voice had a quality when he was displeased that Regan had come to think of as humming. It sounded normal, pleasant, teasing, to most people, but when it took on that light, singsong quality, she knew he was unhappy with her, and God, she was so tired of having her every move, every word, every decision scrutinized and found lacking.

"Three glasses of wine do not make me a lush."

"So now you're agreeing it's three?" He finished off her wine himself, and tucked her hair behind her ear, flicking a finger over the pearl earring he had given her for their first anniversary that October. "Why didn't you wear your hair up? I like it best that way."

It was nothing, something a thousand husbands might say to their wives as mere flirtation or playful pouting, but to Regan it was the latest in a litany of disappointments, accusatory glares, and criticisms veiled as suggestions from the man she was supposed to recognize was so much wiser than her. Patronizing words he dropped one by one, like stones of Puritan punishment, letting them settle onto her chest, robbing her of breath, crushing her slowly and painfully. Word after word had pressed, piling on top of one another, paralyzing in their heaviness, rendering her incapable of speech or protest, unable to defend herself, until she knew it was time to leave or lose her voice in her marriage forever.

Shifting her hair out of his touch, she masked her shudder as his fingers fell from her skin. Every touch, every invasion of her personal space, had grown more difficult to endure with each passing day, and it was hard to remember why she had married him, how she could have ever thought herself happy. There was no affection left for him, only the keening and urgent need to flee before she cracked, and lost control.

She was perilously close to it at this goddamn cocktail party.

He rendered a long-suffering sigh next to her. "Fine. Don't talk to me. Don't wear your hair up because I like it. Just be a bitch, I don't care."

Regan said nothing, digging her fingernails into her palms. She hoped they bled. She hoped breaking open her own flesh and feeling the sharp sting of pain would keep her from screaming, would hold the persistent tears at bay.

"But before you prance over to the bar and get another glass of wine, which I have no doubt you're about to do, could you put yourself out long enough to do your duty as a hostess at this party?"

Turning her head to stare at her husband, taking in his good-looking and proportioned features, his tidy and stylish blond hair, his elegant and expensive suit, she waited for him to finish. He would tell her which VIP he wanted her to chat with, which pet project of which partner's wife she was supposed to volunteer to assist with, what invitation for which party she was to extend.

Then she was going to go home to their fabulously trendy condo off Magazine Street and she was somehow going to find the nerve to pack her bags and leave.

He would fight her on it. Dirty. He would twist and bend

the truth, manipulate, and threaten with whatever weapons he had at his disposal.

But she had to find the courage to know that no longer mattered.

"You know John's wife is into all that metaphysical crap and she has that guy here doing voodoo readings as some kind of entertainment. Only no one is getting readings because no one wants to appear to believe in that bullshit. It will make John's wife, and therefore John, happy if you go and have a reading."

Regan relaxed her shoulders a fraction. "Sure, I can do that." It would get her away from her husband and all the mindless chatter of the corporate gathering. "Where is he?"

Retreating into a corner and letting someone tell her she had a financial windfall coming very soon was the perfect way to hide from the party, to regroup and gather herself to get through the rest of the night.

"He's in the interior courtyard. Don't worry, you have to pass the bar to get there."

With that, he dismissed her by turning around and walking away, a smile on his face and his hand out to shake, but not before he put that hand on the small of her back, thumb pressing into her flesh. To anyone watching, a sweet gesture of intimacy, to her, a stamp of his ownership, a tactile reminder that she had let her fear drag this out too long. He expected to touch her, and she cringed at it.

Forgoing the bar out of a childish and pointless defiance, Regan crossed the elegant room, a former residence in the French Quarter turned restaurant and caterer. Her heels, a forty-dollar bargain on sale at a boutique on Chartres, slipped a little on the wood floor when she took the slight step down to the brick courtyard. Teetering, she grabbed the doorway for balance, not daring to look back to see if her husband had seen.

Lush. The word echoed, stinging like a slap.

He would criticize her later in the humming voice, call her an embarrassment, lock the liquor cabinet in their condo again and put the key on his key chain. Regan knew she didn't have a drinking problem, and she wasn't in denial or deluding herself. She enjoyed a good glass of wine, singular being the key, and occasionally she indulged and had several glasses. Being anything close to drunk was something that happened to her maybe once a year.

But it didn't matter if she never drank a single drop. Then he would say she was embarrassing him by not tasting Mr. So and So's wine collection, or for acting evangelist in front of Mr. Big Shot, who was giving a toast.

Never right. She would never do it right. And he was always in control, of her, of her life.

"Are you okay?"

Regan's head snapped up from studying the uneven bricks of the courtyard as she clutched the doorway and regained her balance, her equilibrium. The source of the voice was a man sitting in a wicker chair, leaning back casually against its rich red-striped cushion. He was about thirty, his face, his skin, his hair all an indistinguishable blend of several ethnicities. Whether he was white, black, Latin, Arab, she didn't know. What she did know was that whatever melting pot his genes had been served from, it was a delicious combination.

The man was gorgeous and she was acutely embarrassed that he had seen her stumble.

"I'm fine," she murmured. "I just didn't realize there was a step down, and these stupid shoes . . ." She bent her knee and lifted her foot to point at one of the culprits. "They're new and not scuffed yet, so they slid on the wood floor . . . Together it was a bad combination."

He gave a small smile. "Practically deadly."

Regan felt a blush staining her cheeks and she was mortified. What was she, fourteen? It was just nerves, the night, her whole marriage culminating in her constantly feeling unsure, apologizing for all her actions, no matter what they were. She was practically to the point of apologizing for existing and that scared her. Showed her how much her marriage had damaged her. This man's voice was casual and teasing and she should take that at face value, not try to backpedal and soothe the way she would with her husband.

"I'm lucky to be alive," she told him.

The smile twitched. She had amused him, she could tell. But it was dangerous to be alone in the dusky courtyard with a good-looking man, regardless of how innocuous it seemed. It was the wrong time to anger her husband, and anyone he perceived as competition would infuriate him. "Do you know where we're supposed to go to get the readings? John's wife—you do know John, I'm assuming?—she arranged for someone to be here and I'm supposed to have a reading."

"Supposed to?" His eyebrow rose. "Well, if you're *supposed* to, have a seat."

Gesturing to the table in front of him with an empty chair on the side opposite his, his hand moved from its hidden position behind the table to rest on top of it. She realized he was holding a deck of tarot cards, and the sweat that had been between her breasts broke out again with a vengeance. Of course he was the voodoo practitioner. That explained his plain black shirt, his dark jeans instead of a suit, and why she'd never seen him before.

"Oh, right, absolutely, thanks." Regan cleared her throat and moved to the empty chair. She folded her hands on the table, then in her lap, then on the table again, crossing and uncrossing her legs. It was hard to look at him, his serious, steady eyes a brilliant pale blue, a color so unusual and opaque it was mesmerizing. His hands moved over the worn deck of cards, shuffling them, but his eyes were trained on her.

"Nice pearls," he said, his voice a low, rich, masculine

timbre. Not gravelly, not so deep it was gruff, but a solid, male sound, pleasing to listen to. "Your husband has good taste."

Her hand shot to her throat to feel the necklace. "Thanks. How . . . how do you know I'm married?"

"You're wearing a gigantic diamond on your ring finger. Doesn't take the cards to reveal you have a husband."

"Oh, right. Duh." Regan tried to laugh, but it was brittle, and his hands paused as he watched her. He was a still person, sitting with little movement, no fidgeting or adjusting, and it made Regan squirm even more.

"Can I see it?"

"See what?" Regan looked at him blankly.

"Your ring." He held his hand out.

"Oh." Flustered, Regan glanced at her wedding ring. She never took it off. She hadn't taken it off since the day her husband had placed it on her finger, and she wasn't sure she wanted to take it off now. But neither did the idea of holding her hand out to this man and letting him run his fingers over her skin, her diamond, appeal to her. That seemed too intimate, too odd. Dangerous.

Of course, that was ludicrous, there was no danger there, and it was equally absurd that she didn't want to remove the ring. She was planning to leave her husband. She was. Soon. So there was no reason she couldn't take his wedding ring off for a minute.

"Sure." Before she could change her mind, Regan yanked the band off and dropped it into the voodoo priest's outstretched hand.

The sense of giddy relief that flooded her when the symbol of her marriage left her possession caught her off guard. She sucked in a few rapid breaths, amazed that she could feel so much lighter, so much more confident in her decision to leave, after something as simple as removing the ring.

"Shuffle the cards." He pushed the deck across the table

to her as he turned her ring over and over in his other hand, giving it a cursory glance before resting it on the table, out of her reach.

Regan eyed the ring, wanting to ask for it back, then stopping herself. It didn't matter. It wasn't like he was intending to steal it. Let it sit there on the crisp white table-cloth for a minute. She took the cards and shuffled them carefully, precisely. They felt different from regular play-ing cards, softer, pliable. The colors had faded, and they looked dirty to her, not the fresh dirt of a recent soiling, but the indecipherable grim of years and years of handling.

"Cut the deck in three piles," he told her, when she stopped shuffling and held them out to him.

Trying not to think about washing her hands posthaste, Regan cut the deck as directed, staring down at the cards. It was too difficult to look at him. There was something about his eyes, probably the result of the unusual light color, that made her feel like he was seeing her with altogether too much clarity. He wasn't buying the careful image she pre-sented to the world of happy wife, a classy, pulled-together modern woman.

A glance up showed he wasn't looking at her, but at the cards as he picked a pile and started laying them out in a pattern. He had a strong jaw and high cheekbones, a long narrow nose, and a perfectly proportioned mouth, with lips that had just a hint of flushed color to them. There was some-thing so primal and male, and yet so beautiful about him.

"Do you like what you see?" he asked.

"Excuse me?"

"The cards." His hand indicated the spread on the table.

Regan saw nothing but pictures and swirls of color, all strange, meaningless images. "I don't know anything about the cards. I'm Presbyterian."

There was a short pause, then he actually burst out laughing. "Now that was funny."

"I wasn't trying to be funny." Irritated, Regan sat back in her chair. She didn't need this random man to laugh at her.

But he immediately stopped, his smile eradicated by her words. "I know. You never try to be funny, do you? You don't think you're witty. You're afraid of being judged, so you hide behind platitudes and social correctness and never say what you're really thinking."

A hot flush rushed over Regan. God, that was a little too close to home. "I don't know what you're talking about. And there's nothing wrong with being polite."

"You do know what I'm talking about." He tapped a card, the upside-down images blurring. "You try very hard to please all the time, you always have. But maybe you need to please yourself sometimes."

Leg bouncing anxiously under the table, Regan shook her head, not even sure what she was denying. "I like myself just fine."

His voice lowered. "And so do they, *cherie*, so do they. They never expected you to replace your sister."

Regan's body went completely still, the heat rushing through her extremities, hot saliva flooding her mouth, the unexpected buzzing in her ears and a sweeping dizziness making her question if she might actually faint. But she swallowed hard and the blurry world sharpened again. "I don't have a sister."

He was a hack, that was all. Just guessing, throwing out vague pronouncements, the kind that anyone could interpret however they chose.

"But you did," he murmured, eyes on her while his hands pushed the cards together in a pile. "We don't need these. I know all I need to about you. You had a sister, and when she died, the fire in you extinguished. You turned down the volume on your personality so that you wouldn't hurt your parents any more than they had already been hurt. You wanted to be perfect."

Now the tears did dribble out, unwanted, humiliating, as Regan bit her lip to prevent it from trembling. "How could you know about my sister?" she whispered. "Did you do research on me? It's very cruel to bring her into a form of entertainment."

He shook his head. "I'm not trying to be cruel. I'm trying to release you. Your parents don't expect you to be perfect or to be your sister. They love you, just as you are."

The stranger's words lacerated her, and she wanted so much to believe them. Regan put her hand over her eyes, trying to push back the tears. "Of course they love me," she managed to choke out. She knew that.

"They won't understand, but they won't be angry."

"What are you talking about?"

"The decision you're weighing right now. Your parents may not be happy about it, but just remember they love you."

"What decision?" The heat suffusing her had turned to a chill, crawling across her skin like encroaching winter.

His fingers landed on her wedding ring, and he rocked it on the table, back and forth, back and forth. "You know what I'm talking about."

Regan wanted to snatch the ring from him and leave, abandon his crazy pronouncements and dirty tarot cards and retreat from the courtyard. But she stayed in her chair, curious as to what he would say next, mesmerized by the casual way he fondled the symbol of her marriage. On her hand, it spoke volumes. On the table, it was just a pretty ring that held no power.

She jumped, the sensation of someone touching her shoulder sending her whirling around. "Something touched me!"

"It was probably a plant brushing you," he said mildly.

Regan swept her gaze left and right, squeezing the spot on her shoulder where she had felt distinct pressure. "There are no plants within three feet of me."

Even before the words were fully out of her mouth, she felt it again, this time on both of her shoulders, as if someone was standing behind her and resting their hands on either side of her head. She leaned forward in her chair, a little panicked as she looked around again, but the sensation remained.

"Next you'll tell me it's my sister watching over me," she hissed, suddenly angry. She didn't need this, not when she was already so close to the edge, anxiety her constant companion. This was just bullshit power of suggestion, taking advantage of people's emotions for profit.

But he shook his head slowly. "No. No, that's not what I am going to tell you. Your sister died an innocent child, and she is at peace. You, however, are not. Death is harder on the living than the dead."

That wasn't news as far as she was concerned. The feeling of being touched moved down her arms, as if she were being rubbed in a gesture of comfort, and Regan's eyes went wide. She had the craziest goddamn feeling that it was him touching her. But that was absolutely impossible. He was over there, and she was here, and his hands were on the table in clear view.

The air around her shifted, and she turned to her left for no apparent reason, instinct telling her someone should be standing there when of course they weren't. "What . . ." The word died on her lips, goose bumps racing up her arms as the invisible embrace came at her from the front, like a hug.

Regan's chest swelled in and out rapidly with the frantic tenor of her breathing. She didn't move, afraid to reach out and feel nothing, more frightened still of reaching out and feeling something that wasn't visible. The tendrils of touch went up and down lightly between her shoulder blades, and somehow she recognized it as a man's touch, physically intimate. It wasn't the touch of a relative or a friend, but that of a lover.

It was that ridiculous thought that launched her to her feet. How in the hell could the touch that didn't exist be qualified? If it didn't exist, how could it be so distinct as to belong to a lover?

The chair she'd been sitting in fell backward from her sudden movement, smacking to the bricks with a bang. She thrust her hand out. "My ring, please."

He rose to his feet as well, but slowly, and she was appalled to see what sitting had hidden from her view. Not only was he attractive in the face, but when he uncoiled to his full height, it was evident he was a fine specimen of male perfection, toned and tall and broad-shouldered. His soft worn jeans hung just right as he reached out, her ring in his hand.

"Just remember, if you're going to wear it, wear it of your own free will."

She had no answer to such a cryptic remark and she held out her hand. The ring dropped from his palm to hers, its weight heavy, the stone cutting into her flesh as she closed her fist around it.

"Thanks," she said, turning to leave, righting the chair she had knocked over.

Regan had taken three steps when he said softly from behind her, "You're welcome."

Pausing, she turned, realizing that for all her striving for social perfection since she'd been old enough to say "manners," she had committed the cardinal sin of a first meeting. "I'm sorry, what is your name?"

"Felix Leblanc."

A name as unusual as the man. "I'm Regan Henry Alcroft. It's a pleasure to meet you." Though pleasure wasn't exactly the adjective to describe it. Confusing, a little scary, maybe even a tinge electric. Arousing.

"The pleasure is mine."

It wasn't suggestive or flirtatious, yet she felt the unmistakable jolt of desire between her thighs at his words, his voice. God, she needed to go. She crammed her ring back onto her finger and headed for the door, the lights and laughter of the party spilling out into the courtyard.

"Watch your step back in, Regan Henry Alcroft."

Feeling like there was more to that comment than the straightforward meaning, Regan chose to pretend that she hadn't heard him. A sick churning in her stomach, she swiped her eyes free of tear remnants and steeled her shoulders to navigate the party, and the life she had chosen.

❦

Felix watched Regan wipe under her eyes, smooth her hair, and enter the main room of the restaurant, immediately swallowed up by the crowd.

He sank back into his chair, flicking at his tarot cards with his fingers. He should have given her a generic reading, made her smile and laugh with his charm and entertaining predictions. That was what he was good at, making women feel better about themselves, amusing them and lightening whatever load of burdens they were hauling around. It was both his gift and his curse. Both what he had bargained for and what he would give back with no hesitation if he could.

But he hadn't done that with Regan Henry Alcroft. He had been intrigued by the paradox she presented. There was something so edgy and powerful in her eyes, the glossy vehemence of a snake about to strike, yet she carried herself with uncertainty. Her simple black dress, her traditional pearls, her pin-straight rich brown hair would be elegant on some women, and he supposed they were on her as well. But mostly they were wrong. They didn't match the essence of her person at all, and he found it odd that her best features, those chocolate brown eyes and full lips that would be the envy of any actress, were features she chose to ignore, not highlight. She'd worn muted eye shadow and lipstick in neutral beige, and while Felix was no makeup artist, he did know that a pop of rich red on those luscious lips at a cocktail party would be more flattering.

So he had told her what he had really seen in the cards, what he really thought.

In couched terms, of course.

But she had resisted the truth, as mortals always did.

And she clearly had no idea what her wedding ring was, or its power.

Or who she was married to.

It wasn't his place to tell her.

Let Regan walk back into the party and do whatever she intended to do. If he had learned anything after more than a hundred and fifty years of life, it was to resist the temptation of a woman with pleading in her eyes.

It meant nothing but trouble, and he had no intention of watching another woman die. Not that Regan was Camille, but she shared the same yearning, unhappy quality, and that was a dangerous combination for a man, an immortal, like him.

And Regan belonged to Alcroft.

But that hadn't stopped him from touching her, had it?

Two women in their fifties came into the courtyard, arm in arm, looking at him with a mixture of nerves and excitement. Felix pasted a smile on his face. "Would you like a reading, ladies?"

Regan's appeal was irrelevant.

He was never going to see her again, and that was the way it had to be.

He was a demon servant, and this endless existence of casual relationships and peddling hope to paying customers was what he had condemned himself to for eternity.

❧

"Please," Regan begged, hating the pleading in her voice, but needing to leave the party with such a sense of urgency, she was trembling from head to toe. "I have a splitting headache. I'm doing more harm than good by trying to talk to people. They're going to think I'm rude or an idiot or both."

Her husband took a deep breath, his teeth clenched. He was clearly trying to keep a lid on his anger. "Fine. Have the staff call you a cab."

Relief coursed through her and she gripped the clutch she had collected from their table. "Okay, thank you. I'm sorry, I am. But like I said, I'm barely stringing a sentence together—"

He cut her off, not looking at her, but scanning the room, smiling and nodding at acquaintances who glanced his way. "I heard you," he said tightly under his breath. "Just go. And take some goddamn aspirin so I don't have to listen to you complain when I get home."

Heat flooded her cheeks. As if she ever complained. About anything. "Of course. But I don't think I have enough money to take a cab."

For the first time he actually turned and looked down at her, disbelief on his face as he shook his head. "Fucking unbelievable. You have an inheritance that rivals the state of Louisiana's annual budget and you can't be bothered to put ten bucks in your purse? Common sense, Regan, learn to use it."

She said nothing. Just waited, angry, but more eager to leave than to delay a departure by protesting or defending herself. Not that she ever argued.

He sighed, reaching in his pocket for his wallet. Pulling out two twenties, he handed them to her. "You owe me for tonight."

Of course she did. Nothing was given freely.

"I'll see you at home." He kissed her forehead. "Geez, you're clammy. Get some rest." Brushing his knuckles across her cheek, he said, "I love you."

Regan's stomach flipped again. Oh, God, she had to say it back . . . she had to force the words out somehow. She didn't love him, and she wasn't even sure when she had stopped. But those feelings didn't exist anymore, if they ever really had, and that saddened her, panicked her. "I love you, too," she murmured, avoiding his eyes by pretending to pick lint off of his tie.

Then trying not to run, she waded through the restaurant to the front and surged right past the reservation desk. They were in the French Quarter on a weekend, surely she could find a cab without having to wait around for one to be called, and she needed the cool air outside. Sucking in deep breaths of the crisp December air to settle her stomach, she walked up St. Anne's, carefully avoiding the sidewalk holes with her heels. She'd forgotten her coat, but she didn't care. It was in the fifties and she had goose bumps in her sleeveless dress, but the lower temperature felt good on her flushed skin.

After a minute, she snagged a cab and settled on the seat, closing her eyes after giving her address to the driver. What a disaster of a night. How many more just like it would there be before she had the courage to leave her marriage?

What was the matter with her? Why couldn't she just get the cojones to walk away, to hell with the consequences?

Eyes snapping open, she stared down at her wedding ring. When it had been off, she had felt . . . lighter. Free.

Herself.

Angry with Beau, herself, the whole situation, she yanked the ring off her finger. Tears back in her eyes, she opened her purse and tossed it to the bottom, below a used tissue. She didn't want to wear the ring. Didn't want to see it. So beautiful, so binding . . .

Regan's stomach crawled up in her throat again. "Pull over!" she yelled to the driver.

"What?" He glanced back at her in confusion.

"Pull over, I'm going to be sick." Regan was already

opening the door as he headed to the curb, and she violently threw up the wine and the very little dinner she'd eaten.

It splashed her arm, her hair, and all over the street. Shuddering, she hung there for a minute after the heaving stopped, then wiped her mouth and shut the door. "Okay, you can drive."

The sooner she got home the sooner she could pack her bags and move out.

Chapter Two

"I'm totally moving in with you."

Regan Henry thrust up the latch to unlock the French doors leading to her bedroom balcony and shot her best friend Chris Davidson an amused look over her shoulder. She was 98 percent certain he was joking, but even after a decade of friendship sometimes the other 2 percent of randomness he exhibited threw her. "You're moving into my bedroom?"

"Yes, and you can't stop me." Chris spun in a circle in the middle of the almost empty master bedroom of her newly purchased nineteenth-century house, his shoes squeaking on the wood floor. "This is the biggest bedroom I've ever seen in my life. A whole football team could shack up in here with us, and think how much fun that would be."

His eyebrows went up and down suggestively and Regan laughed as she shoved open the glass doors and felt the warm spring breeze sweep over her. She set down the bottle of wine and plastic cups they had brought and flicked the switches by the doors, trying to find one that turned the outside lights on so they wouldn't be sitting in the dark. "Neither one of us could date a football player. *So* not our type."

Not that she was ready to date, but she would be someday, and it wouldn't be a professional athlete, she could pretty much guarantee.

"True. I prefer men who can read."

"You're disparaging an entire sport, you know." Regan closed her eyes and breathed deep the night air. The scent of flowers from the neighbor's hanging baskets filled her nostrils, and God, she felt good. The deep satisfaction at having a big, expansive house, a gallery that oversaw the narrow streets of the French Quarter, a space that was just hers and no one else's, was intoxicating.

Freedom.

Giddy, overwhelming, exhilarating freedom. It was hers again. All choices, good and bad, were hers alone to make since she had left her husband Beau that night of the law firm's Christmas party. It had been an ugly three months, filled with daily communications from him that had vacillated between coaxing, pleading, charming vows of love, and pure venomous anger. She had caught him off guard by moving out that night, but it hadn't taken him long to regroup, and he had used every weapon in his arsenal from the emotional to the financial to get her to come back to him.

She hadn't, and she was more proud of that than anything else she had accomplished in her life. Not that he was resigned to their divorce or cooperating one iota, but she was through the worst of the paperwork and details of separating her life from his. She was moving into this house in the morning, and she was a cocktail of emotions, nervous and excited all at once.

Everyone but Chris thought she was insane for filing for divorce—her parents, grandparents, coworkers, her female friends. Chris had held her through her tears of fear over the future, and the grief of having to acknowledge that her marriage had never been what she had thought it would be when she spoke her vows. He had been there to comfort her and had popped open the champagne, the only person in her life who had ever thought Beau was not the perfect man for her. The perfect man, period. Tonight Chris was here to get a sneak preview of her impulsive real estate purchase and to break in her balcony with the wine and a couple of wrought iron chairs. They had been walking down Magazine Street after dinner when Chris had spotted, and promptly bought as her housewarming gift, the heavy scrolling chairs sitting outside an antique shop.

Impulsive. Chris had always been impulsive, and now she had the right, the ability to be that way too. To do what she wanted, when she wanted.

"Produce a professional football player for me that has read *The Kite Runner* and I'll take it back," Chris said, dragging the chairs over to the French doors, making her wince.

Hardwood floors didn't take kindly to wrought iron chair feet.

But a quick glance reassured her he hadn't scratched the floors, and she told herself it didn't matter anyway. No husband to yell about the ruined floors.

"For all you know," she told Chris, "there's an NFL book club. And I think I saw some commercial where football players were promoting a literacy-for-adults program. You hate it when people make generalizations about you for being gay—you shouldn't do the same to an athlete."

Though she had to admit, she seriously doubted locker room chatter involved literary fiction, but she could be wrong. She had definitely been wrong before. At least once. She glanced down at her empty ring finger and felt the urge to grin at its nudity.

Chris rolled his eyes. "Thanks, Oprah Pollyanna Winfrey.

The trouble with being so damn PC all the time is that there's nothing left to make fun of, and frankly, everyone needs a good laugh at someone else's expense once in a while. It keeps people from bottling it up and going all Unabomber."

Then he waved his hand as he abandoned the chairs in the doorway behind her and walked over to the chest of drawers that had been left in the house by the previous owners. "But it's too early in the night to debate, it's not even ten yet, for Chrissake, and the wine is still corked. Can we talk about something else? Like why are there just random pieces of furniture that don't belong to you in the house you bought? This is the third thing I've seen, though it's not as ugly as that bench downstairs. That waste of wood needs to be taken out back and put down."

Regan squeezed around the chairs and moved over to stand by Chris, running her fingers over the smooth marble top of the chest of drawers. "Let's just agree not to invite a football team to hold a book club in my bedroom, and I think we're good. As for the furniture, these are pieces that have been in the house since it was built. The previous owners told me this bureau must have been brought in through the windows of this room before the glass was put in, because it's too big to go through the doorway. I think when the movers come with my stuff tomorrow I'll have them carry the bureau over to the exterior wall and put it between the two windows."

She thought it was a beautiful piece and had been thrilled when the sellers indicated it had to stay with the house because removing it would risk damage to the chest of the drawers, or the house itself. The marquetry and the use of multiple woods fascinated her, the gilt bronze mounts and brass locks adding a drama to the already elaborate piece. But by far the most interesting feature was that the doors opened to reveal drawers, which pulled out and to the side, exposing mirrors at the back of the opening.

There was absolutely no purpose to them, a whimsy added by the cabinetmaker.

Regan was ready for a little whimsy in her life.

Chris started opening the doors and drawers and peeking inside. "Well, you know this thing has to have a secret compartment somewhere."

"Do you think so?" Regan opened the opposite door and stared at the drawers. They didn't appear to be hiding anything to her, but she would love to find that the chest of drawers contained a trick, a little bit of mechanical magic. She had to admit that was her private hope, that somewhere in the huge house she'd bought that was way too big for one single woman, she'd find something of intrigue. Letters, old clothing, anything that spoke of the past. It was part of the lure of a two-hundred-year-old house—discovering what secrets its walls contained.

"Of course it has a hidden compartment. All of these antiques in big old Southern houses do. My grandmother Ebbe had one almost exactly like this, and she hid her hooch in the drawer behind a drawer."

"Why does it not surprise me that your grandmother had a liquor stash?" Regan rubbed her hands on her dark trouser jeans. Secret drawer or not, the bureau was covered in a thick layer of dust. She had paid a service to clean the house after the previous owners had moved out three days earlier, but clearly they had made the decision that their job didn't include furniture.

Not that it mattered, she reminded herself. The dust could layer up so high she could grow potatoes in it and it didn't matter because there was no one to criticize.

"Everyone's grandmother has a liquor stash. It's the American way." Chris was opening and closing doors and drawers and feeling along the grain of the wood.

"I know my grandmother doesn't. You know how uptight she is." Regan pictured her Chanel suit–wearing, churchgoing, etiquette aficionado grandmother sucking alcohol from a flask, and shook her head. It would never happen. She would at least use a glass.

"That's exactly why she *is* wound so tight. She's jonesing for the next drink whenever she's with her family and can't reach the gin bottle. Having to wait for the end of dinner so you all will get the hell out and she can take a swig makes her cranky."

Regan laughed. "My grandmother would be horrified at such speculation. And our bottle of cheap pink wine." Yet somehow, it gave her a childish glee to think that her proper, by-the-rules grandmother Henry, would need to hit the hooch to get through family night. Those nights were sometimes interminable—the same conversations, the same politeness, the same avoidance of anything controversial or relevant or emotional.

"I really think it's ridiculous we had to buy a twenty-five pack of plastic cups just to get two to drink out of," Chris said, still poking his fingers around the bureau. "We probably could have just bought two wineglasses somewhere in a souvenir shop instead. Then you could have had kitschy Mardi Gras wineglasses on display in the dining room of your eight-bajillion-dollar house."

It never bothered Regan when Chris referenced her money. She had it, plain and simple, the result of an inheritance from her maternal grandparents, and he treated it as such. She hadn't earned it, didn't deserve it any more than any other human being, yet it was hers, and there was no envy from Chris. "The house cost *nine* bajillion dollars," she joked. "And we're so cool that we're being chic with our plastic cups . . . we're retro, not kitschy." She ran her hands over the middle drawer, then for some reason felt compelled to pull it all the way out. Except that it stuck, so she yanked harder.

"Exactly," Chris said. "And if we really want to be pretentious, we can only drink like two sips out of each plastic cup, then get new ones."

"That wouldn't be—"

Regan cut short her forthcoming speech on environmental consciousness when she realized the drawer she had been tugging had swung to the right on a hinge. Behind it was another one.

"I found it! Look, I found a drawer behind a drawer."

Chris abandoned his own search through the bureau and turned to see, looking more satisfied than surprised. "Told you so."

"I'm glad you did." Regan opened the drawer, which was a perfect replica of the one in front of it, swag design and all.

"Do you think it's safe to drink one-hundred-year-old hooch?"

A shiver rolled over Regan as she peered into the dark depths of the secret compartment and spotted the shadow of an object. "We're not going to find out tonight," she murmured as she reached in and carefully pulled out the dusty item tucked away. "It's not liquor at all, but a book. A journal actually, I think."

It was black leather, about an inch thick, and the cover had the initials CAC embossed in gold foil on it. A faded pink ribbon was dangling out of the top, marking a spot midway through the book. As she carefully opened the first page, Regan's anticipation increased. There was writing, spidery formal handwriting in black ink, the careful penmanship of centuries past.

"Oh, my God, it is someone's journal. This is so cool."

"What's it say?"

"'June 28, 1878. I received this journal for my twentieth birthday today as a gift from Mr. Tradd, the man my parents wish for me to marry. I imagine it will be so. I shall become Mrs. Tradd before the end of the year unless something unforeseen occurs.'"

Regan ran her finger down the yellowed page, immediately feeling sympathy for the long dead author. She knew what it was to feel parental pressure, to drift into marriage simply because it presented itself. "She doesn't sound thrilled about getting engaged, does she?"

"Not particularly. What else does she say?"

"That's it for that entry." Regan turned the page. "'June 29, 1878. I went to the hospital with Mother again today to give them the fresh linens the church has donated. I wore my emerald green dress with the black ribbons, newly arrived from Paris. This was an error in judgment as the streets were swollen with summer rain and I fear the hem will never recover.'"

"Well, someone leads an exciting life. The next page is probably a description of the cold cuts served for lunch." Chris continued to fiddle with the bureau. "Maybe the booze is in another drawer."

Regan smacked his arm and closed the book, pressing it against her chest. "Come on, let's go outside and open the wine since you're clearly your grandmother's descendent and need alcohol. Maybe the journal gets more interesting as Mr. Tradd courts her."

"Yeah, sure. 'Went in the carriage. Saw a play. Had my underpaid servant put my hair up in the latest fashion.'" Chris rolled his eyes and followed her onto the balcony. "Flip to the middle while I open the wine. Look at what I do for you . . . chairs, cheap wine, plastic cups, and a corkscrew. Never say I didn't give you anything."

"And you're always so humble about it. Thank you." Regan sat down in the chair Chris had dragged out and tucked her straight hair behind her ear. The heels of her black sandals scraped across the wood floor as she stretched out, journal in her lap. She opened the book at random and started to read. "'August 12, 1878. I tasted his nectar for the first time last night.'"

"*Nectar?*" Chris said when she paused, frowning herself at the word. "Did she take up beekeeping for a hobby or is that implying something totally different?"

"She has to be talking about honey. I mean, she didn't sound remotely sexual before."

"Maybe someone stole her journal, or maybe she learned a trick or two from Mr. Tradd. Keep reading."

Regan cleared her throat and focused on the tight, slanted writing. "'It was not as I expected, rather salty and bitter, but I understand the principle behind swallowing his fluid—I consumed his sexual energy, took his magic inside me, and it was terribly exciting. I cannot wait to see him again, I must convince him to allow me to conduct my own spells . . .'"

Regan was so flabbergasted she stopped reading. "Hello. Wow. I really didn't see that coming, even after the word nectar was dropped."

Chris stared at her, the bottle between his legs, hands suspended in the act of twisting the corkscrew, eyes wide and mouth open. "And speaking of coming . . . it seems our little Victorian socialite was learning the art of fellatio between piano lessons and visits to the poor."

"So much for the cold cuts," Regan said. They looked at each other and started laughing. "I could totally make a bratwurst or Vienna sausage joke here, but I won't."

"I wish you would." Chris went back to the cork and pulled it out. "But if you're not going to, give me the next entry. This journal just got way more interesting."

"Okay, okay." Regan found her place again. "'I must convince him to allow me to conduct my own spells, or if he proves uncooperative, perhaps I will do them on my own, without him. At times, he becomes too domineering, and he must understand I am no longer a naïve girl, but an angry woman.'"

"Uh-oh. Angry woman alert."

Regan felt the edge of uneasiness. This didn't even sound like the same person as the first few simplistic entries. She turned a few more pages and saw that the writing had grown sloppier, as if the author were writing faster, with no concern for appearance. There were notations in the margin, so spindly Regan couldn't interpret them.

"'Must get rid of Mr. Tradd, he has become nothing but a nuisance. F was happy to tell me how, because he knows if I ever marry Mr. Tradd, my money will belong to my husband, and he will surely curb both the time and money that is spent on my so-called heathen activities with my black lover.'"

Geez. That was no trip to the hospital for charity work. Those were the words of a defiant woman. Regan could understand if the author was in love with another man, the pain and heartbreak of being forced by her parents to marry a man of their choice, their station in life, but this didn't sound like love. It sounded like . . . anger.

"Whoa. Our Victorian lady has some serious balls under her skirts," Chris said. "I think I would have liked her."

That was a courageous move for the late nineteenth century—having an interracial affair—but something seemed so off to Regan.

"But why is she angry?" she wondered. "Because she can't be with him? I can't say that she really sounds like a woman in love."

"What does a woman in love sound like?" Chris asked.

"Happy."

He snorted. "Oh, really. Love makes most people I know, men and women, neurotic, not happy."

Regan really didn't want to believe that was true, but in her own case, it had certainly been dead accurate. "That's such a positive outlook. I'm sure Nelson—you remember who he is, the man you live with and are in love with— would be thrilled to hear it."

Shrugging, he gave her a grin. "I'm happily neurotic."

"Is that what we're calling it?" Regan took a sip from her wine, smiling at the plastic cup. She could have as many glasses in whatever container she wanted and no one could disapprove. Setting the cup back down, she continued to read.

"'It is half past midnight and I just returned from Mr. Tradd's and I am exhilarated! I did as F said. I planted my left foot in front of his house and spun around nine times. I scooped up a handful of dirt where my foot had been and threw it at his front door, then ran like the wind to my landau waiting up the street. Such a thrill! I was so pleased with myself and so aroused that even though I did not have F to satisfy me in the carriage, I did so myself. Ah, to feel so alive when all I have longed for is death . . . it is a strange, unpleasant mystery.'"

Regan snapped the journal shut, discomfort rushing her. "We shouldn't be reading this." It was voyeuristic, to be speaking this woman's thoughts out loud over cups of wine.

"She's dead!" Chris protested. "What difference does it make?"

"I don't know. But I feel like reading this out loud, together, is sort of like making fun of her. And she was clearly struggling through some difficult times."

When all I have longed for is death . . . not the words of a happy woman, and Regan didn't feel right reading about her pain.

"She's bat-shit crazy is what you mean."

Maybe. "Struggling," Regan repeated. "It's like poking around in someone's head. It makes me uncomfortable."

"She was a rich white woman having premarital sex with a black man and dabbling in voodoo in 1878, and yet she was writing it down in a journal for anyone to find. So I don't think you should feel guilty about reading it."

"You think she's talking about voodoo?"

"It sounds like it to me—spells and dirt tossing. Maybe her paramour was Haitian."

"He could be. I can't say I know that much about voodoo." Regan carefully set the journal in her lap and took another sip of her drink, telling herself the heat in her cheeks was from the wine, not from the memory of the one time she'd made contact with anyone in the voodoo realm. "Did I tell you I asked Jen to find a voodoo priest for my fund-raiser?"

"Oh, really? That's cool. Is he going to do divinations and make mojo bags or something?"

"I don't know. We haven't booked one yet. There was one in particular that came highly recommended and Jen is having trouble making contact with him." That was stretching the truth. It was Regan who had suggested Felix Leblanc to Jen Dengler, their friend and Regan's event planner.

She wasn't sure why she had mentioned his name to Jen, but when they were planning the fund-raiser for the Save Our Cemeteries organization that Regan worked for, they had decided on a quintessential New Orleans theme. They were having zydeco and jazz music, Cajun and Creole food, Mardi Gras decorations, and a voodoo priest. Which had immediately made her think of Felix.

"Isn't the party in two weeks? He's probably already booked."

"Probably." But Regan had to try, because she wanted to see him again, if for no other reason than to tell him thank-you. It had been his asking to see her ring and her removing it, something he probably wouldn't even remember, that had given her the courage to leave Beau. She was curious to see if Felix would intuitively know that her marriage was over.

Not that she believed he had told her anything other than vague pronouncements. She didn't.

If she were brutally honest, she'd admit she had been attracted to him that night, and a small part of her wanted to see if that had been a weird anomaly or if she would see him again and come to the same conclusion—that he was hot, and she wanted to have sex with him. Not that she would ever act on it, but she was intrigued.

"Hit me," she said to Chris, holding out her empty cup.

"So . . ." he said, as he picked up the bottle and poured. "How are you doing? Is Beau-Beau the bastard behaving himself?"

She shrugged. "If calling me a greedy bitch is behaving, then yes."

"How can you be greedy?" Chris refilled his own cup. "You're the one who has all the money! What an asshole."

"That would be accurate." But sitting on her own balcony, of her own house, it didn't matter nearly as much. Their divorce probably wouldn't be final for months because of Beau's stalling. They had been legally separated since January 1, and he had fought and been as petty as humanly possible through the whole process, but money was good for a lot of things and eventually they would get it settled. Regan had hired one of Beau's chief rivals for her attorney, and he had gone for the jugular.

Thank God she had listened to her father and had Beau sign a prenup before their wedding.

"He wanted a lump-sum settlement for all the money he said he'd spent on me over the year of our marriage and six-month engagement. But since I paid for our condo with cash, I'm offering that to him free and clear. My lawyer says the judge can't argue with my generosity."

"He doesn't even deserve that."

She shrugged. "Maybe not. But I don't care. I just want out." The wine was warming her from the inside out and she had a happy little buzz going. "He sucks."

Chris laughed. "Oh, my God, I love hearing that come out of your mouth. That's totally worth the nine-ninety-nine this wine cost me. Why did you ever marry the putz in the first place?"

"I don't know." It was a question she had asked herself many times. Regan looked into her wine cup. No answers in the pink fizz. "I was twenty-eight, ready to settle down, have a family. He was charming, had a successful career, my family loved him . . . he treated me well when we were dating. It was just easy, I guess, and I thought I was in love with him."

"I always knew he was an asshole." Chris studied her over his glass. "You know if you had stayed, eventually he would have gotten physical. Mental abuse almost always turns to physical."

Regan shuddered, both fear and relief riding up her spine. "That's part of the reason why I left—fear of how far it would go. Though I don't know that he would have ever gone there. It really was more just that I couldn't be what he wanted and I was so damn tired of trying to please him. I've wondered a lot why he ever married me . . . he really didn't seem to like me the way I am."

There was a pause while they both reflected, then Chris waved his hand in dismissal. "Well, you're everything I want, and you're an amazing friend. And thank God you did leave, because these chairs needed a home. Think of all the awesome parties we are going to throw in this house. Wait until Mardi Gras next year, we'll blow the roof off this place."

Glad he had lightened the mood again, Regan grinned. "I would kind of like to keep the roof. But a party would be fun." Sinking back in her chair, legs stretched out, she sighed in contentment. "If I wind up old and alone in this massive house, will you take pity on me and move in with me?"

"Only if the football team is here too."

"Deal."

She raised her cup to his and they bumped them together, wine sloshing out and splashing their fingers. Regan laughed. "I'm loving life right this minute."

It was the first time in a long, long while she could say that and mean it.

"I wish to go for a drive," Camille told one of her footmen as she came down the stairs, gloves in hand. "Have the landau brought around immediately."

There was a pause, the footman glancing toward the clock hanging over the rosewood table in the foyer. "Miss?"

Camille's temper flared. Everyone always telling her what to do, how to live. There was no one left on this earth who had the right to an opinion as to how she behaved, and she hoped the servants, the ladies in society, would all choke on their disapproval.

She glared at the footman from the bottom step. "Are you now feigning a hearing impediment? You heard me, you insolent laze-about. Yes, I am well aware of the hour, and you will do as you are told without opinion or hesitation."

He was already stammering an apology and scrambling to do her bidding, which gave her great satisfaction. She had been stripped of all of her loved ones, but she had been left with the cloak of copious wealth, and she did appreciate the security it provided, the power within her own household. But because of her sex, having money also brought the burden of society's rigid rules, and the fawning attention of men seeking to claim both her hand and her fortune.

The thought of marriage was abhorrent.

A husband would seize her assets, control her spending, and dictate how her time was spent.

Most of all, a husband would forbid her from seeing Felix, and she was not going to give up that peculiar pleasure—no, necessity—for anyone.

The voodoo practitioner had shown her how to awaken the delicious desires of her ripe body, and he was taking her through the labyrinth of magic, down the dark road *that blurred the lines of this world and the next, where at the end she would have her family once again with her.*

Strolling across the marble floor to head outside for her ride, Camille tossed her gloves on the Louis XIV chair that resided next to the front door. It was hot as Hades outside and she had suddenly realized there was absolutely no reason to follow convention when she was on a mission to rid herself of an unwanted suitor at nearly midnight. Why suffer through damp palms when there was no one to see her? Besides, she would soil the gloves when she threw dirt at the door.

Mr. Tradd wanted both her hand and her fortune, and she was no longer inclined to give him either, so she was going to conduct her very first spell—a ritual to rid herself of his bothersome presence in her life.

Her parents had wanted her to marry him, but he was two things she could no longer tolerate at this point in her life—he was both boring and bereft of money.

It was time to make the stuffy social climber disappear. The thought of doing so made her smile in satisfaction as she went out the front door and took the hand of her footman to step up into the landau. His eyes widened at the contact with her bare skin, and feeling more than a little wicked, Camille drew her fingers across the length of his palm before releasing him.

Desire replaced the shock in his eyes, and she gave him a saucy smile before turning to look out onto Royal Street. Perhaps after she had given her virginity to Felix, she would play with the footman. He was quite attractive, and displayed a rather impressive figure beneath his coat. There would be no disapproval from him for her behavior if she were on her knees before him, she could virtually guarantee. She laughed aloud, shifting on the seat against the sudden rush of arousal.

"Mr. Tradd's residence," she told her coachman, who had the good sense to neither protest nor hesitate.

Her suitor lived in a well-appointed house in the American district uptown, giving every appearance of having ample funds, but Camille knew it was a façade. He was using the last of his ready cash to let the house, and within months he would be solely reliant on his income as a banker to survive, hence his desperate desire to marry her. Camille found it amusing that a banker had no money, but not amusing enough to bind herself to him in marriage.

As far as she was concerned, he should have had the good sense not to lose all his money gambling.

When they pulled up to the crossroad of his street and the main thoroughfare, Camille ordered her coachman to stop. "I'm going for a quick stroll," she said. "I shall return momentarily."

"Miss, I don't think that you should go alone."

But she ignored him, vaulting down with no assistance, and set off at a quick pace along the street, her linen gown swirling around her legs, her skin dewy from the humidity. She had chosen to wear dancing slippers instead of boots so that she could remove them in front of Mr. Tradd's, and she did just that as she approached the lawn in front of his residence. The street had gaslights, which allowed her to see, yet weren't strong enough to alert any neighbors to her presence should they glance outside.

The door of his Greek Revival home was red, which made her laugh. It was the color said to ward off evil spirits, but it would not prevent her from infusing his household with her magic. Of course, she knew she wasn't evil, just determined. But perhaps the magic was evil. It was of no importance to her as long as her goal was achieved. She would fling the very flames of Hell at his house if it would rid her of his presence. She padded across the dry lawn, slippers in hand, toes unaccustomed to the feel of the hard ground. Since the rainstorms of early July, when the fevers had come, the summer had been dry, which would suit her purposes.

Throwing her arms out, she tipped her head back and did a slow pirouette, resting all her weight on her left foot as she completed a full rotation.

Nine, eight. She stared up at the wide-open sky, thick, dark clouds rolling in as she chanted softly, "Mr. Tradd, Mr. Tradd."

Seven, six. Warm air rushed over her face as she spun faster, commanding, "Be gone, be gone."

Five, four. "Stay away, stay away." Dizziness enveloped her, but she focused on the sky, on her desire.

Three, two. "From me, from me."

One. "Or die."

She ground to a halt, her head swimming, body listing to the left, off balance from spinning, and she smiled at the sensation as she righted her head and black spots danced in front of her eyes. Reaching down, she yanked up a piece of the foliage and the dirt beneath it.

Taking aim, she hurled the handful as hard as she could at his front door. When it made contact with a satisfying thwack, Camille let out a triumphant cheer. She had never, never in her entire life of being the perfect daughter, the perfect lady, thrown anything, and it was exhilarating.

And she'd made her mark.

Laughing, she grabbed her slippers, picked up her skirts, and raced off down the street as fast as her legs could carry her. Moisture dripped down her back and her corset shifted on her breast. Pins fell out of her hair from the jostling, allowing the long tresses to tumble loose, and her hand was covered in dirt and grass.

She had never felt so free or powerful, bare feet scraping and tearing as she ran over the stones. When she arrived at her waiting carriage, she was not in control of her speed, and when she tried to jump up onto the step, she slipped and smacked down onto the stones.

Her coachman gasped and was getting down to assist, but she paused on the stones, hands and knees on the *ground, head staring at the muddy step, the sting of pain in her palms and beneath her skirts. Her lungs burned from the exertion and she'd lost a slipper, but at that moment, the acute sharpness of pain merged with the exhilaration of breaking all the rules, and she had never felt so alive in her entire life.*

It was crystalline, heady, the wild thrill of freedom, and she didn't want it to go away, to recede and leave her floundering in grief and loneliness.

The coachman lifted her, and she let him, but once settled in her seat, she bunched up the front of her gown, the volume of the fabric still covering her legs, but allowing her access to her inner thighs. Stroking herself as the carriage lurched forward, she felt the surge of desire, the perfect way to continue the thrill of her adventure.

As she buried a finger deep into her slick heat, Camille didn't bother to prevent a small moan from escaping her mouth. The coachman turned, eyes widening, hands almost dropping the reins. She stared him straight in the eye and smiled, her hand moving faster.

"Holy Mary, Mother of God," he murmured.

But Mary and her son had abandoned Camille as surely as her parents and sisters had.

She closed her eyes and disappeared in the frenetic burn of physical pleasure.

Chapter Three

❧

Regan woke up in her hotel room with a start. Glancing at the clock glowing on the nightstand, she tried to quiet her racing heart, her inner thighs throbbing with unsatisfied desire. 6 A.M. She had been dreaming.

It had been the most vivid one she'd ever had, placing her in the point of view of someone else, which was odd. In her dreams, she was usually still Regan, sometimes in her body, sometimes watching herself, but invariably herself.

In this dream it wasn't that she was Camille, in the truest sense, but she had been watching her, privy to all her thoughts. She had felt every emotion, every physical sensation, including Camille's desire.

Regan shifted her hand off of the front of her damp panties, evidence of her unmistakable arousal. Strange. Though not surprising, considering it had been months since she'd had sex. Maybe it was just a very imaginative sex dream. Pushing a sweaty clump of hair off her forehead, she felt under the pillow next to her for the journal she and Chris had found in the chest of drawers. It was still there, safe.

She had checked into a hotel right around the corner from her house the day before. She'd had no intention of staying in her new place without a bed to sleep on. Chris had offered her a couch to crash on for the night, but he lived Uptown and she wanted to be close to her house so she could meet the movers at eight in the morning. When she and Chris had called it a night and parted ways at one in the morning, both more than a little drunk, she had grabbed the journal before catching a cab, not wanting anything to happen to the one-hundred-plus-year-old book.

Maybe she should have stayed with Chris, because alone in the dark hotel room she was disturbed at the tenor of the dream, the manic desperation of it still clinging to her. She wasn't sure what it said about her psyche that she could take the scraps of what she'd read in that journal and spin them into such a clear scene of the event, that she had made the woman even a little more nutso than she had appeared in the later journal entries they had read.

And that she would masturbate along with her dream. That was a first.

Where the name Camille had been plucked from in her subconscious, she had no idea either. She'd never known anyone by that name, and while the author of the journal had the initial C, she had never written her name in any of the entries Regan had read, so she had no explanation as to why her brain would ascribe that name to the dream figure.

Dreams were random, that was all. Nothing more, nothing less.

Flicking the lamp on next to the bed, she sat up against the pillows, her fingers running over the black leather cover of the journal, over the embossed initials CAC. While Camille might be random, it didn't surprise her that she had inserted Felix's name into her dream as that of a voodoo priest.

He tripped around the edges of her thoughts chronically

since she'd met him, and he had grown more attractive with time than he probably was in reality, if she wanted to be honest with herself. The months since their brief meeting had been harsh and emotional for her, and as she tried to stay strong in her fight against Beau, and look down a future that might result in her never marrying again, the idea that there would be men like Felix, men she could feel desire for, intrigued her. At some point a year or two from now, she would date and have sex again, or at least Lord, she hoped she would. It was nice to know that fundamental spark in her still existed, because despite the circumstances of that awful night she'd met Felix, and the strange conversation they had shared, Regan had been attracted to him.

She would never date Felix. Men like him didn't have interest in plain, politically correct women, and given the fact that their worlds were wildly different, she doubted that they would have a whole lot in common. Yet the one thing she didn't doubt was that he would be amazing in bed. It was the eyes, the way they had met hers without ever wandering away, the intensity in them, the focus. Eyes like that had to belong to a man who would give and demand a dedication to pleasure.

Not surprising then, that in her dream she would cast him in the role of voodoo priest and forbidden lover, when she was clearly undersexed.

And she would like to see him again, just once.

Regan tried to close her eyes, but the image of the fictitious Camille, features indistinct, down on the cobblestones in front of her carriage, muddied and covered in sweat, full of triumph, kept her from relaxing back into sleep. It was unnerving, disturbing, the vividness reminiscent of a nightmare more than a casual dream, the clarity of the event not the usual mishmash of random thoughts, but purposeful.

She had been under a lot of stress and had restructured her entire life. A graphic dream was normal.

But that didn't erase the unease she felt at the memory, nor did it settle her back into sleep. What if it was some horrible metaphor for her life, her marriage to Beau? The feelings of entrapment, the desperate urge to flee, the yearning for freedom . . .

Disturbing. Plain and simple. And she didn't want to think about the past, or the damage her marriage might have somehow done to her. Wide awake and tense, after another five minutes of staring at the ceiling, dream rewinding and rolling over and over in her head, Regan gave up and threw the covers back. If she wasn't going to sleep, she might as well get some coffee and shake off the last remnants of the wine.

Ten minutes later, she was dressed and checked out of the hotel, the doorman hailing a cab for her as she waited on the curb, the journal tucked in her overnight bag. The street was quiet in the shadows of the early morning, or the late night, depending on your perspective. They were only a block from Bourbon Street, after all. She pulled her sweater a little tighter around her against the chill and glanced down Royal Street, pleased to be back in the Quarter despite the tension the dream had created.

Beau had disliked the French Quarter, thinking it was noisy and dirty and filled with undesirables. She would have never been able to convince him to live here. Yet she loved it for its authenticity, for its acceptance of all kinds of people, its tolerance of the unusual. It had always felt like home to her, though she'd never had the courage to live here before. Her parents would have found it odd, her friends would have raised eyebrows at her.

But since she had left what they all considered the perfect husband after little more than a year of marriage, a few more raised eyebrows meant nothing at this point. So she had bought her house, and she was excited to fill it with furniture and make a home for herself.

Jumping in the cab that pulled up in front of her, Regan

tipped the doorman and settled on the seat, mouth dry from the wine the night before. She needed coffee. "Café du Monde, please," she told the driver. It was open twenty-four hours a day, and she relished the thought of sitting there in the morning quiet having her coffee and a beignet.

She was supposed to meet Jen, an early riser, at seven to go over some details for the fund-raising party, and she decided to text her to meet at Café du Monde instead of her house. After typing the message and hitting SEND on her phone, Regan glanced up. They were about to pass her house and she wanted to just take in the view of its grand gray façade.

It was a ridiculous purchase for a single woman, she knew that, and Beau and her parents and grandmother had told her over and over in no uncertain terms how stupid it was to have six thousand square feet to wander around in by herself. But this house had always excited her imagination with its majestic beauty and its grand courtyard that faced the cross street. The Juliet balcony jutted out over the foliage like a feminine curtsy before racing in either direction in the more traditional New Orleans gallery.

"Can you turn right here?" she asked the driver as they approached the front of her house on its corner lot.

"Sure." He turned, and they passed the side of the house, where the Juliet balcony and courtyard were.

Regan realized her bedroom light was on. She and Chris must have left it on in their preoccupation with picking up used plastic cups and the empty wine bottle. The angle made it impossible to see into the windows, but she knew the light would only show her empty bedroom to the curious passerby, so it wasn't anything to worry about anyway.

So why was it bothering her? She frowned and looked at the courtyard gate, suddenly doubting if she had locked it.

"Can you stop a second?"

She leaped out as soon as he braked, not waiting to

answer the question on his lips. Testing the gate, she was reassured to see that it was locked. No one could possibly get in. Climbing back into the cab, she mentally scolded herself for getting paranoid.

"Lady, you can't just pull on gates like that. It's someone's house, not a museum," the driver said, giving her a frown.

That lightened her mood considerably. She felt both pride of ownership and pleasure that a cabdriver would be looking out for her property. Locals had a love-hate relationship with tourists. Everyone loved the business and the influx of revenue, but it was hard not to be irritated when drunken revelers were scaling your gallery poles or hitting you in the face with beads they'd scooped up off the ground. And every local knew you never touched anything that had landed on the streets.

"It's my house," she told him with a smile. "I just bought it and I'm moving in today."

He shot her a look of disbelief, his bushy gray eyebrows rising to meet his hairline. "You bought this big old house? Where are you from?"

Regan realized she'd distracted him, and she started to wonder if he had any intention of pulling back out into traffic. She could really use her coffee. "I'm from here. I grew up in the Garden District."

"Then why were you staying in a hotel?"

"I'm moving in today and I stayed in a hotel so I'd have a bed to sleep on."

He still looked suspicious, but he seemed to relent short of asking to see her settlement statement from the title company. "Well, it's a big house, but you won't be alone in it."

"Actually, I will, I'm single." For which she was grateful on a daily basis.

"I meant the spirits. Everyone knows this house is haunted." Leaning over his steering wheel to stare up at the balcony, he pointed. "That's where she died, you know."

"Who died?"

"Some girl. Threw herself off that balcony over a hundred years ago. Boy trouble. You know how that goes."

"No, actually I don't." She'd never once felt the urge to throw herself off a balcony. Run like hell? Yes. Scream witlessly into a pillow? Definitely. Throwing herself off a balcony to shatter every bone on the stones below had never once occurred to her.

Maybe she was normal after all.

But she was already questioning that again an hour later when she was staring across the powdered-sugar-laden table at Jen, saying, "Ask him again."

Jen made a face over her coffee cup. "Regan, I can't. He said no, what am I supposed to do? Threaten him? Use a spell to coerce him? He's the voodoo priest, not me."

"Well, maybe he didn't understand what the event was," Regan said, crumpling up a napkin on the sticky table in front of her. She couldn't believe Felix had said no to doing readings at her party. "Did you give him my name?"

"Um, yes." Jen set down her coffee cup.

"So give me the address to his store then. I'll go and ask him in person. He just can't say no." Regan wasn't sure why it was so important, it just was. But she realized a second too late how her determination could be misconstrued.

Definitely too late. Jen's brown eyes were curious. "You're going to walk into his shop and ask him in person? Are you freaking kidding me? What's the big deal? We knew it was a long shot to get anyone on such short notice."

"He's just really good, that's all," Regan said, the words sounding lame to her own ears.

Given that they had been friends for twenty years, Jen wasn't buying that for a second. "When did you meet him, by the way? You never said."

Shit. "At a Christmas party." She strove for casual,

taking a big bite of her beignet and occupying her attention with shaking powdered sugar off her fingers.

"Which Christmas party? I don't recall you going to any except for the one Beau's firm threw."

"It was that one." She blotted her mouth and blinked at Jen. Time to change the subject and quick. "So, have the tabletop decorations gotten in yet? I know I said I wanted ten rounds, but I'm thinking we should go with twelve. The living room is huge and I don't want it to seem empty."

"Nice try." Jen moved her finger in a circle. "But let's back up to the moment of meeting the voodoo priest that you're clearly dying to have at your party. If my math is right, which it is, you met this guy the night you left your husband. Would you care to explain that to me?"

"What difference does that make?"

"Hello! It makes a huge difference." Jen sank back in her chair, her beignets forgotten. "Oh, my God, you slept with him, didn't you? That's what this is all about. You panicked in your marriage, had a fling, left your husband, now you're thinking the answer to all your problems is with this guy you don't know jack-shit about."

"I did not sleep with him! And my leaving Beau had nothing to do with meeting him. We barely exchanged five words." The doughnut sat in her gut like an anchor, and Regan crossed her arms over her chest, feeling belligerent. "Can't you just accept that being married to Beau blew and that's why I left him? Why isn't that good enough?"

"It's not good enough, I'm sorry. You had this great husband who was madly in love with you, who catered to your every whim, and you just threw him away for no apparent reason. Relationships don't always go your way every single second of the day, Regan. You have to work at them and appreciate what you have. Do you know how many women would have loved to be in your designer shoes?"

Regan's arms fell to her sides as she stared at Jen,

stunned. "I see. I didn't realize you thought I was such a spoiled brat."

Her friend sighed, tucking her caramel-colored hair behind her ear. "I'm sorry, that didn't come out right. I don't think you're a spoiled brat. You're very generous and not even remotely pretentious. I just don't see what it is you want. I mean, how could you not be happy with him?"

Picking at the damp coagulated sugar on her half-eaten beignet, Regan swallowed the twin lump in her throat. "Maybe," she said softly, "because he was the wrong man for me. Maybe, because he made me feel horribly inadequate and intensely lonely. And because no matter how good it looks on paper, a marriage that does that to you is not a good one."

Jen stared at her for a long minute then tossed her napkin on the table. "Shit. I'm sorry."

Knowing that was a major concession for Jen, Regan nodded. "Thanks."

But Jen was already rifling around in her handbag, which she had carefully set on the empty chair next to her, on top of a layer of protective napkins she had spread out. Powdered sugar was a fact of life at Café du Monde, stuck to every surface and scattered all over the floor. It was the price you paid for the luxury of beignets caked with the addictive stuff.

"Here." Jen shoved a piece of paper at her.

"What's this?"

"It's the address for Felix Leblanc's shop. Take it. Do whatever you want with it."

Regan grinned as she glanced down at it. Orleans Street. "Thanks." She could have looked it up herself, but it was touching that Jen had given it to her, no matter how begrudgingly.

"And for God's sake, if you start screwing the guy, can

you please be discreet about it? If Beau finds out he'll hurl an adultery charge at you so fast your head will spin."

"But we're legally separated."

"Like that will matter to him?"

True. "I'm not going to have sex with him. I just want to talk to him."

Jen finally cracked a smile. "Famous last fucking words."

❧

"Is there anything else you'd like to know?" Felix said, knowing precisely what the girl in front of him had spent twenty minutes working up the nerve to ask.

She was a plain, shy girl in her early twenties, the kind who had been dealt an unfair hand by fate. No amount of makeup could mask the squareness of her jaw, there was no way to alter the closeness of her eyes, and no cream that could fix the stretch marks that had already appeared on the peak of each of her breasts. This was the kind of young woman who had spent her life being judged as less than attractive, and had clearly retreated into shyness as a result of harsh societal standards of beauty.

He would have to coax the question from her.

"No, I guess that's it," she said, shaking her head, even after her friend nudged her with her shoulder. "Thanks."

"Don't you want to know about your love life?" he asked, smiling at her. "Most people do."

The sallow yellow shirt that didn't flatter her ruddy complexion slipped and she tugged it, covering the bulk of her cleavage back up. "Oh, well." She laughed, a self-conscious, sad sound. "What love life?"

At one point in his life, back when he was young, mortal, greedy, he would have flirted and flattered for the sole purpose of ensuring repeat business. If you gave customers what they wanted, they kept coming back. It was a basic business principle.

Now he did what he did simply because everyone needed some kind of hope. Everyone needed to believe that there was one person out there for him or her, a soul mate.

If they didn't have hope, they became Felix.

And the world didn't need another one of him.

"We are talking about six, maybe nine months from now," Felix said, his smile pleasant, not flirtatious. He never flirted with customers anymore. That was something that had died back in the nineteenth century with Camille, as had the desire for money. For any of the things money could buy.

The girl was trying not to look too interested. "Oh?" she asked.

"That's when you're going to England!" her equally unattractive friend said in an excited whisper.

"Exactly," he said, with a confidence he didn't feel. But he had learned that confidence could create an illusion that could create a reality. If he bolstered this girl, maybe she would go off to England and take a chance and talk to a man she was interested in, and maybe, just maybe, she would find some kind of happiness.

Or at the very least, get laid. That never hurt either. Felix couldn't always shake his cynicism, and he figured sex was better than no sex even if it came without a declaration of love and a promise of forever.

"There is a man, outside a castle . . . a tour guide, maybe? He likes your accent."

The friend giggled. "Do we have accents in Georgia?" she said with a rueful grin.

"You're wearing a navy shirt when you meet him." Might as well steer her in the direction of a better color for her complexion.

She frowned. "I don't have any navy shirts. I like bright colors."

"Maybe I'm wrong about that," he said, soothingly,

knowing she would be out shopping that very afternoon for navy. "But he shares your interest in horses."

"Oh," she said, her voice breathy, expression thoughtful. "That would be . . . nice."

The two girls sighed and exchanged a look of contentment. Maybe the fantasy would be enough. Or maybe just the idea would spur confidence in her, and that was worth a few words of encouragement from him.

The doorbell tinkled the arrival of another customer and Felix wrapped up the reading. He couldn't see who had entered the shop, since he did readings behind a screen, but he could care less if someone robbed him of every last voodoo doll and scented candle in the shop. It was meaningless to him.

The girls thanked him with smiles, dropping a five-dollar bill into his tip jar. Not that he could keep it. Most of it went to the master, not to his pocket. But he expressed his thanks anyway, smiling and wishing them a good day as he escorted them around the screen.

They walked toward the door, scooting around the new customer, and he opened his mouth to say hello.

Then he realized who it was and his greeting died on his lips.

Regan Henry Alcroft.

Just who he didn't need to see.

She was wearing expensive jeans, boots with heels, and a black sweater. Along with a tentative smile.

"Hi. I'm not sure if you remember me, but I was at a function you gave readings at . . . you gave me a reading. I'm—"

He cut her off, not wanting to prolong this, not wanting to feel any compassion or desire for her. "Regan Henry Alcroft. I know who you are."

She was startled, but then she recovered, dropping her large handbag down onto the floor at her feet. "Actually, it's Henry. Just Henry."

"Excuse me?" He didn't follow her thought, preoccupied with wondering if it was coincidence that she was in black again, or if she preferred black and white clothes.

"I've dropped the Alcroft. My divorce will be final in a few weeks, I hope."

Well, well. Felix's eyes automatically fell to her ring finger. It was bare. Alcroft hadn't mentioned a divorce in progress, but then why would he? The master gave no explanations to the servant.

"Do I offer congratulations or sympathy?" he asked, leaning against a display table a few feet away from her.

"Congratulations." There was a pink stain on her cheeks, and she looked nervous, but pleased with herself. "It's a good thing and it was my decision."

"Then congratulations. May Regan Henry be very happy." Far, far away from him.

She smiled. "Thank you."

"So are you just passing by?" he asked. "In need of a potion to win more in your divorce settlement?" He didn't think for one minute she had just been strolling down Orleans Street and walked into his shop by accident. She had sought him out, and damn it, that made him uncomfortable. Her being anywhere near him was dangerous, for both of them.

"No." Regan shook her head. "I don't need a potion. I wanted to ask you a question, but first I want to thank you."

Felix could feel the coil of tension in him tighten. "For what?"

"For the reading that night, at the Christmas party. I'm sure you had no idea that I was thinking about leaving my husband, and well, it sounds stupid, but when you asked to see my ring, and I took it off, the freedom I felt then was the push I needed to get the courage to leave. So thank you. I might still be with him if it weren't for you."

The hot burn of anger spread out through Felix's body.

When the hell would he ever learn? He should have never, ever gotten involved with Regan that night. He should have been smart and given her a generic reading, not brought up her ring, or her sister, or her free will. He had acted out of compassion and concern, but in this case it would only bite them both in the ass, and he had known that.

He'd known that.

But he'd done it anyway, because he had seen the pain in her eyes and he had been unable to stop himself.

Now they would both pay unless he made it clear he wasn't worth her praise. "Don't thank me. I didn't do anything," he told her gruffly.

"Oh, I know not intentionally," she said, her fingers fiddling with a fertility doll in a bowl on the table to her right. "But . . ." She looked at him, so earnest, her dark eyes shining. "It doesn't matter. What matters is that because of you, I left."

And may she never speak those words out loud again. "What did you want to ask me?" he said abruptly. "If it's about your party, I already told your employee no."

He was being rude and caustic, and he hated it, but it was the best thing to do. It would keep her away from him in the future. Trying to ignore the confusion on her face, he stared at her coldly, waiting for her response.

"Yes," she said, clearing her throat. "It's about my party. I know you told Jen no, but I was hoping that you would change your mind. It's an important fund-raiser. All the proceeds go to the Save Our Cemeteries organization, which preserves and restores our historic cemeteries. The pay is more than reasonable, I think, and we'd only need you for two hours."

"No."

The pink on her cheeks deepened. He thought she would finally slink off, but Regan had more backbone than he'd given her credit for. She straightened her shoulders and asked, "Why not?"

"Because I don't want to."

Her lip curled at his behavior and they stared at each other for a long moment, before she looked away. It wasn't fair. She was a beautiful, intriguing woman and he could only look, not touch.

Though why he would even bother to lament life's unfairness at his age and experience was ludicrous. He knew better.

"I see." Her voice was all wealthy ice princess. "Well, if it's not too much trouble, would you at least point me in the direction of some research materials?" Regan lifted her bag and dug around in it, pulling out a black leather book. "I found this personal journal from the nineteenth century in my new house and I'd like to research some of the spells in it. I'm pretty sure they're voodoo spells."

Hating that he had put that reserve into her normally sweet and melodic voice, Felix put out his hand. "No, it's not too much trouble. Can I see it?"

"Of course." She handed him the book. "Thank you."

He flipped the book open to the first page.

June 28, 1878. I received this journal for my twentieth birthday today as a gift from Mr. Tradd, the man my parents wish for me to marry. I imagine it will be so.

Felix's entire body went still, heat rushing into his head, his mouth, the shock so palpable he could taste its acerbic bitterness on his tongue. No. It couldn't be.

But he flipped a few pages and it was.

Camille's journal.

The voice of his long dead lover reaching out from the past in her formal handwriting and increasing madness. "Where did you get this?" he asked, his voice tight.

"In the chest of drawers in the house I just bought. The

chest is original to the house, and it had a secret compartment, which is where this was hidden. A pretty cool find, isn't it?"

Or disturbing, depending on your perspective. "Where is your house?"

He knew what she was going to say, even before the words left her mouth. Felix could picture the room in the house on Royal Street, the elaborate scrollwork on the chest of drawers shadowed by the many candles Camille had lit, his altar resting on top.

"Royal Street, here in the Quarter. It's on the corner of Ursuline, the big gray house. I just bought it."

"I think I know the one," he said, trying to keep his voice normal, forcing his shoulders to relax. "It's a beautiful house."

"Thanks. The movers just left. I knew I didn't have enough furniture to fill it, but I didn't realize how much I really need to buy. I'm going to be an interior designer's best friend for the next few months."

What a horrible, ironic, coincidence that she would buy that house, of all the properties in the Quarter. Or maybe it wasn't coincidence at all. So very few things were.

"I don't see any spells in here," he said, fingers gripping Camille's journal, the innocent and innocuous words of the days before her family's death blurring before him. It was painful to read even one of the bland, pleasant entries, devastating to realize what Camille had been when he had met her, and what she had become.

Guilt, for his greed, for his role in her madness and death, rose up in his throat, threatening to choke him.

"They start in the middle. I haven't had a chance to really read the journal, I just found it last night, but when I have more time in the next few weeks, I'd like to research the spells, and see if I can figure out who the owner is."

Felix flipped to the middle of the book, knowing precisely who the owner was.

> *To Cause a Rash*
> *Boil the root and bark of a tree.*
> *Drop in nine black peppercorns and boil it down*
> *again.*
> *Sprinkle it over the person's food.*

"Can I keep the journal for a few days?" he asked. He wanted to see if there was any evidence of his existence in Camille's life. That would be seriously unfortunate if she had addressed him by name in her journal.

She made a face of obvious reluctance. "Actually, I'd prefer to keep it myself. Maybe I could make some copies of it for you?"

Regan was already reaching out her hand to take the book back, and Felix opened his mouth, having known he would even as he knew he shouldn't. "How about I just meet you and we could go through it together?"

Her face split into a pleased smile. "Sure. That would be great, thank you."

"The coffee shop on Frenchman?" A public place was smarter, though maybe not safer. He wanted to walk through that house again, wanted to see the balcony, feel if there was any sense of Camille in its walls at this point, but it wasn't a good idea at all. Divorce or not, Regan Henry was still entangled with Alcroft, and if he heard that Felix was alone with her in that house, of all places, it would not be pretty.

Plus he wanted to see how Regan fit into the puzzle of the demon world, what her role, obviously unknown to her, was before he walked into the heart of that house and the past.

"That would be lovely," she said with another smile.

Lovely was not the word he would have chosen, but as he handed back to Regan the damning book that he hadn't even known existed, he thought it was the perfect way to describe her Ivory soap beauty.

"As are you," he said, the words flowing from him as naturally as sap from a maple.

Chapter Four

Felix watched Camille stroll around his shop in her smart fashionable gown, her hands stroking across the fronts of glass jars containing herbs. She wore a proprietary smile, taking pleasure he knew, in the fact that her being there was not acceptable by anyone's standards.

She liked to flirt with danger and he was happy to oblige her.

"What can I do for you this fine day, Miss Comeaux?"

"Oh, so formal," she protested with a playful pout. "There is no one here, Felix, surely I can be Camille to you."

Leaning in front of her, allowing his arm to brush her breast, Felix moved back the jar that she was at risk of knocking to the floor. "Have a care with the snake's blood, Camille."

She shivered in delight. "Say it again."

"Snake's blood?" he teased.

"No, my name."

Pressing his lips to her soft, delicate neck, he murmured,

"Camille. Camille. Camille." He could feel her pulse jump beneath his touch.

"That is more the thing," she said, her voice breathy, her fingers digging into his arms. "But our pleasures must wait. I have come for a very important reason, you know."

Felix straightened and flicked his tongue over her bottom lip, enjoying the shine he left on the pretty pink flesh. "No, I was not aware anything is more important than my mouth on your body."

Her eyes darkened with desire, the peaks of her pert breasts rising and falling rapidly above the bodice of her gown. "You are very bad and I won't be dissuaded from my purpose."

"What purpose, precious?" Felix drew his finger across her décolleté, watching as goose bumps rose in the wake of his touch. He appreciated her physical perfection, the beauty of her young and ripe figure, and her willingness to share it with him. He was greedy, he knew that, and wasn't ashamed of it.

You either took what you wanted or you spent your life longing for it. He had no wish to leave his desires unsatisfied, not when they were so easy to acquire. The only thing preventing anyone from possessing what he wanted was the sticky and misguided issue of morality, and Felix had abandoned his long ago.

Perhaps he'd never had it. His mother had certainly never displayed any moral reservations when it came to survival.

"I wish to irritate a certain Miss Janise who has been rather outspoken in her dislike of me."

"And what have you done to poor Miss Janise to generate such animosity?"

Camille gave a moue of disgust. "Poor Miss Janise, indeed. She has barely a penny to her name, yet somehow she is all the rage in every ballroom this summer." She pulled back from him, her hands smoothing down the front of her gown. "Everyone blathering on about how beautiful she is, how accomplished. What has she done, save simper behind a fan? The girl cannot string two intelligent words together, and yet she has had the audacity to have doors closed to me!"

So that was the crux of the problem. Camille's misconduct was beginning to have repercussions and she was choosing to blame it on Miss Janise and unfair gossip. "Miss Janise will marry and find herself in a delicate condition," he said, mocking the polite phrasing for a woman who is carrying a child. He would never understand society's obsession with pretending men and women did not take pleasure in each other's bodies. "And she will be out of your hair and out of your league."

"That's just it! I have no wish for her to marry well. She does not deserve it." Camille paced across the shop and picked up a random voodoo doll and set it back down.

Felix came up behind her, lifting her soft blonde curls and letting them fall through his fingers. "She will live a boring and predicable life, whereas you were made for adventure."

She whirled around and moved out of his touch. "I want to cause her to become ill so she will miss the Hansons' ball this Saturday. I need a spell."

He had no doubt she thought she did. And since he wanted her money, Felix saw no reason that Camille couldn't have what she wished, just as he took what he wished. "I have just the thing for you. Two dollars is all it will cost you."

"Two dollars?" Camille gave him a look of reprimand. "Felix, that is rather high for a close and personal friend." Yet she was already reaching into her reticule.

"Which is why I discounted my standard price. It will be worth it, Camille, when Miss Janise is suddenly afflicted with a horrible head-to-toe rash and dares not show her face in public for a fortnight."

Her eyes lit up. "A rash? That is brilliant."

"Indeed. All you need is tree bark and peppercorns, which I happen to have, and ill intent, which you have." He slid the money from her hand into his pocket and hooked his finger in the front of her gown, between her creamy breasts, and pulled her over to him. "One splotchy, itchy Miss Janise coming right up."

She laughed and threw her arms around him. "We are quite the pair, aren't we?"

"We most certainly are."

A match made in greed.

So wrong, yet so right.

❦

"It's a beautiful house," Regan's mother said begrudgingly as they walked out into the courtyard to say their good-byes.

"For twelve people," her father added, his hands in the pockets of his khaki pants.

Regan tried to end the visit on a positive note by saying, "Or me." She'd just spent an hour giving them a tour and having her mother criticize all her furniture placement while her father calculated maintenance costs on a house that size.

She was exhausted and just wanted to close the courtyard gate on them and sink onto her couch, which was placed exactly where she wanted it, thank you very much.

Her mother, wearing a red pants suit even though she'd had no plans that day other than this visit, fluffed her short, chic gray hair. "I know it's none of my business."

That was such a promising start to a sentence.

"But honestly, Regan, can you just give me one good reason why you're throwing away your marriage to Beau? It's not too late. He'd take you back, I'm sure he would. Just tell him you panicked, you got confused, he'll understand."

There it was. Yet again. Her mother's conviction that

she had suffered some sort of temporary insanity. Regan crossed her arms over her chest then realized her action, and purposely dropped them. She didn't need to defend or protect herself. "I didn't panic. I didn't get confused. Our marriage wasn't working for me."

"So you just gave up? Like that?" Her mother snapped her fingers. "The shine wore off the new toy so you threw it away?"

When had she ever behaved that way? Her entire life she had caused no ripples, had always done what was expected of her, and respected all of her mother's rules and desires. Regan could be totally honest in saying she had been a passive child and teenager, not a brat. That was no doubt partly the result of her sister's death at the age of six. Regan had never wanted to add to their grief, had never wanted strife or tension. Felix had been right about that in his reading of her.

"No," she told her mother carefully, determined not to lose her temper. "It was a mistake. I never should have married Beau in the first place."

Her mom opened her mouth, but her father interceded. "Mary," he said, a soft warning in his voice. "It's time for us to go."

"Thanks, Daddy," she said. "Thank you for dinner."

He gave her a kiss on the forehead. "Talk to you soon, princess."

"Bye. Bye, Mom. I love you both."

"I love you, too, Regan," her mother said, her disappointment so apparent it undid Regan's carefully constructed façade.

Knowing she was going to cry, she waved and retreated into the house, shutting the door behind her and locking it. Rude, no doubt. And something she would hear about later, but God, she couldn't stand that look on her mother's face. The implication that Regan had left Beau purely on some juvenile impulse, a bratty plea for attention.

Did her mother even have one clue about who she was?

Regan wandered through the enormous gourmet kitchen and wondered, did she really know herself?

Who exactly was Regan Henry? And who had Regan Henry Alcroft been? That was easier. She had been fictitious, a woman who didn't actually exist. A woman who had never really been, and would be no more.

Her family's reaction to her divorce was what she had been expecting, no matter how much it distressed her. But Felix's reaction in his shop hadn't been what she'd been hoping for.

Regan climbed the stairs to the second floor, her hand gripping the rich mahogany balustrade. She wasn't sure what she had expected, but it wasn't such coldness.

Then again, why would he care about her marriage breaking up?

It was more than a little embarrassing to think how frequently he had popped up in her thoughts over the last few months, and clearly she was just a random customer to him. One of hundreds he saw in a year. Nothing special to make her stand out in his mind.

Though he had remembered her.

And he had said she was lovely.

It was artificial flattery, nothing more, and she needed to remember that.

Stepping into her living room, she went over to the box she had purposefully avoided unpacking before her mother had seen the house. It would have led to another argument, and Regan could only handle one at a time. Ripping off the tape, she opened the box and pulled out the picture frames, then removed them from their Bubble Wrap one by one.

On the creamy buffet she used for storing candles and magazines in her living room, Regan arranged the photos of her childhood. Her and Moira at the beach. The two of them lying in a hammock together. Wearing twin grins in another picture, mouths rimmed with chocolate ice cream.

The formal picture of the Easter that Regan had been four and Moira six, before the diagnosis. They were both dressed in yellow chiffon, white gloves, rosebud purses clutched delicately in their laps.

Her mother didn't approve of Regan displaying pictures of her sister. It was too painful, her mother claimed. But for Regan, it was a way to hold on to the good, to the wonderful memories of sisterhood, of happy times, and the fast friendship that only siblings can share. In these pictures they were two little girls living life to the fullest, and that was the way she remembered Moira. Even when she'd been dying of leukemia, all her hair gone, Regan had memories of Moira singing along to the TV in the hospital, grinning in delight at the treat of a Popsicle, and offering for Regan to snuggle under her covers with her, then tickling her.

It was a mystery how her father felt about his oldest daughter's death, because he was silent on the subject, but her mother's opinion was clear—the hole in her heart had never healed and she didn't appreciate being reminded of that.

The mother-of-pearl frames surrounding the treasured photos were expensive antiques from her grandmother on her mother's side, passed to Regan at her death. Another point of contention between Regan and her mother. Bad enough she had pictures of Moira lying about, but to stick them in her grandmother's frames . . . to her mother, that was heaping grief on grief. For Regan, it was comfort, a way to keep them both close, to show respect.

She pulled a small crystal lamp out of the box, placed it on the end of the buffet, and plugged it in. Surveying the tablescape, she arranged a few frames, then was satisfied. Considering what a long day she'd had, that was good enough for tonight. She'd tackle the real unpacking tomorrow.

For now, she was going to sit on her balcony and go back to the beginning of CAC's journal. She didn't want to read it out of context, but wanted to read the author's whole story, from start to finish. She was meeting Felix the next day, and she wanted to at least have some questions ready for him about voodoo so he didn't think she was using the journal as some sort of excuse to see him.

Which maybe she was. In part, at least. She really did want to understand the journal, but there was no denying she also wanted to see him.

For some reason, her dream from that morning popped into her head, and she felt the flicker of arousal spark between her thighs. Her body was clearly sending her a hint that it didn't appreciate being neglected.

Unzipping her boots in her bedroom and tugging them off, she flung them on the floor at the end of her bed. The room was a disaster of boxes stacked on boxes, but she had a bed, and she'd put sheets on it, so the rest could wait. Except for one thing. Rustling around in the box she'd marked with a heart drawn in marker, she pulled out the stuffed monkey, its ear tattered, tail perilously close to falling off.

It was her sister's and it belonged in the bottom of her nightstand, close to where Regan slept. She would have preferred it on the bed, but didn't want to hassle with hiding it every time her mother came over, because invariably one day she would forget, and that would be disastrous considering that her mother didn't even know she had Patrick the monkey. When she lived with Beau, she had kept it tucked away as well because she hadn't wanted to explain anything to him, to share the pain of her loss.

Maybe that should have been a red flag to her, that she couldn't be vulnerable with him.

She supposed it had been.

Tucking the monkey into the nightstand, on his yellow blanket, she took the journal and headed out onto her balcony. Regan flipped past the first two entries she had read with Chris and read two more that outlined normal day-to-day tasks. It wasn't until she got to the entry on July 2 that Regan got her first glimpse of understanding as to what had happened to this poor girl.

Mother died this evening. I can barely write for my shock. We dined as usual, all seven of us, and all was well. Within two hours she was poorly, and now it is midnight and she is gone from the fever.

I cannot express my grief. My mother, gone. It is beyond comprehension.

Regan sighed, her heart going out to the girl who had written those words of pain. She understood all too well the grief, confusion that death brought.

July 3, 1 am. Jeanne-Marie has the fever now and is quite ill. Her moans are pitiful and I fear greatly for my sister. Father recalled the physician who left after my mother's passing, but we have heard the fever has taken the city in earnest and it may be some time before he can return. I can only pace and pray.

1:47 am. Lord help us, both Isabel and Frances have the fever as well. The physician has not returned.

2:01 am. Jeanne-Marie has passed after a brief, but horrendous struggle. Her cries of agony are burned onto my consciousness. I am utterly devastated. My beautiful mother and sister gone from me forever.

4 am. Clara is afflicted as well.

7:17 am. Just finished preparing the mourning room for Mother and Jeanne-Marie. I am moving in a fog of shock and exhaustion.

8:03 am. Frances has joined my mother and Jeanne-Marie.

> *10:12 am. Father has the fever.*
> *10:23 am. Clara dead.*
> *Noon. Isabel dead.*
> *5:19 pm. Father dead.*
> *5:20 pm. All dead, save me. I pray my time will*
> *be soon.*
> *July 5, 1878. I did not die.*

"Good God," Regan whispered as she read the last entry. Those words, scrawled onto an otherwise empty page, told the entire story.

Here was a twenty-year-old girl who had lost her entire family, four sisters and her parents, in less than twenty-four hours. It was unimaginable. No one could recover from that kind of staggering loss.

Regan shivered, leaning back in her chair to stare blindly at the house across the street from her.

Her heart broke for the girl who had endured such a horrible tragedy. The girl might be long dead, but Regan wished she could offer her some measure of comfort. But there could be no words to make someone feel better under those kinds of circumstances. It was beyond horrible.

And it had happened in her house.

She sat up straight in her chair. It had happened in her house. All those people had died here, somewhere within these walls. The mother and father probably right there in her bedroom. They had suffered and died from yellow fever.

Regan wasn't sure how she felt about that. Of course anytime you buy an older home, you have to recognize that at some point someone probably died there, but to know for sure that they had, and in such a tragic montage of death, well, it was a totally uncomfortable feeling.

Though maybe it hadn't happened here. Maybe the girl had moved here afterward. Maybe it had been a fresh start. Maybe she had married someone other than the undesirable Mr. Tradd.

Regan would have to do a little investigating, but she could find out who had owned the house in that time period and see if she could research the family.

But the question was, did she want to know?

Logic told her they most likely had all died here.

The taxi driver's story popped into her head. He had mentioned a young woman who had killed herself by jumping off the balcony. Maybe that was true, though it wasn't over a boy. Maybe it was a young woman who had struggled to continue after she lost her entire family and eventually gave up the fight.

Regan would have to read the rest of the journal to see if there were any clues as to what had happened to the author.

She got up to go inside and snag a Diet Coke so she could keep reading. Passing through her bedroom, she glanced over at her bed. And stopped cold.

Patrick the monkey was on her bed, right in the middle, propped up on her pillows.

She let out a shriek and almost dropped the journal. "Oh, my God."

Stuffed monkey's didn't move by themselves.

Someone must be in her house.

Panicking, she felt her pocket for her cell phone, darting her gaze around the room, but not seeing anyone or anything else of suspicion. Setting the journal down on the chest of drawers, she rushed back out onto the balcony and shoved a chair in front of the French doors. Digging her phone out with trembling fingers, she dialed Chris at the same time she walked the length of the balcony, checking for any intruders through all of her windows.

She saw nothing but empty rooms, the phone up to her ear and ringing. When she passed her living room, she realized that if someone was in the house, they could reach the balcony through that set of doors, but then again, why would anyone chase her onto the balcony?

Chris answered his phone. "Hey, can I call you back?"

"No! Don't hang up. I think there's someone in my house!"

"Are you serious? Well, fucking call 911 then!"

Good point. "Okay, I'll call you right back. Answer the phone."

"Of course."

Regan called 911 and explained she thought she had an intruder then called Chris back. "They said they'd send someone over to check it out."

"Where are you?"

"On my balcony with a chair shoved against the door." Regan paced back and forth, checking the windows inside. All the rooms were still empty. "I figure if someone comes out here, I can scream for help at least."

"Why do you think someone's in there? Did you hear a noise? Because, sweetie, it's a big old house. It's going to make noises."

"I know that." Talking to Chris was calming her down. At least a little. All it took was one glance into her bedroom and a glimpse of the stuffed monkey propped so carefully on her bed to freak her out all over again. "It wasn't a noise. I had put something away in my nightstand, then I went outside to read the journal. When I came back in half an hour later, it was sitting on my bed."

"What is it?"

She hesitated, but Chris knew the truth, so she told him. "It's Moira's stuffed monkey. I had just put it away, and I was thinking about the fact that I wish I could keep it on the bed . . ." Her words trailed off as a chill snaked its way up her spine. "Oh, my God . . ."

"Did you say any of that out loud?"

"No." She didn't even want to think what that meant.

A knock on the door downstairs startled her. "I'm up here," she called over the railing to the police standing on her front step. "Chris, I'll call you back. The cops are here."

"Call me right back," he warned. "And I'm coming over. I'll be there in twenty."

"You don't have to do that." But she hoped he would insist, because she suddenly didn't want to be alone. "I'm coming down," she called to the police.

"I'll be there. Nelson will be heading to bed in like five minutes anyway."

"Bed? It's seven o'clock."

"He's old, remember?"

"He's not old, he's in his mid-forties."

"Old."

Oh, please. But she had no time to debate it with him. "And on that note, I'll call you back," she said as she jogged down the stairs and skidded to a halt at her front door. "Hi, thanks so much for coming so quickly. I just moved in here and I thought maybe someone was in the house. I . . . I heard a box fall over in my bedroom." For some reason, she didn't want to tell them the truth, though she realized how lame that sounded.

But they were nice enough about it and did a search of her whole house. "Nothing here, miss. No sign of any sort of forced entry and your back door was locked. Was the front door locked when you opened it to us?"

She nodded. "Yes, definitely."

The older cop shrugged. "Must have been the wind or plain old gravity. Is your husband going to be home soon? Are you okay by yourself?"

"I'm not married," she said, and reflected on how different that statement felt than it had two years earlier. Then, those words had been a regret. Now, they were a relief. "But I have a friend coming over."

"Good. Lock her up nice and tight after we leave, and try to relax. It takes a few weeks to get used to the sounds of a new house."

"Thanks, I will."

"Have a good night."

"You, too." Regan locked the door behind them and frowned. So there was no one in the house. She hadn't imagined the monkey had moved and she knew beyond a doubt she hadn't moved it herself.

She called Chris back. "Hey, cops just left, there's no one here."

"Thank God. I'm coming around the corner right now."

A minute later his blond head popped up in front of her door. She opened it and said, "I'm not crazy, I swear."

"Of course you're not crazy. You're like the least crazy of any person I know, and I know a lot of bat-shit crazy people, so that's saying a lot."

"So . . . before you say anything else, just come upstairs and tell me you see the monkey on my bed. Let's just establish that first." Regan shoved her cell phone into the front pocket of her jeans and ran back up the stairs.

Chris followed and a second later he was standing in her bedroom next to her. "Yes, there is a monkey on your bed. No doubt about it. So you were reading the journal, then you came back in and the monkey was there?"

"Yes."

"What was in the journal?"

"I was actually reading about how the girl's whole family died. It was horrible. One day they were all alive, the next all of them were dead, except for her. My heart was just breaking for that poor girl, left all alone."

Chris wiggled the button on his blue golf shirt and frowned. "So you first thought you would like to have the monkey on your bed, but you put it away anyway. Then you're sitting there feeling sympathy for the girl whose family died. Then the monkey is on the bed. Are you thinking what I'm thinking?"

Regan shook her head. "I don't know what to think." She knew what Chris was going to say, she just wasn't so sure she wanted to hear it spoken out loud.

"It's a ghost. Most likely the author of the journal. That was a gesture of comfort. You offered her comfort, and she gave it in return."

All the hairs on Regan's head stood up. "Do you really think so? That her spirit is here?"

"Why not? This was the scene of the greatest tragedy, the most pivotal event of her life. It changed her indelibly."

"I've never been sure if I believe in ghosts or not."

"Maybe you should start believing," Chris said, not looking at her, but smacking her in the arm.

"Why?"

"Because the French doors are opening by themselves," he whispered.

Regan snapped her gaze from the bed to the doors and felt her mouth slide open in shock. The doors were opening, not the back and forth movement from wind, but a methodical swing of both doors simultaneously, like someone had a hand on each of them and was pushing.

"Chris." She felt around for his arm, not taking her eyes off the doors, but wanting physical contact with him.

"Yeah?"

She squeezed his hand when she found it. "Will you stay here tonight?"

"Am I going to need a garlic necklace?"

They watched the doors finish their slow journey outward then stop when they were fully open. Regan jumped involuntarily when the door stops dropped down onto the wood floor to maintain the open position.

"No," she whispered, shaking her head. "That's for vampires. I think we just have a ghost. One who apparently needs fresh air."

She had wanted to find something within the walls of her old house, and it looked like she had.

"Maybe they know where the hooch is hidden."

"I'll let you ask."

"So what do we do?" He squeezed her hand back, his

own voice a low murmur. "I feel like I'm waiting for the other shoe—or in this case, monkey—to drop."

"I think we go out onto the balcony and act like nothing is wrong."

"Well, I'm good at that. I act like nothing is wrong on a regular basis. But what if we walk through her or something?"

They shuffled forward, still holding hands.

"Oh God, don't say that."

But even as she was speaking, Regan felt a gust of air sweep over her, so cold and empty that it felt like the breath was being sucked right out of her lungs. She stopped, unable to move, the sensation frightening and unlike anything she'd ever felt, her hair whipping across her face like she was outside in a sharp wind. Then the air seemed to snap, and the rush of cold was gone as quickly as it had appeared.

She looked at Chris, unable to speak. His eyes were round, his breathing heavy. "Did you feel that?" he asked.

Regan nodded, still speechless.

"Screw the balcony. Let's go get dinner and a drink."

"Good idea," she said, swallowing hard.

They edged forward, flicked up the doorstops, and pulled the French doors closed, then practically fell over each other getting down the stairs.

"I bought a haunted house," she told Chris as they burst out onto the street. She was stunned, and not sure how she felt about the whole thing.

"Yes, you did. And for nine bajillion dollars. Guess you can't even get haunted houses for cheap anymore."

Chapter Five

Felix stood outside the coffee shop for a second, watching Regan through the window. She had her bag cuddled in her lap and she was reading a magazine—a pretty woman, and yet unremarkable in many ways. Just another attractive twenty-something mortal woman.

What was her connection to Alcroft? Why the hell had he married her? And what perverse chain of events had Felix set in motion when he had asked her to take off the ring that bound her body and soul to Alcroft?

It was hard for him to believe that her husband would readily give in to a divorce. If he had wanted her, he wouldn't have appreciated her being the one to walk away. If Alcroft was fighting the divorce, Felix was wading into dangerous, shark-infested waters.

But he had told himself that it was in his own self-interest to see what was in Camille's journal. If he could protect Regan at the same time, all the better.

He walked in, strode around the front of her table, and sat down across from her.

Regan looked up with a tentative smile, her hair up in a ponytail. "Hi, how are you?"

She was wearing dark jeans and a white shirt. It was a casual outfit, yet somehow she still managed to look pulled together. Beyond pulled together, and veering in to uptight. Muted. It wasn't that she was emotionally reserved, because he didn't get that impression, but it was as if the clothes she chose were intended for someone else, for a corporate woman.

He didn't know what Regan did for a living, if anything, but he didn't for one minute think it was a corporate job.

"Hi. How was moving day?"

She made a face then laughed. "It's over. Thank God."

It had been a long time since he had thanked God for anything. "We always wish for the end of things, don't we?" he said, just thinking out loud, but the smile fell off her face.

"Maybe," she said.

There was a long pause, and he knew he'd made her uncomfortable. Well, he was uncomfortable, too. He was taking a huge risk meeting her in public. Meeting her anywhere.

"I'm sorry," she said, breaking the silence first as she fiddled with the coffee cup in front of her. "I'm tired from the move, and well, I didn't get much sleep last night. Do you want to go up and order a coffee?"

As if coffee could improve his lack of social skills. He'd had them at one time. He'd been the favorite pet of bored New Orleans society ladies, and he had charmed and talked his way into their hearts and their purses. Not anymore. Never again.

"I'm fine. Were you up late unpacking?" There had been something . . . a flicker in her eyes when she had mentioned her sleepless night, and he was curious what it meant.

"Oh, it was stupid." She waved her hand in the air dismissively. "I thought someone was in the house and I freaked out. I called the cops and I called my friend to come over. He ended up staying the night and since I don't have my guest bedroom made up, he ended up sharing my bed, and he snores. He's gay."

Then she gave a laugh. "Not that you need to know that. But the point was I didn't get eight hours of sleep."

He didn't need to know it, but it confirmed that she wasn't letting another man into her bed already, so soon after the end of her marriage. It didn't suit her to leap into another relationship, and he was arrogant enough to believe that if she wanted a hookup, she would have come to him. That was the power that had been granted him, after all, and he saw it on her face—she was attracted to him, as they all were.

Felix was attracted to her too, the first woman who had piqued his interest in a long, long time. But he would never touch. Not with her still legally bound to Alcroft, not while her ex still wanted her.

"Someone broke into the house? Was anything stolen?"

"No, nothing was stolen. I don't think anyone was in the house after all. Well, not a thief." She bit her lip. "I have a weird and random question for you, but I figure given what you do, what you practice, you're open-minded, right? I mean, you believe in the unexplainable, don't you?"

Felix found that amusing. "I believe in a lot of things. I believe there are things out there that not only can we not explain, we could never even imagine them in our rational day-to-day lives." Like the existence of demons, and the possibility of immortality. He had no idea what she was dancing around telling him, but nothing would surprise him. "I won't judge, Regan."

She glanced around them. "I don't know if I should say it here."

The coffee shop had a dozen patrons in it, some with laptops, some reading the paper, some chatting with each other, all different types, from the heavily tattooed and dyed woman in her early twenties to the graying businessman.

"No one here cares."

With a nod, she said, "You're right. Of course no one cares what I'm saying. And it sounds crazy, but I think, maybe, if ghosts exist, I have one in my house."

Somehow that wasn't what he had expected her to say. He had thought it would have something to do with her ex-husband, not a restless spirit. Feeling a flicker of intrigue that it could somehow be Camille, he said, "Really? What happened?"

Her expression was uneasy and she lowered her voice. "Something, an object, moved in my bedroom while I was outside on the balcony. I had this thing put away in the nightstand and when I came in, it was sitting on my bed. A stuffed animal that belonged to . . . my sister. It . . . it was like whoever they are they were trying to comfort me."

Huh. Comfort wasn't Camille's style. She would have watched an infant tumble into the dirt and just stared at it in curiosity, a self-protective trait he had to assume came from losing her family. Felix had only met Camille once before the fever outbreak, and she had seemed thoughtful and proper then. It was only after her family had died, when she'd been stripped of her security and love, that she'd had no compassion.

If it wasn't Camille in the house, it was probably just one more lost spirit wandering around. "I see. I believe that's possible. So you think the spirit is benevolent?"

She hesitated, but then nodded. "Yes, I do. There was no bad feeling attached to it, you know what I mean?"

"So you don't want it removed? Because if you ever feel it's become malicious, I can exorcise it."

Her eyes went wide. "You can do that?"

"Sure." Evil be gone. It was an old tenet of voodoo, and with his power, it actually worked. For other people. Not for himself. Never for himself. There was no spell to undo his connection to evil.

"I don't think so. Not yet. I just want to wait and see."

She laughed nervously. "If I have the guts. I ran out of there like someone yelled fire last night."

Felix wasn't sure what to think. Maybe it was just a regular old haunt. But maybe it was something more, maybe it was Camille. But he wouldn't know unless he went to the house, and he wasn't about to do that unless Regan was truly scared. "If you ever feel uncomfortable, let me know. There are some spirits that will drain your energy, your peace of mind, your ability to sleep, like a spiritual anvil around your neck. You don't want that."

"Geez, no, I don't want that. Thanks." Smoothing the hairs back along her temple, Regan picked up her coffee and sipped it. "But I'm sorry, I didn't drag you here to whine about weird goings-on in my house. I wanted to ask you about the journal I found."

"Very clever of you to find it. It's been hidden for a long time obviously." And very clever of Camille to keep the journal from him. He wouldn't have approved of her writing down his spells, their liaisons. It must have amused her that last night to know that he was standing right next to the hidden journal. He could even hear her laughter, see her saucy smile.

"Here it is." Regan pulled the journal out of her bag and handed it to him with a nervous smile. "It's probably a good thing you're not drinking coffee. I want to be very careful not to damage it."

Felix took it reluctantly. He needed to know, needed to see whether he was mentioned at all or not, but the yellowed pages sucked him back into the past as he flipped through them, and the past was a place he never wanted to return. "What is it you want to know?"

"I want to understand voodoo, why she was doing it. And if these are legitimate spells."

"All spells are legitimate if the person using them believes in them."

F is coming over tonight. Finally. The time is here.

Guilt crashed into him, the intensity catching him so off guard that he slammed the book shut in anger.

Regan reacted, jumping a little in her seat at his sharp movement.

It had been a mistake to meet her. There was nothing he could do to help her, and he was putting them both in jeopardy.

"Look. You can't understand these spells without understanding voodoo. Is that what you really want? Because I can recommend some books for you to read."

"Really? That would be great." Her cell phone rang in her purse, her ringtone a classical piano piece.

He frowned. "That's your ringtone?"

"Yes. Sorry." She was digging around in her purse and checked her Caller ID. "This is my lawyer. Do you mind if I take it?"

"No, go ahead." Though the ringtone still bothered him. It didn't sound like her. But then what made him think that he knew a damn thing about Regan?

He didn't. She was just an average, pretty woman that he knew nothing about and never would.

Because she would never tell him and he would never ask.

❧

Regan tried to ignore the frown on Felix's face as she answered her phone. It was rude, she knew that, but she had been playing phone tag with her lawyer for two days and she really wanted an update. Besides, she was starting to think it had been pointless to ask Felix to meet her. What could he really tell her about the journal? It was voodoo spells, end of story, and she was feeling a little stupid for wasting his time.

"Hello?"

"Hey, it's Richard. You're not going to believe this."

"What?" Lord only knew what Beau had called her now or tried to claim she had done.

"Beau dropped his requests straight across the board. His lawyer says your offer of the condo and the cash settlement is more than generous."

"Are you serious?" Regan sat straight up, a grin splitting across her face. "Did he sign the papers? Am I actually going to be divorced soon?"

Felix was staring at her, making no secret of listening to her conversation. But she had answered the phone in the middle of their meeting, and besides, she didn't care if he overheard. The news made her ecstatic. God, she could be divorced in a matter of weeks.

"Yep, he signed the papers. I still don't trust him, Regan. He's up to something. But as it stands right now, yes, you'll be divorced before hurricane season. Hell, you'll be divorced by the end of the week if I can manage it."

Make that days. She could be divorced in just a couple of days. Now that was the best news she'd heard in a long time. "That's fantastic. Thank you, Richard. And really, what could he possibly be up to?" she asked, trying to scoff, hoping it was just Richard being paranoid.

"I don't know. But I like to be cautious. It comes with the job."

Felix was waving his hand in front of her to get her attention. She looked at him, startled, and mouthed, *What?*

"Tell him to look for hidden assets."

"Excuse me?" she said to Felix.

"What?" Richard asked.

"Tell him that your husband doesn't want to fight the settlement anymore because he's afraid you'll discover his hidden assets in the Caribbean and Switzerland," Felix said.

He was being rude to interrupt, and he couldn't possibly know anything about Beau or their divorce, but something about the look in his eyes had Regan saying, "Richard, do you think he could have hidden assets? I seem to remember something about the Caribbean and Switzerland."

"Ah." Richard made a sound of satisfaction. "That would explain the sudden cooperation. He could be worried we would uncover his true financial status."

Uh-oh. Regan realized immediately that she shouldn't have said anything. "If he does have money hidden, I don't care," she assured her lawyer. "I just want the divorce, that's all."

Felix frowned at her.

Richard didn't seem to like her statement either. "Hey, I know, Regan, but come on. If the guy's trying to smoke a few mil past us, we shouldn't let that fly. You just offered him a shitload of money. If he doesn't need it, we should withdraw our offer."

"No. Forget I said anything. I don't care about the money."

There was a big pause. "Alright. I'll keep you posted. Ciao."

Regan hung up the phone and glared at Felix. "What do you think you're doing? You completely threw me off balance in the middle of a very important phone call."

"He's hiding money."

"One, how do you know? Two, who cares? I don't. I just want a divorce."

"How do I know? I know," he said, leaning over the table so that his face was closer to hers, "because I have the second sight. I'm intuitive, or whatever the hell you want to call it. And you should care because he was a shitty husband and you shouldn't have to pay off an asshole to get out of your marriage."

His vehemence shocked her. Regan was having trouble thinking with him in her space. She could see the dark

stubble on his chin, feel the warmth of his breath, watch
the pupils expand in his blue eyes.

He withdrew, falling back against his chair, and she felt
irrationally irritated with him. "How do you know he was
a shitty husband? Maybe I'm just a bad wife. Maybe I'm
just flighty or fickle."

Felix shook his head slowly. "No, there is nothing flighty
or fickle about you at all. And he had to be a shitty husband
to put that look in your eye at the Christmas party."

"What look?" Regan turned her cell phone around and
around on the table, nervous and not sure why.

"Fear. Desperation. Like a caged animal."

Jesus. That was so accurate she was horrified. Who
else had seen that in her? "Well, then you should understand why I don't want to risk screwing up my divorce. If
he's going to let it go through uncontested, I am beyond
happy."

"You deserve more," he said simply.

Regan felt the hairs rise on her arms. It was the first
time someone had put it quite like that. Her family and
friends argued with her that she shouldn't have left. Chris
wanted her to stick it to Beau. But no one had ever told her
in such a straightforward way that she was entitled to better
in her life.

"Thank you," she said softly, feeling comfortable with
him, truly comfortable, for the first time. Then she looked
at him, curious about the man in front of her. She supposed
she believed in fate, and somehow, it just seemed that she
and Felix had been destined to cross each other's path. But
who was he, how did he live, who did he spend his time
with? "So tell me about yourself, Felix."

"Nothing to tell. I run a voodoo shop. Nothing more,
nothing less."

That couldn't possibly scratch the surface of his life,
but she wasn't surprised that was his answer. He seemed
reticent about himself. Perfectly willing to talk about her,

but dismissive about himself. "Do you have a girlfriend? A special someone?"

Felix gave a short laugh, though there didn't seem to be a lot of amusement in it. "No. Any woman who would date me would undoubtedly *deserve more.*"

That was annoying. Men always dropped lines like that, and she found it to be false self-effacement. They didn't really believe it, they just didn't want to work at a commitment. It also chafed that it seemed directed at her, like she shouldn't get any ideas about the two of them having any sort of relationship.

"So is that a warning?"

He shook his head slowly. "No. It doesn't do any good to warn anyone anyway. We all do as we want, for the most part, regardless of the danger."

Maybe that was her problem. She hadn't known what she wanted, so she had done what she had thought she'd wanted, regardless of the danger of it being a mistake, and married Beau. Could that be the real danger? Never knowing the truth of what you wanted? "What if you don't know what you want?"

"Everyone knows what they want, whether they acknowledge it or not. You have to be honest with yourself."

What she wanted, right at the moment, was him. She could be honest with herself, but she wasn't about to be honest with Felix about it, so she made a noncommittal sound.

He had shifted his weight in the chair so he was leaning forward again, and it unnerved her. Regan fought the urge to back up, to create distance. It felt like he was challenging her and she wanted to hold her ground. Her skin tingled, her nipples hardening. There was such a sexual energy surrounding him, and she couldn't help but respond to it. Or maybe it was just that she found him attractive and she hadn't had sex in four months. Either way, she was always very acutely aware of her body around him.

"There is no memory with less satisfaction than that of some temptation which we resisted."

Indeed. Regan was very, very tempted by Felix, and while she knew she should resist, doing the smart thing gave absolutely no satisfaction to a woman in desperate need of a good lover.

Chapter Six

Felix tugged at the tattered cuff of his shirt, hoping the sleeve of his jacket would cover the flaw. Not that anyone would see the embarrassing evidence of his poverty.

He shouldn't have come tonight. He was in a foul mood, feeling a familiar swell of jealousy at the casual wealth of those in the ballroom as he watched through the windows. So entitled, every last one of them, and yet most had never done a damn thing to earn their money. Their easy lifestyle was an accident of birth, as was his reverse fortune.

Yet they took great delight in looking down on him and his mother.

His mother. The glow of the gas lamps and taper candles turned the room into a tallow cloud of faces and figures through the glass, and it was impossible to pick her out of the crush. It made him sick to think what her purpose was there tonight.

It wasn't fair. His father's death. His father's wife using the courts to have his mother stripped of the house his father had given her, free and clear. Not fair, none of it.

And it was agonizing to think that no employment available to Felix could ever earn enough money to prevent his mother from being forced to take this present course of action. She was nearly forty-five years old, her beauty still intact in his eyes, but a softer, more mature beauty, and she was being forced to compete with ripe twenty year olds for the prize of a wealthy benefactor.

His mother had been the mistress of his father for twenty-seven years. Felix had always known the arrangement. It had been neither a dirty little secret nor something his mother had been particularly proud of, but they had always been an affectionate pair, and Felix had felt secure in their amiability with one another. It had never seemed cheap or harsh or mercenary, and he had grown to manhood in the knowledge that if laws and money and society were not as they were, his parents would have married and been faithful to one another.

Had he longed for acceptance and a different sort of security for himself and his mother? Of course. But he had known enough to understand he was fortunate for his station in life.

But that was before his father's death. Now his sweet and intelligent mother was reduced to flirting and casting about for a man to sexually service in order to feed herself, and it was devastating. A reality he wasn't prepared for.

The long-simmering and mostly ignored resentments he had felt growing up were boiling up and over to the forefront. Yet he had no idea what to do to stop this madness, to find his way in a world that would no longer accept him without his wealthy white father's wheel greasing, or how to retreat to a laborer's life, where he was equally unwanted, both for the lightness of his skin and the quality of his education.

Felix's stomach churned, from fear and disgust as well as deep and painful hunger. He hadn't eaten in three days, and while his mother was imposing on a friend for shelter, Felix had assured her he could manage, so as to not be a burden to her. In reality, he had slept in the alley for the past seven nights. Six months ago various friends had opened their doors, but now he had surpassed their generosity.

"You might be able to see better if you entered the ball-room," an amused voice said from behind him.

Turning quickly, Felix's head spun. The lack of food and sleep combined with the sharp movement blurred his vision for a split second in the sudden darkness after the lights of the ballroom. Slapping his hand against the bricks of the house behind him to reestablish equilibrium, he blinked and swallowed the bile that had risen from his empty stomach. There was a man in front of him, dressed all in black, the cut of his coat and trousers elegant, his hat at a jaunty angle. He looked to be in his late twenties, and when he pulled back his coat to reach for his tobacco, Felix saw a gold pocket watch that gave off a gleam even from five feet away. The walking stick he carried swung back and forth casually, its owner seemingly unconcerned with the way it scraped the cobblestones.

A rich man, no doubt.

Felix fought the urge to tug at his own coat sleeve again and started to move past him, intending to leave without speaking. He had no desire to either be heckled or arrested for vagrancy.

"Do you know the story of Aladdin's lamp?" the man said as Felix skirted him.

"Excuse me?" Felix paused, the voice quiet yet commanding in the courtyard, compelling him to respond.

"I'm sure you do. Aladdin is granted three wishes from the genie of the lamp. If you were to request three wishes, what would they be?"

He scoffed, head swimming again. God, he needed to sit down. Just sink to the ground and rest for a few hours, then he could think what to do. There were no answers to *be found staring into the play palace of the rich, or talking to a stranger dressed in black. "I have no wishes."*

"Oh, no? Perhaps a house of her own again for your mother . . . a new wardrobe for yourself . . . never having to wonder where your next meal will come from?"

Anger, humiliation surged in Felix. "How the hell do you know about my mother?"

He shrugged. "I've followed you. You seem like the kind of man I'm looking for in my line of work."

Feeling weaker by the second, Felix shook his head, straining to hold his shoulders up, to hang on to the last vestiges of pride he felt. "I understand how that bargain works. I do your thieving or dealing for you, take a small cut, than you toss me to the authorities to placate them for your illegal doings. Leaving me in prison, my mother on the streets, and you rich and happy. No thank you."

Felix turned to leave, irritated that he had allowed himself even one second of hope. Organized crime was not a temptation.

"You misunderstand." The man stepped forward, his hand outstretched as he stepped into the square of light cast from the window. "Allow me to introduce myself. I have different names, but all you need to know is that I am the man who can give you your three wishes and then some."

Before Felix could reject the handshake, the man's flesh gripped his and a pulsing warmth rippled through his fingertips and palm, racing up his arm. "What . . ."

Felix tried to pull back, break the contact, but the grip was ironclad, and when he tugged harder, panicking, he looked into the man's amber eyes, their glow bright and vibrant like a cat's, and his own vision blurred again.

When it cleared, he was standing in a tidy house, filled with tasteful and expensive furnishings, his mother smiling up at him from her position on a velvet sofa. Her fingers played with a diamond pendant dangling from her neck, her gown a rich gold that complemented her coloring.

Only his mother wasn't smiling at him, but a different him. Felix watched himself stroll into the parlor, dressed in dapper evening clothes, affixing his hat to his head.

"Enjoy your evening, cher," *she told him, the other him, her smile pleasant and content.*

"I will, thank you, and you should do the same." *He leaned over and kissed her cheek, his well-shined shoes squeaking on the hardwood floors.* "I'm off to dinner at my club. I have a taste for étouffée this evening." *He rubbed his stomach in anticipation.* "And a glass of wine or two."

Felix could feel his own anticipation for the meal, feel the pleasure of the innocuous domestic scene, smell his mother's floral perfume, and see the crisp newness of his gloves. He even turned and saw the exterior street through the floor-to-ceiling windows. The houses across the street were well maintained and attractive, and a couple strolled by, an idyllic neighborhood scene.

"Are you taking the carriage?" *his mother asked his other self.*

"I'm of a mind to walk. Have a wonderful evening."

His mother nodded, and then she and he were gone, the parlor receding, the room disappearing like a carpet being rolled up and hauled off. There was a brief moment of darkness, where Felix hovered in nothing, then the sound came first, of ladies laughing, their sweet high-pitched voices unnatural in the emptiness. The visuals returned, rushing back at him in a blur of color, like butterflies' wings, and he was in a different house, surrounded by proper ladies.

They were attentive and twittering, their chairs arranged in a circle in front of him, their expressions rapt as they batted eyelashes and flicked fans in the summer heat.

"That is fascinating, Mr. Leblanc," *one brunette said. The girl next to her whacked her arm with her fan, and the original speaker made a moue of distaste at her friend.* "What? It is."

The friend who had smacked the brunette said, "Mr. Leblanc, I fear that your intelligence so greatly exceeds my own that I am having trouble following your lesson. Perhaps you might be so kind as to repeat your thoughts again for me at the end of the session?"

Outrage played over the brunette's face and she sat up straighter. "I think I could benefit from additional instruction as well, Mr. Leblanc. Would you be so kind?"

They were flirting with him, that was clear, and he felt his own smug satisfaction in the scene. Then Felix saw the cashbox behind him on the piano bench, the lid slightly askew. It was stuffed with bills, hundreds of dollars, and he knew that it was his money.

He was rich and he had everything he had ever wanted. Everything he had ever wanted . . .

The scene crackled in front of him, the sound that of fabric tearing, and then it was gone and he was back in the grip of the man with many names, the glow of his amber eyes dimming. He dropped Felix's hand, and the loss of that vise-like grip had him stumbling backward in the courtyard, his skin throbbing where they had touched, not from pressure, but as if it had been warmed from the inside out. Felix glanced down, afraid his hand had been seared, but it looked perfectly normal. It just felt as if it had been shoved into the fire.

"Who are you?" he whispered to the man.

"The genie of your lamp," he said with a smile. "I have shown you what I can give you."

Felix shook his head. "I don't understand . . . how . . ."

"Your mother raised you with voodoo secretly, didn't she?"

He didn't answer, the warnings of his mother too engrained in his mind. They were never to tell his father.

Of course, that no longer mattered.

"Yes."

"Then you understand the gods and goddesses and that

if you please them, they will help you achieve your desires. That is me." The man turned his hand over so his palm was up, and on it rested a wedge of bread. "For you."

Fear and fascination mingled together, and Felix's heart raced. He should walk away, turn his back on whoever and whatever this man was. Because he knew that you never got everything you wanted without paying a price, and this man, this creature, would exact a high price, he was sure.

But his mouth watered at the thought of eating the warm, crusty bread, and he could smell its yeasty freshness. His stomach growled, an aching pit of desperation, and his hands trembled from exhaustion and hunger. The warnings his brain were whispering were drowned out by the urgent cries of his stomach, and getting lost in the vapid fog malnourishment had created in his thoughts.

He reached out, stretching his arm, hand trembling, saliva filling his mouth, and he accepted what was being offered him, with no real understanding of what that even was.

❦

"Do you regret any temptations you've resisted?" Regan asked him, crossing her legs, her fingers flitting over the top of her coffee cup.

He'd made her nervous.

Felix smiled at the irony. "No, for me it's the opposite. I wish I had learned fortitude earlier in life. There are a number of things I should have resisted."

His greed had driven him to accept the demon's bargain, his greed had led him to his dalliance with Camille. And he had paid for both. Harshly.

"I'm not sure I've ever really been tempted to do anything," she said in a thoughtful tone. "I've never been a risk taker. I guess marriage was a temptation, but like you,

I wish I had resisted that urge." She shrugged like it no longer mattered. "Have you ever been married?"

"No. Never even tempted."

Regan laughed.

Felix smiled at the sound. She had an innocent, joyous laugh. Regan was an interesting woman to be around. Despite what she was doing, starting a new life and fighting Alcroft tooth and nail to get out of her marriage, there was nothing cynical or bitter about her. Anxious, yes, but not hardened. He found that intriguing, refreshing.

Every minute that he sat there in clear view in a public place increased his risk of being caught with her, of facing retribution, but he didn't want to leave. There was a quiet peacefulness about just sitting there with her, and he enjoyed her company. But he didn't want this to turn into yet another temptation he wished he had resisted. Punishment would be swift and harsh and painful.

Then again, Alcroft had given up, accepted a divorce. Maybe it had been his pride that had led him to resist the end of their marriage, instead of genuine affection or an agenda. Maybe he wouldn't care what or who Regan did now.

Or maybe that was a horrible rationalization on Felix's part.

He tapped the cover of Camille's journal, the initials mocking him. "Are you going to try to research who this belongs to?"

"Yeah, as soon as I have some time. There are some clues. The date. And the fact that her entire family died that year in a yellow fever epidemic. Her grief is so stark, so palpable. It just broke my heart to read about it."

What the hell was he supposed to say to that? "I'm sure."

"I've been wondering if it happened in my house . . . if all those people died there."

"Would that bother you?"

She shook her head slowly. "I guess not. I mean, it was a long time ago. It's just a house, four walls and all that. But I'm not going to lie, it makes me sad. I don't want my house to have been a sad house."

"Houses don't have emotions."

"But people do."

"More than they should."

"Are you a cynic?"

That was a label he could definitely own. "Oh, undoubtedly."

But she shook her head, a small smile playing about her mouth. "I don't think I believe you."

"Believe it." He opened the damn journal so that he wouldn't have to see that optimism, that misplaced belief and trust in him. She had no fucking idea what she was staring at.

"You're not going to try to do any of these spells, are you?" he asked her.

His spells. Taught to him by his mother, and peddled to bored society ladies who had paid him piles of money to cures their illnesses, to increase their sex drive, and to capture that certain special man.

He had never believed in what he was doing, but had reveled in the reward of their attention and all that cold, hard cash. Now seeing his so-called magick written in Camille's handwriting just made him feel anger at himself, at the disgusting man he had been, using all those women for material gain.

But those were not new feelings. Guilt, anger, and bitterness were his closest and dearest friends, walking every step of his endless existence right alongside him, arms entwined with his.

"No, of course not." She played with the black rope necklace she was wearing. "That would never even occur to me."

"Good. Now I need to head out," he told Regan, slapping the book shut and standing up. He couldn't do this anymore, just sit here and talk like they were two normal people in a normal world.

"Okay, sure," she said, looking a little bewildered. "Umm, thank you, for meeting me and for the information."

Felix handed her the book. "Why don't I e-mail you those book titles? You can read about voodoo and I think that will help you read the journal. My guess is she was just a bored socialite dabbling in it for something to pass the time."

Regan nodded. "That would be great, thanks." She pulled out a business card and handed it to him. "Here's my contact information."

It was a black-and-white card. Felix was not the least surprised. Then a perverse impulse had him saying, "Take down my number. In case you need to call me."

There was a pause where she stared at him, then she picked up her phone. "Great. Thanks."

After he gave her his number, Felix moved closer to her to let a man past him in the aisle. His knees brushed her and she pulled away, shifting her legs to the opposite side of the table leg. He couldn't leave it, her, like this.

"Regan."

"Yes?" She looked up at him, clutching her phone.

"I will do readings at your party. If you still want me."

It was meant to be an apology for his rudeness in cutting their conversation short. But he didn't lie to himself. He wanted to see her again, despite the risk.

Maybe because of it.

For whatever reason, Regan Henry had been pulled into his and Alcroft's world, and yet she had no idea she had been. It wasn't fair to her, and Felix wanted to understand why she was involved, to learn what her role in the odd triumvirate of Camille, Alcroft, and himself was. Felix didn't believe in coincidence and she was here, dragged unwittingly into their world, with no way to defend herself.

He didn't know if he could, but he felt compelled to protect her.

She gave a small smile. "Yes, I still want you. At the party."

"Good. And if you feel nervous in the house, you can always call me. I can give you some herbs to calm you even if you don't want to remove the spirit."

"Okay, thanks." Her head tilted.

He had the oddest compulsion to kiss her. If not on the lips, then the forehead.

She would accept it, he knew that instinctively.

But Felix knew it would be greedy to take anything from Regan, and if there was anything he fought against, it was his own greed. The flaw that had brought him to subjugation.

"Have a good day," he said softly, and fought the urge to sigh. There was something so painfully innocent about her, so inherently good, and he wanted to just sink into her, soak up that hope and joy, and restore all the noxious holes inside of his soul.

But down that road lay disaster and disappointment.

And he'd already had enough of those.

Without another word, he left her alone in the coffee shop.

Chapter Seven

Camille had been lax in wearing full mourning, and she knew the ladies had remarked on it. But honestly, it was the height of summer and who wanted to be wrapped in layers of black crepe? Besides, the dark color sallowed her complexion, so she had chosen to generally wear white with black ribbons and to hell with anyone's opinion. But on this day she was calling on a poor Miss Janise, who had not been seen about in days and was rumored to be ill, so she was dressed in full black for effect, the grieving Miss Comeaux.

Everyone had spent the summer staring at Camille with pity and mortification, Miss Janise being a veritable ringleader of such social strikes, and she thought it quite satisfying that now it would be her turn to cast sympathy at the wretched cow.

Her maid knocked on the front door of the Janise household, and the butler who answered informed them that Miss Janise was not accepting visitors.

"Oh, but I must see her," Camille declared, brushing

past the butler. Being thought of as eccentric and outside the boundaries of social propriety allowed her delightful liberties. "I must see for myself that she isn't as ill as everyone is saying."

"She is expected to fully recover," he told her, blustering along behind her as Camille strolled toward the stairs.

Mounting the steps one at a time, her boots making a delightful sound of authority as they rang on the marble flooring, Camille shot the butler a look over her shoulder. "I am sorry, but I just have to see for myself. She is such a dear friend, and I cannot think of what I would do if she were to die. All my family died, you know, and I have no one but my friends," she told him, knowing that would shame him into shutting up.

It worked. His jaw dropped, then he nodded, stopping at the foot of the stairs. "Yes, Miss Comeaux, I am most sorry for your great loss."

She was damn sorry, too, the miserable little jackass, a tick starting in her eyelid. But she recovered, thrusting aside her anger. "Thank you."

The sight of Annabel in bed, covered in an oozing beet red rash, washed away the rest of her animosity. Fighting the urge to laugh, Camille affixed her expression into one of sympathy and horror . "Oh, my dear! I had heard you were ill and so I came right away."

"Camille," Annabel said, her body slumping down lower on her bed, her hand fluttering in front of her pocked face in embarrassment. "Whatever are you doing here?"

Annabel shot her maid a look of distress, but there was nothing a servant could do, and the girl just stared at them with wide eyes.

Coming around the side of the four-poster, Camille came right up to Annabel and took her hand, so that she could get a proper look at the witch's splotchy face. It was thoroughly disgusting, the sores open and weeping, covering at least 50 percent of her face and neck, and Camille was very, very pleased. It had been difficult shaking the potion onto Annabel's scones without detection the week before, but this was so worth the effort.

"You poor thing, I am most distressed for you. I heard you were ill and I had to ascertain for myself that you were not in any real danger, and also I thought to offer my assistance."

Annabel was trying to discreetly remove her hand, but Camille held on tight. "That is so thoughtful of you, but I am expected to recover. There is nothing that can be done but wait for the . . . ailment to recede."

"I see. Well, then I am much relieved. Though you do look very uncomfortable." Camille made a slight gesture to Annabel's face. "Do they hurt?"

Tears were in her foe's eyes. "No. They itch a little, but mostly it's just a huge inconvenience. I am beyond bored."

"Oh." Camille waved her hand in the air in dismissal. "Absolutely nothing of interest has happened in society this week. Only that Mr. Perkins became engaged to Miss Hanson at her family's ball last night."

Watching Annabel's face contort in shock as she realized she had lost the battle for Mr. Perkins's affections would have been worth two hundred dollars, let alone the measly two Camille had forked over to Felix. A sob of distress came from Annabel.

Camille leaned in and studied the lesions on Annabel's face. "My dear, I hope these won't scar," she said with false concern. "What a tragedy that would be for one so lovely as you."

And she would learn the pain of social ostracizing just as Camille had.

Annabel began sobbing in earnest, and Camille thought it was such a pretty, satisfying sound. Perhaps she should make people cry more often.

꧁꧂

Regan sat up straight in bed. Blinking, she looked around the room, disoriented. God, another dream so real, so intense, she felt like she had been there. She had seen the crusty, oozing sores on Miss Janise's face, and smelled the bitter medicinal lotion that had been rubbed over the girl's skin. She had heard the rap of Camille's boots on the floor, and felt her sick satisfaction at having reduced her enemy to tears.

How could Regan feel those emotions, ones that didn't belong to her and that she, frankly, found offensive? And what was rolling around in her subconscious that she could take a simple entry in Camille's journal for creating a rash and spin it into such a detailed story? There had been no indication why the author had written it down, other than the cryptic remark that it had worked, though she had never mentioned on who it had been used. Regan still didn't even know why she kept giving her the name Camille. It was an odd name to pluck out of thin air and it made Regan nervous.

Kicking back the covers, Regan stood up. She needed a glass of water and a new T-shirt to sleep in. The one she was wearing was damp with sweat, another disgusting side affect of these new vivid dreams. Regan flipped open her cell phone on her nightstand and sighed. Two A.M. She had to work the next day and she was wide awake and then some.

Padding to the adjoining bathroom, she flicked on the light and squinted, the bulbs blinding. She leaned over the sink to splash some water on her face, the cool liquid hitting her hot skin and flushing away the perspiration. When she stood back up she glanced in the mirror.

And screamed.

Oh, my God. Her face was covered in a rash, open sores oozing fluid, a patchwork of lesions all over her cheeks, forehead, chin, and neck. Regan fell back, knocking the towel rack, her hands flying to her face. She could feel them, the sticky wetness of the rash beneath her fingertips.

It was everywhere, a road map of a rash, one she'd had no indication could be appearing when she'd gone to bed.

Stepping forward cautiously, she studied her face in the mirror, droplets of water still clinging to her chin and eyelashes. "Holy shit," she murmured, every hair on her arms standing at attention.

Where had it come from? And if she had just had an allergic reaction to something, how could she have dreamed about the very same thing? Could her mind somehow have known even asleep what was bursting forth on her body?

A whoosh of air from behind her, the prickling sensation of eyes on the back of her head, had her whirling around.

What she saw in the doorway had her knees buckling.

It was a young blonde woman in a black Victorian mourning gown, a small smile on her pretty and delicate face.

The vision wasn't solid, more like a projection of a picture into the air, her tiny feet in high boots hovering just above the floor.

Regan couldn't speak, couldn't move, couldn't breathe. She just stood there, suspended in the surrealistic timeless moment, she and Camille.

It had to be Camille.

It was Camille.

The dress, the strange smile, this was how she had pictured Camille heading to Miss Janise's house. Only that had been a dream. Just a dream. There was no Camille or Miss Janise.

Maybe this was a dream, too.

Yet it didn't feel like a dream, but a frightening and strange reality she didn't understand, she and a ghost, an imprint on this house, who was somehow now reaching out from the other realm and connecting with Regan.

She wanted to ask the woman what she wanted, why she

was there, who she was, and how she had died, the questions streaming through her mind rapidly, but her mouth remained closed. It felt like the violence of her voice breaking the silence of their assessment of one another would be inappropriate.

It was Camille's move to make, not hers.

Regan had no idea how long she stared at the unmoving translucent figure, but she finally succumbed to the irresistible urge to blink, and when her eyes opened there was nothing in the doorway. Regan shot forward and glanced into her bedroom and in the other direction, toward the hallway. Nothing. Obviously.

Goose bumps dancing all over her arms, she went back into the bathroom, realizing that with the light on behind her, she shouldn't have even been able to see anything in the shadowy darkness of the doorway.

Not that such details mattered to a ghost, she supposed.

A glance in the mirror stopped her thoughts abruptly and scattered them in shock.

The rash was gone. Her face was exactly as it had been when she'd removed her makeup before bed, her complexion a little uneven without her foundation, merely one small pimple setting up camp on her chin.

Wanting to scream again, she realized all the air was locked in her throat. Backing out of the bathroom, the reflection of herself, eyes wide, skin clear, chased her as she stumbled into her room.

"Jesus, I'm going crazy," she murmured out loud, then regretted the sound of her frightened voice ringing in the dark silence.

Flipping on every light she had, both overhead and lamps, as she went, she jogged to the nightstand where her cell phone was. She had entered Felix's number in the coffee shop, though at the time she hadn't been sure why he'd offered it, after springing out of his chair like he had suddenly realized she bored him.

But he had said to call her if she needed to talk.

She needed to talk.

And for very obvious reasons, she thought this was something Felix would have a better understanding of than her friends.

It was incredibly rude to call him at two in the morning, but Regan was freaked out so thoroughly, all her social graces vanished as completely as the figure in black.

He answered right away. "Regan, what's the matter? Did something move again?"

Regan immediately felt relieved that she had called him. He didn't think she was insane. "I just had a dream that the girl who wrote the journal was visiting the girl she used the rash curse on. And then I woke up and I went into the bathroom and I had a rash. The same rash. On me. Then I saw a woman standing in my doorway, a spirit, in Victorian mourning clothes, and then my rash was gone. And I don't even know that she actually used that rash curse on another girl . . . Why in the world am I having these dreams? And how could I have a rash, then not have it? It was so creepy, so . . . scary."

She barely took a breath as she blurted it all out, then paused, panting, waiting for him to comment. Glancing around her bedroom, she saw a shadow play across the chest of drawers. Letting out a scream, she backed up and collided with her nightstand. "I think I just saw something."

"Alright, it's okay. Why don't you go into the living room and turn on the TV and I'll be over in ten minutes."

Regan instantly felt better, and she swallowed hard. "You would do that?" She was both touched and relieved. Part of her felt like she should protest and demur, but she couldn't manage it. She didn't want to be alone.

"Yes, I would do that."

"Thanks." She blew out the breath she'd been holding. "Thanks."

Glancing at the time on her phone as she hung up, she

tried to gauge how long she would have to wait until Felix got there. He lived only a few blocks away, but he probably needed to get dressed, then he would walk . . . the quiet of her house closed in around her as she anticipated having to wait ten minutes or more. She kept touching her face to feel for sores and glancing toward her bathroom, expecting to see the girl in black again. Her bedcovers were destroyed, tossed in every direction, a sign of a restless sleep.

The house was dark and achingly silent around her. The air seemed to move, the quiet absent of any individual sounds, but becoming a presence in and of itself, as if her house were breathing, in and out, in and out.

God, she was losing it. She needed to do something, distract her mind, occupy her hands, so she dragged on jeans and changed her T-shirt with trembling hands. Darting her eyes left and right, she went into the living room with her iPod and speakers, flipping every light on as she went, and turned on some music. At first, she put on classical, what Beau had taught her to appreciate, but it was too lilting, too haunting for her mood. Flipping through her menu, she selected pop dance music and turned it up to a healthy volume, hoping it would overcome the silence of the room.

Then she started contemplating placement on the walls for her photographs. Using the level and the hammer gave her a focus, though she kept glancing over her shoulder.

It wasn't the sense that someone was watching her so much as she had the feeling she wasn't welcome in this house. It wanted to be alone with itself, its own aging plaster and long-held secrets.

Which was crazy. Giving the house emotions was crazy. Even Felix had thought houses didn't have emotions.

Regan forced herself to methodically measure, hammer, hang. She had one photo up over the console table, awaiting its trio of companion photos, when the doorbell rang. Her phone vibrated at the same time. She opened the text from Felix as she headed downstairs for the door.

I'm here was all his text said.

A shiver ran through her at the words. It suddenly occurred to her that she didn't know anything about him at all, really. Who was to say he wasn't psychotic? He had been a party hire for the law firm, nothing more. No one could vouch for him personally.

But he seemed to know how to deal with whatever was in her house, and she was truthfully more afraid of that than him.

❦

Felix stood on Royal Street and stared up at the house that he should have never been allowed entrance to. He hadn't been born a slave, but his mother Louisa had, the child of a mulatto slave and her French owner. Louisa had followed in her own mother's footsteps and became the mistress of a wealthy Creole, with Felix the result of their arrangement.

Back when Camille had inherited the house in front of him from her parents, Felix had walked the narrow fence of social conventions between two worlds. He was wildly popular with the New Orleans society ladies for his spells and voodoo gatherings, but they always came to him. None of their doors were actually open for him to enter.

Except for this one. Camille had defied all rules of convention and insisted he perform his rituals within its walls.

Despite the wealth of his father and his clients, Felix had never seen how the rich really and truly lived until he had entered this house. Even though his own father had been fairly generous with both his money and his affections, frequently visiting Felix and his mother at the house he had purchased for them on North Rampart, Felix had never seen his father's house.

It was that social distinction, that sting of humiliation that had driven Felix more than a hundred years ago, fostering his greed, and leading him to make destructive choices.

Now he was back at the house on Royal Street, not a greedy and arrogant young man, but an immortal demon servant, chained for eternity in servitude, and he would do anything to give it all back.

Yet there was no way out.

And while it wasn't at all smart or self-protective to be ringing the doorbell of what was now Regan Henry's house, he felt defiant. He had done what he was told, and it got him nothing. A century of servitude and he had absolutely nothing but bitterness and a complete loss of hope that he would ever enjoy anything in his life again. Showing up here might earn him punishment, but could anything be more miserable than his day in, day out endless existence of peddling voodoo to tourists?

The memory of the vast, echoing darkness crowded him, pain leeching across his body slowly, a hot, fiery lava of agony. Yes, there were worse punishments than selling trinkets to tourists. Much, much worse.

Yet Felix was very curious about Regan, about what was happening in her house, and he was willing to take the risk to satisfy that curiosity. And if he were honest with himself, he would admit it was way more than curiosity. He wanted Regan in a way he hadn't wanted a woman in longer than he could even remember.

He wanted to see if her whole body would go as pink as her cheeks in her arousal, if she would let go of her inhibitions and scream in pleasure.

Or if she would stay muted, a dim version of herself in a black-and-white world.

But Regan wasn't the kind of woman who would enjoy casual sex, of that he was certain. She would want a relationship, and he had nothing to offer her.

And the way he felt about her, intrigued and protective

and fascinated, made him question if he could have casual sex with her either.

Which made his standing on her stoop even stupider.

The door swung open for him. Regan was practically bouncing on the balls of her feet, and she looked like if he gave her one indication he would allow it, she would throw herself into his arms.

So he folded them across his chest.

"How are you?" he asked as he stepped into the foyer and glanced over into the dining room. The house had changed since he had last been in it. Different flooring, different paint colors, giving a varied overall impression. It seemed lighter, less oppressive.

It was also ablaze with every light the three-story house had. "I see you're not worried about your electric bill," he added.

She gave a nervous laugh, tucking her hands into her front pockets. "Emergency circumstances. Look, I'm sorry. I feel like a complete idiot for freaking out. Last night I called the cops and I didn't think I could do that again without being fined or something. And my friend Chris is great, but I can't keep calling him either."

"I don't mind," he said.

"Well, come on in. I don't know what I expect you to do or say. I'm sorry, it's so rude of me to be bothering you like this. It was just so weird."

"It's no big deal. I wanted to give you something anyway." Felix pulled out the three photocopies he had folded and crammed into the back pocket of his jeans for Regan. He had known this was all information she could, and would, find on her own, so he figured he would save her a step and save himself the trouble and discomfort of having to lie.

"Oh, what's this?" She glanced curiously at the papers, but she didn't take them from him.

"It's some information I found on the house." This very house that he had never expected to be standing in again.

Regan said, "Oh, wow, great, thank you. Let's go upstairs. Would you like a drink?"

"No, thank you." A drink was not what he needed or wanted. Felix watched her walk in front of him, appreciating the curves of her body. She was thin, but not boyish, and she had a very cute backside. He had the urge to cup her ass with two hands, and then slide a finger between her legs and feel that warm heat. Of course, she would throw him out of her house if he did that without warning.

Or would she? She wanted him, he had no doubt of that.

It was an entertaining what-if, to consider taking Regan to bed, burying himself inside her.

And the temptation to touch Regan distracted him from the memories of this house. Of coming in through the courtyard and being led up the servants' stairs in the back. He had come up these main stairs only once, when he had gotten as bold as Camille. It had been that last night. He had knocked on the front door and walked in with all the arrogance of youth, the two of them addicted to defiance and danger.

"The family did die here," Felix told Regan. "That's pretty clear from the quick research I did."

She stopped in her living room and turned to face him. "Really? Why? What did you find?"

"I looked up who owned the house in that time period then searched newspaper articles relating to the owner. Your house was purchased by a wealthy businessman named Francois Comeaux in 1867. Searching his name, I found several articles that show he died in the yellow fever epidemic of 1878, along with his wife and four daughters. Only one daughter survived, his youngest, Camille."

Regan blanched, every inch of color draining from her face in a split second, her knees buckling. The change was so sudden and severe, he actually looked behind him to see if something or someone was standing behind him, but the stairwell was empty. So what the hell had he said to cause that kind of reaction?

"Regan?" he asked, moving forward quickly, his hand crumpling the papers as he grabbed her elbow to steady her when she looked ready to drop. "What's wrong?"

"I think I'm going to faint," she said, swallowing hard, her hands clawing toward him to find purchase.

"I've got you. You're fine," he reassured her in a soothing voice, using both hands to grip her, shaking her a little. "Look at me."

She struggled for a second, her eyes rolling in and out of focus, but then she managed to lock her gaze with his.

"You're okay," he murmured.

Taking a deep, shuddering breath, she nodded. "I am. I'm okay. Sorry. I'm okay."

"Lie down for a second." He guided her to the sofa, which she sank onto without a word, looking intensely grateful to give up the fight to stay standing.

She lay on her side, tucking her hands under her cheek on the cushion. "I'm sorry."

"Don't be sorry." Felix sat on the sofa next to her waist, perching precariously. Brushing back some of her hairs that had fallen loose, he leaned over and set the crumpled papers he'd been holding onto the end table. "What happened?"

"You're going to think I'm insane."

Hardly. "Hey, no judgments, remember? You're talking to a guy who sticks pins in dolls and dances with a snake."

"You dance with a snake?" She looked intrigued by the concept. "Why?"

"Never mind. I'll tell you later. Right now you're going to tell me what it was I said that made you look like I'd kicked the wind out of you with my boot."

She took another deep breath. "Okay. I've been flipping

through the journal, but I haven't read most of it. In what I have read, the author never mentions herself by name, only those around her. Her initials—CAC—are on the cover, but that's it. And with my moving in yesterday, I haven't had a chance to do any research on the house. So I had no way of knowing what her name was."

"Okay." Felix wasn't sure where this was going, and he waited for her to continue.

Biting her lip, she tore a piece of the tender flesh away with her teeth so aggressively a bead of blood appeared.

"I dreamed about her, that I was seeing things from her perspective. In the dream she left this house in a carriage and went to Mr. Tradd's house, her suitor she referred to in the journal, and she spun in his yard nine times and threw a clump of dirt at his front door. That's easy enough to explain because I had just read that entry in her journal, though it was odd how detailed it was in my dream, even beyond what she wrote. I didn't realize I had that good of an imagination."

Felix watched the blood on Regan's lip trickle into the cracks and crevices of her abused flesh, mixing with the moisture already present and causing a red puddle to bead over her bottom lip. He had an idea of what she might say next, and he didn't think he wanted to hear it.

"But the strange thing is, I knew her name was Camille in my dream," she whispered. "When I woke up, I thought I must have just plucked some C name out of the ether. But what are the odds I would use the very same name in my dream? There was no way I could have known that was her name, I'm convinced of it. And there are dozens of much more common C names for my brain to pluck out at random. So when you said Camille . . . it freaked me out."

So Camille had managed to find a conduit through Regan's dreams. Or maybe it was Alcroft under the guise of Camille.

Either way, it was much worse than he had imagined.

He wiped the blood off of her lip with the pad of his thumb, unable to stare at it any longer.

"What are you doing?" She jerked beneath his touch, causing him to smear the blood on her chin.

"You're bleeding." Felix rubbed the new stain off her chin. Her skin was such a perfect, delicate shade of ivory, her tiny nose pert and delicate. Her dark eyes, framed by lustrous eyelashes, were clouded with confusion.

"Oh." She sighed. "You think I'm nuts, don't you?"

"No, not at all. I have no answers for you, but I believe you." He definitely believed her. She was right—there was no way she could have known Camille's name if it hadn't been written in the journal.

Someone was clearly poking around Regan's house and in her thoughts, but whether or not it was a long-dead Camille or a very much alive Alcroft, Felix just didn't know.

What he did know was that it infuriated him that either one would pull someone as innocent and harmless as Regan into their games.

Which meant that despite all his reservations about getting involved, he was going to stick close to her until he knew exactly what was going on.

"So then you had another dream tonight."

"Yes. And this one was even more embellished. That journal had nothing about who Camille . . . I guess I can call her Camille . . . who Camille used that rash spell on. Or how she did it. Yet I had this very vivid dream about her visiting this girl, a Miss Janise, and gloating over the rash."

In the deep recesses of Felix's memory, the name struck a cord. Camille's rival. "Did she mention Miss Janise somewhere else in the journal?"

Regan shook her head. "No. And I'm starting to think

I'm losing my mind." She gave a nervous laugh. "I'm sorry. I shouldn't have called you. You must think I'm a mess, but I . . . I just didn't want to be alone."

She wasn't alone.

Someone was with her.

And it made Felix very, very worried for her and for her soul.

Chapter Eight

Regan had always thought she was an independent woman, but the dreams, this house, they were making her nervous, and that was both upsetting and embarrassing. Now she had almost fainted right in front of Felix, and she was clinging to her sofa cushions like she would float away without them as an anchor. She wasn't sure he'd ever actually seen her when she wasn't at her absolute worst.

"We've all had our moments where we don't want to be alone," he said, his light eyes darkening. "Stop apologizing. You do it constantly."

She did. She knew that. It was ingrained in her from Beau, and maybe even from her mother. But did he have to make it sound like such a criticism? She was pretty sure there were worse flaws than saying you were sorry. "Okay, geez. I'll never apologize to you again."

"Petulance doesn't suit you," he said softly. "I didn't mean it to sound insulting. I just think you should hold your chin up a little higher . . . please yourself from time to time instead of worrying about everyone else. Don't worry about what I think, what anyone thinks."

Regan studied Felix's expression. He looked concerned, nothing more. She did think he believed her about the dreams, about seeing the apparition, which was a huge relief. Her ex-husband would have scoffed and made fun of her for thinking such a thing, but Felix didn't seem to think anything of it at all. But then, as he had pointed out, he was a voodoo priest.

An incredibly good-looking one. Now that the shock had worn off, Regan was altogether too aware of the fact that she was lying on her couch only a foot away from him. He was wearing jeans and a long-sleeved white shirt, with a gray T-shirt over it. He wore a large cross necklace on a leather string, which she found interesting given his voodoo religion, and a silver band around his index finger. Overall, there was an inherent masculinity, a rawness to him that was very appealing.

"Thanks for believing me," she said. "I appreciate it."

"No problem."

His finger brushed her bottom lip again, causing her flesh to tingle and her nipples to harden under the unexpected touch. "More blood?"

"No." He shook his head. "I just wanted to touch you."

Uh-oh. Regan sat up, panicked. That sounded flirtatious, and she had no clue how to engage in flirting with a man like Felix. Way out of her league, her comfort zone, her planet. "I'm feeling better. Thanks for keeping me from hitting the floor."

The smile he gave her, the corner of his mouth tilting up, told her he knew precisely what she was doing—that she was bolting.

"Sure."

So what if she was running? It was the smart thing to do. A man like Felix flirted just to flirt, it meant nothing, and she wasn't savvy or experienced enough to play that casual game. She was too emotional, too easily attached to people. Or so her therapist had told her.

It was probably true. She was incredibly invested in the people she let into her life, and she wasn't a good candidate for meaningless flirting. In retrospect, it wasn't hard to see how she had wound up married after a brief six-month relationship. She sought attachments.

Tugging down the bottom of her shirt, Regan dropped her legs to the floor. "Are you sure you don't want a drink? Just a soda or something?"

He shook his head. "I don't need a drink."

"It's not a problem," she protested, standing up. "I stocked the fridge this morning. I have water, all the soft drinks, beer, wine."

"Don't wait on me," he said. "I'm not thirsty."

Puzzled by his choice of words, Regan shook her head. "It's not a big deal. What would you like?"

"Nothing," he said through clenched teeth. "I don't want anything."

What the hell was that supposed to mean? It sounded like he was talking about much more than a stupid bottled water. "Okay," she said, mystified. "I'll be right back. I need a Diet Coke." Then she thought about going downstairs to the kitchen by herself and hesitated. "But before I go, please tell me you don't see a rash on my face."

The corner of his mouth turned up as he reclined on her sofa, one arm up along the back. "No rash."

"Maybe I was still dreaming when I thought I saw the rash," Regan mused as she wandered back over to the photos she'd been hanging, deciding to forgo the soft drink. "They are really vivid dreams."

"Most dreams are. We just don't remember all those details by the time we wake up."

Regan stood there, not sure what to do with herself. Or him. She had called him, he had shown up, and now she had no clue what to do with him. "That's true."

Then they fell into silence, the music she'd been listening to an obnoxious frenetic pulse surrounding them. It was only adding to the agitation of her mood and she hit the OFF button on her iPod remote.

"You've done some unpacking," Felix commented, rising to his feet and strolling to the center of the room. "It looks good. Very black-and-white, but I suppose that's no surprise."

"What do you mean?" Regan frowned at him. She looked around. She did prefer neutral-colored furnishings, a lot of ivory with black and beige accents, but she went in for texture more than color. She had natural elements like a sisal rug, a chunk of coral on her coffee table, and white feathers holding a cluster of bird eggs under a bell jar.

"You're very black-and-white. Your clothes. Your personality. It stands to reason that your decorating would be the same."

"You make that sound like an insult," she said, turning to pick up another photo to hang—black-and-white at that. "I think it's soothing. The room is harmonious. And if I was totally black-and-white, I wouldn't be scared of the weird things that are happening in my house. I would explain them away logically or I would embrace them. The fact that I'm both anxious and excited about it proves I look into the shades of gray."

"I suppose that's true," he murmured, coming up behind her and taking the framed photograph from her. He studied it, and the one on the wall, and then flipped through the stack she had piled up to hang.

Felix did a small circle, looking at additional larger pieces of art she had propped on the floor against the wall, waiting to be hung. "You collect cemetery art. That I didn't expect. Is death so very black-and-white to you?"

Regan couldn't even answer the question because she was struck dumb by the fact that he had called her photographs a collection of cemetery art. She hadn't even really realized that all the photography and art she owned was in fact images from cemeteries. She had always been drawn to the still quiet beauty of the monuments, the statues, and the crumbling tombs, and was well aware of each individual purchase. But to say that indicated she was a collector of cemetery art, well, that made her uneasy.

"I work in historic cemetery preservation and restoration," she said. "That is what the fund-raising party at my house is for. So it only stands to reason that I would be drawn to photographs of them."

But while the words were logical, she doubted the veracity of them herself. How could she have never noticed that her interest was at the exclusion of all other subjects? Why was it that she had never bought one green pastoral scene? Even her largest piece, one she considered to be a portrait, was actually that of a weeping angel statue in the Metairie Cemetery.

"Sure, that stands to reason. It's something that is clearly important to you. But why? Why does restoration of historic cemeteries matter? Why shouldn't we just let them crumble to the ground tomb by tomb, the heat and humidity restoring the bricks, the marble, the bones of the interred back to the earth?"

It was a question her mother had asked her many times, though not in the same way. Her mom had always suggested she save historic homes instead of dirty old cemeteries. She had never bothered to try to explain it to her mother, but she turned and looked at Felix. Maybe he would understand. He certainly seemed open to different ideas, if his choice of occupation was any indication.

"Because they're beautiful, peaceful tributes to humanity. When they were built, each tomb mattered to the people who built it. They invested money, time, love into erecting a place for their loved ones to spend eternity, and it seems the height of disrespect to just let them, and the remains they contain, be destroyed."

"I see. Do you know much about Victorian mourning practices?" he asked, not looking at her, but arranging the photos on the table in a grid.

"No, not really."

"Before the Victorians, before anyone really understood how disease was transmitted, when someone died their body was discarded as quickly as possible. The thought was to get them as far from the living as possible so they didn't spread death. The fear of death was greater than the fear of showing disrespect to a loved one. Then in Victorian times, even though they really had no better understanding of disease, they created elaborate death rituals, huge, lengthy periods of mourning, and the interest in spiritualism and contacting the dead rose. What they were afraid of was life, living without the dead."

Regan watched his fingers move, long and beautiful for a man, masculine yet not stubby or dirty or hairy. Elegant, in a way, the silver ring he wore simple and well suited to him. He brushed them over the glass gently, his care in touch so different from his voice, which frequently sounded gruff and almost angry. Felix was a gorgeous man, and unlike any she had ever met. The men she'd been raised with, who moved in her social circles, blurred into a tie-wearing mass of confident, entitled materialists, their focus almost invariably themselves and their professional success.

She had never met a man who spoke the way Felix did about any manner of strange things and made it sound casual, conversational. And he never talked about himself, which was a foreign concept to her. Men she knew thought of themselves as their favorite subject.

It didn't sound like he was finished, so she said nothing, just waited.

He seemed to find a pattern he liked with the photos and reached for a nail as he continued speaking. "Can you imagine being in mourning for a year, which meant wearing black every day, never attending balls or parties, not getting married during that time or doing anything that might be considered too much fun, and then maybe being out of mourning for only a month before some other unfortunate relative died and you had to haul out the black crepe again."

She stood there mute, while he tapped the nail with the hammer, sending it into the wall, and hung the photograph, stepping back to check its position. She was equal parts fascinated by what he was saying and by the fact that he had just taken it upon himself to hang her photos in the way he liked.

Felix turned and stared at her, unsmiling. "Fear of death versus fear of living. A strange shift in society, don't you think? Though easily explained by circumstances. But I find myself wondering which applies to you. Are you afraid to die or are you afraid to live?"

The anxiety Regan had felt before Felix entered the house returned full force. The telltale trickle of sweat was back between her breasts, and her throat was constricted, the urge to flee reminiscent of her final months with her ex-husband.

"I . . . I don't know." For some reason her right hand went to her left, to twist the wedding ring that was no longer there. When she realized what she was doing, she dropped both hands. "I've never really thought of my fears in either of those ways."

"What are your fears, Regan Henry Alcroft?" he asked, picking up another photograph, one of Marie Laveau's tomb, ironically enough.

The voodoo priest held the voodoo priestess's final resting place in his hand.

"I'm afraid of snakes," she said carefully. "And my name is not Alcroft."

"Perhaps that is your real fear . . . that living sometimes is far too similar to death. Empty, pointless, lonely."

It was a horrifically accurate description of her marriage, yet Regan saw the pain in his eyes, the stark bald suffering of a lonely man. She reached out and touched his arm, thinking to offer compassion, to let him know she understood, that she could be a friend, someone he could talk to. "Are we talking about me or about you?" she asked gently.

"We're never talking about me. That subject is not open for discussion." He moved his arm so that her hand dropped away from his skin.

Regan felt bewildered, wounded. "Yet you can ask me personal questions?"

"Isn't that what you want from me? Someone to talk to, someone to explain the mystery of life and death and the spirit world to you . . ."

Felix moved toward her, abandoning the photograph on the table, his steps slow, but purposeful. "Or is there something else you want from me?" His voice was hypnotic, yet mocking, and she didn't understand what he was doing, the point of the conversation, what he wanted her to say.

She shook her head. "I don't know what you mean. I don't want anything from you."

"Yes, you do." His hand lifted up and connected with her hair, pulling the strands she had tucked behind her ear out, his touch gentle, seductive. "You want me to fuck you, don't you?"

Yes. But hearing him say it out loud, so crass, so matter-of-fact, Regan felt the burn of humiliation, followed by anger. "It's time for you to leave," she said, now the one to back out of his touch, out of his space, breaking contact with his manipulative, mesmerizing eyes.

"Don't be offended. I'm just saying what we both know."

That was just what she did not want to hear, him pointing out that she was a pathetic undersexed divorcee who was dangling after the hot guy she couldn't have. It was beyond embarrassing to realize she had been so transparent, so unsophisticated and obvious. "Get out," she said, tightly.

She'd rather face the spirits in her house alone than have him there for one second longer.

Felix gave her that half smile he so frequently wore. "Sure." He moved around her, his shoulders brushing her, and his mouth leaning in close to her ear. "But just for the record, I want to fuck you, too."

Regan shivered, goose bumps rushing up her arms from disgust, arousal, fear, she wasn't sure. Maybe all of the above.

Then he grabbed the research papers he'd brought for her and crumpled them in a ball, taking them with him. Without a single glance back he was gone, the front door slamming a brutal exclamation point to his departure.

❧

Felix burst out onto Royal Street, swearing at himself. What the hell was he doing? He had intentionally pissed Regan off, knowing she would throw him out. He had needed to get out of there. Looking at her wide, innocent, compassionate eyes was torture.

And he knew torture.

He had been fine. Distant, in control, listening to her story of what had happened in her house—Camille's house. Then suddenly she had looked at him, like she saw the truth. Like she knew he hurt, and wanted to comfort him, of all things.

My God, it had been so tempting, so fucking tempting to let her. But he knew the real truth. There was no comfort for him, and no woman would ever really be capable of giving to him. That was his curse. They could take, but they could never give.

What he had done, bargain for the right to take, meant he had been served the same in kind—no woman would ever want him. They would just want.

It was a brutal distinction, and for a split second he had seen something else on Regan's face, a false promise, and he needed to squash that hope in himself before it sprouted. She was no different. It would never be different.

He knew that. Had chewed, swallowed, and digested that bitter lesson a hundred times over.

Felix's footsteps ate up the short block to Bourbon Street. He needed a drink.

He started to turn right, to head to Lafitte's, a dark moody tavern, but he changed his mind and turned left, letting the neon lights of the flashier bars splash over him. The street was still jumping, partygoers stumbling in and out of clubs, clutching plastic cups, wearing Mardi Gras beads.

The thought was to be anonymous, to go unnoticed on the busy street, but all it did was remind him that he was alone, always alone. He told himself this was his world, that of entertainment in exchange for money, that he was the game show host with a revolving door of contestants.

It might be how he had to exist, but it didn't mean he had to like it.

A woman stumbled in front of him and Felix grabbed her arm to steady her. She tried to glance back and thank him, but her eyes were glassy from alcohol, and the movement of her head threw her off balance again.

She couldn't make eye contact with him.

Felix let her go and her friend locked arms with her. They tottered away and Felix cut down Orleans Street and headed home.

There was nothing here for him.

❧

Regan finished hanging every last photograph and piece of art in her living room, pounding viciously into the plaster with her hammer, angry with herself.

Felix had known all along that she was attracted to him.

The thought that he might think she had made up excuses

to see him was a very mortifying fear. It rolled around and around in her head, a refrain of insecurity. Why had he left like that?

Unable to stand it anymore, Regan sent Felix a text message. She wrote, *Thanks for coming over,* and hit SEND before she could change her mind.

Three hours later she finally fell asleep on the couch, Camille's journal in her hands.

Felix never answered.

Chapter Nine

"You look like shit," Chris told Regan over dinner the next night. "You should hit your dermatologist up for something to hide those dark circles under your eyes."

Regan set down her salad fork so she wouldn't throw it at him. "Thanks for the advice. And brutal honesty."

"What are friends for?" He made inroads into his cranberry walnut salad, either totally unaware he had hurt her feelings or not caring.

Chances were, he just didn't care. There was probably a lesson in that for her. She should take a page from Chris's book and worry less what other people thought of her. "I'm not getting any sleep. I keep having those weird dreams, and last night, I think I saw a ghost." She described Camille to him. "It was really unnerving."

That hadn't been the only thing that was unnerving. The image of Felix's face, his light eyes boring into her, popped into her head.

"I think it's cool you have a ghost. Not that I would want to live there, but I think it's very trendy and great fodder for dinner parties. What did you do? Did you try to talk to her or leave the house or what?"

She picked her fork back up and fiddled with it, staring at her mixed greens. "I stared at her until she disappeared, then I called the voodoo priest, the one who is going to be at my party. He came over."

"Oh, really?" Glee crept into Chris's voice. "Is he cute? Or is he like a hundred years old with hairy knuckles?"

"He's not old. He's our age. And cute is not the right word to describe him. Striking is more accurate." Regan shrugged. "He's hot."

"Now we're talking. So he was all reassuring and sexy, controlling the freaky shit in your house . . . Please tell me this is going somewhere interesting."

"Well, we talked. And he's kind of hard to read, but it was nice to have company and he believes me without question about the occurrences in the house. Then he said something I was not expecting."

"Yeah? What?"

It was embarrassing to say out loud, but Regan wanted a male opinion. She dropped her voice. "He said, 'You want me to fuck you, don't you?'"

Chris's eyes went wide. "Hello. That's hot. So you said yes and he threw you against the wall, didn't he? Oh, my God, I'm so jealous."

That wasn't the reaction she'd expected. "No! I told him to get out of my house. Don't you think saying that to someone you hardly know is rude?"

"Umm . . . was it true?"

"Well, maybe, but it's still rude."

"Why?" Chris looked genuinely puzzled. "Why play games? Just say what you're both thinking. I think that's just a time-saver."

Was that really the male point of view or was that just Chris? Regan frowned. "Yeah, but when he said that, I had no way of knowing if he was going to reciprocate the

sentiment, so it made me uncomfortable. Embarrassed.
What if I said yes and he said, 'Thanks for the ego boost,'
and left?"

"See, this is where women need to get a grip. No man
is going to throw a question out there like that unless he
is thinking that he totally wants to nail you. It's like he's
handing you a permission slip to sign. Trust me, if you had
said yes, it would have been up-against-the-wall sex."

There was a pause while Regan contemplated that actually happening. Felix's hands on her shoulders, her waist,
in her hair, peeling off her clothing. His mouth on hers, on
her breasts. The wall hard behind her head, her back as he
stroked her to the first of many orgasms . . .

Regan put her hands on her cheeks and cleared her
throat. That definitely would have been more fun than
hanging art and falling asleep on her couch alone. "Really?
Well, I guess I blew it then."

"Yeah, well, let's be honest here. Are you really a casual
sex kind of girl? You've always been relationship oriented,
you know. Can you really have sex with this guy and not
worry or fixate on what it means?"

She shrugged. "I don't know. Part of me thinks casual is
just what I need after my marriage, but I am fascinated by
him, I can admit that to myself. If I have sex with him, and
it's good, I'm going to want to again, I'm sure. Part of me
thinks maybe it's not a good idea to be involved in any way
with a man right now, casual or otherwise."

"Which might be why you freaked and tossed him out
of your house. It was more self-protection than fear that he
didn't want you in return."

Feeling depressed, she abandoned her fork yet again.
"So I'm supposed to just do what? Never have sex again?
Have sex with someone I'm not even interested in? I don't
think that will work at all."

"You have two choices. Wait until you're emotionally

ready to have another relationship and find a guy you want to have that relationship with. Or you can go for it and shag the hot voodoo dude and hope there's no fallout." Chris raised his wineglass. "I think you can take a wild guess which one I would do."

"Oh, I have no doubt which one you would choose." They were dining al fresco at a restaurant on Royal Street a block from her house, and Regan glanced over at the fountain burbling water over rough, aged stones. "And for me, well, for the first time in my life I'm tired of playing it safe. It's like leaving Beau gave me the courage to rock the boat in more ways than one." She smiled at Chris. "If I was given a do-over, I think I would go for it."

"You still can. Text him. Call him."

But she shook her head. "It's too late for that. I ticked him off. I'm not even sure he'll show at the party."

"He'd better. He made a commitment. Just call him."

Suddenly Regan laughed. What the hell was she worried about? People's opinions? Felix's opinion? If she wanted something, she should just take it and they could all go screw themselves. "Maybe I will. Why not, right?"

Only Chris didn't respond.

She looked at him. "What? I thought you would approve."

"Normally, yes. But for a second there, Regan, I swear to God, you didn't look like yourself. It was like your face kind of *changed* or something. That was freaky shit."

"Drink more wine," she told him lightly, dismissing what he was saying, even as a nervous tremor ran up her arms.

For just a second, she had actually felt unlike herself, full of defiance and anger and selfishness.

None of those were normal to her, yet she had felt them.

Like the dreams.

Only now she was awake.

Felix hated being summoned. Hated that when he had accepted the false promise of security, he had given up his independence, the ability to ever be his own man.

A young, pretty secretary showed him into Alcroft's office, flipping her hair and smiling coyly at Felix the whole time. He barely spared her a glance. Too young. Too obvious. Too not Regan.

"Leblanc, how are you?" Alcroft asked, rising from behind his desk and adjusting his tie.

"Fine." He didn't bother to inquire about Alcroft. He didn't give a shit how he was doing. "I'm here. What do you want?"

"You know, you'd think with all the money you have, you could wear clothes that didn't look like a garage sale leftover from the Seattle grunge days of the nineties." Alcroft moved around his desk and leaned against it, displaying his designer suit and Italian shoes.

Felix was wearing jeans and a T-shirt, what he always wore, and it was who he was. At least who he was now. There had been a time when he had reveled in the sharp clothes money was able to buy, the elegant watches, shiny shoes, ebony walking sticks. But they had come with a price, and in the end, Felix had shed his materialism.

Ironic that while he had outgrown the trappings of greed, he was owned by the biggest purveyor of that particular sin—the demon of greed.

"Did you ask me here to discuss my fashion sense?"

Alcroft gave him a smile, and it wasn't a pleasant one. Felix steeled himself, forcing himself to maintain a relaxed stance, his hands loosely in his front pockets.

"No. I asked you here because I want to know why the hell you are doing your little voodoo bullshit at my wife's fund-raising party."

Now Felix did relax. "Because her party planner called me and invited me to do it."

"And that's all?"

"Sure. It's no different from the law firm party. Just another way to make a quick buck."

"And it's just a coincidence that she is my wife?"

Alcroft didn't seem to know that Felix had seen Regan personally, and he wanted to keep it that way. "Actually, no, not a coincidence. I thought maybe you had something to do with it. That you wanted me there."

The demon laughed. "I suppose I could see that. But no, I had nothing to do with it. I don't want you around my wife. You can do her damn party, but you're not to have any contact with her, do you understand?"

"Why?" he asked, knowing it would piss Alcroft off, but not caring. "What do you think I'm going to do?"

"Nothing. You can't do anything. But Regan is a weak woman, and we all know how easily they fall for your Creole charm."

"I don't have any charm left, Alcroft. I wouldn't worry about it if I were you." Hell, Regan had thrown him out of her house, after all. She hadn't seemed to think he was the least bit charming two nights ago. It wasn't smart to rile the demon in his cage, but Felix couldn't resist. "Though I did notice she has dropped your last name. Trouble in paradise?"

Alcroft's eyes narrowed. "You could say that. Regan left me, ironically enough the night of the law firm party when she had a reading with you. Could there have been anything you might have said to her that encouraged her abandoning a very happy marriage?"

"She left that night? Right before Christmas?" Felix gave Alcroft false sympathy. "I'm sorry, that must have been very difficult and embarrassing for you."

"Watch it," Alcroft said, in a soft voice. "You forget who you're speaking to."

"Oh, I know exactly who I'm speaking to. I never, ever forget." Felix forced a casual shrug. "I didn't say anything to her about you, other than to tell her the necklace she was wearing was pretty. We talked mostly about her sister."

Alcroft rolled his eyes. "Of course you did. She blathers on about that stupid dead kid every chance she gets. But she must have had a reason for leaving me."

Disgust rippled through Felix. "Maybe it's because you have a block of ice for a heart and you refer to the sister she loves as that stupid dead kid."

But Alcroft just laughed. "Like I ever said that to her. No, I was a damn good husband. She is my tenth wife, after all. I've gotten good at satisfying a woman's material and physical needs."

No mention of emotional needs, of course.

"And she's the first wife who has ever left me. There has to be a reason, and you'd better hope it has nothing to do with you."

"Maybe she just isn't as weak and pliable as you thought she was." Regan was that paradox, appearing so even and passive, yet Felix knew there was an iron core to her.

"Stay away from her," Alcroft said. "I'll show you no mercy, and trust me it won't be worth it. She's terrible in bed. It's like fucking a blow-up doll."

Charming and sensitive as always. And Felix didn't believe for one second that Regan would disappoint in the bedroom. More likely Alcroft didn't know how to coax pleasure from her. Whereas Felix knew he could. Knew he would. "Then why do you want to stay married to her?"

"Who said I did?" Alcroft tilted his head, a smile turning up the corner of his mouth. "So what do you think of Regan buying Camille's old house? Great memories there for you, huh?"

He'd been waiting for Alcroft to bring that up. "I find it an amazing coincidence."

"It's no coincidence," Alcroft said, picking up a paperweight off his desk. He turned it in his hand, over and over, then lifted it up high. The crystal sculpture had turned into an opaque image of Camille's—Regan's—house. "I've always liked that house. Such a pretty balcony, isn't it?"

The words were soft-spoken, innocuous, but Felix heard the warning. He wasn't exactly sure what it meant, but it was a threat, to Regan, and the cold fissure of fear trickled up his spine. "What are you doing?"

Alcroft tossed the miniature house into the air, and when it landed in his palm, it was just a crystal rock again. "What? Nothing. Nothing at all." He smiled. "Just remember that while I'm not nearly as fond of Regan as I was of Camille, I still don't want to hear that you laid one of your filthy fingers on her. Not now, and especially not later."

Felix didn't understand what the game was, but he knew one was in play, and Regan was nothing more than a poker chip to Alcroft.

"You may own me and my filthy fingers." Felix held up his hands, flashing the silver binding ring he wore. "But you don't own Regan anymore."

"I own everything," Alcroft told him, his eyes glowing the amber hue of his hatred. "Never forget that."

Not waiting to be dismissed, Felix said nothing, just turned and left.

For the first time in a hundred years he realized that while Alcroft owned his actions, his money, and his immortality, he didn't own Felix's soul.

He was going to protect Regan from his own fate regardless of what it cost him.

❦

There was no light. No sound except for the staccato of Felix's breathing and the rustle of his clothing as he shifted occasionally.

He had thought he had been set on a stool when he had arrived, yet there was nothing beneath him, no furniture, no ground, no sense of the bottom, the top, the walls, or anything other than an infinity of darkness. Plato's Myth of the Cave melded with Dante's Inferno, a vast empty chasm of quiet, shadows, and the occasional lick of the flame of pain.

Felix had no concept of how long he had been suspended in nothing . . . whether a day or a month or a year he couldn't say, only that he was slowly and increasingly going mad, like Camille had in the torture of her grief, every second an agonizing suspension of time, every moment endless in its nothingness.

There was no food, yet he wasn't hungry. No water, never thirsty. He had no need to relieve himself and no sexual desire, a strange physical lethargy coupled with acute discomfort stretching each minute that much longer. He was aware of every inch of his body as a heavy, crushing burden, simply struggling to hold himself upright as weighty as balancing a tree trunk on his shoulders for months on end. No longer attempting to move, he hung, suspended, like a ham in the slaughterhouse, swaying, blood trickling down his sweaty back from the latest slash of pain.

His thoughts moved quickly, like cockroaches scrambling across his brain, purposeful and startling in their approach. They didn't belong to him, and came and went as they pleased, scattering with the unexpected glare of lacerating agony. The pain was like being thrust into the heat and light of the sun after the darkness, pricking and burning, slashing and tearing, sometimes here, sometimes there, never in the same place twice, the pattern so random as to not be a pattern at all, maddening in its anticipation.

The fear intertwined with the pain, which kicked the numbness with the force of a boot heel, bringing back the fear, which preceded the pain, until there was nothing but numb, fear, pain, the trio that confirmed Felix still in fact lived.

He wished, when his mind was not screaming, for

death. If it were bestowed upon him, he would embrace it, caress it, make love to it as a groom does his bride. Without hesitation he would fall into it, accept the oblivion, the freedom of a true nothingness.

His hands had found their way to his neck, had tried to choke off his life breath, to end the infernal agony, but they didn't have the strength to complete the task, not even enough to produce the bliss of unconsciousness.

It simply went on and on and on . . . until it didn't.

Felix blinked and he was in the parlor of his own house, sitting on the sofa, body still stiff and wracked with the aftereffects of pain, but clean and whole.

Alcroft stood in front of him in evening clothes. "You're released from your punishment. But if you ever touch another woman I have chosen as my own, it will be much, much worse. Ponder that, slave."

Felix did.

Chapter Ten

Chris paused in front of Regan's house. "Are you okay being here alone?"

She shrugged with an aplomb she wasn't sure she felt. "Sure. I'm fine. I do love this house, you know. It's been a ten-year dream to live in it, and I'm not going to let a ghost scare me."

So she said. Her racing heart didn't seem to get the instant message from her brain.

He looked unconvinced, too. "Hey, you have a package on your doorstep."

Regan glanced down and saw the bubble mailer propped against her front door. "Geez, I think I need to talk to the mailman about that. It's a miracle it didn't get stolen."

She picked it up and winced. "It's from Beau."

"The bastard. Maybe it would have been better if it had been stolen. What is it? A knife for you to shove in your back?"

Ripping open the packaging, she slid the interior box

out and frowned at it. "It's a box of chocolates. And a note that says, 'I love you.'"

"Lame. Like a fifty-dollar gift is going to make you change your mind."

"Especially considering he just agreed to the divorce. My lawyer said this afternoon it will be official, all filed and done." Regan shoved the gold foil box back in the mailing envelope. "I would say it's meant to be a truce gesture, but that doesn't strike me as something Beau would do."

"Hardly. But who cares about him? Just eat the chocolates and burn the note. So, are you going to call the voodoo guy to celebrate your divorce going through? And does he have a name, by the way? I'm tired of calling him voodoo dude."

"His name is Felix." Regan unlocked her front door, juggling the envelope under her arm. "And no, I'm not going to call him. What the hell would I say? Hi, I do want you?"

"That seemed to be your plan back there over dinner." Chris leaned against the wall and lit a cigarette. Taking a deep drag, he said, "Regan, something strange is going on here in this house."

"I thought you quit smoking," she told him.

"I did. This is just a vacation from quitting. And don't avoid the subject."

"What am I supposed to say?" Regan shoved the door open and turned to him, hand still on the knob. "Yes, something strange is going on. Is it paranormal activity? Is it me, drinking too much wine? Being completely stressed out over my divorce? I don't know. But I'll go crazy if I just sit around thinking and freaking out about it."

"I'm just worried about you. Remember that movie *Poltergeist*? What if they're punching a hole into this world with the intention of taking you back to theirs?"

Great. Just one more thing she needed to worry about,

being sucked into her walk-in closet and disappearing into the world of the dead. "Good night. I'm going to bed. I love you." She kissed him on the cheek.

"Love you, too." Chris blew smoke to his right. "Call me if you need me. Or if you have hot sex and you want to tell me all the juicy details."

"When have I ever given you details of my sex life?"

"When have you ever had sex with a voodoo practitioner? There's a time to start everything."

"True that." Regan smiled and started to walk into the house. "Bye, sweetheart."

"Bye, babe. Talk to you later."

Regan paused, glancing up and down the street. She had the unmistakable sensation of eyes on her, watching.

"What?" Chris asked, following her stare curiously.

There was only a man walking his dog a few doors up and he wasn't even looking in their direction. Looking up at the balconies across the street, Regan saw they were all empty. "Nothing."

Just paranoia, her new best friend. She closed and locked the door and went up the stairs, determined not to turn on every single light she encountered. The moonlight was streaming through the entryway windows, illuminating her ascent. She didn't want to be afraid of her house. She wanted to believe that Camille was reaching out to her. Maybe the dead woman just wanted someone to acknowledge what she had suffered in her young life. Maybe she wanted to comfort Regan or at least share in their mutual pain of having lost a sister.

Or maybe Camille was simply what people referred to as an imprint—a ghost who was trapped in the house reliving her last days on earth over and over. There was no purpose to an imprint, they weren't even aware of what they were doing.

Yet somehow she knew that wasn't what Camille was. The monkey on the bed, the image behind her in the doorway, the rash . . . those weren't repetitive flashes, they were intentional actions.

Heading to her room, Regan decided to take the chocolates with her. She would watch a little bit of TV now that she had hooked up her flat-screen, and eat the candy in bed. That seemed like a perfect way to thumb her nose at Beau's gift. He would be appalled at the idea of eating messy melting chocolate in bed. Maybe she would even smear a little on what would have been his pillowcase, just because she could.

Childish, maybe. But she had earned her petty defiance.

Ten minutes later she was in her pajamas, a romantic comedy playing on the DVR, the box of chocolates open in front of her, a glass of red wine on the nightstand. She was debating a cream-filled versus a cherry-covered dark chocolate when she decided she needed to rest her eyes for just a second. Dinner had given her a full stomach and the sleepless nights were definitely catching up with her.

The remote sliding out of her hand, she fell asleep.

❦

Camille filled the crystal flute with water and set it on the chest of drawers. Her parents' old room was dark, the only light that of the moon streaming through the French doors. She was in her shift, straining to see the parchment paper in front of her as she wrote in bold, large letters "COURAGE" in dragon's blood ink. Rolling the paper and then dipping it into the glass, she watched the liquid darken, the ink washing off the paper to swirl into the water.

The blood of her enemies, that's what it was, everyone who had betrayed her, who had spoken out against her, the very rules and conventions of society themselves, and her biggest foe of all—disease. She concentrated on the water, on focusing all her fears into that glass, all the things, people, emotions that had ruined her life.

She would ruin them in return. Make them powerless by making them a part of her. She would triumph in the ultimate victory, that of death.

Picking up the glass, Camille drank her bloody courage.

Two swallows and it was gone, inside her, flowing throughout her whole body.

She stepped over to the French doors and flung them open, pushing the doorstops with her bare feet to force the doors to stay. Feeling the power already, she climbed onto the wrought iron railing of her balcony and perched there, arms flung wide.

The breeze kicked up her hair, her shift, and she closed her eyes, her head sinking back. The night, the moon, the other world kissed against her cheeks, and she laughed, embracing it.

Soon she would be with her family again and she wouldn't be alone in this big empty house anymore.

⁂

Felix took the corner of Ursuline Street for the fifth time, intending to walk past Regan's house yet again. He had no idea what he was doing. He had been pacing and stalking the outside of her mansion since right after his meeting with Alcroft. He had no idea what he was expecting to see or why he didn't just go up and ring the damn doorbell, but he just kept trolling the block, again and again, waiting for something.

The only thing he'd seen so far was the FedEx guy deliver a package and Regan return home with a blond man in a red golf shirt. Felix had hung back and watched them chat for a second on the doorstep, the guy smoking a cigarette while they talked. They gave each other a cheek kiss for good-bye, and Felix had wondered if it was the friend she had mentioned, the one who had spent the night with her the day she had moved in.

Then she had paused before going in and Felix had instinctively known that she had sensed his presence. He had ducked into the doorway of an art gallery and cursed himself. When she'd gone in, he'd started another circuit around the block.

What the hell was he doing?

Glancing at the screen on his cell phone as he approached the side of her house, he saw it was almost eleven. Maybe he should just send her a text message. Though he had no idea what it would say.

Hey, you're in danger, though I'm not sure from what. Your ex-husband is a demon, and the ghost in your house is my crazy nineteenth-century client and lover.

Somehow he doubted she would think anyone was crazy but him.

Which maybe he was.

What did he really know about Camille or Alcroft's intentions? Nothing. He just knew something was off, something was in motion, and he couldn't let Regan be hurt.

Shoving his phone back in his pocket, he looked up at her house, at the balcony overlooking her courtyard.

And would have had a heart attack were he capable of such a thing.

Regan was sitting on the balcony railing, legs dangling over the side down toward the cobblestones of the courtyard. She was in a nightgown, her dark brown hair not controlled the way it usually was, but whipping around in the wind.

Jesus Christ. Felix started running, afraid to call out to her and startle her, but terrified that she could slip and crash down onto the ground below. Tugging at the gate, he knew it was locked even as he rattled it back and forth. Regan was meticulous about locking all her doors. Keeping an eye on her, just perched there so still, hands gripping the railing, Felix reached up and grabbed the gate, pulling himself up the length of it.

Regan didn't seem to be moving or looking at anything. She was just sitting there, not even reacting when the wind grabbed the bottom of her nightgown and lifted it, exposing her thighs and a flash of panties. Grateful for his immortal strength, Felix scaled the top of the fence, slicing his hand on one of the spikes but ignoring it. He dropped down onto the stones of the courtyard and ran for the interior stairs that led to where Regan was dangling.

She didn't seem to see him, and Felix realized she had to be sleepwalking. Slowing his pace at the top of the stairs, he approached her as quietly and swiftly as possible. He hesitated, not sure how to grab her in such a way that she would fall backward with him, and in no way did he want to startle her so that she struggled with him and fell forward.

Breathing hard, he actually surprised himself by offering up a quick prayer. It had been a long, long time since he'd done that.

Reaching out with both arms, he got them positioned around her middle and whispered, "Regan."

She didn't respond, and he moved in closer to her, tightening his grip on her. "Regan, you need to wake up."

Suddenly her head whipped around, cracking him in the temple, the unexpected pain causing his grip to loosen. She wobbled and screamed and Felix panicked, her hair blinding him. He squeezed her against him, and felt her sliding down the front of the railing.

"Regan, lean back!" he yelled, her motion propelling him forward so that he slammed against the railing.

The iron fencing rattled against his weight, and she screamed again as he yanked her as hard as he could. Her one knee hooked on the railing and she was dangling upside down, her nightgown falling over her chin, arms flailing, but he had her on the right side of the balcony. Swearing, heart pounding, he dragged her the rest of the way until they both thumped onto the wood floor.

"Holy shit," he said, sucking in a few breaths as he pulled her so that her head and shoulders were lying on his leg.

"Felix?" she asked, her eyes glassy with sleep and confusion as she stared up at him. "What's going on?"

"I think you were sleepwalking." He brushed her hair off her face and leaned over to tug her nightgown down over her bare breasts. He couldn't get it past her waist because of the angle but he didn't think it mattered. She was wearing panties and they were deep enough into her courtyard that someone would have to be staring pretty intently from the sidewalk to get a flash.

And he wasn't exactly feeling sexual at the moment so she had no worries from him.

"I was sleepwalking? I never sleepwalk." She shifted and winced. "Oh, my leg hurts."

"I'm sure you're going to have a hell of a bruise tomorrow, but at least better than the one you would have had if you'd fallen off that railing." The image of her sitting there, vacant, was replaying in his head. God, if he hadn't been walking by . . .

"I never sleepwalk," she said, still looking dazed. "I came outside?"

"Yes. Come on." He nudged her gently. "Let's get up and get you back inside."

Regan struggled to her feet then yanked her nightgown down. "Sorry."

"For what?" Felix stood up, forcing his shoulders to relax.

"For my nightgown." She gestured to indicate it had been bunched up, her pale cheeks staining pink.

"Give me a break. I wasn't even looking," he said, irritated.

"Of course you weren't," she said, crossing her arms over her chest. She looked back at the balcony. "What happened?"

"I was walking by and I saw you sitting on the railing, facing out. You almost gave me a fucking heart attack. Were you dreaming?"

"No." She frowned, shaking her head. "Not that I remember. I was watching TV and I fell asleep. That's all I remember."

"Alright, let's get you back in bed and we're shoving a chair in front of the door so you can't leave." Felix put his hand on the small of her back and pushed her toward the doors to her bedroom.

When they stepped into the room he smelled it immediately.

Demon.

The scent was cloying and overpowering in her room. Felix grabbed the back of her nightgown and brought her to a stop. "Hold on. Stay here." Going into the room, he did a quick sweep and saw no one.

But there was no denying the smell . . . a demon had been in her room and had left something of himself behind to create that kind of stench. But Felix didn't see anything obvious or out of the ordinary.

Then his eyes landed on the chest of drawers and what was resting on top of it. "What is this?" Felix moved toward it, the very bureau Regan had to have found the journal in, the one that had been in the room the night he had been here with Camille.

He ran his hand over the marble top of the chest of drawers, remembering it with candles burning on it, the shadows dancing over its handles and glossy finish. Only now it held a wineglass with a piece of mailing envelope crammed in it, red droplets spattered over its marble surface. A pen lay next to the glass, and the envelope she had ripped a piece out of and shoved into the wine was lying carelessly beside it. "What is all this?"

"I . . . I don't know. When I fell asleep the glass was on the nightstand next to me. I'm sure of it."

A quick glance at her pale face, her trembling lips, showed she was telling the truth. "And the envelope?"

"It was on the bed. I got a box of chocolates in the mail and I had pulled it out of the envelope on the bed to eat them while I was watching TV. Felix, how . . . how can they be over here? Did I do this in my sleep?"

"Apparently." He plucked the torn envelope out of the glass and uncurled it. There was writing on it. Smeared from the wine, but still legible. *Courage*.

What the hell . . .

"Was the glass empty?" he asked.

"No. I barely took two sips before I fell asleep."

But she clearly had drunk it after she'd fallen asleep. After she had done a courage spell. Put your fears in blood, add your courage, and drink it.

"This is a voodoo spell," he told her.

"What?" She got that look again, the one she'd been wearing when she had almost fainted on him before, and Felix grabbed her with both hands to steady her.

Swallowing repeatedly, she whispered, "What do you mean?"

"It's a spell to rid yourself of fears." And all it had done was increase his.

"How . . . how could I do that asleep? I don't even know any spells."

"Was it in the journal?" Camille's little legacy. And possibly Camille's trapdoor into the land of the living once again.

"No. I haven't read very much of it. And I don't remember there being anything like that." Her arms furled tighter around her breasts. "I don't understand what is happening."

Neither did he. Not exactly. If the journal was Camille's access to Regan, and mortality, then why did the room stink like demon?

"You said you were eating chocolates? Where did they come from?"

"My ex-husband sent them to me."

Bingo. Felix went over to her nightstand and eyed the box of chocolates. Grabbing a piece, he broke it open and almost gagged. The scent was even stronger, a bitter salty venom. The fucking bastard had sent her a very lovely box of chocolates with his semen inside each little piece of candy. The ultimate binding tool—sexual fluid, inserted right into her food so she would consume it.

Disgusting. Absolutely the lowest form of manipulation in Felix's opinion.

Knocking the box to the ground, he stepped on the chocolates and crushed as many as he could with his heel.

"What are you doing?"

"I dropped them."

"No you didn't. I saw you throw them down," she said.

He ignored that. "Did you eat any?"

"I don't think so. I was going to, but I fell asleep. Why? Is something wrong with them? You can't possibly think Beau is trying to poison me."

"Of course not." She'd be of no use to him dead. But why did Alcroft want Regan? Just to win?

"So why did you crush them? Felix, I'm totally freaked out." She pulled her hair back and wound it into the shape of a bun, then stared at him with huge, frightened eyes. "How could I not remember shoving paper into my wineglass?"

He realized he was just scaring her more than she already was. Walking toward her, he schooled his features into what he hoped was reassurance. It wouldn't help if she was afraid of him, too. "It's okay, Regan, it's okay. Lots of people sleepwalk. You hear stories all the time of people leaving their house, or thinking an easy chair in the living room is the toilet. It doesn't mean anything."

She managed a shaky laugh. "Well, at least I've never thought my chair was a toilet. Just that my balcony railing is a park bench."

"Hey, you're safe." He rubbed her arms, wanting to take

away that look on her face. She had goose bumps, and she shivered when he caressed her. "You've been under a lot of stress."

Not that he thought for one minute stress had caused her to dangle off that damn balcony, the same one Camille had fallen from and died. He suppressed a shudder. If he had been a minute or two later, he might have found Regan broken on the cobblestones in the exact same way.

She seemed to have the identical thought at the same time. "What if you hadn't shown up right then?"

"But I did. And we had our *Titanic* moment there. I felt like Jack hauling you over the side of the ship." He tried to inject lightness into his voice. "Though you're much prettier than Kate Winslet."

"Hah, right. She's gorgeous." Regan stared at his chest, biting her lip.

"And so are you." Felix ran his finger up her arms, under the sleeves of her nightgown. "You're more than gorgeous. You're beautiful."

"Aren't those the same thing? And you don't have to flatter me to distract me."

Felix almost laughed at the irony. "Oh, trust me, I gave up false flattery a long, long time ago. And while gorgeous implies a sort of overblown beauty, being beautiful is more delicate, more poetic, less overtly sexual."

"You don't think I'm sexual?"

He should have known that would be what she extracted from what he had just said, had tried to explain. It seemed that the honesty of his compassion and concern, the truth of his attraction, was more difficult to convey than all the fake sentiments he had whispered to women over the years.

Felix shifted his hands to cup her face. "Regan. I think you are very sexual. But it's not an in-your-face stripper kind of sexual. It's coiled like a snake under your elegant exterior, and I have no doubt that you're the woman every man craves—the lady in public, the tiger in private."

"I'm really not," she said, her tongue flicking out to nervously lick her bottom lip in a way that made his muscles tighten. "My ex-husband always said—"

Like he gave a shit what Alcroft thought. He cut her off by shifting his fingers over her mouth. "Shh. Why do either of us care what your ex-husband thinks? I only care what *we* think. And I think that I can't leave here tonight until I've at least tasted you."

Maybe it wasn't the way to deal with the fears of either one of them, but Felix didn't know how to offer comfort. It wasn't something he had ever really learned to give. His mother had cosseted him, taught him to take, encouraged his spoiled greed. But he wanted to give . . . wanted to make Regan understand she was an amazing woman.

He wanted to take that look off of her face, to hold her and make her relax, to feel the beauty in herself that he saw.

He also wanted to reassure himself she was alive and well, despite whatever the hell Camille was doing to her.

And he just wanted her.

Without waiting for a response, Felix leaned forward and kissed her, a slow, seductive press of his lips on hers. Closing his eyes, he sighed with pleasure. She tasted better than he could have imagined, like wine and sweetness, her lips a perfect fit to his, the intimacy intoxicating. It had been so long, and she was so much. The most amazing woman he had ever encountered in his long and ultimately pointless life.

"Regan," he breathed, taking in her floral scent. Felix kissed her again, harder, still holding her face in his hands. "You're delicious."

She made a sound of approval, her hands rising to twine around his neck. She kissed him back, her legs shifting in closer, breasts beneath her cotton nightgown pressing against him. He enjoyed the taste, the touch, the sound of her, knowing it couldn't go any further, knowing a kiss would have to be enough.

Then she made a fatal error. She opened her mouth.

Just a little more . . . he would take just a little more then be done. But then his tongue slipped between her lips and he knew a little would never be enough. He wanted his tongue, his hands, his cock on her, in her. Almost more than anything he had ever wanted. But he just might have been able still to show restraint and walk away and not involve her in the mess of his life, his soul.

Except that Regan groaned and met his tongue with hers in a teasing little flicker, at the same time she thrust her inner thighs against his erection, her hands entwining his neck even more.

It was that shift, that moment of her acquiescence that made it impossible for him to resist. She had given in, abandoned herself to the kiss, the moment, to him, and Felix found that the hottest fucking thing he had ever seen, felt, known in his life.

So he was going to ignore everything rational screaming in his head to stop, to think, to walk away, and he was going to give her pleasure.

Felix stepped back and took her hand, planning to lead her to the bed.

But Regan shook her head, her eyes slumberous with desire, lips shiny and swollen, nipples tight against her nightgown. "No. Against the wall."

Oh, no, she didn't. Felix almost groaned out loud. She had to know how unbelievably sexy that was. "Whatever you want, beautiful," he told her, and pushed her back until she hit the nearest wall, his lips on her neck, on the cleavage he revealed by yanking down the neck of her nightgown.

He was going to give her exactly what she wanted and then some.

Regan couldn't believe she'd just said that out loud. She'd told Felix to take her against the wall. But it had just slipped out, the culmination of a very weird night, fear that she was losing her mind, fear that she could have died.

Chris's suggestion for what to do with Felix had popped into her head, and she had wanted it. Wanted rough and raw sex that screamed she was alive.

When Felix yanked her nightgown over her head and tossed it on the floor she felt just that way. Alive, drowning in pleasure, needing it now, ripping the fabric of fear off of her. His mouth closed over her nipple and she gasped, digging into his shoulders with her nails. It was a blur of sensation, of fast, hard desire springing up and driving her to tug off his T-shirt, to claw at the button on his jeans, take down his zipper, while he kissed, sucked, nipped at her breasts, neck, mouth.

His finger slipped inside her panties, and deep into her slick desire. Regan threw her head back and tried to moan, but her breath was gone. His other hand yanked down her panties and lifted her thigh to rest on his.

Then he was in her with a hard thrust that liberated her voice and had her groaning in ecstasy. He was big, powerful, pushing inside her wet body with rhythmic, forceful pumps, his breathing hot next to her ear.

There was no time, no room for words in the tight, hot cocoon of pleasure, her back crammed against the wall, his body over her, against her, in her.

When he skimmed his thumb over her clitoris, she came with a cry, the intensity startling, overwhelming, and she tightened her grip on him, her whole body a taut string of desire as it wracked her.

"Regan," he said through gritted teeth.

Then she felt the pulse of his orgasm, a ragged moan escaping him, and she smiled, reveling in her own aftershocks and the triumphant female power of knowing she had caused him to come undone so quickly.

His hand slapped on the wall and he shuddered deeply as he throbbed inside her. Both of their voices quieted into ragged breathing before Felix shifted and gave her a soft kiss.

Then he smiled. "Was that what you had in mind?"

Regan nodded, giving a small laugh, her shoulders sagging. "Oh, yeah." It amazed her that he was still inside her, her leg propped over his, that he had wanted her as much as she'd wanted him. He was so good-looking it was almost painful to look at him, astonishing to think that she, the quiet woman who worked hard to never rock the boat or do anything wild or outrageous, had done just that.

But she didn't feel like herself lately. Or maybe she felt more like herself. Despite the fears, the doubts, the odd occurrences in the house, she felt intensely free, alive, excited to discover who exactly Regan Henry was beyond dutiful daughter and trophy wife.

It seemed the real Regan had just stood up and had sex against the wall.

Chapter Eleven

"You're amazing," he said, nuzzling in her neck. "And I'm going to do that again in about five minutes, slower this time."

"You are?" Regan shivered, her inner muscles contracting on him at the thought of a repeat performance.

He groaned. "Damn, don't do that yet."

Felix pulled out of her, causing her to sigh in disappointment, then he bent over and skimmed her panties back up from where they'd been held captive at her ankles. He brushed his lips over her stomach in a gesture that struck Regan as intensely intimate, and she curled her fingers into his short hair as he came back to her mouth and kissed her hard.

"Why don't you get in bed and I'll be right back," he said, stepping away from her, his jeans still undone, belt clanking to the side, but everything important tucked back into his black boxer briefs.

She hadn't even really had a chance to see him naked, to see his smooth erection. She'd just felt it, deep inside her. A fresh rush of moisture between her legs had her unfolding herself from the wall so she could head to the bed. But she couldn't take her eyes off him as she went. He was so freaking gorgeous, his bare chest toned and broad, his cross necklace dangling down, a barbed-wire tattoo around each of his biceps.

Felix gave her a smile and kicked off his shoes, then headed toward her bathroom, jeans riding low on his hips. He had another tattoo on his back between his shoulder blades, an elaborate scrolling word, but in the dimness of the room she couldn't make out what it said. Climbing onto her bed, she tossed the two chocolates she had been debating eating before falling asleep off the bed onto the carnage of the original box.

He hadn't just thrown the chocolates on the floor, he had clearly stepped on them too, crushing both box and candy alike. She had no idea what the hell that had been all about. He couldn't possibly be jealous of her ex-husband. Beau was just that, her ex, and she and Felix had never even so much as kissed before tonight. It was way too premature to think that she could inspire jealousy in him. Yet he had trashed the sweets, no doubt about it.

Whatever. She didn't need the calories glomming onto her backside anyway. Not to mention that accepting any gift from Beau gave her a knot in her stomach, no matter how inexpensive, innocuous, or mouthwatering it might be. It was a connection to him, and frankly, she wanted to sever all of those.

Regan crawled under the covers and sighed in contentment, the sheets cool on her hot body. It was completely bizarre that she didn't remember what she'd been dreaming about or getting out of bed and drinking the wine. Going outside had been so dangerous, and she hoped the sleepwalking was a onetime incident. But at the moment, she refused to stress about it. She had a hot man in her bathroom who was planning to have sex with her again pronto. She could worry about her new nocturnal habits later.

Lying there, head sinking into her pillow, she debated turning the lamp on or not. It would be nice to see him better, and the bulb was soft and filtered by the shade. She had no desire to expose herself under harsh overhead lights, but a little bit of light on the subject—namely him—would be nice. Leaning over, she turned the knob and winced when the sudden brightness hit her in the eye. She flopped onto her side, away from the light, to let her eyes recover.

And screamed.

There was a snake in the bed with her. Right next to her, brown and big and scaly and staring at her with its little black beady eyes. It moved, its body gliding up toward the pillow next to hers, its head turning to watch her, like it was tracking her, and Regan's scream froze in her mouth.

She was terrified of snakes and, as such, had never been able to look at them long enough, even in pictures, to learn which were poisonous and which were safe. But it didn't matter. Venomous or not, she felt with absolute certainty that she was going to die, either from an actual bite or from pure, lacerating fear.

"Regan, what's wrong?" Felix came up next to the bed in his boxers, frowning. "Are you okay?"

The snake was between them, turning toward the new movement Felix had made.

"A snake. There's a snake in the bed," she managed, still unable to move, afraid if she did it would turn and strike.

"A snake?" Felix leaned over the bed, right over the reptile itself, and yanked all the covers back. "Where?"

"Right there!" She pointed to the snake, which was inches from his chest. "Felix, move!"

My God, was he blind?

"Regan." Felix looked at her in concern, having tossed all the bedding onto the floor after shaking it vigorously, all while the snake lay exposed right on the sheets in front of him. "There's nothing in this bed."

The snake shot upward, its mouth striking and landing

a bite on Felix's arm. Regan screamed again, propelled into movement. Scrambling backward off the bed, she tumbled to the floor, wondering how you killed a snake. After struggling to her feet, she was glancing around for a weapon and her cell phone to call 911, when she suddenly realized Felix wasn't writhing in pain or battling to knock a snake off of him.

He was just standing there staring at her, puzzled, no signs of pain.

And no signs of a snake. In the bed or anywhere else.

Regan stopped at the bottom of the bed and burst into tears. What was happening to her? She was going absolutely crazy.

Felix moved toward her. "Regan, it's okay."

"No, it's not!" She covered her bare chest with her arms. "I saw a snake in bed. I saw it bite you. And it's not there! I've lost my mind."

"Didn't you tell me snakes are your greatest fear?"

"Yes."

Felix reached for her and she winced.

"Hey. You aren't afraid of *me*, are you?"

No, she definitely wasn't afraid of him. If anything, she was fighting the urge to throw herself into his arms for a little bit of support from those firm shoulders. Which was interesting because it wasn't like he was a comforting sort of man. There was an edge, a reserve, a coldness to a lot of his words. Then other times, it seemed like he just looked at her and there was a connection . . . an understanding. An acceptance of her.

Tonight, he had been there for her, when she had been tottering on the balcony, and when she had needed to be touched.

"No," she whispered. "I'm not afraid of you." What she was afraid of was that she was losing her grip on reality, the solidness of her mind suddenly melting down into a mass of jumbled nonsense. She was afraid she was imagining everything. That there were no ghosts, that it was all her, suddenly breaking out in a rash of insanity.

"We don't know exactly what happened when you were asleep, but it's clear to me that you tried to do a courage spell, which means swallowing your fears. I think that given your state of semiconsciousness, what you did was simply to manifest your fears. You created a snake in the bed."

Regan turned that one over and over in her head. It sounded strange and out there, and yet oddly reassuring. "So you think that by trying to conquer my fears, I just conjured them instead?"

"Exactly." Felix wrapped his arms around her and pulled her against his bare chest.

"But why am I doing these things asleep? It would have never occurred to me to do any sort of spell, let alone one to dispel my fears. I don't know any spells, Felix." Her hands were crunched between her chest and his, yet she had no desire to drop them, to open herself fully to him. She needed a shield, however imaginary, between them for protection.

She wanted to give in, to let him hold her, but somehow that would be giving up control, admitting that she was tottering on the edge of some kind of mental breakdown.

"Those who are dead are never gone," he said calmly in her ear, his fingers caressing her back lightly.

Goose bumps traversed her arms like an electrical current racing along a wire. "Excuse me?"

"You believe that just as much as I do. Otherwise you wouldn't work to restore cemeteries. You wouldn't collect art that reflects the beauty given to assuage grief. The dead are always with us. Physically, in things like your sister's stuffed monkey and in the photos we save, a tomb dedicated to them, or a journal. Spiritually, in that their lingering presence affects our behaviors and decisions, and sometimes, appears in the form of them pressing into our world, either as a ghost, or in our dreams."

It was moments like this that she looked at Felix and marveled that there were men like him, and that she had never encountered a single one before. It was like somehow he crawled inside her head and made sense of her convoluted and mostly secret thoughts. It was thrilling, yet unnerving in its danger. She could fall for him very, very easily, and that was something she knew she just couldn't do.

"I would agree with that, I suppose. I guess I never thought about it in exactly those terms, but yes, the dead are with us. Though I'm not sure what that has to do with me seeing a snake that didn't exist." Regan pulled back against his arms for release. "I want my nightgown." She felt too exposed standing there in nothing but her panties.

He continued to hold her, making it impossible for her to leave him and get her clothes. "Regan. I think Camille is using you, in your dreams, to revisit this world she left so long ago."

She stopped trying to back up and stared at him, her mind screaming that was impossible, insane, ridiculous. The other part of her, the one that had seen Camille, the one that believed her sister's spirit was sometimes with her, felt the weight of the truth of Felix's statement. It wasn't logical by most standards, but something was going on in her house, in her dreams.

It was either Camille Comeaux or Regan was going mental, and if she had to chose, she hoped it was a nineteenth-century beauty reaching out from the dead, not her own mind cracking under pressure.

"How can she do that? I mean, I understand seeing her floating in the hallway, or the French doors opening, but how can she be in my dreams?"

"I don't know, *cherie*, but it seems she is. The question

is, are you comfortable with her being here, or do you want to try to rid the house of her?"

Geez, that seemed brutal. "I don't think she's malicious, Felix. Just angry at her loss, maybe confused that she's dead." Regan ran her fingers over his hard chest, musing. "I wonder how she died."

Felix stiffened beneath her, and she looked up. His face looked pained. Regan dropped her hands immediately. She was touching him too tenderly and he clearly didn't like it.

"Maybe she just wants me to see what happened to her. Maybe she wants comfort," she said.

"I don't know. But she is clearly a powerful spirit to manipulate your dreams and move objects. I think you should be careful."

"And how exactly do I do that?" She was all for being careful. She didn't relish the idea of being tomorrow's news because she'd fallen off her balcony. "Eccentric Heiress Kills Herself in Midst of Divorce from High-Powered Attorney." She could see it now.

That would be enough to make Regan come back as a haunt.

Feeling a little hysterical, she finally pulled away from him and snatched her nightgown off the floor.

"I'll protect you," he said, his voice even, serious, pale blue eyes glassy in the dim lamplight.

And she believed him.

Which scared her even more.

❦

Regan looked wild-eyed and terrified again. Or maybe *still*. Felix had tried to calm her down, but he wasn't sure how successful he'd been. "Let's lie down," he told her. "Have a glass of wine together."

It took her a second to respond, her nightgown clutched in front of her, but finally she nodded. "Okay." She turned her back and pulled her nightgown on over her head.

Felix didn't bother to look away, even though she clearly wanted some privacy to dress. He watched her arms go up, showing off her creamy white back, her narrow waist, and the tight backside in her cotton panties. He wanted another taste of her, a longer, more exploratory foray into her sensuality, her body.

Whether by fate or choice, he had wound up here with her, and he was already in too deep to back out, despite the consequences.

"I'll go get the wine," he said. "Is it in the kitchen?"

She glanced over at the chest of drawers, where the empty glass still sat. "Actually, I don't think I want a glass of wine. But I can go get you one if you want it." Moving over to the bureau, she lifted the glass and swiped her hand across the surface. "Damn it. I stained the marble. A hundred-plus years it sits in this room, and I'm here a week and I ruin it."

"I'm sure there's a way to clean it." Though Felix wasn't sure why she gave a shit. It was just a thing. A box of wood with a marble top, nothing more. Though truthfully he did know why she liked it. Regan wasn't materialistic, she was sentimental.

Which meant Felix was the absolute worst man to have in her life.

But here he was.

"I'm spending the night," he told her, shoving his jeans down and stepping out of them. "And I never do that."

She frowned, rubbing her fingers together where they must have gotten sticky from the spilled wine. "So what do you want, a cookie? Don't stay if you don't want to. I don't need any favors."

"Why? Why don't you need favors?"

Slapping the wineglass down on the floor next to the bureau, she said, "Because favors from a man you've slept with come with a price. It's code for 'you owe me.'"

"But you would accept a favor from a friend at face

value? Say the friend who spent the night with you, you would believe his favor was given freely?"

Regan stood back up. "Yes. But that's different."

"Why? Oh, I know why. Because your ex-husband was an asshole, and he did a number on you."

"I don't want to talk about my ex-husband. I want to talk about you. So why don't you ever spend the night?"

Shit. Regan had effectively turned that right around on him. Felix moved toward the bed, grabbing all the bedding he'd hurled to the floor when she'd been panicking. "Spending the night leads to expectations that I can't meet."

"But you're willing to risk it with me?"

Tossing the mess of sheets and blankets back onto the bed, he kept his back to her. "You and me, we're both damaged. So neither one of us has any expectations."

"Why the hell does your tattoo spell out 'GREED'?" she asked, horror mingling with curiosity in her voice.

Felix whirled around and saw her stricken expression. It made him turn back to the bed again in shame. He'd forgotten about his tattoo, his own personal branding. There was a story he told everyone, and then there was the truth. For some reason, he found himself giving Regan the truth. "I used to be greedy. I wanted money, power, material possessions. And I got them. But it wasn't worth what it cost my soul. So this is to remind me that my greed is behind me."

"I see," she said.

He sensed her moving up to him, and then her fingers were fluttering across his skin, tracing the letters. Felix stood still, enjoying her touch, yet unable to shake the shame of who he was, what he had done.

"Maybe I should get a tattoo," she whispered, her breath tickling his shoulder. "Only mine would read 'Stop Being a Doormat.'"

Felix laughed, turning to take her into his arms. "I don't think anyone who leaves Alcroft and fights through a divorce is a doormat."

"Do you know him?" Regan asked, head tilting slightly.

"Yes." Felix left it at that, cursing the fact that he'd brought the demon's name into what they were doing here, together. "Now get in bed." He pushed her so that she lost her balance and fell backward onto the mattress and crumpled covers.

"Ah!" she yelped, before launching a pillow at him. "Jerk."

Glad to see she was grinning, Felix just smirked. "And don't you forget it."

Her smile turned tender then disappeared altogether as she lay on the bed looking up at him. She whispered, "I think you're nicer than you'd like to admit."

Felix lost his grin as well at her words. He wanted to scoff, to protest, to tell her the truth, that he had never been a good man, that he tried to find ways to be decent in this life he had to live, but that in no way was he a man of quality.

But he didn't want that look on her face to alter. For once, he just wanted to close his eyes and believe that he could be worthy of the love or at least affection of a wonderful woman.

Climbing onto the bed, he ran his hand up her leg, her thigh, drifting over the front of her panties. "Is this nice?"

Her breathing had already altered, becoming more audible, her eyes widening as she watched him. "Yes."

"I can make it even nicer." Felix leaned forward and brushed his lips over her panties, taking in the scent of her arousal.

Then he jerked the cotton to the side to expose her to his view. She was slick with desire already, her dark curls dewy. Skimming his thumbs down either side of her, Felix flicked his tongue over her swollen clitoris. Regan gave a soft moan and her fingers made their way into his hair.

His cock swelled at her reaction and at the taste of her, so elemental, so sensual. He knew he was good at this, knew that he could please a woman, and he enjoyed that. But he had never needed to know he could satisfy a woman as much as he did with Regan. It mattered. And that scared him at the same time it thrilled him.

Moving his tongue first slowly, then faster, Felix listened to Regan responding, to her increased moans, her rapid breathing. He felt her body tighten, shifting restlessly beneath his touch, felt her fingers dig deeper, her back arching as he licked and sucked at her. Her flesh grew warmer, her body damper, her cries louder.

Felix felt his own body stiffen, his grip on her thighs tighter as he reveled in her pleasure. He wanted to shift up and plunge his erection into her, but he wanted to have her shatter on his mouth more.

When he sucked her clitoris, she did, calling out his name in such a raw voice it made a chill rush over his hot body. Slowing his tongue down over her slick folds, Felix pulled back as her orgasm petered out, intent to replace his tongue with his cock inside her warm and wet body.

Only Regan stopped him by reaching down and closing a hand around his cock, putting her other hand on his chest to prevent his forward motion.

"No?" he asked, disappointed in more ways than he could describe. But it had been a long and emotional night. Maybe she just wanted to go to sleep. He couldn't be selfish and withhold that from her simply so he could get his rocks off.

But sleep wasn't what Regan had in mind. She had sat up and was moving forward, her mouth open . . .

Felix stared down at her in shock as she touched his cock with her lips in a small kiss. No woman had done that, done this, in over a hundred years. They always took. They never gave. And it wasn't right to ask. But Regan's lips were separating, head lowering, as her hot, smooth mouth slid over the length of him.

Felix closed his eyes and gritted his teeth at the agony

of pleasure. Damn it, it felt so good, better than he remembered, all-consuming. But he had to force himself to say, "You don't have to if you don't want to."

She looked up at him, her eyes glossy with desire, her lips wrapped around his cock, shiny and damp, her hair falling in her eyes. She pulled back just enough to say, "Oh, I want to. Trust me."

That alone almost sent him careening over the edge. The look in her eye matched the conviction in her voice, and Felix was stunned. She meant it. She wanted to suck him, and that was the hottest damn thing he'd ever experienced. Despite his curse, somehow this woman wanted to give him pleasure instead of just taking it.

So he put his hands on the back of her head lightly and watched her as she took him into her mouth over and over, her mouth slicking him, the sensation hot and tight and explosive. Felix felt the edges of his control starting to splinter, both his physical and emotional barriers disintegrating. He should stop her, it, this . . . everything between them, but he couldn't.

It might be selfish, but just once, he wanted to share, to feel that bond of intimacy, to be one, instead of two separate people moving through life alone.

He wanted to fall in love, and be loved.

Knowing he was going to lose it, Felix pulled out and pushed at Regan's shoulder.

"I wanted to . . ." she started to say.

But Felix shook his head. He couldn't finish that way, or he might never recover.

Regan saw the fierce look of determination on Felix's face and swallowed her protest instead of him. Falling back onto the bed, she had barely hit the mattress when he was inside, entering her with a brutal thrust that had her gasping.

"Oh," she said, her eyes lolling into the back of her head, her fingers fluttering in the air, their path toward his hair forgotten.

"Open your eyes," he said in that rough voice she had gotten accustomed to, as he moved inside her with hard rhythmic pushes.

Regan forced her eyes open and looked into his cerulean ones.

It was at that moment, when her orgasm burst, and his followed on the heels of hers, that she fell deeper into the abyss of pleasure than she ever had in her entire life.

Chapter Twelve

Regan wasn't sure what the rules on cuddling with Felix were, so she lingered on her side of the bed, satisfied and replete enough that it didn't even really bother her that they weren't touching. He had just kissed, sucked, and caressed her enough to save her from touch deprivation for the next year.

Except that Felix reached over and pulled her onto his chest. Even better.

"How long have you had your shop?" she asked, curious about him, about his lifestyle, his beliefs. He fascinated her, and she loved to hear him talk.

"Forever." His thumb skimmed her upper arm.

Well, that was specific. "Were you raised in New Orleans?"

"Yes. On North Rampart Street."

"Really? That's such a different world from the sub-urbs, so exotic almost. I don't think I know anyone who was raised in the Quarter. What did your parents do for a living?"

"My dad was a businessman, but he didn't live with us. I don't think his wife would have appreciated him living with his lover and their illegitimate child."

No, that was not a suburban family arrangement. It shocked her, but Felix didn't say it with any particular emotion. He just sounded sleepy, relaxed.

"Oh, I'm sorry."

"For what? It was a long time ago. My parents were together for twenty some years. My father just wasn't going to divorce his wife for financial reasons. It worked well enough for them."

Regan pondered that. She didn't think for one minute she could share her lover with another woman. Call her selfish, but she wanted to be her husband's priority, his love, his passion. Which made it an even greater mystery why she had married Beau. Then again, that was the picture he had painted for her. The reality had been harshly different. She wondered what marriage to a man like Felix would be like.

Not that it was wise to contemplate that, even in theory. She would just wind up hurt. But that didn't stop her from snuggling closer to him, caressing his chest with her fingertips the way he was touching her arm.

"Were you raised with voodoo or did you do that on your own as an adult?"

"My mother practiced in secret and she taught me. My father wouldn't have approved. It wasn't until he died that I decided to make a living at it."

"Are you glad you chose this career path? I think it sounds freeing, to be able to take your passion, your beliefs, and earn a living with them."

"It's not a career. And if I had to do it all over again, I would change a lot of things. Selling dolls to tourists isn't fulfilling. That's not voodoo."

She raised her head off his chest and looked at him, wanting eye contact, wanting to understand him. But he was staring at the ceiling. "What *is* voodoo?"

"Do you know," he said, his fingers still tracing patterns on her skin, "that the voodoo God Danbala is as old as humanity, and as such, he no longer speaks . . . he uses the hissing of the snake to communicate. So the chanting of the ceremonies is that of the snake."

Sometimes in her conversations with Felix, Regan felt like she'd missed a directional signal, indicating they were turning right or left. This was one of those times. "Snakes. Great," she said. "My favorite."

"If you listen, it might have something to tell you of value."

He had definitely gone left and she was still standing in the intersection. "You want me to listen to a snake?"

Felix finally turned and looked at her. "Your snake. Listen to your snake."

She'd get right on that. Feeling frustrated, Regan said, "This is all new to me, you know. Until I bought this house, I was just an average twenty-nine year old woman who liked to shop for sweater sets and pencil skirts and enjoy a good meal in a nice restaurant. I don't understand all of this . . . otherworldly stuff."

"Yet you collect cemetery art and believe in ghosts. I don't think you were ever quite the nonbeliever you'd like to think you were."

Maybe she didn't know what she had been. Who she was now. Or where she was going. This divorce was supposed to be a new beginning, the end of drama in her life, and yet she felt like she was being plunged into something bigger than her, in her very own house. Something she didn't understand at all.

And she was, as of two hours ago, sleeping with a man she didn't understand at all either.

"Maybe you're right." Regan rolled off of him and onto her own pillow, suddenly feeling petulant.

"Go to sleep, Regan, and dream of happy things. Dream of playing on the beach with Moira."

Heart rate jumping, Regan flipped back over and stared at him. "How did you know my sister's name was Moira? I never told you that."

He frowned. "I don't know. You must have told me."

Not knowing anymore what was real and what was imagined, Regan flopped back down, suddenly wanting to cry. "Did I tell you she died of leukemia when I was four? She was only six. That stuffed monkey was supposed to be buried with her. I was afraid for Moira, being closed in that box, and I didn't want her monkey to be in the dark either. And I wanted to keep something of her because they told me I'd never be able to see her again. So I took the monkey and hid it before my mom could take it to the funeral home."

Felix shifted closer to her and brushed her hair off her face. Regan closed her eyes tightly, trying to stave off the tears. She had no idea why she'd just told him that. She had never admitted the full truth of Moira's monkey to anyone, not even Chris.

"Oh, *cherie*," he murmured. "I'm so sorry you had such a huge loss at such a young age."

His lips drifted over her forehead and Regan sighed. It was a relief to finally unburden herself of the truth, even if it didn't change it.

"It's time to let go of your guilt. Your guilt for living, for laughing, for keeping a toy when you were young and confused. Just let it go, and do whatever you want with your life."

Swallowing hard, Regan forced her eyes open. It amazed her that a man she had known for such a brief amount of time could understand her better than her parents or the man she had married.

"Is that what my snake says?" she asked lightly.

Felix smiled. "Yes."

Then he kissed her, a soft lingering press of his mouth

on hers, before retreating to the other side of the bed. "Go to sleep, beautiful Regan. Release your snakes."

Regan closed her eyes again, and felt Felix's hand reach over and brush her cheek. Sighing, she quieted her mind and let it all go.

*

Felix watched Regan sleeping, her hands tucked up under her cheek. He couldn't believe he'd ever thought her ordinary looking. She was a delicate, ethereal beauty, her compassion in her eyes. She was the kind of woman who loved with all of her heart, even at the risk of having it hurt.

He wasn't doing her heart any favors by being there with her. She was still vulnerable from her bad marriage, and she was falling for him, he could see it in her expression when she spoke. It was just infatuation, obviously, since that was all women ever felt for him. They merely took, never gave. And it would fade.

Yet with Regan, for the first time since he received his immortality, he was tempted himself. There was something about her unselfishness, the way she asked about him, seemed genuinely and truly interested in him, that was puzzling. Pleasing. It brought to the forefront the loneliness he'd been ignoring and taunted him with possibilities that could never be.

He wanted a woman to love him. To really and truly love him.

But that was something he was never entitled to, what the consequence of his greed was. No woman could love him.

Yet, when he watched Regan, at peace in her sleep . . . he ached for her to give him that.

She wasn't like other women he'd dated, women who simpered and flirted and laughed. Women who thought he was strange, but were willing to overlook it for the sake of hot sex or to brag to their friends that they'd nailed a voo-doo practitioner. No woman, then or now, had ever under-stood him, or even desired to understand him.

Until Regan.

He had been telling the truth about spending the night with women. He had never, not in his entire existence, slept in the same bed all night with any woman. In the previous century, it hadn't been possible or practical given the stric-tures of society and the fact that most of his lovers were wealthy white women. Then in later days, he hadn't wanted to. It was much easier to leave after sex, still in control of his emotions, than to hang around hoping for intimacy that would never arrive.

While he intended to stay the whole night with Regan, it didn't look like he was actually going to sleep. He was wide awake, body satisfied but mind restless.

By being there with her, he had done something he couldn't take back, and while he wanted a lot of things—wanted to protect her, wanted to enjoy her company, wanted, wanted, wanted—he was worried.

If his presence caused her pain, he would never forgive himself.

Climbing out of bed, he shook his head at himself. He'd told her about his mother. His parents. He never did that. Never. He wasn't sure what had possessed him with Regan, except that maybe it was because she was the first to ever ask.

Moving in the dark to the chest of drawers, he touched the cool marble top, looking at the sopping piece of torn paper that he'd tossed on top of the original mailing envelope.

"Camille," he said, under his breath, so he wouldn't wake Regan. "Are you here?"

The room was silent. There was no movement at all, including from Felix, as he stood still and listened, watched, felt.

Nothing.

There didn't seem to be any presence in the room, and the only sound was the soft whisper of Regan's breathing.

"Camille," he said again, more forcefully. "Show yourself."

No response, not even a rustle of a breeze.

He almost walked away, climbed back into bed with Regan, but he realized if he never dealt with the past, how could he ever find a future? Some small, stupid part of him still wanted to believe that one did exist for him. Hope was too strong of a word for it, but if righting the wrongs of the past made the present more tolerable, he would embrace that.

Besides, he owed Camille.

Opening one of the French doors, he glanced back at Regan. She didn't even shift on the bed, but slept deeply, the covers up to her chin.

He stood in the doorway and faced the room. "Camille, I'm so sorry. I'm sorry for any part I had in your pain and suffering. Most of all, I'm sorry for your death. Talk to me. Tell me what it is you want."

Felix sat down on the floor in the house he should never have entered and waited for an answer.

He never got one.

❧

Regan woke up with a start, the light streaming from the windows onto her face. She was late for work. She had to be. It was too bright for it to be before eight A.M. Sitting up, she stopped frantically shoving her covers off when she caught sight of Felix on the floor in the open French door to her balcony.

"Good morning," he said.

He was still in his boxer briefs, his knees up, elbows perched on them, his cross prominent on his chest.

Have mercy, she could not believe she'd had sex with

this man. Such amazing, world-tilting, multiple-orgasm sex. Surely this was retribution for all the so-so sex she'd had with Beau.

And he'd stayed the whole night, which she hadn't expected, even though he had said he would. Of course, she wasn't exactly sure what he was doing on the floor.

"Good morning." She smiled, a little nervous. What the hell was she supposed to say to him? She'd had a total freak-out meltdown on him the night before and afterward had asked him to do her against the wall. Then followed it up with embarrassing confessions of reptile delusions and her childhood theft of her sister's stuffed animal.

"Did you sleep okay?" she asked, then berated herself mentally. That was such a lame, polite, ridiculous question.

He shook his head. "I didn't sleep."

Regan blinked. "At all? I'm sorry, wasn't the bed comfortable? Did I steal the covers? Or snore?"

"Why do you always assume that anyone else's discomfort is your fault or responsibility? Nothing you did kept me from sleeping. Nothing."

O-kay. She felt her cheeks start to burn. Maybe he had a point, but did he have to make it sound like such a flaw? He almost sounded angry with her. "Good. Glad to hear it."

He stood up, and she immediately forgot why she was irritated. He was physically perfect. Absolutely perfect. That was both exciting as hell and intimidating in the extreme. "Any reason you were on the floor?" she asked.

"I couldn't sleep and I didn't want to disturb you. There was a nice breeze coming from outside."

So he'd just sat there half the night? If only she could figure out how to be so zen. She suffered from nervous energy most of the time and found it hard to be still, to quiet her body and her mind.

"Oh. Good. A breeze is good." Regan climbed out of bed, wanting to avoid feeling like she was waiting for him to kiss her. Or worse, waiting for him to make future plans with her. "I hate to rush you, but I really have to get to work. I slept later than I should have and I'm going to have to fly to get there on time. You're welcome to stay and take a shower if you'd like, and there's coffee in the kitchen."

That sounded casual, calm, collected. She hoped. Like a woman who had one-night stands and didn't think twice about it.

"I'll head out with you," he said, already pulling on his jeans. "But thank you."

"Okay, great." Feeling more than a little awkward, Regan grabbed some clothes from her closet and went into the bathroom. She didn't have time to wash and dry her hair, but she couldn't skip the shower. Not when she could smell Felix on her skin as she pulled off her nightgown. His scent was all over her body, and she still felt the remnants of him between her thighs.

So much for safe sex. That more than anything proved the state of mind she'd been in the night before, because she'd never even had sex with her ex-husband without a condom. Blame it on the sleepwalking and the snake, because it was totally out of character for her to be so irresponsible.

Jumping into the shower, she removed Felix from her body with cucumber-melon shower gel. Maybe by the time she was done, he would be gone. Then she could avoid the whole question of whether they would see each other again or not.

No such luck. When she came out of the bathroom ready for work, he was sitting fully dressed on her bed, which he had made. Wow. She had never actually seen a man make a bed before, which probably said something about the company she'd been keeping.

"You ready?" he asked.

"Yes." Regan glanced around the room for her purse and didn't see it. She must have dropped it on the kitchen counter when she'd gotten the wine the night before.

"What are you doing tonight?" he asked as they headed for the door.

Regan stumbled a little in her peep-toes. "Oh, I have dinner plans with my friend Jen." Damn it. But at least he had asked. That was something.

"Good. You won't be alone."

Or not.

"Remember to push a chair in front of your balcony door when you go to bed."

"Isn't that a fire hazard?" she asked, feeling a little cranky as she went down the stairs, him behind her.

"No. You have smoke detectors. If one goes off, you get up and move the chair and go outside. It's better to have a chair there and have to move it on the very slim chance of a fire than to find yourself dangling from the railing again."

She hit the wood steps a little harder with her shoes. Did he have to be right at the same time he was blowing her off? "Okay, you're right. Chair it is."

"Did I do something to make you angry?" Felix asked as they hit the landing of the foyer.

"No, of course not." Regan realized she'd forgotten to stop in the kitchen. "Shit. My purse. I'll be right back."

Furious with herself for wanting more, Regan went left into the kitchen. She had gotten to have sex with Felix, that should be enough. He had been there emotionally, too, when she had needed him. It was ridiculous to expect or crave more.

She'd never been a discontent person. Even being married to Beau hadn't been about feeling discontent, but about being belittled on a regular basis. She was generally easily pleased and happy.

So why was she so worked up about Felix?

Because it had felt good to be with him. Both in bed and out.

Her purse was on the counter as predicted and she

grabbed it and spun around on her heels. Felix was in front of her.

"Oh! Geez, I didn't realize you followed me." She grabbed her neck. "You scared me."

"I'm sorry." Felix pointed to the kitchen door. "But I realized it makes more sense for me to leave from the side of the house since I'm going that way."

"Right. Sure." Regan mentally rolled her eyes. She was just full of inane comments this morning. "Thanks. For last night."

Yikes, that didn't sound right. She cleared her throat. "For saving me, I mean. From falling off the balcony. And for the . . . other stuff. The snake, I mean."

"Regan." Felix moved closer to her, his arms reaching out and resting on her shoulders.

"Yes?" She fought the urge to back up. It was really difficult to think straight when he was so close to her.

"I'll call you."

He kissed her, a nice long kiss, his tongue making its way into her mouth and teasing hers. Then he pulled back. "Bye. Be safe."

She watched him open her kitchen door and exit without a glance back. *Be safe? I'll call you?*

What the hell did either of those mean?

❦

"It means you've been dumped," Chris told her in no uncertain terms as he sipped his gin and tonic.

"No, you haven't!" Jen protested. "Don't listen to him. He's a man."

"Which is why she should listen to me," Chris said. "I understand the male psyche."

Regan sipped her glass of wine and frowned at her friends. They were in the courtyard at Pat O'Brien's playing tourist. Chris had wanted to go out, but Regan hadn't been able to stomach the idea of a club or bar with loud music, so they had compromised. Now she almost wished she had stayed at home because this was not what she wanted to hear.

"What makes you think I've been dumped?"

"He didn't make plans to see you again. He said he'd call you. Lame." Chris waved his hand. "Look, I don't mean to be a bitch—"

"Yes, you do," Jen interrupted, smirk on her face.

"Shut up," he told her. "I have the floor right now. You can give your opinion after I tell you all the truth you don't want to hear."

Regan smacked at the plant frond that kept invading her space and tickling her shoulder. "Wow, I can't wait."

"So, anyway," he said with a pointed look in Jen's direction. "If he wanted to see you again, he would have made plans. Plain and simple. And come on, what are the odds he would be walking past your house when you're about to plunge to your death? He was totally coming over to see you."

That had never occurred to Regan. "You think so? Why would he be coming over without calling first?"

"At midnight? Hello! Fuck-fest. He was totally going to do the whole, I was walking by, your light was on, thought I'd say hi, blah, blah, blah. Boom, you're in the bedroom."

"The way your mind works disturbs me," Jen said, sipping her hurricane. She adjusted her white tank top for the tenth time. "I shouldn't have worn this shirt. My boobs look huge."

"They do," Regan admitted.

"Massive," Chris agreed.

They both started laughing.

"Thanks," Jen said, crossing her arms over her chest. "I think that's a bachelor party over there. They all keep looking at me and my boobs."

Chris rolled his eyes. "Oh, whatever. It's only ten o'clock

and they're halfway to shit-faced already. By the time we leave here they'll all be vomiting in trash cans so you don't need to worry that they'll be hitting on you."

"There's a beautiful image." Regan curled her lip. "Can we get back to me please? What should I do?"

"Um, nothing." Chris pointed his swizzle stick at her. "Chalk it up to a good time and move on. If you call him, you'll look needy."

"I was afraid you'd say that." She knew it was the truth, and the absolute last thing in the universe she wanted to be perceived as was needy.

"I would call him," Jen said. "He probably has no idea if you're receptive to the idea of seeing him again or not. He may be thinking the same things you are because you didn't give him any clear signal you wanted to see him again. What harm is there in calling him?"

"Don't listen to her! If you call, he's going to slap you in the 'never want to talk to her again' box. He'll think you're all about a relationship. Whereas if you don't call and you bump into him three months from now, you can totally have sex with him again."

That was so not the way Regan thought; she had to repeat Chris's sentence in her head twice to make sure she understood it. How would zero contact result in future sex? It boggled the mind.

"You're seeing him next week at the party," Jen said, slapping her drink back on the wrought iron table. "Oh, my God, he's not going to cancel, is he? That will screw my whole entertainment schedule up."

"I hope not. I mean, he would have told me, right?" Though she didn't know why she would assume he would tell her. What did she really know about him, after all?

Nothing, and she was annoyed with herself for spending the whole damn day glancing at her cell phone every ten minutes to see if he had called. Which he hadn't.

"Probably."

"Thanks for the reassurance." Regan fiddled with the rim of her glass. "So let me ask you this. Assuming he never calls me again, what does that mean? What went wrong? I mean, I thought the sex was, well, great. Did he not like the sex?"

"That's not what it means at all. It just means you had great sex, but he's not looking for a relationship. It's not like you were dating, you know. So if he liked the sex, he'll probably call you in a few weeks and see what you're doing."

"A few weeks?" Great. Fourteen days of wondering if she had sucked in bed.

"And keep in mind that if he does call you it will be for sex. You've established yourself as a booty call since you slept with him so fast after no actual dating."

Regan knew Chris was right, but she didn't want to hear it said out loud. "Do we have to use the term booty call? Can't we just say we're two adults who wanted to have sex with each other?"

"Call it what you want."

"Regan, do you want a relationship with him?" Jen asked, looking skeptical. "I mean, it's only been four months since you left Beau. I don't think it's such a hot idea to jump right back into something serious."

"That wasn't my intention." She didn't think. Hell, she didn't know what her intentions had been. She had just known she wanted Felix, plain and simple.

"Then why do you care if he calls or not?"

"Because I don't want to be rejected. I had enough of that in my marriage."

Her friends made those faces, the ones that showed you had revealed too much. They both instantly went into sympathetic.

"Sweetie."

"Oh, Regan."

She waved her hand. "No, it's fine. It is. That's why I left after fourteen months. And no, I don't see myself in a relationship with Felix, but no, I don't want to be blown off either. Who would?"

"It's not being blown off," Chris insisted. "It's casual sex. We had this talk . . . I knew this wasn't an outfit you could wear."

"I guess you were right." She drained her wine. "So what do I do?"

"Nothing. You do nothing."

"Okay, I've got to agree with him now," Jen said, playing with her caramel-colored hair like she could somehow get it to cover her cleavage. "I think maybe you should wait awhile before you wade into sex and dating. You'll either wind up in a rebound relationship or in a string of meaningless hookups."

Just when she thought she couldn't feel any worse, her friends managed to make her feel just that way. "Thanks. This has been very helpful. Just resign myself to celibacy for an indefinite period of time."

"Just a few months. Get your head back on straight."

Jen might have a point. God only knew Regan's head was not on straight.

She was seeing reptiles in her bed and heading out for balcony strolls she didn't remember.

It was better to focus on decorating her house, working, and spending time with her friends and family.

So why did that feel so incredibly unsatisfying?

"Where's the waiter?" she asked. "I need a refill."

Two hours later, Chris and Jen walked her home on their way to the parking garage to retrieve their cars. They had managed to have a great time, despite Jen's fears coming true and the bachelor party hitting on her, and they were navigating the sidewalks of the Quarter, joking and laughing with each other.

Until they got to the corner of Ursuline and Regan came to a complete stop.

"What's the matter?" Jen asked.

"He's sitting on the stoop across from my house," Regan whispered, pulling them back into the shadow of the building.

"Who?" Chris asked, bewildered.

Regan fussed with her hair, then checked her phone. He hadn't called. Yet he was sitting outside her house.

"Felix," she hissed.

"Really?" Chris popped his head around the corner. "Ohmigod. He is smoking hot."

She knew this. Knew it very, very well. "I told you!"

"Why is he sitting across from your house?" Jen asked, peeking around the corner for her own look. "Whoa. Hot is right."

"I have no idea why he's sitting there. What do I do?"

"Well, we can do two things. You can pretend you don't see him and we'll just sail on past to the front door. Or you can glance over, pretend to see him for the first time, and wave and go and say hello. Your choice."

Regan bit her fingernail. She had a slight buzz going on and was feeling a little vulnerable. Like if she spoke to Felix she would say something incredibly stupid. "Let's just pretend we don't see him. I don't know what to say to him." Maybe it wasn't the mature thing to do, but everyone was entitled to a moment of immaturity, weren't they? She was going to claim hers.

Taking a deep breath, she said, "Okay. Let's go. Don't look left, anyone."

"Do you think it's a coincidence he's sitting there?" Jen asked in a low voice as they started walking, crossing the street.

"Hello!" Chris made a face. "I don't think so."

Could they walk any slower? They were only halfway across the street and Regan's heart was racing, afraid Felix would suddenly call out her name, and then she'd be forced to confront him, feeling flushed and weird and insecure.

"Slow down," Jen hissed at her. "You're practically running."

Great. By the time they got to the cover of her house, Regan was stress-sweating. "Did he look? That was horrible."

"How would I know if he looked?" Chris asked. "I didn't look. Sweetie, you need to get a grip."

"You think?" she asked sarcastically. It took two tries to get her key in the lock, and after a quick good-bye, she retreated into the house and leaned against the door.

Yeah. Getting a grip was a solid plan.

After jogging upstairs she changed into pj shorts and a T-shirt, turned out the light, and went over to the balcony doors. Hanging against the wall to the left of the doors, she leaned and peeked out through the glass. Felix was still sitting there.

Taking Moira's monkey out from under the nightstand and hugging it, Regan climbed into bed and tried to sleep.

Two hours later she was still staring at the ceiling.

Tossing back the covers, she crossed the dark room, and strained to see the street. Her nose was against the glass before she spotted him. Still sitting there. Staring up at her.

Regan drew back so fast she tripped over the ivory silk drapes.

What the hell was he doing? Did he honestly think she was going to sleepwalk again? And if he did, why didn't he just knock on her door and come inside?

Because while he wanted her safe, he didn't want her.

That was a fun thought.

Determined to get some sleep and stop running on three hours a night, Regan got back in bed and closed her eyes.

When she woke up in the morning, she was lying on the floor of the bedroom down the hall, one completely empty of furniture, with no idea how she had gotten there.

Chapter Thirteen

Camille snapped at her maid, "Hurry up, damn it."

The fool was taking a veritable hour to get Camille out of her evening gown, and she wanted to be in bed. Now. She had taken liberties with the remains of her father's liquor cabinet, and now that the best of the floating, buzzing sensation had worn off, she felt sick to her stomach and dizzy. It was time to lie down.

"Yes, miss. Sorry, miss."

The maid started unlacing her corset more swiftly, which only resulted in chaffing Camille's skin. "Never mind." She jerked away from her. "I'll sleep in it for God's sake. Just get away from me."

She wanted no one touching her anymore. No one but Felix.

Gown pooled at her waist, corset loose and gaping at her breasts, she glanced at her bed and felt a fresh wave of anger. She had shared this room with Isabel, and the other bed stood still, empty, its coverlet untouched for months.

This house taunted her, every inch of it filled with memories, with clothes and trinkets and furniture that had meant something to each of her sisters, her mother, her father. It mocked her with its daily silence, rooms big and daunting, bereft of conversation, of laughter, of music, of the clang of silver at the dinner table.

Lurching toward the door, she flung it open and went into the hall.

"Miss, you're not dressed!"

Camille whirled back to her maid, and only by the greatest restraint managed to prevent herself from slapping the insolent cheek of the pretty and concerned girl. What the hell did she know? Had she had her heart torn out of her chest, yet had to still live, to breathe, to function without it?

The maid backed up, fear replacing concern.

Lowering her hand, Camille gave a shriek of frustration and ran out of the room. She passed her parents' room, her sisters' rooms, the long-empty nursery, and went to the room at the top of the stairs, the one that overlooked the Rue Royale. Her hand trembled on the doorknob, but she forced herself to open it and enter. She shut the door behind her and paused to let her eyes adjust to the darkness.

The sickroom, which had become the mourning room. It was still draped in black, the mirror covered. Camille tore the black fabric off and stared at her dim shadow in the glass. If it were possible for spirits to become trapped in a mirror, she prayed with all her heart and soul they would look back at her. That she could see the face of one who loved her, who valued her.

There was nothing but her in the reflection, corset drooping, gown crushed at her waist, hair half in pins, half undone.

She took the fabric and laid herself on the bed with it,

crossing her hands in an X on her chest, the black cloth draped over her lower half, silent tears running down her cheeks.

Camille never slept in her own bed again.

❦

For the third morning in a row, Regan woke up on the floor of the front bedroom, body stiff from sleeping on the hardwood.

"Oh, my God," she groaned, rolling onto her side, muscles protesting. What the hell was going on? And if she was suddenly sleepwalking, why did she have to keep picking the same room that had no furniture? It was killing her back.

The only plus was that the room faced Royal Street, so the morning sun streamed in, preventing her from oversleeping for work. Other than that, the whole thing was miserable and frustrating.

As was the fact that every night when she went to bed, Felix was sitting across the street from her house, watching her.

At first it had seemed odd but strangely thoughtful. Then it had just seemed weird. And now it was making her angry. Sitting on the sidewalk practically stalking her was not acceptable. Normal people picked up the damn phone and called each other if they had concerns. They didn't hover on the fringes of your life, watching you, instead of trying to have actual person-to-person contact.

She was going to do something about it. She wasn't sure what, but it needed to stop. It was damaging her already fragile peace of mind. Bad enough to have amazing sex with a man and then have him blow you off. Even worse to have amazing sex and then have the man practically pitching a tent in your bushes. It only wanted a pair of binoculars in his hands.

What made it even stranger was that he *knew* she knew

he was there. She was absolutely sure he saw her glancing out at him night after night. Wouldn't most men slink off in shame or explain themselves? Felix didn't seem inclined to do either.

Regan hauled herself off the floor and winced. She was going to deal with Felix, but first she was going to have to deal with this sleepwalking issue. If for whatever reason, she was going to keep winding up in this room, she was going to have to put a bed in here. There was a full-size bed in another one of the bedrooms that she had deemed a guest room, but she was going to have to move it to this room and hope that if there was at least a bed present, she wouldn't keep waking up on the floor.

She'd been in this house eight days and she had yet to get a single night of quality sleep. It was making her cranky.

Or maybe, just a little bit crazy.

❧❦❧

So cranky, and possibly crazy, that after another party-planning meeting with Jen that afternoon, Regan found herself heading to Felix's shop to confront him. The sign outside was wooden, giving the appearance of being hand-painted. It said simply "House of Voodoo." The bell over the door jangled when she entered.

The layout of the store, the items on display, were familiar to anyone who had grown up in New Orleans or visited frequently. Some voodoo shops went for the fantastical, displaying gruesome dolls, catering to tourists who wanted a thrill or a chill. Others were designed to attract tourists more interested in a spiritual souvenir, and those who wanted to burn a candle for luck or love or money.

Felix's store was somewhere in between the two. He had candles and altars to the gods and goddesses of voodoo. There were beautiful dolls handmade by local practitioners and artists. But there were also cheap manufactured dolls, chicken-foot key chains, and Marie Laveau refrigerator magnets. It was an odd mix, the baskets of inexpensive items on tables up front, the back dedicated to the altars, candles, expensive dolls, and a built-in case of herbs.

Maybe it was good business sense. Put the disposable tourist trap items in front for a quick sale. If anyone bothered to go all the way to the back of the store, where Felix did his readings, they were probably genuinely interested in voodoo, or aspects of voodoo.

Regan liked the back of the store better herself. The herbs smelled pungent, the candles sweet, the altars comforting and beautiful, with all their various offerings of money, perfume, honey, cinnamon, lipstick, depending on the god or goddess, tumbling in front of them. It was quiet, peaceful, as Regan wandered around, no sign of Felix.

Standing in front of Dantor, the goddess who helped women invoke strength in themselves according to the placard in front of her statue, Regan tried to ignore the pounding of a sleep deprivation headache and the anxiety she felt about confronting Felix.

She was reaching for the dragon's blood ink, curious what it was and what it did, when she heard, "Regan."

Whirling around, she almost dropped the vial before putting it carefully back on the shelf. "Hi," she said to Felix, who was standing in front of her, not looking particularly surprised to see her.

His expressions were irritatingly difficult to read. She had no clue if he was pleased to see her, indifferent, annoyed. He was just . . . there. Casual, good-looking, in his usual uniform of jeans and a gray T-shirt that showed off his muscular chest.

"How are you?" he asked.

All her years of training to be polite almost had her saying that she was fine, but at the last minute she stopped herself. If her relationship with Beau had taught her anything, it was that she was no longer content to be silent. That if she had feelings or wants or opinions, no one would ever know unless she spoke them.

"I've been better," she told him honestly. "I'm here to see if you're still planning to be at the party since I haven't heard from you."

"Of course I'll be there." He was standing a few feet from her, his hands in his front pockets, and the way he said it, like there was never any doubt, irritated Regan.

Adjusting her handbag on her forearm, she crossed her arms over her black sleeveless tank. "Great. I'll have Jen call you then with the final details. Now maybe you can explain to me why you've set up camp outside my house."

There was still no reaction from him. "I just want to make sure we don't have a repeat of the other night."

Of her dangling off the balcony or the sex? It was so hard to believe that her safety was really the sum total of his motivation. "So you're just going to watch me every night? That's hardly practical. Or normal."

He shrugged. "No one has ever accused me of being normal."

"That doesn't give you an excuse to behave however you want."

His head tilted and his voice shifted, went lower, a fissure of anger creeping into it. "Oh, and how would you have me behave, Regan?"

That knocked her off balance. She fought against feeling flustered. Needing to feel in control, she fought to revive her anger, so she wouldn't crumble. "I would have you call me after we had sex."

"So that's what this is about?" he asked, his hands falling out of his pockets as he took a step closer to her. "You didn't call me either."

Regan clutched her handbag in front of her, swallowing hard. "You're right. I didn't. But first of all, you said you would call me. And when you didn't, I didn't know what to say to the man I imagined a snake in front of and then came home to see him sitting outside my house three nights in a row. It made me feel a little insecure and unnerved, and I don't think that's just me. Most women would probably feel the same way."

"Fair enough." Felix stopped right in front of her and gave her a small smile. "I was going to call you."

Yeah, right. "Well, now you don't have to bother because I'm here and we've established that you're still attending the party and that you're going to stop watching my house every night."

There. She'd said it. She was in control, she was not going to be passive and hide behind her curtains every night, wondering and worrying what he was doing, what he was thinking.

"I'm not going to stop watching you," he said. "I need to know you're alright. Has the sleepwalking happened again?"

Regan bit her lip, not wanting to admit the truth.

"So that's a yes. Which means I'm going to keep an eye on you whether you like it or not."

"It's not your responsibility. You need to sleep, you have your own life. You must have better things to do than sit on the sidewalk all night." She still didn't know whether to be flattered that he cared about her safety, or completely creeped out.

"Just because it isn't my responsibility doesn't mean I won't."

My God, he was so stubborn and hard to understand. Regan made a sound of frustration. "So, if you want to make sure I'm okay, why don't you do it from the inside?"

"From the inside?"

"Yes. Watch me sleep from inside my house. Actually get some sleep yourself. You can put bells on me so you'll wake up if I get out of bed." She hadn't really meant to suggest that he spend the night with her, but now that she'd thrown it out there in irritation, she was going to back it up as a more sensible plan than sidewalk loitering.

"Share your bed? Every night?" Felix reached out and touched her pearl necklace. "Is that what you're suggesting?"

She shivered, desire already pooling in her inner thighs, shoving her anger aside. "Sure. For a few nights anyway. Until you're satisfied I'm not going to balcony surf again."

"I think it's safer for me to stay outside on the street."

Rejection smacked her in the face and she stiffened. "Why? What is that supposed to mean exactly?" She was tired of his riddles and half statements, and while her instinct was to retreat, out of his touch, she stood her ground, determined yet again not to be passive anymore.

"It means that if I'm allowed into your bed, to spend all night next to you, I might not want to leave. Ever."

Oh, my. Regan lost the ability to breathe. She had not expected him to say that. She didn't know what she'd expected him to say, but it most certainly was not *that*.

"It could be dangerous," he murmured. "To me."

"I've never invoked fear in a man before," she said, letting her arm and her bag drop down so she could be closer to him.

"I'm very afraid of you . . . afraid that you are the one woman who could make me want to stay the night, every night."

It could be a line. Regan didn't care. She wanted Felix, regardless of what her friends or her head might tell her about getting involved with a man like him, regardless of whether or not she was capable of having casual sex, or if she was ready to be involved with anyone this soon after her divorce. Her body had experienced a passion she never had before with him, and she wanted it again, for whatever amount of time it was available.

"Confront your fear. Swallow it," she told him, amazed she'd managed to shove the bold words out of her mouth. "Like you told me to do."

Felix gave a soft, sexy laugh. "My own advice thrown back in my face. I like it. And you're right, of course. Why miss the opportunity to lie next to you from the basic primitive emotion of fear? I'm cautious, not stupid."

He had shifted again subtly as they talked so that they were now standing close, bodies brushing. Regan put her hands on his waist, wanting to feel him. She was tired of always trying to please, of walking the narrow fence of propriety, of putting everyone's needs ahead of her own. This was her life, and she could live it on her terms, without hurting anyone.

Chances were the only one who would get hurt was her when Felix inevitably pulled the plug, but she was willing to take that risk.

"You are so sexy," he whispered, lips brushing against her cheek, teeth nibbling her ear.

"Thank you." She wasn't sure what else to say to that, and she was concentrating on breathing evenly as his teeth did interesting things to her flesh.

"So I'm staying the night." He slid his tongue inside her ear, hands moving up and down her sides.

It wasn't a question. But she still confirmed, "Yes."

"Come upstairs. I'll pack a bag."

He was going with her right then? Her desire kicked into overdrive, but even as her body applauded the idea, she asked, "Don't you have to stay in the store?" She didn't want to pull him away from his business.

"I can close whenever I want." He kissed her neck. "Do you notice any customers in here?"

"No." Though she couldn't say she'd really been looking, which was a little disconcerting. She'd never been one for public displays of affection. Though affection was a misnomer for what they were doing.

"Then let's go upstairs." Felix pulled back and started to move to a door she had assumed led to a storage room.

"Aren't you going to lock up?" It would be really easy for someone to stroll in when they were upstairs and steal hundreds of dollars' worth of merchandise.

But Felix looked unconcerned. "I suppose I could. Not that it matters."

"Don't you care?"

"Not really. It's only money. And if someone needs a love oil so desperately they're willing to steal it, I say more power to them and their libido." But he did move toward the front of the store.

Regan knew Felix didn't want to be greedy, but there was such a thing as business sense. But it wasn't her business or her money so she said nothing, even as she thought locking the door against thieves wasn't exactly a major inconvenience, and she was glad he was going to take the two seconds to do it.

Watching him walk toward the door to lock it, Regan stared at his butt and thought about how it had felt to scrape her nails across that tight muscle when he was thrusting inside her. Blowing her hair out of her eyes, she shifted in her black sandals and said, "Do you have any condoms?"

He paused in the act of flicking the lock over. Then he turned around, that sensual smile he had perfected so well on his face as he moved toward her. "Regan Henry, why would we need condoms? Tell me."

She knew what he wanted her to say. His words about her black-and-white world popped into her head. Did she want to always play it safe, with a life that coordinated perfectly, everything interchangeable? Or did she want to risk adding something that could throw life off balance, add a splash of color that didn't fit into her décor?

"So that you can fuck me," she said.

That was the splash of red, of purple, of citrine, in her neutral palette.

His blue eyes lightened. "That can definitely be arranged."

Felix watched Regan perch on the end of his bed, looking a little uncomfortable as he packed an overnight bag. His small apartment was cramped and cluttered, but he didn't think that was what was bothering her. It was both what she had said to him downstairs and the fact that she had discovered his odd little habit of shoving money in random places around his apartment. He'd seen her pull a wad of cash out from where it had been sticking out from the bottom of the mattress, then hastily shove it back.

He didn't feel compelled to explain it to her. He had already revealed way too much with Regan. He cared about her safety, about her. Despite everything he had learned over the years, she had somehow managed to find a way into the heart he had thought was jaded beyond caring.

It was disconcerting. And it made him angry.

So his life had sucked before she had entered it.

At least it had been even. Calm.

Boring.

Empty.

Damn it. Felix yanked open his dresser and grabbed a pair of boxers and clean socks. He shoved them into the bag.

"Do you rent this apartment and the store?" she asked, her legs crossed in her white cotton skirt, perfectly manicured toes swinging up and down.

"No. I own them."

"Wow. That's impressive. We all know it's not cheap to have a property in the Quarter."

"I'm not poor," he said, peeling two twenties off the stack of bills sitting on his dresser and cramming them into his pocket.

"I can see that," she said. "Since you have money all over your apartment. You probably have a thousand dollars in the ashtray alone."

"I don't smoke, so why waste the storage space?" He was being an asshole, he knew it, but he couldn't seem to stop himself. It wasn't fair that he would feel this way about *her*. It wasn't fair that of all the women he had encountered in his long lifetime she had to be the one to act like she actually gave a rat's ass about him.

Why couldn't it be just any woman? No, it had to be Alcroft's ex-wife. The woman living in Camille's house. It wasn't fair and he was angry that it wasn't and angry that he cared that it wasn't.

"It just seems that a bank might be a better option. Especially if you have a guest over who ashes your savings into oblivion."

"I don't have guests." A T-shirt and a fresh pair of jeans went into the bag. He walked the short distance to his bathroom and rooted around for his toothbrush and toothpaste. Screw the razor. He'd go scruffy.

When he came back, Regan was glaring at him. "What exactly are we doing here?"

"What do you mean?" he said, even as he knew exactly what she meant.

"You're packing to stay with me overnight, probably more than one night, and yet you're acting like you're irritated to even be in my presence. This isn't going to work. I don't have to put up with this."

She stood up, her shiny black purse clanking against her leg, as she readied to brush past him indignantly.

Felix sighed. "Regan, don't go. I'm sorry. I'm not irritated to be around you, I just . . ."

"You just what?"

Maybe he should just tell her the truth. Tell her who and what he was. Maybe that was the only way to save them both from pain. Just open his mouth and explain that he was over one hundred and fifty years old, enslaved to a demon in exchange for his worthless life. Let her know that she was possibly in danger from the ghost of Camille and that her ex-husband had sent her chocolates filled with a special little semen surprise.

Then she would conclude he was insane, walk out, and they would never see each other again.

But he couldn't do it.

Because Regan was vulnerable without him watching her back. She was involved in a world she knew nothing about, and Felix had no idea what her role was meant to be yet. He would never forgive himself if something happened to her.

And because he couldn't deny himself her. He just couldn't. It had been too long since he had felt the soft touch of a woman, since he had allowed himself to lie next to someone, to talk about himself. The loneliness was an ache he had managed to ignore until Regan had forced him to feel the bleed of the open wound being alone had sliced in his life.

"I don't know how to do this," he told her honestly.

"Do what?"

"This!" He pointed to her and to himself and back to her. "Have a relationship. I haven't had one in a hundred years and I don't know what the fuck I'm doing."

She relaxed a little, her shoulders dropping. "A hundred years?" She smiled. "Wow, you're older than I thought."

If she only knew.

It was clearly a teasing joke, but it struck a nerve with Felix. "I'm being serious, Regan."

"Okay. Fine. I'm being serious too. So you're uncomfortable. I am too. But being belligerent and aloof isn't going to help us figure out how to deal with our feelings and each other."

Rational and beautiful. If she told him she cooked, he was lost. Hell, he was already lost and he knew it.

"That's true. I can't argue with that."

"Let's not argue at all."

Argue was definitely not what he wanted to be doing. "I have a better idea of how to put my tongue to use."

Her eyes darkened. "Show me."

Avoiding difficult conversations with sex. He was good at that.

"Sit down." He stepped forward so that she automatically moved back.

He didn't kiss her. He didn't touch her. He just stalked until she hit the edge of his bed and sat down, her shiny proper purse still hooked over her arm. Felix pushed up her white skirt, exposing her pale, firm thighs.

Regan gasped, but she didn't stop him.

Yanking on her knees, he dragged her to the very edge of the bed and went under her skirt, snapping the string of her white panties so he could pull them to the side. He had to taste her, had to sink his tongue inside her and feel how wet she was for him.

When he flicked over her, he got his answer. She was damp and ready already, a juicy treat just for him. He could hear her ragged breathing, feel her fingers digging into his shoulders.

He licked and sucked with urgent, intense strokes, needing to express his overwhelming and chaotic feelings for her, wanting her to understand that he couldn't control this, what they were doing, where they were going. Her hands shifted to his chest, pressing against him like she couldn't take it, like she wanted him to retreat.

Felix pushed against her resistance and bit her clitoris. Regan came hard, with a beautiful loud cry that echoed in his dingy apartment, her thighs trembling.

Her hand closed around his necklace, and as her body rocked and her muscles contracted, she yanked and broke the chain.

The cross his mother had given him tumbled down to the floor as her perfect little purse knocked him in the side of the head.

Chapter Fourteen

❧

They went to dinner. Had a normal conversation about her job, the fund-raiser, his love of jazz. They walked to a bar on Frenchman to listen to some live music. Then back to her house where they watched an action flick on DVR. Like two normal people dating. It was so ordinary it was unnerving.

When he took her bare feet and started massaging them, Regan was pretty damn sure she'd fallen down the rabbit hole.

But she also figured she might as well enjoy it while she was in the hallucination.

Not that it was *exactly* normal. She'd never had sex with a man the way she did with Felix, raw and intense and shattering. And insatiable. She wanted him again, more, all of him.

It was scary and exhilarating, and she didn't want him to leave, at the same time she had no idea what to really do with him in her house.

"God, that feels good," she said, twisting on the couch so her legs stretched out fully. "Thank you."

"You have very cute toes." He rubbed each one thoroughly then gave her pinky toe a kiss.

Now she was really in a parallel universe. One where she had a gorgeous man who wined and dined her and made love to her in her beautiful house, who didn't care one iota about her money, and who made her forget all about her lack of sleep.

"So tell me about the sleepwalking. Do you remember it?"

Or not.

Regan sighed. "No, I don't remember it. I just keep waking up in a different bedroom. It doesn't seem dangerous. Just annoying."

He stopped rubbing her feet. "Which room?"

"The front one. It's totally empty. I don't have any furniture for it yet, so I wake up on the floor." She realized she could make a plea for a backrub too. "It's killing my back."

"Do you want me to rub that?"

Score. "Oh, you don't have to."

"I don't mind. Lay down on your stomach."

By the time Felix had rubbed every inch of her body and slid into her from behind, tripping off a catastrophic orgasm, Regan was positive she would sleep so solidly she wouldn't move all night.

But the next morning she woke to Felix gently shaking her awake in the same front room.

"We need to talk about this," he said, once she had rubbed the sleep from her eyes and sat up.

"I don't want to talk about it."

What was there to say? People sleepwalked. Just because she had suddenly started meant nothing.

But she knew that it did.

She just didn't want to face whatever it was.

"What do you want for breakfast?" she asked as she stood up and tried to discreetly stretch her stiff muscles.

Felix let the subject of sleepwalking drop. "I don't know. We could just go to the coffee shop."

"I was going to make you breakfast. Are you a bacon-and-eggs kind of guy?"

Felix, who was bare-chested in his boxers, just stared at her. "What do you mean . . . you're going to actually cook for me?"

He looked so shocked she laughed. "Yes. I can cook, you know." And she needed to buy him a new chain for his cross necklace as soon as possible. She felt guilty for breaking it during sex, and his chest looked so bare without it.

"Yeah, but . . ." Felix shook his head, then he smiled at her, a smile so open and honest and happy she felt a river of emotion swell up inside her. "I would love bacon and eggs. If you don't mind. If it's not too much trouble."

"Of course not." Regan moved into his arms and rested her head on his shoulder. "I want to do something for you for a change. I want to . . ." She hesitated, unsure how to convey what she was feeling.

"You want to what?"

Regan looked into his eyes. "I want to be there for you. I want to be with you. Maybe I shouldn't say that, maybe it's too soon."

But he shook his head. "It's not too soon. It's what I want, too. And maybe this is going to sound weird, but thank you."

Tilting her head, Regan studied him. "For what?"

"For being you. For being willing to put up with me." Felix brushed a kiss over her lips. "For actually liking me."

"Of course I like you," she said, returning his kiss with

one of her own. His lips were warm, his eyes still sleepy. "I like you a lot."

"And I guess I can't ask for anything more than that."

⌘

On her lunch break, after picking up a new chain for Felix's necklace, Regan ran over to the public library, determined to do some more research on Camille. There was something about the girl . . . something about her losing her family in Regan's house, that had her curious to find out what had happened to her. Regan could ask Felix, since he'd done research on the house, but then she would be forced to confront both of their fears over her sleepwalking.

She had never sleepwalked in her entire life, and that she was doing it now felt somehow connected to the spirit of the dead girl. It felt like Camille wanted to tell her something, that she wanted her death known, grieved. Maybe it was as simple as that. The girl who had died after her entire family had probably had no one to genuinely grieve for her, and maybe if Regan gave her that, she would pass on to the other side, or whatever it was spirits did.

And Regan could reclaim her house and her sleep.

A quick search of death records online showed that Camille Comeaux had died in October of 1878, a mere four months after her family had died in the yellow fever epidemic.

Frowning, Regan shifted in the hard chair, the hush of the library settling around her. She had to find out how Camille died. It was possible she had died of disease as well, either the same one as her family, or something else. Prior to antibiotics, death was common from illnesses that were easily cured in the modern era of medicine.

But something told her Camille hadn't died a natural death.

Searching the newspaper archives with the dates a few

days after the one on Camille's death certificate, Regan found confirmation of her fears immediately.

HEIRESS DIES BY OWN HAND!

Camille Comeaux, the youngest daughter of Francois Comeaux, who perished in our city's latest battle against the dreaded yellow fever along with his wife and four daughters, has joined her family in death. Her broken and bloodied body was found in the courtyard of her home, where she landed after jumping from the balcony above, her goal to take her own life sadly successful. Witnesses report Miss Comeaux leapt to her death as nature intended her, with a snake around her neck. Gossips foreshadowed an unfortunate ending for this grief-stricken girl, as her behavior had been suspect in prior months, with whispers of the consumption of spirits and wearing white while in deep mourning. A once great family comes to an unceremonious and inglorious end with her untimely demise.

Regan shivered as she stared at the computer screen. Suicide. Off the Juliet balcony Regan had once found so charming. The very balcony she herself had been sitting on in her sleep like it was a sofa at noon.

It was too coincidental to be random. It was too bizarre to believe it could be anything but.

And a snake around her neck?

Jesus. Regan grabbed her purse and ran to the ladies' room, afraid she was going to throw up. Careening into a stall, she knelt on the cold tile floor and breathed in and out, determined to swallow her nausea. It didn't make sense. None of it made any sense.

The urge to vomit quieted, but Regan's mind didn't.

It was insane. All of it.

Or was she the insane one?

Her phone rang in her purse, startling her into jerking back away from the toilet. Fumbling to get it out, she prayed it was Felix. He would be calm. Nothing freaked him out. He would talk her off the ledge.

Oh, God. Poor choice of words.

Regan felt a hysterical laugh burble up inside her.

Without checking to see who it was on the phone, she answered. "Hello?"

She would talk to anyone if it meant she didn't have to be alone with her disturbing thoughts.

"Hi, Regan, how are you?"

It was Beau. Regan squeezed her eyes shut. "I'm actually not feeling very well, Beau. I think I have a stomach flu. Can I call you back later?"

There was a pause and she knew he was getting his anger under control. "The stomach flu or morning sickness perhaps? Has your new boyfriend knocked you up already? I know how much you always wanted kids."

Oh, no. The nausea returned full force, and dropping the phone in her lap, Regan leaned over the toilet and hurled the contents of her hurried lunch into the bowl. She heaved four or five times, her body ensuring that every last bit of food and fluid was evacuated. When she was sure she was finished, she wiped her tearing eyes on the sleeve of her black cardigan and took a shaky breath.

Shuddering, she reached for her phone. The asshole was actually still on the line.

"Well, that was charming," he said.

"I'll call you back," she managed, running her finger over her saliva-splattered lip.

"No, you won't. So you're going to sit there and listen to me now."

"I'm in the public restroom. I'm not doing this with you

right now." Hopefully, they could do this never. She had no desire to discuss Felix with her ex-husband.

"I'm impressed," he said, like she hadn't spoken. "It didn't take you long to find an idiot willing to put up with your petulance and your overdrinking. Though I have to say I'm surprised you went for the voodoo guy. He doesn't seem your type . . . a little dirty for your tastes. And aren't you worried he's fucking you to get to your money?"

That pissed her off enough to have her hauling herself off the cold floor. "It's none of your damn business. And don't tell me you're living in celibacy because I won't believe you."

"He'll get bored with you, you know. You can't hold the interest of a man like that."

Regan paused, hand on the stall door. Damn it. He had hit on her very real fear. She did worry that she was too staid, too ordinary, too boring for Felix. But she wasn't about to let Beau know that.

"Or maybe he won't hold *my* interest," she told Beau. "Like what happened for me with you."

It felt good to say it, to hear the pause where she knew she'd shocked him, where she'd landed a direct hit he had never anticipated she would sally at him. She strode out of the stall, head held high.

When he said, "Bitch," Regan only smiled at herself in the mirror above the sink.

"Asshole," she said in return and hung up the phone.

It felt damn, damn good.

❧❧❧

Felix had been planning to meet Regan for dinner after work, but he knew something was wrong when he spoke to her on the phone. She sounded anxious and unfocused. So knowing she wasn't planning to leave her house for another thirty minutes, Felix decided to meet her there instead and walk to the restaurant with her. It would give them time to talk, and he could ferret out if something was bothering her.

She had given him the key to the courtyard gate, and he used it, sending a text message to her so she wouldn't jump out of her skin when he came in the house. Heading into the kitchen, he didn't see her on the first floor, and didn't hear her on the second. The house was so damn big, he could wander for ten minutes before he found her, so he sent her another text asking her where she was.

My bedroom was her short response.

Now he was really worried. She didn't sound like her usual cheerful self at all. Felix bounded up the steps and jogged down the hall to her room. He skidded to a stop in the doorway.

Regan was sitting on the edge of her bed, face pale, still dressed in the Capri pants and sweater set he had seen her leave for work in that morning. Normally when she got home she changed into jeans. But she was just sitting there, legs crossed at the ankles, staring down at her hands in her lap.

"Hey."

She looked up. "Hi."

"What are you doing? Is everything okay?" He looked around the room for any outward signs of an interaction with Camille. There was nothing out of the ordinary in the room, everything neat and tidy the way she had left it that morning. Regan was always neat, unlike him.

Wondering if she was even awake, Felix started walking toward her. It was then he realized she had her left hand up and was staring at it. Or more accurately staring at the wedding ring she was wearing. He sat down next to her on the bed and took her hand, studying the expensive and elegant ring.

Running his thumb over the diamond, he asked, "Why are you wearing your wedding ring?"

"Beau called me today. He was quite horrible. He knows about you. I'm not sure how, but he does."

Felix fought the fear, the memory of pain, of pressure, of darkness flooding over him. It didn't matter. He had known what he was risking, had known there was no way Alcroft wouldn't find out at some point. Felix was practically living with Regan. And it was worth it. She was worth it. Being with her brought him the closest to happy he had ever been.

"I take it he wasn't exactly thrilled that we're seeing each other?" Felix had no doubt Alcroft had been scathing in his opinion of Felix.

"No. He told me I didn't waste any time finding some fool willing to take on the mess that I am."

"That's anger and jealousy. You are not a mess, Regan. You're an amazing, giving, compassionate woman." Felix watched her twist the ring on her finger and fought the urge to reach out and yank it off.

"He asked if you had gotten me pregnant. Isn't that an odd thing for him to ask?"

Felix's heart almost stopped. "Did I get you pregnant?" He had no idea how he felt about that. He had never thought he would have children, but maybe, with a woman like Regan . . . A whole different vision of the future popped up before him in ten seconds.

"No, of course not. I'm on the pill."

The family-man future disappeared as quickly as it had appeared. It was ridiculous anyway, totally impractical and irresponsible for him to even consider bringing a child into this world. "Right."

"I just thought it was weird that he would ask that." Regan still sounded unfocused, her voice distant and reserved. She kept lifting her hand and checking out the wedding ring.

"So what about that phone conversation had you coming home and putting on your wedding ring?" he asked, gently. It needed to come off. The longer it sat on her finger, the greater potential there was for her to fall back under the influence of Alcroft.

"I'd never taken it out of the evening bag I'd thrown it in the night I left him, and I came home thinking I should pull it out and sell it. That it was time to deal with it instead of keeping it tucked away in a purse. I felt ready to handle getting rid of it, instead of ignoring it. This is a valuable ring . . . I can swap it for different jewelry or just take the cash."

Felix waited. There was clearly more and he wanted her to say it unprompted.

"So I took it out and I just thought it feels so good not to wear it . . . what would it feel like back on my finger? I put it on, and it feels heavy and oppressive and awful, and yet, it's like I can't take it off. It's like it's whispering to me, asking me if I made a mistake, even as my brain knows I did not make a mistake. I could never go back. Yet every time I think I should pull the ring off, my hand never moves."

That was all he needed to hear. Reaching over, Felix tugged the ring off her finger. It would be better if she took it off herself, but he wasn't about to wait around and see if that happened or not.

"Ouch!" she protested. "You scratched me."

"Sorry." Closing his fist around the ring, he dropped his hand down on his thigh so the ring was nowhere near her, and leaned over and kissed her ring finger and the tiny scratch he had made removing it. "Don't put his ring on again, please."

Regan shivered and looked at him with wide eyes. "Felix, that was so weird. It was like the second you pulled it off, I felt this pain, then relief. Just instant relief. I sound crazy, don't I? All the time, I just sound insane."

"No, you don't." He lifted the ring and looked on the inside for the inscription he knew would be there. "*Ego own vos.* Do you know what that means?"

"It means 'we belong together' or something like that. Beau said it's Latin."

"The literal translation is much less romantic than what he told you. It actually means 'I own you.'"

"'I own you'?" Regan's eyebrows shot up. "No, that's not romantic at all."

"It's a binding ring. When you wear it, you feel compelled to be with the person who gave it to you."

Regan looked at her bare hand. "A binding ring? But wouldn't that mean it had a spell put on it? That's totally not like Beau at all . . . he wouldn't believe in something that out there."

Which went to show you how well she knew the man she had married. She had been lured and blinded by his charm and the very spells she didn't think he would believe in. "You'd be surprised what people will do."

"That's true. And it did make me feel that way . . . like I couldn't take it off. It was weird." She shuddered. "This has been a very weird day. Hell, every day has been weird since I bought this house. Do you think it's cursed?" Regan pressed her temples. "God, I can't even believe I just said that out loud."

"I don't know what is going on in this house. There is definitely something here, and it's wise to be on guard. But not all things that have happened in this house are weird." Felix took her hand into his and stroked it. "It's where we found each other, after all."

"That's true." Her eyes softened as she looked at him.

Felix loved that look she got, the one that said she did care about him, more than just as a means to an end, but him. The man. The person. She cared about him. "If none of these weird things had happened, we probably wouldn't have met again after the Christmas party. And what a shame that would have been."

"That would have been a shame. Having you here, with me, well . . . it's been amazing, Felix."

When had anyone ever told him his presence mattered? Intense, powerful feelings welled up in him. He kissed her, a soft, gentle press. "I just want you to know that I'm falling in love with you."

Her breath hitched. "Are you serious?"

Felix gave a soft laugh. "Oh, hell yes, I'm serious. When have you ever known me to say something I don't mean, especially when it comes to emotion?"

He didn't know where it could go, how long it could last. He didn't know if Alcroft would kill him or exact a long and painful punishment. And even if he survived that and Regan didn't think he had abandoned her, Felix didn't know how any sort of relationship between them could last, given that he would never age.

But he wanted her to know. He wanted her to see and feel and believe that he loved her.

And he wanted to enjoy the pleasure of her company, the contentment she brought him, while it lasted. It would go sour, he had no doubt of it, but for now, he could close his eyes, breathe in her scent and affection, and feel happy.

"I'm falling in love with you, too," she said, her thumb skimming over his hand. "I think you see me more clearly than any man I've ever been with."

"Thank you," he said, squeezing her hand harder and leaning in to press his forehead against hers. "For making me feel alive again."

Regan pulled back, expression puzzled. "What happened to you? Who hurt you? You can tell me anything, you know."

He hadn't meant for her to come to that conclusion. It wasn't the truth, not exactly. "No one hurt me. I hurt myself with some bad choices. I'll tell you about it someday. Just not today."

She paused, like she was going to press, but then she nodded. "Okay. I'm here for you."

"I appreciate it." Felix stood up, her hand still in his.

"I have something for you." He hadn't bought a woman a gift in a very long time and he felt suddenly insecure. "It's no pearl necklace, but I saw it and I thought it would look pretty on you."

Felix pulled the hot pink scarf out of the bag and draped it around her neck. "It seems like a lot of women are wearing these now and this color with your eyes . . . I just thought it would look nice."

And he was going to shut up because he sounded like an idiot, and he felt even stupider.

Regan smiled, a soft pleased smile. "You bought me a pink scarf? That seems very appropriate. I love it, thank you."

"You're welcome." He almost said that he would give her anything, anything she wanted, anything that was within his grasp, but instead he just kissed her softly.

"I have something for you, too." She turned and rustled around in her purse before pulling out a small brown bag. Opening it, she withdrew a chain necklace and held it up. "For your cross. You must miss wearing it."

Felix stared at the necklace, rocking back and forth as it dangled in Regan's grip, and he was speechless. It was such a simple thing to do, yet no one ever did anything for him. Never. Not in a hundred years had anyone walked into a store with him in mind and gotten him a gift. No one had even noticed the nuances of his likes and dislikes, in clothing, food, sex, anything, and yet Regan had. Overwhelmed, he realized that he had just fallen completely and totally in love with her.

She cared about him, and it was the most amazing feeling he'd ever had in his life. He wanted to hold it close and never let it go.

"Thank you," he said gruffly, taking the chain from her. Walking over to the nightstand, he picked up his cross and threaded the chain through the hole. Another second and he had it back around his neck. Turning to her, he asked, "Ready to eat?"

She nodded, adjusting the scarf around her neck.

Funny that they had both given each other something worn around the neck. Were the gifts a binding of their relationship? He tried to ignore the uneasiness that crept over him, the feeling that maybe he wasn't that different from Alcroft. Did love always result in greed? Wanting to own another person's affections, projected emotions a noose around the neck.

It wasn't a pleasant thought and he shoved it aside.

"Don't forget your purse," he told her.

Unsure what to do with it, Felix slipped the wedding ring from Alcroft into his pocket when Regan turned to pick up her purse. If they sold it in a jewelry shop or on eBay, Felix wasn't sure what effect it would have on the new wearer. He thought that the spell would have been intended solely for Regan, so if anyone else put the ring on, they would feel nothing, but he wanted to test the theory first before he created turmoil in some poor, unsuspecting newly engaged woman.

Regan stood up, too. "I went to the library today. I found out that Camille Comeaux died here, too."

Felix paused. "Oh, really?" he asked, hoping he sounded curious enough to prevent her from being suspicious. Yet he didn't want to discuss Camille's death with Regan, now or ever.

"Yes. Just a few months after her family. She killed herself."

"Wow. That's terrible." Felix clenched and unclenched his fists, a buzzing starting in his ears. He couldn't talk about this, not even with Regan. He couldn't admit that he was the only one who knew that Camille had not committed suicide.

"She flung herself off my balcony, the same one I

was sitting on, Felix. Don't you find that just a horrible coincidence?"

"Yes, that is a horrible coincidence. But it is the balcony right off the bedroom. It makes sense that's where you wound up when you were sleepwalking."

"She died with a *snake* around her neck. Isn't that strange and awful?" Regan was losing color in her face as she got agitated, her hair falling out of its twist as she spoke emphatically.

"Huh. That is strange and awful. But honey, she was dabbling in voodoo from what you've read in the journal. It doesn't surprise me that she would want to use it under those circumstances." He couldn't bring himself to say suicide.

"Don't you wonder what happened that night?" Regan flung her arms around. "Right here in this very room?"

No. Because he already knew.

Chapter Fifteen

Felix watched Camille dance naked, his body hardening in automatic response to the erotic vision of the once prim and proper daughter letting go of all her inhibitions and dancing to the rhythm of the drum.

He had watched her increasing agitation and growing madness over the months he had known her, and knew that she wasn't really interested in voodoo. She merely liked the forbidden quality of it, the mystery of the language, the chants and spells and rituals that were so foreign and seemingly primitive to her wealthy ear, raised on subdued religion and sedate ballroom waltzes.

She had no idea the complexity of voodoo, the very real power it could wield, particularly in Felix's hands now that he had the magic of immortality flowing through his veins. He had no intention of doing what she had requested for this evening—raising the spirits of her dead family. That would release a power so uncontrollable, Felix did not want to tangle with it. He was more voodoo magician than true houngan, and he had no desire to blur the lines between this world and the next.

What he wanted was simply to create a ceremony so seductive, so thrilling, that she would be appeased, that she would continue to pass her many coins over to him in vast quantities, that tonight she would finally allow him entrance into her body. He had plucked pieces of various ceremonies, with different meanings, and fused them together in random order to please Camille, but so they would have no consequences.

As she danced, candlelight flowing over her firm, dewy body, Felix began to chant in French.

Take me, keep me from death,
For if you kill me, it's a crime,
Since it is the Great King of Ife,
Where mortals never go,
Who gives us the light of life.

He enjoyed the power of the serpent, enjoyed holding its heavy, dry body in his hands, high above his head. It brought to mind the intriguing and vibrant voodoo ceremonies of his youth, those his mother took him to under strict instructions never to speak of them in front of his father. The secrecy added to the mystery of the elaborate rituals, filled with a language he didn't understand and pleas to gods he didn't recognize, and when the men had brought out the snakes and made them dance, rising like water with the spirit of the deceased initiates, his heart had pounded with the thrill of it.

Just like Camille's heart raced now, her hands high, hair flying around her as she danced to the elemental rhythm of the beat of his foot on the wood floor.

"We call on the Saints to guide you, to answer our plea, in the name of all that is Holy."

Out of the corner of his eye he saw that one of the

housemaids had opened the door a few inches and was watching hunched over, with wide eyes. It gave him a certain satisfaction, a feeling of defiant power, to have strolled in through the front door of the mansion tonight, coolly staring down all the servants, who had eyed him with total disapproval. As far as he was concerned, he had more right to enter through the front than they did. He had the lineage on his father's side, the savvy survivalist skills of his mother's side, the wealth from his own business, and the power of never having to face death.

He would be in this room if he so chose.

Whipping the head of the snake around, he undulated it toward the door. "Danbaala-Wedo!" he chanted to the maid. "Join us, join us."

She gasped and slammed the door shut.

Felix laughed. Invoking fear was intoxicating in and of itself, and he was doing nothing, a nonsense compilation of voodoo, and the power pleased him.

"Camille, stop," he ordered.

She did, her chest heaving, her arms still over her head, her damp hair sticking to her lip.

"Drink from the water of the living. Drink from the water of the dead."

Her movements were unbalanced as she walked, and she lost her footing at the chest of drawers, stumbling before reaching out and regaining her equilibrium by gripping the furniture. She took a long swallow from each of the two jars he had placed between the candles. They were wine, not water, because he had wanted her relaxed, inebriated, so that tomorrow she would remember this in hazy terms, that she would remember the excitement and the "sign" of her family that he would manufacture. He wanted no crystal clarity of events, which might disillusion her.

Selfish, to be sure, but he wasn't done with Camille.

"Now turn in a circle and repeat after me."

For once Camille was serious, listening carefully to him, concentrating on making a slow, complete turn, repeating each sentence after he spoke.

"In the name of Bha."

"In the name of Dan."

"In the name of Lah."

Her voice was slurring, the dancing, the wine, the tight circles she was spinning sending her into a heady trance, and her hands moved down over her breasts, down her belly, slipping through the blonde curls between her thighs.

The snake wrapped around his neck, Felix held the jaw at bay with one hand so it couldn't strike, and reached out with his free hand and covered Camille's. Together they stroked her, fingers gliding together into her hot dampness. She seemed to have forgotten what they were doing, what their purpose was. Driving the pace from languid to frantic, Camille bit her lip as her passion exploded.

He felt the power of her climax begin, and pulled his hand sharply back, to tease and heighten her desire. She made a sound of frustration but managed to please herself, her head lolling back as her shoulders relaxed.

Camille opened her eyes, shiny from wine, and laughed. "It's time, isn't it? I can feel it. I can feel them."

"Yes, it's time. Come to the window." He wanted to see her in the moonlight, wanted the air to tease over her naked body, a breeze that he could point out was the spirit of her dead loved ones.

She did so without hesitation, heading right to the French doors and gripping either side of the door frame with outstretched arms, her eyes drifting closed as she breathed deeply. He stood directly behind her, a watchful eye on the dark street below. They were tucked into the shadows of the trees in the courtyard, and it was very late, but he was still mindful of unwanted attention. If Camille were seen, it would ruin both of them.

"Welcome them home," he whispered in her ear.

Camille started humming a tune he didn't recognize and moved forward, out onto the balcony. *"Let me have the snake,"* she demanded over her shoulder.

"No. It's dangerous."

"Give it to me," she snapped, expression wild, fierce as she stood naked in the moonlight, her hair whipping around her face. *"Please. I can handle it. I want the power. You said the magic comes from within me and you're right. I feel it."*

"No, I can't give it to you." He had his limits and he had no intention of putting her at real risk.

She looked ready to protest, her brow furrowing.

"Turn around," he told her. *"Remember your focus."*

She did, taking another step forward. Then she stopped suddenly and turned back to him, eyes wide, a smile transforming her face. She no longer looked like the angry, desperate, contentious woman he had come to know, but a sweeter, milder, much more innocent version. It was Camille before death had robbed her of love and her sanity, and Felix paused, shocked, humbled.

He hadn't realized precisely how much four short months had ravaged her countenance and the essence of her soul. How much of that transformation was he responsible for? He had taken advantage of the tragedy of her grief and encouraged her behavior.

Now to see her, looking so young, so light, so unburdened, he felt a hot wave of shame and regret wash over him. It was one thing to take advantage when it didn't harm anyone, but to contribute to someone's decline . . . he was selfish, but not cruel. *"Camille, come inside,"* he said gently.

She shook her head. *"No, Felix, they're here. I feel them."* Tears started to stream down her face. *"I smell my mother's perfume. I can hear my sisters whispering, giggling. Can you hear them?"*

"No, sweetheart." He shook his head gently. "That is for your ears only. They've come to comfort you, to tell you they are with you always."

Maybe that is what she needed to regain control of her life, a brush with those from beyond, real or imagined. Felix turned, intending to take the snake and deposit it back in the basket. He thought perhaps Camille needed him to just hold her in his arms platonically more than she needed passion or magic, and he owed her that.

He had taken two steps toward the doors when something about the sound, the movement behind him had him whipping back around before he could even decipher where his alarm had arisen from. Holy hell, what he had heard had been Camille climbing up onto the wrought iron railing of the Juliet balcony.

"Camille! Get down." She was standing on the wrong side of it, feet perched precariously on just a few inches of wood flooring, arms stretched out as she clung to the railing.

Felix moved to erase the distance between them, panicking.

"I see them," she said. "Right in front of me, Felix! It's so good to see them again."

He was reaching for her when it happened. She laughed and let go, her arms outstretched to nothing. Felix tried to grab her, but his fingers slid along her bare skin, nothing to hold on to, and she pitched forward. Lurching forward himself, he climbed up on the railing, desperate to find a way to stop her fall, but it was too late, hopeless, and as a groan escaped his mouth, Camille landed on the cobblestones with a horrific jarring crunch.

The snake he had forgotten about bit his arm.

Felix jerked from the pain and the serpent slid off his shoulders, tumbling over the side of the balcony, following Camille in a surreal tangle of its long heavy body, framed by the stones, the lush green foliage on either side of it.

Down and down it swirled, a freakish unnatural twisting and turning of its elongated body. Frozen, Felix watched the snake finally hit the stones at Camille's feet.

Then he started running down the stairs, the back door of the house opening at the same time he dropped onto the courtyard, skipping the last three steps. The little brunette maid, the one who had been peeking into the bedroom, stepped outside. She took one look at Camille on the ground and opened her mouth to scream. Felix moved to her and clapped his hand over her mouth.

"She fell," he told the maid in a hoarse whisper. "Don't make it worse for her memory. I was never here, do you understand? I was never here and she was sleepwalking and slipped."

The maid just stared at him with wide eyes. He shook her a little. "Do you understand me?"

She nodded quickly.

Felix never knew what the maid told the staff and the doctor who must have been called to the scene of the accident, but within two days the newspapers were reporting that Camille had killed herself, a snake wrapped around her neck as she took her deadly plunge.

But he wasn't around to read the various accounts. He left New Orleans within an hour of Camille's death and didn't return for ten years, during which time he perfected the art of self-loathing.

❧

Regan had scared herself by putting on Beau's ring, and scared herself even more when she'd been unable to take it off. There were strange things happening in her house, in her mind, and she was worried that it was more abnormal, more dangerous, than she could ignore.

Even now, on the street after dinner, she kept glancing down at her bare finger, picturing the princess-cut diamond on it, how beautiful it had looked, how she had heard almost whispers in her head, assuring her of the rightness of its presence. It had been terrifying, that one part of her rational mind had known the truth, that she didn't want to be with Beau, while the other had been like a wicked child, encouraging and coaxing and manipulative, daring her to keep the ring on.

There was something so very insane about it, so not herself that Regan felt the gnawing relentlessness of anxiety eating away at her.

But being with Felix, having his hand at the small of her back, and his calm smile trained on her, made her feel almost normal again. She had the sense that no matter what happened, she could count on him to stand by her, and that was a huge reassurance.

As they strolled down Royal Street after having dinner in the courtyard at the Court of Two Sisters, comfortable and content with each other, Regan realized that she finally understood what was needed to sustain a serious relationship. It wasn't enough just to love. You had to be able to show your partner everything about yourself, good, bad, vulnerable, odd, and know that it didn't matter. You had to be able to trust that at any given moment, he could and would support you, that his love was well and truly unconditional, and that while you weren't always going to like each other every single minute, you were always going to love each other.

She loved Felix. It was as simple as that, and when he had reached out and yanked Beau's ring off her finger, she had known that with absolute certainty. She found Felix the most intriguing, compassionate, self-aware man she'd ever met. She'd seen his good, his bad, his warmth, his cool defensiveness, and she understood that the difference when he showed aloofness had to do with him, not her.

And he was seeing her at her worst, or at least her most vulnerable, and he didn't care. He thought she was worthy, no matter how imperfect she might be. It was so cliché, but she could truly just be herself around him and he still seemed to think she was deserving of his attention and affection.

Her cell phone rang in her purse and she fished it out to check the screen. "It's my mother. I'll call her back."

Felix shook his head, a smile dancing across his lips. "I still can't believe that's your ring tone. It sounds like it could be Harvard's alma mater or something. It doesn't suit you at all."

"What should my ring tone be?" she asked, tucking her phone away and reaching for his hand. She wanted to touch him all the time, just feel his skin on hers.

"You're always listening to pop and dance music. You need something like that on your phone."

Regan made a face. "I'm really too old to listen to that stuff. It's my guilty pleasure, but I can't have it going off on my phone."

"Why not? If you like it, why is it anyone else's business?" Felix stroked her thumb with his as he held her hand and paused in front of her house. "We're home."

Home. A little word, filled with such meaning. She wanted this beautiful house to become a home, to feel like her own, to not make her heart race, and her eyes dart over her shoulders into the shadows.

She wanted Felix in this house with her.

He made the dark corners lighten and the rooms less empty. "Yes, we're home. How does one more glass of wine on the balcony sound?"

"Wonderful."

In two minutes they were out on the balcony, relaxing back in their twin chairs. "I need to get a table," Regan said, crossing her ankles and sighing in contentment, stomach full, the sweetness of the wine they'd grabbed in the kitchen on her tongue. "So many things to buy and do to this house. It's too empty now. I want to fill it up." Maybe that would make the weird uneasiness, the echo she felt, go away.

"There's so many empty rooms, I don't even know where you'd begin." Felix glanced over at her. "Hey, I was thinking . . . how would you feel about living together for real, permanently? I don't have any stuff that would ruin your décor. It's just me and my clothes. But it would be cool to have a key, to know that I'm going to wake up next to you every day."

Regan shivered, clutching her glass tighter. He looked so sweet, so sincere, so intense.

"Do you really want that?" she asked, her heart swelling. She hadn't expected that it would be him who would suggest it. She had thought she'd wait a few months then bring it up herself.

There was something very reassuring in knowing the man you loved was confident in his feelings toward you. And she did love him. She hadn't planned to fall in love, not now, maybe never again, but she had, sharply and quickly, like having the wind knocked out of her.

"Yes. I know it's fast, but I love you. I want to be together."

That was the first time he had straight-out said he loved her, and Regan felt a goofy grin of wonderment splitting her face. "Yes, I absolutely want you to move in. I love you, too. God, I love you."

She laughed, amazed that they had stumbled into each other's life. Amazed that when she tossed out the rules and worries and unrealistic expectations for perfection, she could achieve such happiness.

"Regan," Felix said, his voice deepening, his body leaning toward her.

"What?" she asked, even as she knew. That look he gave her, that burning intense stare, always meant one thing.

"It's time to go in the bedroom."

"Oh, really?" Regan licked her bottom lip, her inner thighs automatically warming at his words, her nipples tightening. "To do what?"

"Stand up and walk in and you'll find out." He stood up and moved the chair out of the way.

Regan could see an impressive erection straining against his jeans, and she didn't hesitate to obey his instructions. She stood up, smoothing down the front of her Capri pants, knowing the minute she tried to pass Felix he would touch her. The thought excited her, and tossed with the fact that he had told her he loved her, had Regan already aroused and he hadn't laid one finger on her.

She kept waiting for the day that their sex was slow and considerate and proper, and so far it had never come. She didn't want it to. It was much more exciting to have Felix wanting and demanding of her, to know that they were both so turned on and so eager that waiting was never an option.

It was that reaction she was anticipating when she brushed past him, and she got it. Regan was in the doorway when his hands landed on her waist and pulled her back to bump against his erection. His hands slid down the front of her pants, down along the vee between her legs, his lips brushing along her jaw.

"I love you," he whispered.

Regan shivered, a soft moan escaping her both from his words and from the fact that he was stroking across her pants in a teasing, coaxing rhythm. Hot saliva filled her mouth and her eyes drifted half-shut. "I love you, too."

He unhooked the clasp on her pants.

Regan started to turn, but he held her in place. She made a sound of protest. "Felix, we're in the doorway."

"No one can see you. Only me."

She didn't think it would take a genius to figure out what they were doing if anyone happened to look up and see Felix thrusting and her pants down at her ankles. Call her crazy, but she didn't want to meet her neighbors that way.

And she didn't want to think about neighbors or worry about having her backside exposed or have any thought in her head other than the fact that the man she loved loved her in return. This wasn't a moment to be self-conscious, but a moment to look into each other's eyes and embrace that connection.

So Regan stepped forward, undoing the scarf he'd given her and dropping it to the floor in a hot pink puddle. Her shirt followed suit. Undoing her zipper, she stepped out of her pants and went to the bed. Before she could climb on it, he was right behind her, nudging her up against the footboard.

"You feel so amazing," he murmured, his voice a low growl in her ear, his necklace cool on her back against the heat of her skin. "I can never touch you enough."

"And I can never have you touch me enough," she said, sighing in pleasure. In more than pleasure, in amazement and awe and the purest form of bliss.

Felix nuzzled her neck, his fingers running up and down her sides lightly, occasionally veering to the front to brush against her breasts and nipples. Their urgency had quieted, and as if by mutual agreement they both hovered in this place of anticipation, a moment to just hold each other and savor.

It was a sweet, sensual embrace, bare flesh on bare flesh, their feelings open and honest. Regan sighed when his fingers stroked her moist inner thighs. "You make me feel so good."

"I hope so. That's the point." Felix pushed deeper inside her with his finger.

Regan moved against his hand, her knees shifting apart. It was amazing to her that with a few touches, a few kisses, a few strokes of his finger he could make her feel this. This sharp, hot, soaking desire to have him in her body, to make her come over and over. "Harder," she begged.

Felix gave a soft laugh. "Oh, yeah, is that what you want?" His finger stilled. "You do it then."

There was a pause, then Regan started to move herself on his finger and Felix felt a fresh jolt of desire. There was something so sweetly sexual about Regan, so free. "I love it that you're not polite when we're having sex," he told her. He wanted her to give in, to feel the freedom, and she did.

"I don't think I'm being rude," she said in a jagged voice, hips moving rhythmically over him.

"Not rude. Just not polite. You're being demanding, taking what you want, and that is so amazingly hot."

Regan stopped pumping on him, and he could feel the tenseness of her interior muscles. She was on the edge of an orgasm but had stopped herself. "Then get on the bed and fuck me."

Felix couldn't prevent a groan from slipping out. That was the first time she had ever said something like that, thrown his own raw, base words back at him, and it was so sexy.

"Yes, ma'am." Felix shifted away and waited until she climbed on the bed, then he moved over top of her.

"Do you want me to lick you or do you want to me inside you?"

"Inside me," she said, her eyes glazed over with desire, lips shiny and moist, legs already spread.

Felix trailed his finger over her clitoris, then farther down over her, teasing lightly, before moving in close to her, his erection resting against her.

"Now," she said, her hips lifting to force the issue.

"Now," he agreed, and he pushed inside her, joining their bodies.

As he thrust harder, Regan looked up at him, joining their souls.

He laced his fingers through hers, joining their lives.

"I love you," he told her.

Regan exploded in a powerful orgasm, her back arching, her body squeezing him, as she murmured, "I love you, too."

And for the first time ever, Felix believed in the power of love.

Chapter Sixteen

Regan rushed around her dining room, checking on the placement of the food as the caterers deposited heaping trays of seafood gumbo, jambalaya, red beans and rice, king cakes, and pralines on the massive table she had bought the week before. The band was setting up on the second-floor landing, the flowers were being arranged on various surfaces, and Jen was running around with a clipboard in her hand looking frantic.

Jumping when someone touched her back as she leaned over, Regan paused in the act of shifting the candlesticks in the center of the table to see who it was.

"Everything looks beautiful," Felix said. "You've done an amazing job."

She smiled at him over her shoulder. "Thank you." What was amazing to her was that when Felix gave her a compliment, she believed him. There was no hidden agenda, or flattery that was covering a criticism. He just meant it. Likewise, when he was angry or upset or uncomfortable, he told her. That was so new to her she had to constantly remind herself not to seek out the hidden meanings with him.

Everything was what it was.

Despite the fact that she was still sleepwalking, and anxiety about her house, the dreams, the visions, still plagued her, the past few days had been calm. Being around Felix was comfortable, easy, and the irony of that made her laugh. When she had met him she could have never imagined that he would be anything but a mystery to her, but once she had learned more about him, it was very, very easy to be together.

Turning, she let Felix pull her into his arms. One quick kiss, one short hug, then she had to get back to work. But it was so nice to just be close to him, to know that this was their house, their home.

The short kiss lengthened, and Regan felt the familiar tug of desire yanking at her.

"You look beautiful," he told her. "The proper hostess, yet so sexy."

That was another thing she believed. When he said she was sexy, she felt sexy. She was sexy. As his tongue flicked over her bottom lip in teasing, Regan felt a sly defiance creep over her. This was her house, her man.

"I'm wearing a skirt," she said, her fingers stroking down the front of his jeans, where he had the beginnings of an erection. A few pumps with her hand on his bare flesh and she knew it would be a full, hard cock, and she could have it inside her, right here, against the table.

Felix pulled back slightly and gave her a quizzical look. "Regan, we're in the dining room with caterers all over the place."

"You can just pull my panties down and no one will know." She spread her legs a little, hitching her skirt up an inch or two to show him what she was offering.

His eyes darkened, but he pulled a little back from her, as if he needed distance to resist the temptation. "I would love to, but it's not a good idea . . ."

"Don't you want me?" she said, the words shocking her a little as they came out. She had never been one to pout, yet she was, her lip jutting forward, her hands still stroking him, as if they were acting independently from her brain.

From her.

"Of course I want you," he murmured. "I always want you." His mouth turned up in that small smile she had been so attracted to from the beginning. "But you have a party to host."

Regan let go of the fabric of her skirt she'd been bunching, so that it fell back down over her thighs to her knees. "I know. Of course I do." Suddenly embarrassed, she glanced around the room to see if any of the hired staff was making note of them. "I wasn't serious."

She hadn't been.

Or had she?

She wasn't sure what exactly had just happened. It wasn't like her to flirt with voyeurism, and especially not here, not tonight, of all nights, at the party she had worked so hard planning.

But now she couldn't quite focus on the thought process, what had run through her head, how she had been feeling, just two minutes ago. "Anyway, I guess neither one of us should be standing around. We have work to do."

Felix stared at her for a second, but he didn't comment further. He just kissed her cheek and said, "Okay, I'm taking my station to wow and amaze your guests."

Regan smiled, her heart pounding a little too fast. Trying to restore her equilibrium, she reached out and squeezed his hand. "Hey, do I get a discount on your party fee now that we're living together? Especially since it will just end up in a pile on my coffee table."

She was joking, just teasing him and trying to shake the

unease she suddenly felt, but he frowned. "My money is not my own, Regan. I have a debt to pay."

Confused, she frowned. What the hell did that mean? "Felix . . ."

But he was already walking away.

She tried to ignore the anxiety that was suddenly crawling all over her, and went to find Jen to see if everything was ready.

An hour later the party was in full swing, over a hundred people mingling in the house. Mounds of food were being devoured on the first floor, the zydeco was ringing cheerfully on the second, and Felix was doing readings for a long line of curious women in the sitting room. Regan was thrilled that the crowd was enjoying themselves, that the house looked fantastic, that the energy of the event was high and festive. It was like the house itself was embracing the soiree, like it was telling Regan this was what it had been designed for, for the joy and excitement of entertaining.

Maybe that was her being fantastical, flush with the success of her event, but it seemed to her that the house was happy.

So was she, her earlier weird feelings dissipating with each compliment on her home and on Felix's charm and accuracy as a tarot reader. Watching women practically knocking each other down to get in line for a reading with Felix made her secretly smile with feminine satisfaction. They weren't just interested in the cards, they were interested in him. And he belonged to her.

Oh, yeah. She was definitely happy.

Then she turned and locked eyes with Beau, a drink in his hand, a smirk on his handsome face.

She shouldn't be surprised. It was a classic Beau tactic. Show up for the purpose of making her uncomfortable, in a venue where she couldn't call him out. But he underestimated her.

Setting down her wineglass on the coffee table, she

excused herself from the conversation she'd been having with two food critics and strolled over to him, a smile pasted on her face.

"Hello, Regan. How are you?" He bussed her cheek.

"Get the fuck out of my house," she told him in a quiet but firm voice, still smiling for the benefit of anyone who might be glancing in their direction.

His own smile froze, then he chuckled softly. "I admit, I didn't see that one coming. But maybe you should order me out of *our* house since we have both owned it now."

"Excuse me?" Regan glanced around, torn between wanting to walk away, and curiosity over his words.

"You bought this house from me. I've owned it for the last ten years."

It was bullshit. It had to be. "That's ridiculous. There were people living here when I looked at the property, a family."

"Renters in town for a movie shoot."

Regan wanted to crack that smugness right off of his face. This was her house, her dream, her future. "You hate the Quarter. And you can't afford this house."

"You shouldn't have signed the divorce papers so soon, Regan . . . a few more weeks of prodding and I have no doubt your lawyer would have uncovered the assets I've hidden." He raised his glass. "I'm almost as rich as you, my dear."

Regan didn't want to believe him, but somehow, looking into his cold brown eyes, she knew he was telling the truth. All those months he had made her feel she had to apologize for her wealth, for making him feel so inadequate, and the bastard had been hiding money from her? He'd made her feel that her major contribution to their relationship was cash, and while he appreciated that, he hated it at the same time.

She turned and walked away, having nothing to say to him, and not sure what would come out of her mouth if she opened it. She would investigate who was behind the trust that she had bought this house from, but she already knew it was Beau. He wouldn't say it if it wasn't true. He enjoyed winning far too much.

Feeling a headache springing up out of nowhere, she decided to run upstairs to her room for some ibuprofen.

Her ex-husband was not going to ruin her party, damn him.

❦

Chris swiped another glass of champagne off the passing waiter's tray as his boyfriend Nelson stood next to him fiddling with his video camera. Videography was a hobby of Nelson's, and Regan had asked for some footage of the party for the foundation's website.

"This house is insanely big," Nelson commented. "I cannot believe Regan lives here alone."

"Well, not alone anymore. Voodoo dude is here like twenty-four-seven these days. I think he's moved in, though Regan hasn't admitted that to me." Chris glanced over at the sitting room, where tall, dark, and tarot was holding court with fawning women. "I don't like him for Regan," he added. "He has a rock star quality that doesn't fit her."

"That's for her to decide, not you." Nelson pushed up his black designer glasses before raising the camera.

Chris rolled his eyes, well aware Nelson was filming him. "Whatever. I kept my mouth shut about Beau-Beau and look at how that turned out."

He saw Regan dashing up the stairs, her face pale, looking on the verge of tears. "Hey, there she is and she looks upset. Come on." Not bothering to see if Nelson was following him, Chris jogged up the stairs himself, wondering why this damn house had so many steps. He needed to work out just to be able to visit her without straining his lung capacity.

Regan was standing in the middle of her bedroom

pulling her hair out of its knot and shaking it loose, her back to them.

"Hey, everything okay—"

Chris stopped speaking when he realized Regan seemed to be unbuttoning her blouse. "Um, Re, hello, your door is open. If you spilled wine on your shirt, you should lock the door. Half those men downstairs are old and undersexed and would love a glimpse of you naked."

It was meant to be funny, but she ignored him, which was totally unlike Regan. She had either spontaneously gone deaf, or something was really, really wrong.

"What is she doing?" Nelson murmured beside him.

"I have no fucking clue." A chill shot up his spine. "Regan. Look at me."

She didn't turn, but dropped her blouse to the floor and began peeling off her skirt.

A weird, crazy idea occurred to Chris, and he acted on it before he had time to consider just how absurd it was. "Camille?" he said. "Turn around."

Regan turned and Chris about wet himself. "Ohmigod," he breathed.

"Jesus . . ." Nelson whispered.

Regan wasn't Regan. They were staring at her body, her hair, but it was not Regan's face. It had changed in a way Chris couldn't explain, the shape and structure just . . . different. The eyes were lighter, the mouth thinner, the expression much more sly than Regan's ever would be. It was like what had happened when they'd been at lunch, only sharper. There was no mistaking this. It wasn't a trick of the light, or his imagination, or a tilt of her head skewing the way she looked.

This wasn't Regan's face.

"Lift your fucking camera and record this," he told Nelson, swallowing the golf-ball-size lump in his throat. Trying to force images from *The Exorcist* out of his head, Chris moved forward slowly. "Camille, what do you want?"

"I want him out of my house," she said, her voice Regan's, yet altered. Angry, petulant, manic.

All the hairs on Chris's arms spiked straight up, and he had to pause to grow another set of balls before continuing forward. "Who?"

"That awful Mr. Tradd. I threw dirt at his door to keep him away and yet he's here."

He had no clue who Mr. Tradd was, but he didn't think it was a hot idea to piss off the possessor. "Okay, we can get rid of Mr. Tradd, no problemo. Consider him gone."

Her head tilted and she frowned. "What?"

"Stop using slang," Nelson whispered behind him.

Shit, of course. "I'll have Mr. Tradd escorted out immediately," Chris said, channeling his inner butler. "Is there anything else you want?"

She nodded vigorously. "I want to *die*."

It was such a plaintive plea, so heartfelt, and anguished, that had she not been squatting in the body of his best friend, Chris would have felt sympathy for her.

"I want to be with them. I don't want him to own me anymore."

What the hell was he supposed to say to that? He didn't want to make Camille angry, and while he wanted to encourage her to leave, he didn't want that to somehow harm Regan. So he just said, "Okay."

"Okay?" Nelson exclaimed to him in a whisper from behind the video camera. "That's the best you can come up with?"

Chris shrugged at him. "I panicked!"

Regan crumpled over, face in her hands. When she stood upright again, it was her face, her expression of confusion, her frown. "Chris?" She looked down at herself. "Why am I standing in my bra and panties?" She glanced over to Nelson. "Nelson! Why are you filming me in my bra and panties?"

"You don't remember what just happened?"

"No." She shook her head. "Was I sleepwalking? Awake?"

The fear on her face had Chris closing the distance between them and handing her his glass of champagne. "Here, drink this. You're going to be fine. Nelson, would you mind running down and grabbing Felix?"

Maybe mojo man could explain to them why Regan's face had melted like plastic into someone else's.

"And bring more booze up with you," he added.

He had a feeling they were going to need it.

Chapter Seventeen

❦

"How long have I been up here?" Regan asked, after draining Chris's glass and handing it back to him.

She stepped back into her skirt and zipped it. "I should get back downstairs." She felt disoriented, but it seemed really, really important to not abandon her guests, especially when the alternative was to actually think about and process what had just happened.

"It's only been a few minutes," Chris said. "The food and the alcohol are flowing so no one is going to miss you for another five. Besides, Jen is down there."

"I had a headache," she told him, retrieving her blouse from the floor and slipping it on. "Beau showed up and I had a run-in with him."

Just stick to the facts. Regan felt weak and shaky and, frankly, frightened. But if she ignored the fact that she seemed now to have taken up sleepwalking while awake, maybe it would go away. It was a futile hope, she knew. The unnerving episodes had been escalating, but what was she supposed to do about it?

"Regan. Something totally weird just happened. We need to talk about it."

Desperate, she tried to button her shirt, irritated that her fingers were trembling. "I don't want to talk about it!"

Damn it, she couldn't get the button into the hole and she was going to cry. "Beau said he owned this house before me, Chris. What if it's true? What if the house I love, my dream house, was owned by my asshole of an ex-husband?"

"Alcroft owned this house?" Felix asked in a shocked voice as he entered the bedroom, Nelson trailing behind him. "Jesus, that explains a lot."

"It does?" Chris said. "It only confuses me. Beau doesn't have the money to buy a place like this, and if he did, why was it a secret, and how in the hell is it possible that out of all the properties for sale, Regan would buy the very one he owns?"

Felix moved toward her and took over the task of securing the buttons she had abandoned. His presence was reassuring, his words were not. "This house wanted you, Regan. That's why you loved it, felt compelled to buy it."

A chill swept over her. "What is that supposed to mean? How could a house want me?"

"Camille's spirit. She wanted a voice, and it seems she's found one through you. Sit down, *cherie*, and let's watch the video Nelson has."

His voice was so gentle Regan was even more alarmed. Something crazy was on that tape. Otherwise Felix wouldn't look like he was prepared to calm her forthcoming hysterics.

"Did it actually record?" Chris asked.

Nelson nodded. "I showed Felix already."

Regan sank onto the edge of her bed, digging her nails into the flesh of her exposed knees. Something was wrong with her. She had known it since the minute she'd moved into the house. The dreams, the visions, the sleepwalking . . . it wasn't normal. If it was a haunting, which she preferred to think it was as opposed to it being her increasing insanity, it seemed more invasive than the stories she had read about and seen on TV documentaries.

Felix sat on one side of her, Nelson the other, the camera in front of them. Chris climbed onto the bed behind her, viewing over her shoulder.

Nelson hit PLAY and there was Chris on the screen, rolling his eyes and making a snarky remark about Beau. Then it cut to her bedroom, to her standing there staring at someone just slightly to Nelson's left, Chris presumably.

Only it wasn't her.

Regan made a strangled noise and leaned closer, touching the screen. That wasn't her face, even though it was her hair, her body, her bra and panties. Something was . . . off. "Can you make this bigger?"

Nelson fiddled with the camera and suddenly the screen zoomed in on Regan, framing her face. Or what should have been her face. The eyes were rounder, the face more heart-shaped, the nose shorter, the very color of her complexion a richer tone, that of a blonde, not the pink pale ivory of Regan's brunette skin tone. It was the most profoundly disturbing thing she'd ever seen, and the icy prickles of fear crawled up her back.

"Oh, my God . . . I don't understand. How could that happen? What is it?"

It wasn't even like her own face was distorted, like a funhouse mirror. This wasn't her. It was as if someone else was inside her body and pushing their face through hers . . . She dug her nails deeper into her flesh, wanting to feel pain, to reassure herself she was real, awake.

Nelson zoomed back out so that Chris moved into view on the screen, blocking Regan until Nelson had shifted the camera to encompass both of them again. "Camille, what do you want?" Chris asked on the video.

Regan shivered, wanting to look back at Chris, ask him why he had thought to use Camille's name, but not wanting to take her eyes off the recording. Chris squeezed her shoulders from behind as he leaned forward to see the camera better.

"I want him out of my house," was the answer to Chris's question, the plea coming from what should have been Regan's mouth, but wasn't. The lips were thinner, the voice hers, yet higher. The words were angry, yet not command-ing. There was a desperate quality to them.

"Who?"

"That awful Mr. Tradd. I threw dirt at his door to keep him away and yet he's here."

Mr. Tradd . . . The journal entry. The dream. He was the dreaded fiancé Camille wanted to be rid of. But what was real and what was the workings of Regan's overwrought imagination? "Oh, my God," Regan breathed. "Is that really her, or is that me?"

It couldn't be her. It wasn't her. That just wasn't her face. Even if she was sleepwalking, even if she was the one over-embellishing the journal entries in her dreams, she couldn't produce *that* effect strictly from imagination.

Someone was inside her, in possession of her body, her voice.

Felix's hand enclosed hers, though she barely noticed. She couldn't stop staring at the video, at the horrific image of herself with another human being layered over her like Saran wrap.

And she had no memory of it.

"Okay, we can get rid of Mr. Tradd, no problemo. Con-sider him gone."

Her head tilted on the tape and she frowned. "What?"

"Stop using slang," Nelson whispered, not visible but his voice clearly audible since he was so close to the camera.

Chris looked back at the camera with an apologetic shrug, before turning to her, Camille, whoever the hell she was.

"I'll have Mr. Tradd escorted out immediately," he said. "Is there anything else you want?"

Camille nodded, making Regan's hair shake forward onto her cheeks. "I want to die."

Regan grabbed her throat, suddenly feeling like she couldn't breathe. She made a gasping sound, well aware she was having a panic attack, but unable to stop it. *I want to die* . . . It echoed in her head, a horrible, agonized cry of a woman in severe emotional pain. Inside Regan.

Felix murmured, "You're okay, it's okay." He shoved her head down between her legs and said, "Take a deep breath. Just open your throat and relax."

Feeling the sting as her nails finally broke the skin on her knees, Regan closed her eyes and tried to relax, tried to drag in air. Spots danced behind her eyelids and hot saliva filled her mouth. She was going to pass out.

But if she did, would Camille take her over again? Would she, Regan, ever get back?

Oh, my God. Hysteria swept over her, and she fought for air, forcing her eyes open, pulling a breath into her lungs. She gasped and coughed, the blackness receding, her chest heaving as she sucked fresh oxygen in and out, throwing herself back up into a sitting position, wanting control.

"Okay, that's good." Felix massaged her back. "You're okay."

Not really. She wasn't even close to being okay, but she was going to stay conscious if she had to slap herself alert. There was no way she was going to just let someone— something—take her over without a protest.

"Rewind it," she asked. "I want to see what I just missed."

"I want to die," played again, and this time Regan narrowed her eyes and drove back the panic. She studied the face on the screen.

"I want to be with them. I don't want him to own me anymore." The first part made sense to Regan. Camille wanted to be with her deceased family. The latter was more confusing. Was "him" Mr. Tradd? And why did Camille feel like he owned her?

"Okay," Chris said.

"Okay?" That was Nelson from behind the camera. "That's the best you can come up with?"

Chris made a face. "I panicked!"

From behind Regan now on the bed, Chris added, "I didn't think it was wise to piss off whatever was in your face, literally."

"Thanks." She patted his hand on her shoulder as they watched her image on the tape grab her head, double over, then stand back up, her face normal, mired in confusion.

"How long do you think that lasted?" she asked, feeling like the only way to process this, to stay sane, was to ask questions, apply some kind of logic to something that was illogical.

"What, like two minutes, tops? There's a timer on the tape, we can figure it out," Nelson said.

"How is she doing this?" Regan asked Felix. "How is she getting inside me? That is what's she's doing, right?"

"It certainly seems that way. I don't know." He shook his head, frowning. "Something is a conduit. This house, the journal . . . I don't know." He turned to Nelson and Chris. "Would you guys give us a minute? I'd like to talk to Regan for a second in private."

"Sure," Nelson said, standing up.

Chris looked to Regan. "Is that okay with you? Are you okay?"

"Yes, I'm fine. Well, as fine as I can be." She gave him a small smile. "Please make sure everything downstairs is going smoothly, and if you see Beau—"

"Throw him out? Throw a drink in his face?" Chris asked eagerly.

That actually came close to making Regan laugh. She couldn't quite manage it yet, but it was important to recognize that even though it felt like everything was shifting and changing around her, some things were static. Like Chris's hatred of Beau, and his sense of humor.

"No. I was going to say if you see Beau, don't start anything with him. Just ignore him."

"Damn."

"Chris." Regan grabbed his wrist as he started to leave. "Thanks."

His face softened. "For what?"

"For not running away like I'm a crazy person. You too, Nelson."

"No problem. And this," Nelson patted his camera, "will be under lock and key. We aren't going to tell or show anyone."

"Thanks," she said.

Felix seconded the sentiment. "And thanks for getting me. Regan is lucky to have friends like you."

Regan knew Chris had been suspicious of Felix's intentions toward her, but he thawed a little at the flattery. "Yeah, you, too," he said begrudgingly.

They walked out and Regan watched them go, unsure what to say to Felix, or where to start. Her emotions were shredded, her thoughts jumbled.

But Felix spoke first. "There's something I need to tell you."

That was never a good start to a conversation. Regan stared at him. "Yes?"

"You know how I said that maybe the house or the journal is a conduit for Camille to enter this world from the spirit world?"

She nodded.

"Well, maybe it's not the house or the journal. Maybe it's Alcroft. Or maybe it's me."

Regan stared at him blankly. "Why would either of you be a conduit for the spirit of a woman who died a hundred and thirty years ago?"

Felix stared at her steadily, his hand twitching on hers. "Because Alcroft and I both knew Camille."

And with those words, he shattered the last of her calm.

"What? That's ridiculous! How could either one of you have known Camille?" Camille was dead long before Felix had been born.

"Because I'm immortal."

Regan fought the urge to throw up, her heart hardening at the realization that the man she loved was lying to her in an insulting and bizarre way when she most needed him to be rational with her.

✥

Felix took a deep breath and thought carefully before he spoke again. Regan was breathing hard, her expression incredulous. He knew he had to tell her the truth—the whole truth—so that they could protect her from whatever it was Camille was trying to do. He also wanted no secrets between them, not about something so important as his whole existence, his history, his punishment, his future, because Felix wanted a real relationship with Regan for as long as it was possible. But there was no easy way to tell someone you were immortal, a product of Hell, and blurting it out had obviously been a mistake.

"What you are about to hear is going to sound fantastical, but it is the truth. Remember that I love you, and I want to be with you, and that I'm telling you for that very reason and because I want you safe, okay?"

She didn't answer, just stared at him with wild eyes.

Felix forged ahead. "I was born in 1851, the illegitimate child of a free quadroon woman named Louisa Leblanc, and her French Creole lover Jean-Paul Arminault. I was named Felix after my father's father, a triumph of my mother over Jean-Paul's wealthy wife. She gave Jean-Paul a son first, and while an illegitimate first son didn't merit my father's last name, I did receive his father's Christian name."

Regan said nothing, but she had shifted slightly away from him on the edge of the bed, her face devoid of color and emotion except for two bright spots of pink on each cheek.

"I had a pleasant childhood," he said, determined to spit it all out before she bolted from the room. "My parents loved each other, we had a house, money. I was apprenticed to a banker since I could pass for white and because my father had friends in high places. I had a love of fine things, and a burgeoning resentment of the doors that were shut to me because of the circumstances of my birth. I was materialistic, petulant. When my father died, we found ourselves without a home, and I lost my job. My mother saw her only recourse as serving herself up on a platter to whichever wealthy man would take her as his mistress. At her age, with a grown child, and no one to protect her, only the deviant or the infirm or the abusive were going to want her, and I knew this, yet was powerless to stop it."

Felix still felt the shame and anger of that night, the horror of knowing he was a man finally, yet he could not take care of his own mother the way she had cared for him. That he had to stand there and let her be used and tossed aside by cold and uncaring men. It had been a bitter tonic on his tongue that night and it still was. "I hated myself for not being able to fix it. I hated that the ache of hunger in my belly was distracting and all-consuming and that I thought of it even more often than I thought of my mother, who was subjecting herself to the rejection and ridicule of men with too much money and too little compassion. So when a man approached me with warm bread and the promise of talent and charm that would guarantee my personal wealth, how could I say no?"

Rubbing the ring on his finger, back and forth, back and forth, Felix smiled at his own stupidity. "They say if something is too good to be true, it usually is. So I was given charm, elocution, access to rich, bored ladies who would pay most handsomely for my voodoo spells and potions, and simply for the privilege and titillation of doing something 'beyond the pale.' I had enough money to buy a beautiful house, to furnish it well, to set my mother up for life, to dress to the nines, and drink the finest wines. But what I didn't realize was that by accepting that piece of bread and that man's offer of all the advantages of immortality, of a life without death, that I was sentencing myself to an eternity of servitude to a man cast out of Heaven and residing in the very bowels of Hell."

Regan still wasn't speaking and it was starting to unnerve Felix. He'd expected that she would either interject a comment or protest or just run out of the room.

"A demon. You know, a fallen angel," he added. "That is what Alcroft is, and I am bound to him, demon servant to demon master, until the world ends." He held his ring up to show her. "Bound by my own greed."

Felix paused, wanting a reaction of any kind.

After a second, Regan gave him one. "You know, when most people feel guilty for past behaviors, they have a few sleepless nights and vow to do better in the future. I think you're the first man I've encountered who has attributed his flaws to a demon. I can see why you're such a good tarot reader. You spin quite a story."

Felix gritted his teeth. "It's not a story. I know it sounds insane, but it's the truth."

"There is no such thing as immortality, and I love how you cast my ex-husband as the villain in your tale." Regan scoffed. "Here I was wondering about my sanity. Yours is nonexistent and I want you to pack your bags and leave."

"Wait a minute." Felix tried to fight his irritation, but a sharpness crept into his voice. "You can believe what you just saw on that videotape—you can accept that a dead woman can come back after a hundred years and enter your body—but you can't believe that demons exist or that immortality is a possibility?"

"That's crazy, yes, but I saw it, I've felt it. And a ghost is, I don't know . . . normal. A spirit that can open a door is a hell of a lot different than you telling me you're sitting here in the flesh, living and eating and breathing like anyone else and yet you'll never die? That's nuts."

Felix jumped up off the bed. "Do you want me to prove it? Is that what you need? Physical proof? I can slice myself open if you'd like and you can watch me heal."

He wished he had the demon ability to let people into his mind, or the ability to levitate. Something, anything, that would prove to the woman he loved he wasn't a complete lunatic.

"If you slice yourself in front of me I'm calling the cops."

Damn. That would not be good. "Wait. I have a picture," he said, frantically patting his back pocket for his wallet. "It's me and my mother. I laminated it a few years ago and I carry it with me. My father had it taken for my eighteenth birthday."

Pulling the picture out, he held it in front of Regan.

She took it reluctantly and eyed it. The spots of color disappeared on her cheeks and her lips pursed. Setting the picture carefully down on her lap, avoiding the dried blood on her knee from where her nails had dug in while watching the video, she swallowed hard. "This could be fake. Photoshop. Or it could be your great-grandfather or something."

Felix sighed. She wasn't going to believe him. "Don't you want to hear the rest of the story?"

"What I really want is for you to leave. If you feel you need to tell me the rest of the story before you go, I won't object."

Ouch. He hated that tone in her voice, that cold, distant look on her face. It wasn't what he had ever received from

Regan, and he couldn't believe that after finding what he had craved so desperately, a woman who would love him, truly love him, he was going to lose her.

"Thank you," he said, falling into the formality she had imposed on the conversation. "I've never told anyone the truth of who and what I am before. I realize it's difficult to accept. But it is the truth."

Pacing back and forth so he wouldn't have to see that stone-cold look on her face, he said, "So the greedy young Felix got everything he wanted. The money, the house, the ability to care for my mother until the day she died, and the adoration of women. If it meant I had to give a portion of my riches to Alcroft as a kickback, it didn't matter. And I could ignore the feeling of being owned . . . it was a loose ball and chain and I was heady with the power, the attention, the money. Until I met Camille."

He took a deep breath, still not daring to look at Regan. "I knew that Alcroft, who was known as Mr. Tradd in those days, was interested in Camille. He spoke about her possessively, confident she would be his wife. But after her family died, Camille had no interest in him. She was only interested in voodoo and me. Really what she wanted in me was a partner, someone who wouldn't say no to the improper things she wanted to do, someone who would encourage her interest in making contact with the dead.

"We were a frighteningly perfect fit, both selfish, both greedy, both insolent and bratty. I almost never told her no, despite how outrageous her requests were, and she relished that. In return, she provided me with stacks and stacks of money, and a companion to straddle the societal fence with. It was a lonely position to be in, caught between two worlds, and Camille's behavior had shoved her outside of proper circles as well. I suppose, in an odd sort of way, you could have called us friends. I never meant for her to die that night. It was an accident. She fell off the balcony . . .

she thought she saw her mother and she reached for her, and before I could even react, she was on the ground."

Felix stopped talking, the pain of failure, of loss, suddenly overwhelming. He wasn't explaining this right. It sounded absurd, and Regan clearly didn't believe one word of what he was saying. She was just staring at him, tight-lipped. Humoring him until she could get him to leave. Hell, she was probably frightened of him, wondering if she should call for help to escort the crazy man out of her bedroom.

God, it hurt. This was by far the worst punishment he had ever received. To have tasted happiness, genuine love, so briefly, then to have to it taken away, it was torture. Worse than the hanging darkness he had suffered through after Camille's death.

That had been maddening.

But this was heartbreaking.

This reached deep inside and shattered him, stripping him of his hope, his future, his dignity, his last remaining sense of purpose in a pointless life.

He hardened himself against the hurt. What had he expected, right? A happily ever after?

There was none for him, and he knew that. Might as well walk away before he sunk to the floor and begged her to understand.

He still had too much pride to do that.

And maybe Regan was his final lesson. Wasn't the ultimate greed wanting another person? He had certainly wanted Regan as his, only his, day in, day out, for the rest of her life.

Possession of another person was the basest of sins.

"I'll just let myself out," he said, when the silence drew on. "Here's your key back." He fished around in his pocket and retrieved it. Setting it down on the chest of drawers that had stayed the one constant in this house for a century,

Felix balled his fist and hit the marble top with a sound of frustration.

Turning to leave, he made the mistake of taking one last look at Regan.

That cold, emotionless face made him sick.

"Where did you get your ring?" she asked him as he moved past her.

"Excuse me?" Felix stopped, confused.

"The ring you always wear. The silver one. What does it mean to you?"

There was no reason not to tell her the truth. "It's my binding ring. It holds me to Alcroft. It has the same inscription your ring had. *Ego own vos*. I own you."

"Why don't you just take it off?" she asked. "You even wear it in the shower."

"It doesn't come off." Felix held out his hand and showed her by tugging on it. It didn't budge a millimeter.

She frowned and reached out with her delicate, long fingers and touched his ring. Then she pulled.

And it came off.

Just like that.

After an astonished second to process what the hell he was looking at, Felix ran his other hand over his bare finger and laughed. Horrible irony. That all it took was someone else sliding it off him? All this time and it was that simple. He couldn't quite believe it.

Regan looked inside the ring and frowned when she saw the inscription. Then she merely handed him his ring back without saying a word.

"I never had a chance," Felix murmured, his heart shredding at he watched Regan shut down emotionally, close him out, withdraw inside herself. "Greed always makes you reach for what can't be yours . . . and I knew you were too good for me. I knew you could never be mine, yet I wanted you anyway. It seems I haven't learned a damn thing in all this time—over a hundred years and I still let greed rule me."

Her mouth opened as if she were going to speak, but then she closed it, her head shaking slightly from left to right as she remained stoically silent.

"Just say something, please. I'm begging you, Regan."

Eyes filling with tears, she said, "How could you do this to me? How could you?"

Her voice was so filled with agony and hurt that Felix felt like he'd been slapped, and he wished he could take back his plea for her to speak.

That expression, those words of anguish, felt like they could kill the man that couldn't be killed.

So Felix walked out of the house he should never have entered and away from the woman he should never have dared to love.

Chapter Eighteen

Regan stared into space from her chair on Chris and Nelson's patio. Nelson was an amateur gardener and he had the courtyard in full bloom, lush reds and oranges popping all around Regan, but she didn't notice.

Her coffee was cold, but she didn't care.

She needed a shower, but she didn't have the energy to take one.

Chris lit a cigarette in the chair across from her, and while she normally wrinkled her nose at the pungent tendrils of smoke crossing in front of her, she didn't even blink.

"Regan." Chris leaned forward in his chair. "This is getting fucking ridiculous. You're like the dawn of the dirty-hair dead. You know you're welcome to stay here as long as you like, but you need to talk to me. This silence is freaking me out and it's not healthy for you."

She stared at him, impassive, trying to work up the energy to respond. Everything was so much effort, so much work. She knew she was in some kind of sleep-deprived depression because it just wasn't normal to feel like it was almost too much work to breathe. Getting dressed ruined her for the day, and chewing her food seemed more trouble than it was worth.

"I can't talk about it." Regan was afraid that once she started to talk, she would start to think, and once she started to think, she would start to feel.

And that was not something she wanted to do.

It had been three weeks since she had seen her distorted face on that video, since Felix had made up the most outrageous story she'd ever heard in her life, and she had learned that loving him had been yet another mistake. That like Beau, she had never really known Felix Leblanc.

She didn't want to think about that. She didn't want to think about the fact that his ring had the same inscription her wedding ring had, or that he knew things, things about Camille that he shouldn't since he had never read her journal.

Her lawyer had confirmed that Beau had in fact owned her house and that he had upward of twenty million in liquid assets in addition to almost fifty million in properties. Regan had ignored Richard's voice mail and subsequent calls.

It didn't matter.

Nothing mattered.

After her debacle of a house party, she had taken a suitcase full of clothes, Camille's journal, and had left her house and its many questions behind. She had been staying with Chris and Nelson, working and doing nothing else, including sleeping. That eluded her completely. This week she'd finally given in to the fact that she was not functioning and had taken two weeks off from work. She wasn't sure what would be better in two weeks, but she couldn't do her job the way she was.

"You're not even going to tell me what went down with Felix?"

"No." How did you explain to your best friend that your judgment was so poor you let a man move in with you who was either delusional or a liar? Or that a small, strange part of you actually believed him? That you thought maybe, just maybe, he could be telling the truth, no matter how bizarre it was.

"And you won't talk about the video." It was a statement, not a question, because Chris knew her answer to that.

"Nope."

"Will you eat something? I swear to God you've lost ten pounds and a cup size."

"Isn't thin in?" she asked, feeling a sudden urge to take a hit off of Chris's cigarette. But she already had enough problems, she didn't need to create a nicotine addiction at the same time.

"Thin is always in. But unhealthy isn't. Your hair is dull, your clothes are hanging on you, and the skin under your eyes looks like you've been beaten black-and-blue and you're recovering. You look bruised and miserable."

At least he was being delicate about it. "I am bruised and miserable!" Regan said in a louder voice than she would have thought she'd have the energy to use. "I feel like I have been beaten black-and-blue. Crazy things happened in my house. The dreams, the sleepwalking, the dangling off the balcony, the face oozing out of my face . . . something got inside me, damn it, and it's crazy and I don't know what to do!"

"Well, you can keep ignoring it, because that's clearly working for you," Chris said sarcastically, before taking another drag on his cigarette. "Or you can deal with it. Kick this bitch out of your house."

"And how exactly am I supposed to do that?" she asked in frustration. "I would love to have my life back to normal. I would love to be able to live in the house I paid a boatload of money for."

"Felix would know."

"Fuck Felix."

Chris's eyebrows shot up. "Okay, then. Apparently whatever happened in that thirty minutes you were alone with him was not good."

"No, it was not good." It was crazy. Crazy. All of it just . . . crazy.

"So how about another voodoo practitioner? Or a priest? Or maybe you can just talk to Camille, and tell her it's all good. That it's time for her to pass on to the other side or whatever they say in that movie *Poltergeist*. Tell her to go toward the light."

Regan knew Chris was just trying to help, that he was worried about her. She was worried about herself, too. But his well-meaning suggestions were just irritating her.

"I'm going for a walk. I'll be back in a few minutes." Then because she felt bad, she kissed Chris on the top of the head when she stood up. "Thank you, for everything."

"Do you want company?" he asked, though he looked perfectly comfortable lazing back in his chair.

"No, I'm fine." Regan walked through the well-decorated but cluttered house and out the front door. There was something claustrophobic to her about all the knickknacks and excess furniture Chris and Nelson collected, so different from her own style of decorating.

Or maybe it was her own thoughts that were claustrophic. Those weren't so easily edited and streamlined as a living room.

She was cutting down the walkway to the sidewalk when she spotted Beau stepping out of a parked car on the street. Damn it. She started to veer in the opposite direction, knowing he had no reason to be in the neighborhood except to see her, and hoping he wouldn't notice her making an escape.

"Regan."

No such luck. Of course he would spot her.

She turned and gave him a tight smile. "Hi. What are you doing here?"

"I heard you were staying with Chris and I wanted to talk to you."

Just what she didn't need, more futile conversation with a man she was definitely growing to despise. "I don't think we have anything to talk about." She kept walking.

Beau fell in step beside her. "I thought maybe we could talk about Camille."

Regan paused and looked at him, the hairs on the back of her neck rising. "What could you know about Camille?"

He smiled at her, and it was an expression she'd never seen on his face before. Sly, and almost menacing. She shivered, wrapping her arms around her.

"Oh, I knew Camille personally, Regan. Before Felix did. When I was known as Alcroft Tradd."

Regan's knees buckled and she fought the urge to gasp out loud, to cover her ears to shut out his words. Was everyone intent on making her doubt her sanity? How could Beau be confirming Felix's ludicrous story? "What are you talking about?"

"You look a little shocked, and at the risk of sounding rude, not the best I've ever seen you. Your hair . . ." He made a moue of distaste. "Anyway, do you want to sit down in my car and talk about this?"

He was standing next to her, casual, smirking, hands in the pockets of his expensive khaki pants, his Italian shoes shined to a high gloss. The thought of being confined with him in his car made her nervous. Like somehow she would be more vulnerable than she was standing here in the sunshine a few steps from Chris's house. Out in the open she felt like she could escape. Both him and his words.

An illusion of safety, but one she couldn't sacrifice nonetheless.

"No, let's just walk." She needed to move so she didn't drop to the ground.

"You don't believe me, do you?"

"That you've been alive for over a hundred years? It is

a little far-fetched, you have to admit." Though what was so hard to wrap her head around was why Beau and Felix would feed her the same story. A mass delusion between two men who she had thought didn't know each other seemed equally as bizarre.

Or maybe they did know each other and they were playing some kind of game with her.

Which really chilled her.

She was walking, forcing one foot in front of the other, her skirt wrapping around knees that still bore the marks of her nails breaking the skin the night she'd been watching the video. She had never been a fast healer. Ironic.

"I'm older than that," Beau said, his voice arrogant and amused. "I'm actually almost as old as time, Regan. Almost as old as God."

Regan stopped walking, glad she hadn't gotten into his car. That was it, she was going back to Chris's. She didn't need to be mocked, and she didn't need to listen to this lunacy. She turned, but Beau stopped her by grabbing her hand.

His fingers wrapped around hers and she tried to tug them away, heart racing, but his grip was too strong. The lush street before her with its pretty cottages receded, and in its place was a dirt path, dust rising up in front of her. Terrified, Regan stopped trying to extract herself from Beau's grip and actually held his hand tighter, needing to know she was still standing, still there, still alive as the world literally shifted in front of her. Beau was solid next to her, and she leaned in closer to him, feeling that even the ground beneath her feet was suddenly unstable.

She blinked hard, frightened, but reality wasn't restored. The dirt road solidified.

"What . . . ?" Regan shrieked when a wooden cart went flying past them on the left, the man driving it wearing a toga, fully three-dimensional and close enough to touch. "Oh, my God."

"It's Rome," Beau told her in a low voice. "See the Colosseum?"

It rose up in front of her between the clouds of dust, a great hulking structure, throngs of people around it, all dressed in ancient robes. Regan stared in astonishment, afraid to move, afraid to speak. It wasn't a picture. It was real.

"We're seeing it through my eyes, the way it felt for me to be standing there," he murmured. "It was a fascinating culture and an exciting city, but I'm just being self-indulgent. I wanted to see it again. Let's move on to late-nineteenth-century New Orleans, which is what really interests us at the moment." Beau raised his hand, with hers still in its grip, and made a waving motion.

The scene in front of her crumpled, the buildings and people that looked so real just disintegrating in a cloud of dust. In its place, brick by brick, in a matter of seconds, the French Quarter rose up in front of her. The gaslights twinkled, the horse-drawn carriages clipped along, and the people strolled in the early evening dressed in nineteenth-century attire, the ladies colorful birds in their hats with feathers, their lush gowns richly detailed with black and ivory lace and trim.

It was so real she could smell the manure in the street, feel the humid heat of a summer evening, hear the murmur of conversation around her. Regan reached her hand out like she could touch a painting, like it would be a flat scene in front of her, but it was just air. The scene was real. Or so it seemed.

"Look, there's Camille."

Regan saw her, the blonde in an elegant hat, the same woman Regan had seen in her bathroom doorway, descending from her carriage in a white gown trimmed in black, her expression haughty and defiant as she let the footman help her down to the street. She looked in their direction, right at them, and sniffed in disapproval.

"She was to be mine," Beau said in a low voice. "My wife. The one I wanted more than all the others that came before and all the women since. But she considered herself too good for me, too exciting, too daring for the likes of me. If only she had understood that nothing is more exciting than a demon. I could have given her whatever she wanted, real or imagined."

Beau made a sound of anger and the scene in front of them disappeared like the one before, and they were back standing on Chris's quiet residential block.

"How . . . ?" Regan swallowed, afraid that she really was going to faint this time. It wasn't possible, what she had just seen, what Beau was claiming to be real. But it was. It was the truth, she knew it beyond a shadow of a doubt. What had just happened was not normal and Beau was something she didn't understand. "What are you . . . ?"

Despite the fact that he still held her hand, she backed up a step, wanting distance from him, from the malice reflected in his eyes.

"I told you, I'm a demon. A fallen angel." Beau smiled. "I would bow, but frankly I'm lazy. Another one of my so-called flaws. Greed is my specialty, my true sin, and the one I will never apologize for. I wanted Camille from the moment I laid eyes on her. It really, really irritated me that Felix got to her first. Here he was my servant, my creation, and *he* was what she wanted. Very irritating. And I've been waiting for an opportunity to right how I was wronged, and I found it in you."

"Excuse me?" Regan glanced at him, trying to retrieve her hand again. He didn't look like Beau as she knew him. His eyes were different. They were a strange amber gold color, and maybe it was just the sun, but she could swear they were glowing.

"The first time we went out to dinner, we walked past the house on Royal, and you expressed a fascinated interest in it. You also had an unusually high interest in death and the possibility of ghosts because of your sister and your job, and you were very malleable, very eager to please. For those three reasons, you were the perfect woman for me to marry, the perfect vessel to bring Camille's spirit into, so she and I could finally be together."

Regan tugged harder on her hand, panicking, but he wouldn't let her go. "You never wanted me, did you?" She had known, the minute she had married him, that something was fundamentally wrong. It had been a gut reaction, an instinct, a feeling of entrapment, and the desperate need to get out almost immediately. But she'd had no idea why . . . what he was. No idea such things even existed, let alone that she had married one.

A demon.

And he had set her up, like a pawn on a chessboard.

She fought the urge to scream for help, knowing it would do no good to draw attention to them and anger Beau. No one could help her.

"I was going to give you the house as a Christmas gift. We would move in together, I would unleash Camille, let her take your body, and we would live happily ever after." He shrugged. "At least until your body got old. Then I'd have to start again. But you screwed my plans up royally by leaving me and getting involved with Felix, who has been more thorn in my side than he is worth. You did buy the house, which worked in my favor, and it definitely appears Camille has been accessing you, so I think maybe we've reached a state of compromise."

"How is that?" she managed to say even though she was certain there was no spit left in her mouth.

"We reconcile and I move in with you. I keep Camille at bay sometimes, allowing you to still be you for the most part, and when I want a little excitement or to have sex, you let her in. It's really the perfect scenario for all of us."

Horrified, Regan managed to finally yank her hand out of his. "That is utterly disgusting!"

He rolled his eyes. "Which is why I don't want to have sex with you. Such a prude."

"I'm not a prude," she said, infuriated. In the short time they'd been together Beau had made her doubt her sexuality, her attractiveness, her entire self, and she would be damned if she would let him continue to insult her. "I just didn't like sex with you. It wasn't satisfying for me."

When his eyes flashed amber gold again, she realized it might not be wise to tick off a demon.

"Oh, and Felix can satisfy you? Is that what you're telling me?"

Regan looked behind her. She was only one house down from Chris's. She was terrified, but at the same time she was so tired of being polite, of being afraid that she would hurt someone's feelings if she spoke the truth, so exhausted from trying to keep the boat from never rocking. If there was anything she had learned through this divorce and her relationship with Felix, it was that she was entitled to be honest. To say and to do and to be whatever she wanted to.

So wise or not, she opened her mouth and told Beau, "Yes. Felix and I had a fantastic sex life. And I think maybe what you need to factor in is that it was never going to be good between us when neither one of us really wanted to be with the other one. You wanted Camille and I was with you under coercion, though I didn't know it. How can there be any passion in that kind of arrangement?"

His eyebrow shot up. "You know, I hate to admit it, but you're probably right."

Encouraged by his agreement, she continued. "Think about it . . . you really wanted Camille, and I was with you because you were clearly exerting an influence over me. My free will was battling with it, just leaving me discontent and reserved. We should have never gotten married."

"Maybe not the way we did. But now that you know the truth, you will agree to reconcile with me."

The one moment where she thought he had actually understood her point of view and might be rational disappeared. She wasn't surprised. It was too easy to think that she could just walk away. "Why would I do that? There's nothing in that scenario for me. You of all people should understand I'd want something for myself."

Beau wasn't looking at her, but across the yard, his expression distracted. "Hey, how long has it been since you've seen Felix?"

"I haven't seen him since the night of my party. Why?"

He nodded. "You broke up? What a horrible shame. Well, don't expect to go running to him now. He's kind of tied up these days."

Something about the way Beau said that triggered fear in Regan. "What do you mean?" she asked in a tight voice. He wasn't making a casual statement, she was sure of it. He knew something, and it wasn't good.

"Just that when you disobey, you're punished. It's very simple. So I wouldn't plan on seeing Felix for a while."

It flashed in front of her, so brief she almost missed it. Felix, hanging in darkness, his face etched with pain, blood and sweat trickling down his bare chest.

She gasped. "Oh, my God, what is going on? Where is he?"

"Prison. One of his own making." Beau pulled his car keys out of his pocket and tossed them into the air. As they lifted, they morphed into a ring. He held it out to show her. "Your wedding ring. I look forward to putting it back on your finger."

Regan stared at the platinum band, jaw gaping open as the diamond flashed in the sunlight. That ring was back at the house on Royal Street. At least she thought it was. She didn't remember where she had put it, exactly, that day that Felix had come home to find her wearing it. She remembered the heavy unpleasantness of it on her finger, yet also the way it had called to her, beckoned. She must have thrown it back in her drawer after Felix had yanked it off of her, freeing her. And yet she was staring at it in Beau's hand. She reached forward to touch it, to convince herself it was real.

But then she saw the satisfaction on Beau's face and she snatched her hand back.

He thought he had won.

But he hadn't.

The ring was gone as suddenly as it had appeared. Just an ordinary key chain again, holding his car key.

"Just think about it," he told her. "It's best for everyone, really."

Beau kissed the top of her head, his lips warm and hard against her skin, and Regan stumbled backward, not bothering to answer. Whirling around, she turned and ran back to Chris's house, exerting more energy and speed than she had in weeks as she ate up the distance. Within a minute she was pounding up the steps of the front porch and slamming the door shut behind her.

"Chris! I need a ride to Felix's!"

❦

The pain was different this time. Instead of being random, a lightning strike of torment he could never anticipate, this time the pain was constant. An endless, ever present barrage of agony, from the roots of his hair to the ends of his toenails.

He was in a rack, being stretched so taut he was surprised he was still in one piece.

Maybe he wasn't.

Maybe this time Alcroft had taken away his immortality and he was in death, in Hell, being punished for his many, many sins.

"Felix!"

The voice penetrated the fog of his pain and his inco-herent thoughts, and Felix blinked, trying to find focus, a glimmer of light to break through the darkness and allow him to see his hallucination. In Hell or merely hanging in insanity, Felix had heard Regan's voice, and he wanted to see her beautiful face just one last time.

But no matter how hard he strained, there was nothing but darkness.

❦

"Oh my God!" Regan came grinding to a halt in the door-way of Felix's bedroom, stunned at the horror of what she was seeing.

Chris crashed into her back. "Why are you stopping—"

His voice changed to a shocked whisper as he looked up and saw what she did. "Holy Jesus. What the hell am I looking at?"

"I don't know." Regan swallowed hard, fighting back the bile that had shot up her throat. She wanted to step forward but her feet seemed to have turned to stone at the sight of Felix, hanging suspended in the air, arms and legs drawn out like he was being pulled in four different directions.

There was nothing holding him at all. He was just . . . there. His eyes were open, but he stared at the floor, and he definitely didn't see her, didn't react to her presence. The only way she was certain he was even alive was because she could see his chest rising up and down rapidly, though he made no sound. Moisture and blood stained his bare chest, and his jeans were dark to the knees, wrung with sweat. His dangling feet were covered in crusted blood, and a glance up showed his fingers were the same.

That's when she realized his nails had been ripped out.

Regan clapped her hand over her mouth and fought the urge to throw up. There was no time for sickness, no time for weakness, no time to debate why none of this was logi-

cal in the world as she had known it. It was real and that
was all she needed to know.

Felix had told her the truth about him, Beau, Camille,
and that meant that everything he had felt for her, the
entirety of their relationship, had been real. This was the
man she wanted to be with, regardless of what he had done
in the past.

That gave her the courage to step forward and circle
around the front of him, trying to assess what she was
looking at. It was an invisible torture device of some kind,
but the question was, how did she get him out of it?

"Felix!" she said, willing him to react. She needed to know
he was still in there, needed him to guide her, to explain how
she was supposed to free him from this binding.

Maybe it would be as simple as removing the binding
rings they'd both worn. Felix had pulled hers off, and she
had slipped his off with no impediment. Maybe if she just
pulled him down it would break the invisible chains holding him.

Regan stepped forward. A second later she was lying
on her back on the floor, almost back in the doorway.
She blinked, struggling to suck in some breath, the wind
knocked clean out of her, with no idea how she had shot
through the air so quickly she couldn't even remember
moving.

"Regan?" Chris's worried face popped up in front of
her. "Are you okay?"

She nodded, dizzy, a gnawing knot of nausea in her
stomach. But nothing hurt, and she forced herself to sit up.
"Yeah, I'm fine. What the hell just happened?"

"You reached out, and bam, you shot backwards like
you'd taken a cannonball in the gut." He reached out his
hand to help her up. "Re, this is serious shit." His voice
was a shaky whisper. "I don't think we can handle this ourselves. I don't even know what I'm looking at."

Regan dragged herself to her feet, fighting to clear the dizziness. "We don't have time to get anyone. And who exactly would we get?"

She moved toward Felix again, fear being replaced by the agony of seeing him so clearly in pain. It was devastating to imagine how he was suffering, and she would help him, somehow, some way. "Go downstairs into the shop. It should be unlocked from the back. Find a book of spells. There has to be something in there about breaking someone free . . . I think it's called uncrossing a spell."

Chris didn't move and Regan looked back at him. He was just staring at Felix.

"Chris! Go downstairs."

He blinked and shook his head. "Right. Sorry. It's just . . . it's like, how can that be real? How is that even possible? But it is and I'm going right now to find a book. Uncrossing. Got it." He put his hands out and repeated the words several times as he left the room.

Regan circled Felix, murmuring, "It's okay. We're going to get you out of this somehow. I'm here." She wanted to touch him, wanted to stroke her hands across his blood-stained face and reassure him, ease his pain somehow. But she knew if she reached out, she would get slammed to the ground again.

"I love you," she told him, moving all around him in a slow circle, too agitated to stand still. "I'm sorry I didn't believe you. I had no faith in what I couldn't see. You mentioned once that I try hard to be perfect for everyone, to please everyone but myself, and you were right. I try to be perfect because I'm afraid that if I'm just me, it's not good enough. That no one will love me."

That was her legacy of being the child who survived, she knew that. And it was a pattern she wanted to break, a limitation she didn't want to place on herself.

"But you do, don't you? You love me just the way I am,

and I didn't believe in that. When you told me the truth about who you are, it was like confirmation to me that if you were making up a crazy story about immortality, everything else you said and did was suspect too. That you couldn't possibly just love me, flaws and all, unless you were crazy. My fears, made real."

Silent tears were running down her cheeks, and she ignored them, just concentrated on walking one foot in front of the other around him so she could reassure herself that he was still breathing. "I don't know if you still want me or not. I don't know how a man who is going to live forever can possibly want to be with a woman who is going to age and die, but I want whatever time is possible with you. Please tell me you want that too."

"Yes."

Regan stopped walking. He had answered her. She was positive of it. Yet when she looked at his face, nothing had changed. He still stared sightless at the floor, his mouth not moving. But she was absolutely certain he had replied to her question with a solid yes, and that made her almost giddy with relief.

Felix was alive in there, and somehow, he had found the ability to reach out and communicate with her, to reassure her.

So she wanted to reassure him in return. Her voice rang with the conviction she felt. "Then I'm going to get you down from this contraption and we're going to be together."

When Chris came skidding back through the door, his arms full of various items, Regan knew she could do this. She would break this spell and bring Felix back to her. This was her life, Felix's life. Not Camille's. Not Beau's.

Felix had told her that voodoo spells were real if you believed in them. She would believe.

"Give me the book," she told Chris.

"I found something in this one." He handed it to her. "I bent the page back. And I got the candles and the grain it says you need."

Regan sat on the edge of Felix's bed and opened the book. She quickly skimmed the spell, then went into action. "Read the steps to me as I do them so I don't have to keep looking at the book."

She made a circle on the floor in front of Felix with the jar of grain Chris had brought up. Over that she dusted rose petals. Glancing up at Felix again, she wiped her sweaty palms on her skirt and drew two intersecting lines across the circle.

Heart pounding, hand shaking, she drew a smaller circle inside the first, then placed a candle in the center, and one on either side as Chris read the instructions out loud.

"Which direction is east?" she asked Chris as she read the directions. She was supposed to light east first, but standing in Felix's apartment, the urgency of the situation pressing on her, she couldn't say with any certainty which way was what.

"I . . . I'm not sure." Chris was staring at Felix, swallowing hard, his hold on the book going slack. Then he pulled himself together and looked out the window of the bedroom, muttering to himself, "The river is there, the expressway is there, Canal Street is there . . . east is towards the window."

"You're sure?"

Chris went a little pale, but he nodded. "I'm sure."

Regan held out her hand. "Let me have your lighter."

He dug it out of his pocket, and Regan lit the candle closest to the east, then the others, murmuring her petition under her breath. "Release Felix, uncross this evil, break these invisible bonds."

She stared at the candles, their undulating flames tiny yet bright and strong in the fading sunlight. They swayed and moved as Regan stood still and prayed to whoever or whatever might be listening to undo the evil that had been done to Felix, to bring him back to her so she could tell him she loved him.

The room sharpened around her, her breathing loud and harsh to her ears, the smell of the burning candles mixing in an overwhelming jumble of scents, and Regan thought she heard whispering. Darting her eyes around the circle, she couldn't tell where the voices were coming from, or what they were saying, but it seemed like they bounced, in a circle, from candle to candle, a chorus of whispers, and Regan felt like it was time.

She left the circle and took a step toward Felix.

"I'm going to touch him again," Regan told Chris. "Watch out in case I go flying again."

But this time when she dragged in a breath for courage and stepped forward, she stayed standing. Her trembling fingers made it all the way up to Felix, and she touched the sweat-soaked skin of his shoulder, felt the heat of his flesh, felt the clammy dampness covering him. Her own shoulders slumped in relief.

"Felix," she whispered.

Moving in front of him, Regan wrapped her arms around his middle, feeling the tightness of his muscles, hearing the labored pain of his breathing. Giving him a hug, she sighed, then forced herself to focus. She didn't know how long she had, so she tugged as hard as she could on his body.

He dropped so suddenly, she didn't have time to react, and they wound up on the floor, him on top of her, her hip slamming into the wood with a sharp jolt of pain. His dead weight was compressing her, and she had cracked her head, but she didn't care. She just needed to know he was okay.

"Felix, answer me." Regan ran her fingers over his back, wiping the sweat from his brow, everything but her hands immobile from his weight pinning her.

He shifted, and his eyes focused on her. "I love you," he said.

Regan gave a sob of relief. "Are you okay?" she asked, staring at him, watching his blue eyes shadowed with pain.

Nodding, he rolled off of her and lay on his side. "I'm fine."

"What *was* that?" she asked. "You were just hanging there."

"Punishment," he told her. "It is what it is. I'm fine."

Regan reached over and kissed him, hard. "It's not fine. He can't do this to you."

Felix stared at her, eyes questioning. "Why did you come here? What day is today?"

"It's April 20th. Is that what you mean? And I'm here because I realized that what you told me is the truth, and I love you. I had to make sure you were okay." A sob choked out before she could stop it. "And you weren't okay."

"Shh." Felix brushed his thumb over her lip. "I am okay now. Thank you. For believing me, for loving me, for rescuing me."

Regan swallowed hard, determined not to lose it. "I'm sorry."

"Why? This is impossible to believe and I understand why you had to break things off."

The last few weeks alone had been so empty, so awful, and Regan wanted to know that Felix just wanted her, in whatever way. "I . . . I want to be with you if you still want to be with me."

"I do. More than anything." Felix gave her a soft smile. "And I need to deal with Alcroft so that we can be together."

He stood up, wincing, and moved gingerly to his dresser, where he pulled out clean clothes. "I'm going to shower and go have a meeting with him." He glanced toward the door, and nodded to Chris, who was hovering with the book still in his hand, sucking hard on a cigarette. "I want you to go with Chris back to his house."

Regan stood up too, pain shooting through her hip. She was worried about Felix's plans, her palms sweaty, heart racing. "You're going to confront him? I don't know if that's a good idea."

"I have to." Felix held his clothes with one hand, his other moving to his face to wipe sweat off his brow.

Regan wasn't sure how much Felix knew, if he knew the purpose behind Beau marrying her. The words made her feel sick, but she needed to make sure he understood. "But it's him, you know, he is the one who is trying to force Camille into me, so that he can be with her again."

"I know. Which is why I need to do this. I have to make sure you're safe, do you understand? It's not fair to Camille either . . . she doesn't want to be here."

Regan thought of the pained plea on the video, Camille speaking through her. "No, she doesn't. But what is he going to do to you?"

Felix just gave her a jaded smile. "There's nothing he can do to me that he hasn't already done. I have to do the right thing, Regan."

What the hell was she supposed to say? She was steeped in a fluid world she didn't understand, where she had no power and no knowledge, yet she was terrified something would happen to Felix. Something horrific beyond anything she could ever imagine.

"Be safe," she whispered. "Call me as soon as you're done."

Then before she could change her mind and beg him to stay, to run away, to pretend none of this existed, she turned and fled the room, Chris on her heels, a wide-eyed stare on his face.

Chapter Nineteen

❦

Felix watched Regan leave, then showered the grime off of himself in two minutes, and got dressed in clean clothes, wincing at the use of his fingers, still tender even though they were healing quickly. Having his nails torn out had been a new form of torture, a layer of pain and humiliation laid down over the agony of that brutal stretching sensation. His body still hurt everywhere, battered and screaming in protest with each step he took, but he tried to ignore it.

What was human pain when before the day was over he was going to die?

❦

Regan argued with Chris. "No, I need to go to the house! You can come with me if you like, or you can go home. But either way, I'm going home."

"I don't think this is a good idea." Chris kept pace with her on the sidewalk, puffing madly on a cigarette. "Did you see what we're dealing with here? This is intense. This is freaky shit. Come home with me and wait for Felix to call you."

Except that Regan's greatest fear was that Felix wasn't going to call her. That something horrible was going to happen to him before he could stop it.

Which was why she was not going to sit around passive and worried, but instead was going to take action. "No." She was fast-walking, and she turned quickly onto her block, digging in her pocket for her house keys.

"At least let me get Nelson's camera. We can be back here in half an hour."

"You go ahead. Meet me back here."

"Don't do anything," he warned. "We want this recorded so Felix can see it if anything happens. And wait outside in the courtyard."

"Of course." She had no intention of waiting outside, but if it got rid of Chris, she would agree to anything. Regan crammed the key in the gate of her courtyard. Her courtyard. This was her house, her life, damn it. No one, dead or alive, had the right to manipulate it.

Running up the curving stairs, Regan paused on the Juliet balcony, hands on the railing, looking down at the spot where Camille had died. "Camille," she whispered. "Tell me how to free you."

There was no answer, not even a breeze stirring the foliage of her trees and potted bushes.

Frustrated, she tried the French doors into her bedroom and was surprised they were unlocked. Then again, that night she had left she hadn't exactly been in a coherent frame of mind. Stepping in, she left the doors open behind her to air the stuffy room out.

And saw that Moira's monkey was sitting on her bed again, his jaunty smile leering at her. She had always thought of the stuffed animal as comforting, but now, it triggered a shiver. There was something ominous about his presence in her still bedroom, like he was patiently waiting for her to return.

It wasn't Moira moving it, that was what made it disturbing. If it had been her sister, that would be different, but this was Beau or Camille manipulating her possessions, her emotions, her peace of mind.

Not sure what to do now that she was standing in her bedroom, Regan dumped her handbag with Camille's journal on the foot of the bed. "I want to help you," she told the empty room, hoping Camille would somehow hear her. "I don't want him to own you anymore either. He's a terrible, bad man, and I want to help you find a way to get away from him and back to your family."

The sense of urgency was pressing on Regan, and she turned in a circle, searching every corner of the room for something, anything, that would indicate Camille was there, that she existed. Maybe Camille was inside Regan for all she knew. Maybe she was lurking inside her body, her soul, her mind, waiting for the right moment to take over.

To own her.

Like Beau owned Felix. Like Camille owned Felix through his guilt. Like the past owned all of them.

The tick of the clock on her nightstand grew louder in the stillness and Regan spun around, sure she'd heard footsteps, but there was nothing.

Just her furniture, the smell of her scented candles, and the dance of dust motes across the sun streak from the doors. The hulking chest of drawers stood at attention and the monkey grinned.

And Moira walked out from behind the silk drapes.

Regan froze, tears springing to her eyes. It was her sister, her big sister, an eternal six years old, wearing her yellow satin Easter dress, white gloves on her delicate hands. Her caramel brown hair was carefully curled, and her lips had the gleam of the lipstick their mother had allowed them to wear that day twenty-plus years ago.

Moira was definitely there, solid, yet something about her shimmered at the edges, a fluidity to her form and movement that said she wasn't real, wasn't of this human world.

"Moira," Regan whispered. "Do you know who I am?"

Her sister nodded, a smile on her soft face. She was Moira before she'd gotten sick, and the tip of her finger came up in her white glove and she pointed. Her lips formed the words, though no sound came out of her mouth. *Baby Re-Re.*

Regan caught the sob before it could escape. She had forgotten Moira's nickname for her, but now she could hear it, a whisper of long ago, the teasing, lilting voice of her sister calling her Baby Re-Re. Making a song out of it, dancing with her, squeezing her so that she couldn't breathe, but Regan feeling happy, always happy, because her big sister loved her.

She nodded. "Yes, it's me. Are you okay, Moira?"

Her sister's head tilted, like the question made no sense to her. She nodded again, and her face and eyes lit up in the most beautiful, angelic smile Regan had ever seen, and she knew that wherever her sister was, it was a place of contentment.

Moira moved forward, her white shoes not quite touching the hardwood. She pointed to Regan's bed, to the handbag lying there.

"My handbag?" Regan asked stupidly, not sure what her sister was telling her. "The bed?" Then she remembered the monkey. "Patrick? Do you want him?"

Moira shook her head. She pointed to the handbag again.

Regan grabbed the bag and dumped the contents out, no idea what she was supposed to do or say, and panicking, knowing she had very little time. Moira was fading, her body transparent.

Her wallet and the journal spilled out. Camille's journal.

"The journal?" she asked, grabbing it off the bed and spinning around to face her sister.

But Moira was gone, and Regan stood in her room, acutely aware of how alone she was, and with no idea what to do.

The French doors squeaked, drawing her attention, moving slightly in the wind.

A snake slithered in from the balcony.

❧

Felix went into the courtyard behind his shop, retrieving a shovel from the shed along the way. With hard, angry kicks onto the metal, he drove the shovel into the ground and displaced enough dirt for a three by three hole.

Then he dropped his binding ring into the hole. Regan's followed suit, making a faint tinny clink as it knocked against his. Regan's ring was worth fifty thousand dollars, but he couldn't in good conscience sell it and potentially release its power on another woman.

It was beautiful and expensive and it represented the ultimate greed—owning another person.

So it belonged in the hole.

Felix pulled a small bag out of his pocket and dumped its contents on the rings. Graveyard dirt. For severing connections. For endings.

Then he refilled the hole with the original dirt, stamped on it with his boot, and tossed the shovel aside.

It was time to confront the demon and send him back to hell.

❧

Regan stood frozen watching the snake. Was it real? Probably not. It was probably just her fear springing it to life. Maybe Moira hadn't really been there either.

But it looked real, so real that no matter how much she told herself it wasn't, she remained paralyzed, standing stock still in front of her bed, clutching the journal.

She could hear her own ragged breathing, feel the clamminess of her palms, and while it occurred to her that she would ruin the binding of the journal by sweating on it, she couldn't move enough to set it back down. Besides, even the small book felt like a barrier between her and the reptile.

It slithered toward the chest of drawers, the very one where she had found the journal. Regan sucked in a breath when she realized there was a glass of wine on the dresser. That hadn't been there before, when she had first entered the room. She was sure of it.

The scented candles on her nightstand and chest of drawers were suddenly burning. Right before her eyes they had flickered to life, as if a switch had been thrown to ignite them. Regan blinked, glancing over her shoulder, wanting to bolt, but unable to make her feet move.

The beat of a drum started from the corner of the room. There was no drum there, no drummer, but she could hear it, a slow, steady, erotic rhythm rising and swelling in the room, around her, over her. Maybe it was in her.

It was then she realized this was the setting of Camille's final night among the living. All it wanted was Felix.

Panic started to set in, her eyes darting around, following the snake, watching for Camille, her heart racing. She touched her face, over and over, reassuring herself she was still Regan. But the urge to walk over and drink the wine was strong, and her foot had started tapping to the music.

She tried to still it, but her foot kept moving, up, down, up, down. The music was calling her, the wine was pleading with her, and despite her fear, she had the desire to reach out and snatch that snake off her floor and dance with it.

It was happening. She could feel it. She was going to live out Camille's last night . . .

And die.

Desperate, Regan flicked open the journal, flying through the pages to find the last entry.

Tonight is the night.

Bile rose in her mouth. Regan dropped the journal on the bed and dug in her purse. She called Felix, but he didn't answer. Then she rooted around for a pen.

She was going to write the final entry in Camille's journal.

❦

Alcroft had agreed to meet him in Regan's courtyard, and Felix knew he would be prompt. He also knew the lock on the gate wouldn't matter to Alcroft, so Felix had very little time. Drawing a circle with a stick over the stones where Camille had landed, he traced a *veve*, or magic diagram, in the center.

He stepped back, into the shadows, when he heard the gate creaking open.

At the same time, he suddenly heard the beat of drums from the interior of the house, sweeping out the windows of the second floor and washing over him.

What the hell . . .

Was Regan in the house?

That had never even occurred to him. She was supposed to be with Chris.

Maybe it wasn't her, but Camille.

There was no time to check or send Regan to safety because Alcroft was entering the courtyard, a smirk on his face.

"So the servant calls the master? I hope this is an apology for releasing yourself from prison before I gave you permission. You can start by groveling at my feet."

Felix moved forward, slowly, holding Alcroft's gaze so

he wouldn't glance down at the ground and see the circle. "I'm not going to grovel. I'm going to ask you man-to-man to release Regan. She doesn't belong to you."

Alcroft took a few steps in his direction, his stance confident, his expression mocking. "Oh, because she belongs to you?"

"No." He shook his head. "She doesn't belong to anyone. She's her own person."

"Well, that's very New Age of you." Alcroft rolled his eyes. "Everyone is bound to someone in a relationship. It's where two become one and all that bullshit. Haven't you heard of a wedding ceremony?"

"It's a partnership, not losing yourself in someone else or in your relationship." It had taken him a hundred years to recognize that, to understand the seemingly subtle difference. Regan didn't want to have Felix or to own him or to change him, but she wanted his companionship, plain and simple. He wanted the same.

"I have partners in the law firm. I want a wife that belongs to me. And I can take her, own her, use her, and throw her away." Alcroft stepped into the circle. "And you can't do anything about it."

Felix moved, hitting Alcroft in the gut with his fist to catch him off guard. As the demon doubled over with an expulsion of air from his lungs, Felix chanted, adrenaline giving him the strength as he moved around Alcroft, binding him to the circle.

But the demon reacted quickly, levitating off the ground several feet. Felix grabbed his leg and landed another punch on his kneecap, which earned him a howl of pain from Alcroft and a kick in his own thigh. Felix ignored the pain from the blow and continued chanting, words so ancient that he didn't even know their meaning. The words of his mother, of the priests and priestesses of his childhood, of all the practitioners who had passed from this life to the next and who united with him to fight the evil.

He believed in them, in himself, in Regan. "I call on the power of Madame Erzulih, all the mysteries, and all the Saints," he said, pulling a vial from his pocket and tossing alcohol over Alcroft's legs and stomach.

Alcroft hissed. "You're an idiot. This won't work."

Yet he was clearly fighting to stay afloat, his amber eyes glowing in the dusky courtyard. Felix hit him in the kidney with every ounce of strength he had, and Alcroft dropped to the ground.

"I vanquish you back to Hell," Felix said, picturing steel cords wrapping around Alcroft's hands and feet.

As Felix pulled a knife out of his pocket, Alcroft writhed around on the ground, his hands and feet bound by invisible restraints. Turn the magic back onto the magician. If Alcroft could bind Felix, he could turn it back and bind him.

Turning the trick back, as his mother would have said.

Felix pictured his mother's smile, her gentle demeanor, as he pulled the knife out of his pocket. He silently thanked her before slashing the knife across his wrist. The pain had him gritting his teeth, but he braced himself against it and squeezed his fist open and closed. Standing over Alcroft, he let his blood drip down onto him.

Alcroft's eyes flashed with anger, and maybe fear. "If I go back, you'll go with me."

"I know," Felix said calmly, resigned to the inevitable. It was time for him to die. He had lived long enough to no purpose, and he would die to save Regan. To release Camille from her torment.

He knelt to his knees and slashed open his other wrist, the blood flowing wet and warm in the humid evening air.

Alcroft lay on his back, breathing hard, struggling against the invisible bonds. "She'll think you abandoned her, you know," he said, the smirk still on his face despite the circumstances. "She'll hate you."

His arrogance irritated Felix, so he just ignored him,

watching his blood drip down onto Alcroft's shirt. His
head was starting to swim. But the wound on his left wrist
was coagulating, so he sliced a fresh one right below it, the
sting of the pain less of a shock this time, more of a heady
triumphant feeling that this would be over.

"She'll move on, get married, have children, live a happy
life hating you, and you'll be rotting with me in Hell."

Felix laughed softly. "That's what you don't understand.
What you're incapable of understanding because you're so
truly selfish." His mouth was hot, and his hands were starting
to feel numb, but he kept his focus, on Alcroft, on the binding,
on the request for vanquishment. "That is what I want, Regan
to be happy. I would do anything to make that possible."

Right then they both heard laughter from the balcony.

Regan.

Felix snapped his head up to see, the movement making
him dizzy.

And wished he hadn't.

❦

Regan's hand was shaking as she put the pen to the yellowed paper, right below Camille's last entry. She didn't
know what had happened that fateful night, Felix had never
had a chance to tell her, but she could guess.

And change the result.

Staying in the middle of the bed, a wary eye on the
snake, Regan wished she had kept a diary at some point.
She had no idea what to write.

Felix arrived, she scrawled. *He brought a snake.*

She stared at her wobbly handwriting. Now what? She
needed to get into Camille's head, Camille's voice.

*He played the drum and I danced. Dancing is a delight.
Here, at home, I can let my hair down and dance the way
I cannot in the ballroom.*

That was better. Regan stared at the French doors. What
had drawn Camille to them?

We drank wine and made love by candlelight.

That didn't sound right, it was too generic for Camille, but Regan had no desire to go into details of their sex, no matter how long ago it was, and she had to assume they'd already consummated their relationship by that point.

Then we stepped out onto the balcony with the snake. My parents were there to meet me, my sisters with arms wide open, smiles on their lovely faces. I've missed them so terribly and they've missed me.

Regan paused, pen on the paper. She could feel it. She could feel the warm breeze, feel the nakedness of her own flesh, feel the hint of laughter washing in like an ocean wave, smell the heavy floral perfume of Camille's mother. Her mother.

The words came without thought, her handwriting slanting and scrolling and beautiful.

I died, but they walked me across the divide between this world and the next, and together we leave the rocky tempest of mortal life behind and dwell forever together in the calm of peace . . .

Regan dropped the pen down. The drums were louder. She had to dance.

The snake no longer scared her. With the journal in hand, she stepped onto the area rug in the middle of the room, in front of the open doors, and moved her hips to the rhythmic beat of the nonexistent drums. The candlelight cast shadows around the room and the snake glided toward her.

Regan ignored him. She wasn't ready for him. Walking to the chest of drawers, she slid the journal back into its secret compartment, and closed it firmly shut. She drank the wine that had appeared out of nowhere, the red liquid warming her as it slid down her throat.

She tore off her shirt, even as she told herself she shouldn't. Couldn't. But it was as it would be and she was powerless to stop it.

One last night she would be Camille then they would both be free.

Regan dropped her skirt to the floor and danced, her hands in her hair. She had never danced alone like this, and there was something freeing, elemental about it. Just her and the music, swelling up inside her. The snake moved around her feet, dancing with her, and she reached down and picked it up.

Holding its head, Regan stared into its eyes, the deep liquid pools of black mesmerizing. There was no fear and there was no Camille.

This was her, Regan, staving off her fear and reclaiming her life.

She walked with the snake, its thick body heavy and draped over her arms. Going through the doors, she moved to the railing of the Juliet balcony and closed her eyes. "Be at peace," she whispered to Camille. "They are welcoming you home."

The wind kicked up, flinging her hair in her face, and yet despite the strands over her eyes, she saw them. Camille, walking forward out into the air, in her black mourning gown, being wrapped in the embrace of a petite woman in a rich ruby gown. Four young women huddled around her, while a man watched paternally from behind. There were smiles and tears of joy and laughter, and Regan felt the squeeze of deep familial love.

Camille turned and smiled and waved in her direction, and Regan laughed, a sob of joy and relief. Tears were in her eyes as she waved back, the weight of the snake shifting on her arm.

Then without warning the railing she was leaning on gave way.

Chapter Twenty

Felix looked up to see Regan standing on the balcony in her bra and panties, her hands out holding a thick, long snake. It was a mistake to look up. Alcroft did the same, and the second Felix saw the railing start to shift forward, he knew it was Alcroft's doing.

"No!" He jumped up, woozy from the loss of blood and the exertion of trying to contain and banish Alcroft.

If he left the circle, his spell would be broken and Alcroft would be free.

But Regan was stumbling, pitching forward, and she was going to fall.

Just like Camille.

Felix moved, but Alcroft grabbed his leg, his hands still bound. "Leave her. Let her die. That's the only way to end this."

"The only way to end it is for *you* to die," Felix said in anger, yanking as hard as he could to escape the grip.

Then he ran forward, breaking free, trying to find the spot where Regan would drop down. She was screaming, her arms flailing, as she lost her balance and tumbled over the side. Felix backed up, stumbling over Alcroft as he gauged where Regan would land. She was going to fall into the binding circle. Felix braced himself, dropping the knife he'd been holding to the ground.

Regan hit him full force and he went down, desperate to keep her from hitting the stones. He hit the ground and gasped in shock when the knife went straight into his back. The pain tore through him and he knew it was Alcroft. One last trick from the conjurer, setting the knife on its handle straight up to impale him.

He couldn't see or feel Alcroft next to him anymore and he knew he should deal with the demon, but Regan was weeping quietly, trembling, and she was his focus. "Are you okay?" he asked her.

She nodded. "I'm fine. I just scraped my leg, that's all." She sat up over him and ran her hand down his cheek. "What are you doing here? You saved my life . . . again."

"I didn't know you were going to be here," he told her, struggling to keep the pain from his voice. "I met Alcroft here." He turned to see what the demon was doing, aware they were in danger if Alcroft had broken the bonds of the binding, fully expecting to see a triumphant grin on the bastard's face.

But there was no Alcroft, in the circle or out. There was only a snake, a cottonmouth, curled up beside Felix, a wallet and car keys lying next to it. Amber eyes glowed up at Felix with hatred and malice, before it uncoiled and quickly glided toward the gate and the street.

Alcroft couldn't shape-shift into animal form, he had told Felix that many times.

Which meant that instead of Hell, Felix and Regan had banished him to the body of the snake. When Regan had fallen with the snake wrapped around her, she'd landed in the binding circle. Instead of vanquishing Alcroft, Felix's spell had bound him to the snake.

He laughed softly. "Regan, Alcroft is in the snake. You're free of him."

"He is?" Regan asked in shock. "How . . ."

"A binding spell. Not exactly what I had planned, but this works. It's over. Now Camille can be released, too."

"She already has." Regan swallowed hard, tears in her eyes. "I saw her being met by her family. It really is over."

Closing his eyes briefly, Felix reached up and ran his fingers over her lips. "I love you."

"I love you, too," she said, her words choked.

"Now will you please pull this knife out of my back?" He rolled onto his side, fighting the nausea that had gripped his stomach and was crawling up his throat. He wanted to vomit, something he never did, and there were spots dancing in front of his eyes.

Regan yelped when she saw his wound. "Oh, my God!"

Felix could feel the warmth of his blood soaking through the back of his T-shirt and seeping across to his elbows and forearms as he lay on the ground.

"Honey," he said, a little confused. He really shouldn't feel this horrible. He should be healing already. "I think I'm going to pass out."

Her face blurred in front of him as he fought to stay conscious, and lost the battle.

❦

"Felix, stop." Regan laughed and pushed his hand away. "You're still recovering. I don't want to tear your stitches."

But she was secretly thrilled that he was here with her in their new rental shotgun cottage on St. Ann, healing and healthy and apparently aroused.

He had scared her senseless when he had passed out in the courtyard. She had still been shaking herself from the fall over the balcony and the realization that Beau had been shoved into the snake she had conjured up when they had collided, and she had been relying on Felix to calm her down. To make sense of all of it for her. Instead, he'd passed out from blood loss.

But in the end, scary as it had been, that wound had shown them that Felix had surrendered his immortality in that courtyard. He was mortal, free of Beau and his past sins, able to live and age with her. Felix knew it as soon as he didn't heal immediately from the knife wound, and somehow, in the midst of bleeding from what should have been a fatal injury for a mortal, he had lost his power to escape death, but hadn't actually died.

But of course that meant he could die now, and Regan looked at him and saw that vulnerability.

She was trying not to let that terrify her, especially given that for most of their relationship, she had thought he was mortal anyway. She hadn't even known an alternative existed, for him or for anyone else for that matter. But watching him almost bleed to death had made her painfully aware of how much she didn't want to lose him now that they had found each other.

"I want you to tear *me* up," he said, his voice sexy and slumberous from his nap.

She had come into the bedroom to see if he was awake since they had dinner plans with Chris and Nelson, and he was definitely awake. In all areas.

"No." Regan made the mistake of leaning over to kiss him, and he pulled her down onto the bed. It was warm and cozy and nice lying next to him, and she would have loved to take her clothes off, but she thought it was definitely too soon after his injury and subsequent surgery. "It's not a good idea."

His finger stroked across the front of her Capri pants. "It's been *forever*."

"I don't want to hurt you," she said, but her protests were growing thinner as his hand slipped inside the front of her pants. It had been weeks and weeks.

"Not being inside you is hurting me," he murmured in

her ear, spooning alongside her, fingers stroking lightly across her clitoris.

Regan laughed. "That's such a line. I'm not sixteen." She glanced around their new bedroom, painted a bright cheerful yellow, and tried to change the subject. "I think I need to buy us some new bedding to match this room. I'd like to stay in this house awhile if that's okay with you."

"I'll stay here as long as you want if you let me have sex with you." Felix was bumping against her backside with his erection in a teasing rhythm that had her shifting restlessly. "If we do it just like this, it won't pull my stitches. Even my surgeon can't argue with that. And he said I should expect a full recovery."

Regan was warring between wanting to be cautious and the need to feel him deep inside her again. It wasn't just the physical, sexual desire, it was also needing the intimacy, the connection that making love brought to them. She wanted him as close to her as possible, to be able to love him, to express her appreciation to him, to the universe, that they'd been given this second chance.

His finger dipped inside her and she bit her lip. "If it hurts at all, stop immediately," she told him, trying to sound firm. "We'll either find a new position or I'll finish you off."

Felix started laughing, his shoulders actually shaking.

"What?" she asked, amused at the joy in his voice, craning to see his face.

"You must love me if you're offering to finish me off . . . that was very romantic, honey."

Felix watched the woman he loved make a face at him.

"That didn't sound right, did it?"

"No," he agreed. "More like giving me oral sex is a chore you suffer through."

"I like to . . ."

Regan paused, and Felix refused to fill in the blank for her. He loved it when she embraced her sexual power instead of shying away from it. If he didn't speak, she would continue, he knew from experience.

"I like to give you blow jobs. Head. Oral sex. Whatever we're calling it." Her fingers ran along the seam of his jeans. "But what I was really trying to say is that I don't want to hurt you by having sex."

"I know, and I love you for it. I love you for a lot of reasons. But the pain is gone, and yes, if it hurts, I will stop." There really wasn't much discomfort lingering from his wounds. Not that the pain mattered when he was so content, so exhilarated by being with Regan, being mortal, able to love her and be loved in return.

He was a free man.

And he wanted to make love to the woman he had been willing to give his life for.

"Okay . . ." she said, her voice reluctant, even as her body shifted forward to make contact with his fingers again.

Felix stroked inside her, closing his eyes to just feel the sensation of lying next to her, his chest against her back, his face buried in her soft hair. "Take your pants off," he whispered in her ear.

As she complied, Felix unzipped his own jeans and kissed the back of her neck. It was such a new feeling to be this happy, he wasn't quite sure what to do with it. Just lying in bed beside her brought him a contentment he had never experienced in his whole long and restless life.

When Regan's skin was blissfully free of clothing, he skimmed his hands over her backside, enjoying the smooth silkiness of her flesh. Shifting her top leg forward, Felix slid inside her, closing his eyes against the rush of ecstasy.

Regan gave a sharp sigh, her head tilting back, and Felix knew that this was perfection, that this moment was worth everything that had come before, that all his sins had allowed him to be here, humble and appreciative.

She moved gently with him, their bodies connected in

a hot sensual slide of pleasure, and Felix picked up the rhythm, slipping his finger around to tease her clitoris. Regan came quickly, her cries soft and ragged, and Felix didn't wait any longer. He pumped hard, gritting his teeth, exploding tight and hard, shattering everything that had come before.

There was only now and tomorrow.

Kissing Regan's shoulder, he relaxed onto the pillow.

"Are you okay?" she asked.

Her concern was a novelty, and Felix smiled, nuzzling the back of her hair. "I'm fantastic."

"Good." She shifted so that she was on her back, facing him. "You know, I've always meant to ask you . . . what was it I felt on my shoulders that first night we met? When you were giving me the reading and it felt like someone was touching me. What was that?"

"I have no idea," he told her honestly. "I'd like to say it was me, but I never had that kind of power. What do you think it was?"

Her voice was thoughtful. "I think it was the promise that someday your arms would be around me, comforting me . . . but that sounds stupid. That's not possible."

"Everything is possible." Felix stroked her hair, studying the varying colors of brown in the sunlight. "Remember I said that voodoo works if you believe . . . this is the same thing."

"Then I believe," she said, shifting so she was completely facing him. "I believe."

So he did.

And he knew they weren't just talking about invisible arms.

❦

Felix held Regan's hand in his as they strolled down the street. The heat of the day was fading and he was wonderfully content, satisfied physically from making love to

Regan, and satisfied emotionally for the first time in a life-time, both with himself and their relationship.

"Are you okay? Should I slow down?" she asked anxiously.

He laughed. "I'm mortal, not an infant. I'm fine. It barely hurts at all." His back still twinged and ached with most movements, and he would always have scars on his wrists and his back, but it mattered little to him. Not when he had been given the opportunity for a whole new life, one rich in love, friends, and hopefully someday, children.

"It's a beautiful day," he told her. "A good day to ask you to marry me."

Regan stopped walking altogether and stared up at him. "Are you serious? Are you actually asking me?"

"Yes. I love you. Be my wife." Maybe not the most romantic proposal in the world, but Felix figured it was to the point.

A smile split her face. "Yes. I will marry you." She threw her arms around him and kissed him, then pulled back quickly. "Sorry, sorry. Did I hurt you?"

"No. You could never hurt me." Felix kissed her back then raised his hand in greeting over her head. "Chris and Nelson are here. They're actually on time for dinner, it's amazing."

Regan whirled around and yelled, "We're getting married!"

"*Shut* up!" Chris said. "I totally saw this coming."

"Congratulations," Nelson said.

"Thanks." Felix shook hands and Regan received hugs.

"I'm starving," Chris said after all the greeting and hugging had subsided. "And I need a cocktail to celebrate. Where are we eating?"

"Nola," Nelson demanded. "I have a thing for Emeril."

No one objected, so they started walking. The path took them past the house on Royal Street, and Felix squeezed Regan's hand.

Regan squeezed back, staring up at the house she had fallen in love with, the one she had just listed for sale. It wasn't hers, it never had been, and the ghosts of the past would always linger. It was time for the house to have a new history, and for her and Felix to build a life together in the tiny colorful turquoise house on St. Ann.

A guide had a group of tourists paused in front of the house, all wearing their tour stickers on their T-shirts. Chris and Nelson wandered ahead, arguing over various celebrity chefs' sexual orientations, but Regan stopped and listened to the guide.

"One of the most imposing and beautiful houses in the French Quarter, this residence has been the scene of many a tragedy and is haunted by more than one ghost. The original owner died in the yellow fever epidemic of 1878, along with his wife and four of his daughters. His youngest daughter survived, only to commit suicide by throwing herself off the balcony a few months later. Her ghost is often seen on the balcony, hair flowing behind her. The cries of her family suffering from yellow fever are often heard late at night."

Regan really doubted that, since she had never heard one word from the Comeaux family, but it made a good story.

The guide continued. "A later owner also committed suicide here, and just a few weeks ago the house was the scene of tragedy and drama yet again. The current resident came down into the very same courtyard you see before you where that young woman died so long ago, to find that her boyfriend had been stabbed by her ex-husband. While she called 911, the ex ran off, and now a couple of weeks later, he's still missing and wanted by the police. Prominent local lawyer and everything. Big scandal."

"Did the boyfriend die?" a teenage girl asked.

"No, he survived, but I'm guessing that relationship is on the rocks." The man winked. "Love hurts, doesn't it?"

Felix scoffed beside her and Regan gave a short laugh.

The guide noticed them. "Listen, y'all, if you want to hear the story, you're going to have to pay for the tour."

Regan shook her head and smiled. "No, thanks. I already know this story."

As they moved down the sidewalk, leaving the past behind, Felix pulled her hand up to his mouth and kissed it. "And it has a happy ending."

Keep reading for a preview of
the next contemporary romance
by Erin McCarthy

HOT FINISH

Coming soon from Berkley Sensation!

Chapter One

"I banged the bride. I feel a little funny about standing up for her husband at their wedding."

Ryder Jefferson almost shot beer out of his nose at his friend Ty's words. Swallowing hard, choking on the liquid and his laughter, he said, "Well, it's not like you slept with her after they started dating, so who cares? In fact, as I recall, she was still dating you when she started sleeping with him. So, yeah, I guess you're right. That is awkward, McCordle, since you got tossed over."

Not that he would ever rib his friend about that if his heart had been involved, but Ryder knew Ty had been half-heartedly dating Nikki Borden at best. It had been a relief to all parties involved when Nikki had trysted with Jonas Strickland and gotten engaged.

Which made the whole thing damned funny now that she had asked Ty to be a groomsman in her upcoming nuptials.

"Screw you," Ty told him, lifting his bottle to his lips, his head propped up on the worn bar with his hand.

"None of us want to be in this wedding," Elec Monroe said, sitting on Ryder's right side, tossing peanut after peanut in his mouth. "But at least we can all hang out together at the reception."

"This is your fault," Ty told him, pointing a finger at him. "You're the one who was friends with Jonas first. You're the one who invited him to your party where he met Nikki."

"And that's where you met your fiancée," Ryder reminded him. "So I can't see how you're figuring it's a bad thing, because if Nikki hadn't met Jonas, you'd still be with her instead of Imogen. Do you want to be dating Nikki 'Where's My Brain' Borden?"

Ty's face contorted in horror and he gave a mock shudder. "Point taken. But it's still weird as hell."

"Nobody's arguing with that." None of them were close to Strickland, yet all of them had been invited to participate in his circus of a wedding.

"I don't mean to be a dick or anything," Evan Monroe, Elec's brother, piped up from down at the end. "But doesn't Strickland have real friends? It's not like any of us are really all that tight with him."

"I'm sure he does," Elec said. "But the truth is, Nikki's pulling the strings here and she wants a splashy media wedding. She has half the top ten drivers in stock car racing in her wedding party. Talk about a photo op."

Ryder had already figured out that was her motivation. He didn't really care all that much, but he did have better things to do than waste a whole weekend wearing a monkey suit. Like watching TV and tossing a load of laundry in. And other stuff, none of which he could think of at the moment. But the truth was, he would do it, and not for Nikki or Jonas.

"Well, I for one feel cheapened and used," he said, amused by the whole situation. He also had a nice beer buzz going, which made him feel much more prosaic about the whole thing.

"You know what? I'm not doing it," Evan declared. "I hate wearing a tux and I always get stuck with the married bridesmaid, so there's no chance of even scoring post-reception sex."

"I'm not doing it either," Ty said, slapping his fist down on the bar. "I mean, what the hell? It's like incestuous or something for me to be standing there, in church, with Nikki and Jonas, and my fiancée sitting on the bench behind us . . . I'm not doing it. Screw it. No one can make me."

"Well, if you all aren't going to be there, I'm out, too." Elec rattled the peanuts around in his hand and wrinkled his nose. "I hate having my picture taken."

"That's because you're ugly," Evan told him, with all the love and affection only a brother can have.

"So it's settled then." Ty sat up and adjusted his ball cap. "We all bail."

Ryder hated to break up this anti-wedding sit-in, but he was going to have to own it. "Not me, guys. I can't bail."

"What? Why the hell not?" Ty asked.

"Because of Suzanne. She's the wedding planner for this crazy-ass mockery of a marriage, and I have to do it. I've gotta support her." He did. He had to support Suzanne whatever way he could since his ex-wife had refused further alimony from him.

He had been busted up about that for weeks, worrying about Suz. She was stubborn to the point where she made the mule look like a pansy-boy.

If she wouldn't take any money directly from him, he was going to do whatever he could to ensure her fledging wedding planning business got off to a solid start. Even if that meant he had to suffer through a whole day of watching Nikki and Jonas delude themselves into thinking their marriage would last forever.

"Sorry, boys, I have to be there."

His friends and fellow stock car drivers gave him various expressions of understanding, overlaid with obvious irritation that he wasn't falling in line with their plan.

"Damn it," Ty said. "Truth is, I have to go, too. Imogen says if I back out, it's going to look like I still have feelings for Nikki or something. She's probably right, isn't she?"

Ty's fiancée Imogen was a brainiac and Ryder didn't doubt for a minute that when it came to matters of logic, Imogen reigned supreme over four guys in a bar at four in the afternoon. "She's probably got a point. If you're in the wedding no one's going to think for a minute you're busted up about Nikki. If you bail, it might look like hurt feelings."

"Well, I sure in the hell don't want anyone thinking that. Guess I'm going to have to do it, too."

Elec gave a monumental sigh. "If you two are in, I've got no excuse for not being there. Jonas is a buddy of mine, and I can't hold it against the guy that he's marrying a woman whose voice is like a cheese grater on my nuts. He's got to be in love, he must be happy, and I should be there to help him celebrate that."

"He's not happy!" Evan said, gesturing to the bartender for another beer. "Have you lost your mind? The man is drowning in a haze of endorphins, that's all. He's going to wake up in six months from his sex cloud and wonder what the hell he was thinking."

"You're such a romantic," Elec told him. "I can see why your love life is such a success."

"Screw you." Evan threw a balled-up napkin at his brother.

"There's nothing wrong with marriage," Ryder said, the words slipping out before he could stop them.

Suddenly all eyes were on him.

"Yeah?" Ty asked, looking at him funny.

"Yeah." Ryder put his bottle to his lip so he didn't expand on his statement. He didn't want to get into it, didn't want anyone to know he was thinking about his ex a lot these days and wondering what exactly had gone wrong.

Evan said, "I still don't want to be in this wedding."

"Guess you don't have to," Elec told him. "But it looks like the rest of us are in."

"What time is it?" Ryder asked, feeling his pocket for his cell phone. "We have to be at that wedding party planning meeting thing at five."

Ty glanced at his watch. "It's quarter till."

"We need to head out then. Should we all ride together? Elec, you can drive since you only had one beer and you've been nursing it for two hours."

"That's cool," Elec said. "We're all going to need a beer after this anyway, so we might as well leave your cars here. Evan, you going or not?"

Ryder settled his bar tab and stood up, hoping they weren't going to be late. Bitching and whining while bellied up to the bar had eaten up more time than he had expected and he didn't want to disappoint Suzanne. Or more accurately, he didn't want to listen to her reaming him.

"I'll go," Evan said begrudgingly. "I'll look like a total ass if I don't."

"True." Ryder clapped him on the shoulder. "Would it make you feel better if we let you plan the bachelor party?"

Evan perked up. "Hey, I wouldn't mind that. I could do that."

As they headed to the front door, Ryder wished that it were that easy to please himself these days. Something was missing in his life, and he was afraid he knew exactly what it was.

Or who, to be more accurate.

❧

"You want fifteen groomsmen and fifteen bridesmaids?" Was she flippin' serious? Suzanne Jefferson looked at her client Nikki Borden, who arguably had cotton candy floating where she should have brains, and knew the girl was one hundred percent serious.

"Uh-huh." Nikki nodded with a big smile. "My big day should be, well, big."

Right.

Nikki's thin, toned, and tanned arms went flailing out, a beatific smile on her youthful face. "Big like the Eiffel Tower. Big like elephants. Big like . . ." She paused, clearly at a loss for more large and lame metaphors.

"Big like the national debt?" Suzanne asked, shifting in her chair at her dining room table, unable to resist.

Nikki blinked. "Huh? What's that?"

Suzanne bit her cheek and squeezed her lips together in the hopes she wouldn't laugh out loud and have Nikki guessing she thought the blonde had bacon for brains. Why the hell Suzanne thought she could go back to being a wedding planner when she'd never been able to hide her emotions worth a damn was beyond her. Oh, wait. She was dead broke—that's why she was pasting on a big old fake smile and listening to the likes of Nikki natter on and on about her perfect man and her perfect proposal and her perfect wedding.

At one time, before her own marriage and divorce, Suzanne had enjoyed the challenge of wedding planning, making sure every last teeny tiny detail was taken care of, and taking pride in the joy on a bride's face on her big day. There had been annoying aspects, sure, but they had rolled off her less cynical back a little easier in those days.

But since she'd spent the past four years working as a volunteer on the board of a charity that funded children's cancer research, she was having a hard time seeing the value in picking the perfect shade of pink for bridesmaid's dresses, or suggesting the happy couple spend thousands of dollars on a cake that would disappear in under four hours.

Not that there was any point in whining about it. This

was life, and she had to deal. She was going to squeeze the shit out of these lemons and force them into lemonade. Suzanne made a notation on her notepad. *Fifteen big-ass bridesmaids.*

Then she added a dollar sign on the end.

That made her feel a little better. She could cash in on Nikki's enthusiasm for excess. "Well, that's perfectly understandable, Nikki. You want to share your wedding with those most important to you, and it's very difficult to cut anyone out." Though from the sound of it, Nikki was planning to ask every cousin, friend, and sorority sister she'd ever had, plus the saleswoman who'd sold her shoes at a discount, and the yahoo who changed her oil to be in her bridal party.

Nikki nodded. "Exactly."

"But normally wedding parties run four to six brides-maids and groomsmen. For a wedding party of thirty, plus your flower girl and ring bearer, that requires a lot of additional planning and coordinating. I'm going to have to increase my fee if that's what you choose to do."

"I understand." Nikki just stared at her serenely.

"By double."

"Sure." Now a smug smile crossed the blonde's face. "Jonas is paying."

"The deposit? Do you have it?"

A check signed by Jonas Strickland passed from Nikki's hand to hers, and a glance down at it showed it was written for the entire original amount Suzanne had quoted to Nikki.

"This is more than the deposit."

"Jonas doesn't like to be in debt. He said to just pay up front. I can get the rest to you in a day or two I'm sure."

Nikki might claim to love Jonas, but at the moment, Suzanne really did. He had just padded her checking account substantially. Her smile to Nikki was very genuine. "That's excellent, thank you. Now you said Jonas was going to be here, right? What time are you expecting him? We can go ahead discussing venues and colors, or we can wait for him."

"He should be here any minute. And I think everyone from the wedding party said they could make it, too."

Suzanne tugged at her red sweater, adjusting her cleavage. Surely she had heard Nikki wrong. "Excuse me? The wedding party is coming, too?"

"Yeah, I thought that would be fun! They can help us make choices." Nikki beamed at Suzanne, clearly proud of herself.

Turning her dining room into sample central was working fairly well. She had access to all her books and menus and fabric samples, but there was no way in hell she could squeeze thirty people into her whole condo, let alone her dining room. There was really only room for her, Nikki, and a fat Chihuahua around this table.

Then again, she glanced down at the check on the table in front of her. For that kind of money, she'd let the best man sit on her lap. They'd shove people wherever for thirty minutes, throw some bridal magazines at them, then she'd get rid of them.

"I'm not good with decisions," Nikki said.

Yet she'd decided to marry a man she'd been dating for six weeks. Huh. That was promising. "No problem. That's what I'm here for, to guide you through the choices. Now let's talk overall tone of the wedding. Do you want it formal, casual, is there a certain location that appeals to you?"

"I want a *Gone With the Wind* theme."

Suzanne's pen paused over her paper, horrific images of hoopskirts, parasols, and skinny faux mustaches popping into her head. "How literal do you want to take that concept?"

Nikki's brow furrowed. "What do you mean?"

"You were thinking like maybe doing the wedding out-

side on the lawn at an antebellum home? But then simple
elegance for the décor?"

"Oh, yeah. That's what I mean. Just like it really was
during the Civil War. That was the Civil War, wasn't it?
Anyway, whatever. Plus I want the big dresses they wore
in the movie, and the guys in those long coats, and horses,
and curled hair, and well . . . all of it." Nikki beamed.

Maybe she'd like cannons, poverty, and runaway infla-
tion in her wedding as well.

The doorbell rang, praise the Lord. Suzanne had nothing
to say at the moment, which was damn near a first for her.

But how in the hell could she slap her name and wedding
planning reputation behind a Civil War–theme wedding?
She'd be stuck doing theme weddings for the next decade,
and everyone who knew her was aware that her well of
patience wasn't very deep.

"I'll get that. Excuse me just a sec, Nikki."

Suzanne hustled to the door and opened it. She blinked
to see Elec and Evan Monroe, Ty McCordle, and right
in front, her gorgeous and annoying ex-husband, Ryder
Jefferson.

"Hey guys, what's up? I'm kind of busy at the moment."

"We're here for the wedding planning thing," Ty told her.

Oh, no. That meant that Nikki's fiancé Jonas had asked
them . . .

"We're the groomsmen."

Damn. Just what she needed. None of them would listen or take her seriously. She'd lose control of the whole
situation.

Ryder brushed past her, dropping a soft kiss on her
cheek, his familiar cologne wafting up her nostrils and acting like a sexual trigger. She smelled Ryder and her nipples
got hard. They were just trained that way.

"Good to see you, babe. And lucky me, I'm the best man
in this wedding."

Suzanne fought the urge to grimace. Good God, this fiasco just got more and more ludicrous. Now she was going to have to spend a fair amount of time around Ryder for the next month, and she just couldn't deal with that on top of all her worrying about her future. He made her crazy, plain and simple.

And there was no way this best man was sitting on her lap.

Ryder handed her a manila envelope. "Oh, and this came addressed to both of us. It's from our divorce lawyer."

Suzanne looked at it blankly. It did have their divorce attorney's name on the envelope, and it was addressed to Mr. and Mrs. Ryder and Suzanne Jefferson. Ouch. It had been a long time since she'd seen her name linked with his, and damn it, it still hurt, which pissed her off. It didn't matter anymore, shouldn't matter. "What is it?"

"I don't know. I didn't open it. Figured you'd want it." He moved past her and the other guys did likewise.

Jonas Strickland was coming up her walk and there was a gaggle of Nikki clones behind him, women in their early twenties, tanned and thin and indistinguishable from one another except for the color of their various sweaters. There was red and yellow and aqua and two in white.

"Hi, come on in. I'm Suzanne," she said absently. "Nikki's in the dining room."

Curiosity killing her, Suzanne ripped open the envelope as she walked behind them, their giggles and chatter a buzzing backdrop. There was a pile of papers that looked like their divorce decree. Okay. She read the cover letter from the lawyer.

And stopped halfway down her hallway, the words blurring in front of her.

Oh. My. God.

She was going to kill Ryder. She was going to rip his arm off and beat him with the bloody stump.

This paper was telling her she and Ryder were not divorced.

They were still married.

"Ryder!" she screamed, aware that her voice sounded like a fair approximation of a banshee.

Everyone in the room looked up at her.

"You know," Nikki said. "I had a thought. I'm blonde."

Elec laughed and Ty elbowed him.

"What?" Suzanne looked at the twit in front of her and didn't bother to hide her irritation.

"I can't do a *Gone With the Wind* theme. Scarlett O'Hara was a brunette." Nikki pointed to her head. "And I'm blonde."

Jesus. "Good point," Suzanne managed to say. "Now would you all excuse Ryder and me for just one teensy minute?"

Ryder gave her an uneasy look, and the guys looked curious, but she didn't care. She had to discuss this with him immediately before her head exploded off her shoulders.

"What's up, babe?" he asked her, moving in really close to her, his hand landing on the small of her back as he guided her into the next room. "If we're going to fight, maybe we should be out of earshot."

Suzanne got two feet into her kitchen, but then couldn't hold back. She whirled and smacked the envelope and stack of papers against his chest. "This says we're still married!"

Ryder's eyebrows shot up. "No shit? Does that mean we can have guilt-free sex then?"

Oh, yeah. She was going to kill him.

ABOUT THE AUTHOR

National bestselling author **Erin McCarthy** has written more than two dozen sassy, sexy tales of contemporary and paranormal romance, including the popular Vegas Vampires novels. Erin also writes paranormal young adult novels under the name Erin Lynn. Visit her website at www.erinmccarthy.net.

NEW FROM

ERIN McCARTHY

Sucker Bet

The *USA Today* bestselling author of *Bled Dry* returns to vampire-filled Vegas . . .

A wild night with a stranger was not in the cards for vampiress Gwenna Carrick.

But that's exactly what happened when she met the ruggedly handsome detective Nate Thomas. But Gwenna's ex-husband is determined to clean house, with Nate the first on his to-off list . . .

M538T0709

Also by

USA Today Bestselling Author

Erin McCarthy

A Date with the Other Side

Haunted house tour guide Shelby Tucker gets hot and bothered when she stumbles upon sexy, naked Boston Macnamara. She knows he's no ghost, though he does make her weak in the knees.

"Sexy, sassy...filled with humor."
—Rachel Gibson

penguin.com

M170T0308

My life...
My love...

My Immortal

By *USA Today* Bestselling Author
ERIN McCARTHY

In the late eighteenth century, plantation owner Damien du Bourg struck an unholy bargain with a fallen angel: an eternity of inspiring lust in others in exchange for the gift of immortality. However, when Marley Turner stumbles upon Damien's plantation while searching for her missing sister, for the first time in two hundred years it's Damien who can't resist the lure of a woman. But his past sins aren't so easily forgotten—or forgiven...

"*My Immortal* is truly a passionately written piece of art." —*Night Owl Romance*

penguin.com

M174T1107